THE
WORLD of
AFTER

THE
WORLD of
AFTER

Stephen
Henighan

a novel

Cormorant Books

Canada Council   Conseil des Arts   ONTARIO ARTS COUNCIL
for the Arts   du Canada   CONSEIL DES ARTS DE L'ONTARIO
an Ontario government agency
un organisme du gouvernement de l'Ontario

 ONTARIO | ONTARIO   Canadian   Patrimoine   Canadä
CREATES | CRÉATIF   Heritage   canadien

The publisher gratefully acknowledges the support of the Canada Council
for the Arts and the Ontario Arts Council for its publishing program. We
acknowledge the financial support of the Government of Canada through
the Canada Book Fund (CBF) for our publishing activities, and the Government
of Ontario through Ontario Creates, an agency of the Ontario Ministry
of Culture, and the Ontario Book Publishing Tax Credit Program.

LIBRARY AND ARCHIVES CANADA CATALOGUING IN PUBLICATION

Title: The world of after / a novel by Stephen Henighan.
Names: Henighan, Stephen, 1960- author.
Identifiers: Canadiana (print) 202003423 8X | Canadiana (ebook) 20200342398 |
ISBN 9781770866195 (softcover) | ISBN 9781770866201 (HTML)
Classification: LCC PS8565. E5818 W67 2021 | DDC C813/.54—dc23

Cover photo and design: Angel Guerra / Archetype
Interior text design: Tannice Goddard, tannicegdesigns.ca
Printer: Friesens

Printed and bound in Canada.

Cormorant Books Inc.
260 SPADINA AVENUE, SUITE 502, TORONTO, ON M5T 2E4
www.cormorantbooks.com

To my mother
To my father
For the Europes I discovered
in their company.

PART ONE

MATRICULATION

He squealed as he blasted carbine-wielding brutes who skulked in tunnels. "How do you find people here respond to you as a Canadian?" he would murmur, turning off his computer and cranking up Spirit of the West on his oversized ghetto blaster.

"They don't have a clue," I said. "I figure it's my business to teach them."

As soon as the words were out, I was the arrogant Montrealer, inflated with bilingual presumption, laying down the law to the boy from the fishing village.

"I bet they don't listen to you."

"Then I insist," I said, knowing that the true object of Doug's hostility wasn't me but Sebastian Castorp, his next door neighbour in the quadrangle at the top of the graduate staircase. Sebastian countered Doug's decibels with chords of classical music. The competitive conversations between the two of them became a spectator sport. Sebastian, the son of a Viennese professor of philology, corrected Doug's assertions with scorn. Their arguments depressed me, not only because the arts versus science formula felt like a high school debating topic, but because their quarrels reminded me of how young my fellow graduate students were. Many Brits started doctoral degrees at twenty-one; most of the English-speaking foreigners were Rhodes Scholars who had arrived in Oxford fresh from being undergraduate class presidents. Coming from Montreal, where graduate programs were thronged with divorced, middle-aged women and men with jobs and families, I hadn't expected to find myself a senior citizen at thirty-two. I avoided the quad at the top of the graduate staircase, ambling through the ancient streets where the serrated spires stood outlined against the cloudy sky and the Tudor beams of the narrow houses squeezed between the castle-like colleges creaked in the damp. I longed for a café life such as I'd known on the Main and Rue St-Denis. But only the Burger King and a few luxury restaurants remained open after dark. Beyond that, I was relegated to the chip wagon or the pub. At twenty past eleven every night, young upper-class Englishmen swung out of the pubs, chanting and roaring and vomiting their way home. In their soft-faced, pout-lipped pallor, they looked like revenants from the Oxford of Evelyn Waugh's *Brideshead Revisited*. Their lives, governed by tutorials, drinking, and dinner jackets, were a retrograde affront to my graduate student Oxford of cross-cultural conversations, where almost everyone was a foreigner.

One noon-time, during the blur of those first days, I entered the refectory for lunch. Dinner, which was included in my residence fees – battels, in Oxford-speak – was served in the College's seventeenth-century dining hall, beneath the hammerbeam ceiling and the implacable surveillance of portraits of wigged Wardens from centuries past. Lunch, paid for on the day, was available in the utilitarian refectory in the College's back quad, which students in the 1970s had dubbed the Ho Chi Minh Quad, a name that student organizations had maintained ever since.

Having paid for my lunch, I navigated the aisles, holding a plastic tray. The only graduate students I saw were Sebastian Castorp, his Australian buddy Stan, and an older-looking fellow with a wave of dark hair riding his forehead. I slid into the vacant seat opposite the guy I didn't know.

I'd barely sat down when an eager undergraduate hurried towards our table. He brandished a fan of red brochures. "Oxford Labour Party. Join up and help put an end to Tory rule!"

Sebastian leaned back in his seat as though avoiding a foul odour.

"I'll take one of those," the man I didn't know said in an East London drawl, "when the Labour Party stands up properly for the working class."

Unfazed by two rejections, the undergraduate directed an expectant gaze through his glasses at Stan and me. "I belong to the Australian Liberal Party," Stan said, in a high-pitched voice at odds with the thicket of chest hair padding his tight white dress shirt.

Feeling sorry for the young man, I said, "I'll take one."

"Americans can't vote," he said, withdrawing the brochures.

"I'm not American, I'm Canadian. As a Commonwealth citizen, I can vote in local elections. Or do you not care about the make-up of Oxford City Council?"

"I didn't think there was any difference," the young man mumbled, ceding me a brochure and hurrying away in search of a more predictable audience.

"You certainly put him in his place," the man opposite me said.

His name was Leon Zamenhof. He lived in the ugly quad at the top of the graduate staircase, but was rarely there because he had a girlfriend in London. For the first time since my arrival, I felt at ease. Here – in contrast to the dutiful Christians, confirmed bachelors, closeted gays, devoted asexual scholars, tortured virgins, and prescriptive born-agains whom I'd encountered until now – was a person with an acknowledged sex life. At twenty-eight, Leon was closer to me in age than the other graduates.

"The Labour Party!" Sebastian said, interrupting our introductions. "This is Oxford! Are we not all Conservative?"

"Not in this college, mate." Leon waved towards the window. "That's the Ho Chi Minh Quad out there. Hamdaw College has produced one leader of the Labour Party and a slew of cabinet ministers. People on the left, if they're coming to Oxford, study here."

Stan, running his hand over his close-cropped skull, said, "Nobody tells you these things when you're back in Sydney. All they say is, 'You've got a place at Oxford.' That was good enough for me. 'You've got a place at Oxford.'"

"We've all got places at Oxford," I said. Stan and I had grated on each other at first sight. Like every Australian I'd met here, he had come to Oxford in ardent pursuit of all I found objectionable about the place.

"We don't even wear gowns to dinner! At Sydney Uni they didn't let you into dinner without a gown. If you came in late you had to bow to the Master to be admitted." He illustrated the gesture, his thick, crescent-shaped nose descending towards a crust of Yorkshire pudding. Mediterranean extravagance burst out of Stan's big, hairy body in defiance of his voice's high-pitched antipodean squeak.

"You have cut your hair, Stan," Sebastian said.

"I keep it short. If it gets curly, I look like a wop. The day I arrived, the porter at the Lodge asked me my name. 'Konstantine Papadopolous,' I says. And he says, 'I didn't expect that name with that accent.' 'I've got a place here at Hamdaw,' I says to him."

"What the fuck do you care what a porter thinks about your name?" Leon flashed a mirthless grin. "What fucking business is it of his? If some wanker gives me a nasty look because my name's Zamenhof, I say, 'Yes, it's a Jewish name. My father's a Jew. Do you have a fucking problem with that?'"

Sebastian looked startled. "I did not think I would meet people like this at Oxford."

Leon stood up. "You wouldn't, would you? You don't have to deal with people like me in Vienna, do you? You took care of that problem a few decades ago."

Grasping the intent Leon had heard in Sebastian's words, I said, "I don't think he meant —"

"He knows what he meant," Leon said. He picked up his tray and left.

I looked at Sebastian and Stan, waiting for them to make amends. When they said nothing, I got to my feet and followed Leon out of the refectory. Outside, feeble sunlight drained through the grey Thames Valley clouds. I caught up with Leon. "What a relief to get out of there."

He stopped, observing me. His build was shorter and squarer than mine; his broad features and long, thick hair gave him an air of being indomitable and, at the same time, bold and dashing. "Fucking wankers. He's the sort of tosser who tells you the Jews burned down the Reichstag. Where do they find such utter *arses*?"

We crossed the perpetually damp, impeccably-mown grass of the Ho Chi Minh Quad and sat down on broad concrete steps overlooking the modern, glassed-in College bar. The bar was closed, the lights extinguished. In the dull day, our blob-like reflections clung to the muted pane like oversized raindrops. "I wouldn't mind a pint right now," Leon said.

I laughed. I hadn't adapted to British pub culture, preferring a glass of wine in a club with jazz music, yet I felt that in Leon I'd met someone human. The year before, accepting at long last that a larger world was not to be found in the confines of English Montreal, where my family had lived for as long as anyone could remember, I had applied on a whim to Oxford. Even as I was filling in forms and applying for scholarships, I recognized the archaic nature of my plan. In an atavistic colonial impulse, I saw Oxford as the solution to Anglo-Montreal stagnation. I knew, though I could barely acknowledge it, that what I really wanted wasn't Oxford — about which I knew nothing — it was Berlin. Since the fall of the Berlin Wall, I had become fascinated by Eastern Europe. I longed to go to Czechoslovakia, Hungary, Poland, to touch the Berlin Wall. I saw moving to Oxford as the first large hop on my road east.

To my surprise, my scheme worked. I was accepted by the university and received scholarships that gave me enough money for four years at Oxford. Now I woke up every morning in a narrow bed flush against the radiator below the window of my room halfway up the graduate staircase of Hamdaw College. Situated in a 1960s building at the back of the College grounds, the graduate staircase led up to a double-tiered fish-bowl of a quad where first-year graduate students lived in glass-fronted rooms that looked out at each other across the concrete. I went up there to hear Decibel Doug and Sebastian argue, but I was glad that my room was on the staircase below the quad, at the front of the building. My window looked out across a balcony at the back of the ancient dining hall, the kitchens and the Fellows' dining room. Waking each morning, I thought, *I'm in Oxford. How did this happen? What's going to happen next? Will I get to Berlin?*

I explained some of this to Leon, in a jocular way, as our raindrop-reflections performed bobbing movements in the glass of the closed-up bar.

"We're all adrift," he said. "Me da' had this tremendous sense of purpose. When he was a young blade he went to fight in the Spanish Civil War. When I graduated from uni, I went out to Greece to teach English."

I said nothing, puzzled to learn that Leon, who must have been born in the mid-1960s, was the son of a man who had been old enough to fight in a war in the late 1930s. "There was a Montreal doctor who fought in Spain," I said. "Norman Bethune. He was a friend of my grandmother's. He became a hero in China. The Chinese put up statues to him."

"The left is wonderful for odd characters — and factional disputes."

I felt him testing the water, gauging my enthusiasm for conversations about the left. I decided to view any confidence Leon displayed in me as a sign of his having overcome British stereotypes about people whose accents they couldn't distinguish from those of Americans. "At some point," I said, risking an assumption of future complicity, "I'll tell you about the woman I worked for in Montreal."

"Women!" He didn't pick up on the part of the sentence I'd expected. "Emily, my girlfriend, was terrified of my coming to live at Hamdaw. Oxford insisted: you have to live here for at least a year for the doctorate. She imagined me surrounded by young nubiles ..."

"Her mind should be at ease."

Our eyes met. I remembered the sunny morning a few days earlier when the newly matriculated graduate students of Hamdaw College, having been instructed on appropriate sub-fusc — the white shirt, collar, and bow-tie to be worn beneath a dark jacket and gown — were summoned to one of the College's ancient doorways to have our group photograph taken. There were about thirty-five of us, some of whom I had not seen before. Having not so much broken up with, as veered apart from Camille, I'd observed the women with a certain discreet, or perhaps not so discreet, hunger. The first disappointment dark it was nearly black with bright blue eyes. The upheaval of 1960s Montreal — nationalist marches, bombings, union activism — had ushered them into the urban world through a door on the left, refocusing their rural tribalism into a socialist allegiance to the oppressed Québécois collectivity. Having left school at sixteen to marry, Camille's union-organizer father and social worker mother became formidable autodidacts who intimidated dinner guests with quotes from Frantz Fanon and Jean-Paul Sartre. Their only daughter — Camille's older brothers lived in Quebec City — was independent, creative, idealistic, self-absorbed. She wrote poems that were published in Québécois literary journals, studied piano, sang in a rock band, dropped out of a degree in French literature at Université de Montréal, then returned to finish law school and practise immigration law. She did all this in an offhand way, as though her attention were absorbed in another sphere, or as if she savoured each experience only in retrospect, once she had moved on to the next activity, job, or lover. She was faithful to me in her feelings over five eventful years, even though she had no patience with expectations of sexual exclusivity. I would sulk in silence during her affairs, or we would drift apart, or she would tell me that this time we would keep seeing each other. I knew no erotic charge greater than that of returning to her bed after she had been with another man. Her half-absent smile, suggesting she was recalling the pleasures of her other lover as I licked her neck, drove me into paroxysms of passion.

Between the fall of the Berlin Wall and the political crises in Montreal in the early 1990s — the Army's stand-off with the Mohawk Warriors at Oka, the monster demonstrations after the Meech Lake Accord collapsed — my bond with Camille thinned. The breaking point, which I later came to think of as

was that, in a reversal of graduate student populations in Canada, there were more men than women. I was surprised by the youth, not only in years, but also in callowness, of my fellow graduates. Nearly all, regardless of their countries of origin, had been drawn to Oxford from relative provincial backwaters. The only exceptions were two American women who didn't count since, being Rhodes Scholars, they socialized mainly with American Rhodes Scholars in other Oxford colleges, preparing the ground for the political careers they would pursue when they returned home. I imagined Camille surveying the men, and decided that she would feel a frustration similar to that which I experienced with the women. It was not simply that none of these women looked like potential lovers, but rather that, lacking experience of love and loss, they were tense, naïve, and puritanical. A certain companionship between men and women, born of an awareness of the games the sexes play, was absent. By leaving Montreal, I'd torn up my life in more ways than I'd imagined. I longed for familiarity and found it nowhere in these portentous turrets and impregnable pale-brown walls. I leaned towards Leon, grateful that we shared a culture of the political left, a sense of humour and an interest in women. As I tried to inveigle him into further conversation, he got to his feet.

"Cheers, Kevin. It's a relief to learn there's someone halfway human on the staircase. Let's have a natter later on. This conversation won't be complete until I introduce you to another bloke I know."

Before I could ask for an explanation, he walked away.

TWO

I HAD COME TO Oxford via Berlin, a city I had never visited. Throughout 1987, 1988, and 1989, Camille and I followed the rumblings in Central and Eastern Europe. I read London newspapers on wicker poles in the McGill and Concordia University libraries and watched CBC News. Working for a small left-wing think tank, I recognized that the regimes whose foundations were trembling in Hungary, Poland, Czechoslovakia, East Germany, Romania, and Bulgaria had been imposed by Moscow's colonialism. Camille was a potent influence in this perception, sending me to the works of Václav Havel and Milan Kundera and to writers like Miguel Sesteaga, prophet of an emerging culturally syncretic Europe. She saw smaller countries' drives towards autonomy as heralding the future independence of Quebec. We sat on the bed of her single large room in La Petite Patrie, watching on her twelve-inch black-and-white television as Hungary turned a blind eye to East Germans in Trabants escaping across its territory to the West, Solidarity ran in a Polish election for the first time, and the protest marches in Prague swelled. My boss, Joan, was suspicious. "The socialist regimes

provide stability and social justice and have local sup
said in a television interview. "Outside agitators surely h
hand in this."

"But those regimes were imposed by the Soviet Union
I envisaged the dissolution of Soviet colonialism as hera
return of the cultural riches of a Mitteleuropa that had e
my imagination through books and films. "*Ils sont en train a
un pays*," Camille said as we watched a Solidarity rally in P
on television. "Now we'll be able to *faire un pays* here in Qu
When we do, I want the people I love to be with me," she'd
taking my hand.

Two years earlier, Camille and I had gone backpacking
Mexico. Now our eyes turned eastward. The cold November ni
the waiter at our favourite Vietnamese restaurant told us,
a shaking voice, that people from East Berlin were going to
allowed to enter the West, we hurried back to her apartmen
turned on the television and watched as men with picks hacke
and pounded at the Wall; jubilant people streamed past abandoned watchtowers. The elation I felt was so powerful that the
gloom that had engulfed me one year earlier, when the 1988
election had confirmed the passage of the Free Trade Agreement with the United States, began to part: a silvery thread of
hope, leading eastward, ran down the core of the darkness. By
Christmas, even beleaguered Romania was free, its dictator
shot by a firing squad. We turned off the television in an uneasy
awareness that these thrilling events were propelling our imaginations in different directions.

Camille's parents had come to Montreal from a village in the
bush near Lac St-Jean. There, pure Celtic Bretons had inter-
married for more than three centuries, reinforcing a culture
of communal belonging and a gene pool that combined hair so

"the end of Before," came in June 1990. Below my rusted balcony, thousands of blue-and-white flags beat against the grey day. Young people draped banners from sidewalk to sidewalk. The crowd covered the four lanes and filled the sidewalks. I watched the procession's bottlenecked slowness, its stop-and-start rhythm. The chants died away, the marchers jostled against each other until, in frustration, they started shouting again. The bottleneck broke and the largest mass of humanity I'd ever seen surged up Rue St-Denis.

"*Le Québec aux Québécois!*"

The crowd blocked the sidewalk outside the door of my building. It would be blocked all day. There was nowhere to go; it was June 24th, *le Saint-Jean-Baptiste*, the most important holiday of the year. Independence marches and flag-waving happened every year on this date, but this year the world had changed. The night before, as the accord to amend the constitution had unravelled, with two legislatures located in time-zones hours apart withholding confirmation of Quebec as part of Canada, I'd ridden the Métro under the St. Lawrence River to Nuns' Island. I'd gone alone, not daring to ask Camille to come with me. At the beginning of the rock concert, the singer who was famous for a song that condemned a circus seal for abandoning his culture ridiculed the time difference between the provinces that were deciding Quebec's fate: "*Dans l'ensemble du Canada, il est trop tard!*" Songs familiar from the radio roared out with fresh fury. I knew that even if Camille had come with me, we would not have been together.

"*Le Québec aux Québécois!*"

I carried a chair onto the pressed-tin balcony and measured the hours it took for a quarter of a million people to march past a single spot. Camille was down there in the crowd; at some point during the day she would pass beneath me. Maybe she would step in the door for a visit. Or maybe today was not the day to accept a hug from an *Anglais*.

The low clouds pressed down, funnelling the marchers up the street. The balconies opposite mine were hung with bed-sheets on which slogans had been hand-printed in smudged black letters: *Vive le Québec Libre, Ne Touchez Pas à la Loi 101*... Blue-and-white flags sprouted from the sooted brick of the walk-ups.

All day I waited for Camille. She must have marched past, she must have seen me. There had been many silences between us over the years, but never before had her diffidence been bolstered by a quarter of a million pairs of feet. The marchers kept coming, shouting in fury and jubilation, until the grey clouds were streaked with black. Flags and banners remained after the people had gone. As darkness fell, I slipped back into my apartment. My Before was gone. A world had ended, releasing me to explore the world that came next.

Over the next few months Camille had two affairs in a row without returning to me in between. It was difficult for me to remember whether this was the cause or the consequence of my decision, a year after that St. Jean Baptiste rally, to apply to Oxford. My application hurt her worse than any sexual dalliance. "*T'es plus anglais que montréalais*," she sobbed. I received her wounded stare as a jab in the chest. As an Anglophone, I had the whole English-speaking world at my disposal. She saw my decision as a rejection not just of Montreal but of our shared conception of life: an urban Québécois life, which could take place nowhere other than Montreal. In no other city in the world could she be herself. My assurances that I would return after Oxford rang hollow. She knew that the city I really wanted to see was Berlin. If I'd had more money, or maybe more initiative or self-confidence, I would have headed straight to the city that incarnated my hopes for a world renewed rather than taking the safe route of applying to a graduate program in England.

I'd been accepted at Hamdaw College to write a thesis on politics, studying how societies grounded in a chronological conception of history were fraying and disintegrating with the end of the Cold War. Every day I had a new idea about my proposal, which, rather than meshing with my other ideas, spurred me off in a fresh direction. Beneath my changing plans hummed the first chords of a panic that I didn't know why I was here.

I was in my room on the graduate staircase, listening to BBC reports on the crisis in Yugoslavia and the threats to the new Russian government of Boris Yeltsin, when Leon knocked on my door. He was on his way to dinner with Tina, a young woman from Westmount. As we walked towards the dining hall through a dark drizzle, he let slip that he thought I might find her congenial because we were both from Montreal. In fact, I had met Tina the day of my arrival. She had asked me which schools I'd attended; I'd recited this motley list, concluding with my master's degree at inner-city Concordia University. "Concordia to Oxford," she'd marvelled, in an accent that already sounded English. "That's quite a leap!"

Tina had studied with the Québécois elite at Collège Jean-de-Brébeuf, completed her undergraduate degree at McGill and her M.A. at Harvard. She had spent a year studying international law in Paris on a scholarship before coming to Oxford to study business law. She was a snob, but she was not a prude. She was politically progressive and widely-travelled, and had a boyfriend in Paris who was a prince in the United Arab Emirates. Assertive and sexy, she flaunted her waved blond hair and her body tapered by competitive-level tennis. She and Leon shared a flamboyance and life experience that intimidated the proper schoolgirls and schoolboys from England, Canada, Australia, Germany, South Africa, Zimbabwe, Italy, and Japan who occupied the surrounding rooms in the fishbowl quad, and trailed behind us as we joined the queue — British words were already filtering into our vocabularies — to enter the hall for dinner.

Three very long rows of low, heavy, varnished oak tables set end-to-end stretched from the door of the dining hall to the stage, where the gowned Fellows and their guests ate at High Table. The twenty-odd first-year graduate students who resided in College ate at the low table closest to High Table. The students entered the hall at seven-fifteen; the Fellows and their guests congregated near the fireplace, then ascended to High Table at a signal from the Warden. Our meal lasted forty-five minutes; theirs went on for nearly four hours, running through four courses in hall before moving on to the Old Library, then the Senior Common Room. We were aware of these rituals because every now and then graduate students were invited to eat at High Table.

As we sat down, Tina pointed. "Look at that jacket."

In an effort to make Hamdaw conform to their expectations of Oxford, Sebastian and Stan began the term dressing for dinner in jackets and ties. Our ridicule forced them to tone down their garb to dress slacks and dress shirts; the rest of us wore blue jeans and sweaters. Tonight, Sebastian had returned to the charge, donning a high-collared grey felt jacket with green piping that gave it a Prussian air.

"Oi, Sebastian," Leon said. "Is that a hunting jacket?"

"I am a member of the Oxford Fox Hunting Society," Sebastian said.

"Do you hunt foxes in Vienna?"

Sebastian stiffened his spine as Tina asked him whether he could ride a horse.

"Why do you need a horse to hunt foxes?" Cindy, the shorter and darker of the two American Rhodes Scholars, asked. "Don't you just waste 'em?"

Laughter erupted as pseudo-English pomposity and Yankee know-nothingness exposed themselves in succession. The roar of undergraduate conversation echoed up to the rafters of the hammerbeam ceiling. A tall, serious young German woman explained that Germany, a more democratic country than Austria, rarely produced people with Sebastian's pretensions.

"I wonder what's happened to Alex," Leon said. When I looked askance at him, he said, "The bloke I wanted you to meet. Another Canadian chap."

"But also Russian," Christa, the German woman nearest me, said. Then, catching her breath, "There are very many Canadians here."

"There's a certain way they treat you over here," Decibel Doug said, "if you're North American."

He directed his smile at Cindy.

"The fusion of our elites with those of the United States," I said, repeating a line I had written in more than one report for Joan, "is the biggest threat to Canada's liberal political culture."

Tina and I smiled at each other, surprised to agree. The white-haired, dark-waistcoated dining hall supervisor reached over Tina's shoulder, and deposited a tight-lidded silver serving dish containing chips – what I used to call french fries – on the table.

Christa described her work in a children's camp in Poland the previous summer. Farida, who had been born into a Lebanese merchant family in Zimbabwe, commented on African children. Farida and Priscilla, the white South African Rhodes Scholar who was a competitive rower, shared a tense, bottled prudishness. They treated each other with disdain. Priscilla's disdain was shrill and haughty; Farida's was thick-voiced and scornful. The vulnerable immediacy with which Farida grappled with her upbringing stirred my sympathy, drafting me, in a tentative way, into an older brother role that I had never dared to assume with my own sister. Oxford was still so foreign to me that finding myself developing emotional ties to people here felt almost troubling.

At the end of the meal, Leon caught my eye. "Fancy a natter?"

We walked to the back of the College, climbed the staircase past my room, went around two tight bends and up to the featureless quad. Leon's room was on the upper tier. As he drew the curtain on his glass wall, I glimpsed Doug's computer lighting up on the other side of the quad. "It's a pity Alex wasn't there," he said, waving me to the standard-issue armchair.

"Is Alex the very tall, thin guy I saw on the day of the matriculation photo?"

"That's him. Needs some flesh on his bones." He reached for a bottle of Irish whiskey and poured us each a shot. "He's Russian. My dad was born ... not in Russia, but in what was later the Soviet Union, in Lithuania. His parents tried to immigrate to America. They didn't get past Dublin because of the First World War. After the war they moved to Motherwell in Glasgow, then to East London. Before the age of eighteen, my dad had lived in three of the biggest slums in the British Isles. That's what made him a Communist."

The wary look in Leon's eyes gave me an impression of someone who revealed himself easily and had been stung by this habit. "How old was your father when you were born?"

"Over fifty." He laughed. "He was married with four children when he ran away with me mum. She was twenty-two. They met in the Labour Party and didn't get married for yonks —"

"That's why your father fought in Spain. My maternal grandfather was going to fight with the Canadian contingent, the Mackenzie-Papineau Battalion. Norman Bethune convinced my grandfather to go, but my grandmother got pregnant with my mother. Or that's what I've been told. The rumour was that Bethune was my mother's father. He was a terrible womanizer."

Having planned to tell Leon about my work for Joan, as a way of confirming my leftist pedigree, I found myself describing my relationship with Camille.

He smiled. "It sounds so *French*. An open relationship. Emily wouldn't give a toss for that."

The thought that his father and my grandfather could have met in Spain unsettled me. My paternal grandfather, a rum-swilling, chain-smoking bilingual Irishman from Verdun, who had trained as a medical technician, was long dead. He had known Norman Bethune when the doctor was a researcher at the Royal Victoria Hospital, before he decided that the causes of tuberculosis were social rather than microbial. It was my maternal grandfather, a halfhearted lawyer and enthusiastic activist, who had met Bethune after his politicization, and nearly gone to Spain with him.

Was Leon's father still alive? Seeking an alternate way of asking this question, I said, "Are your parents still together?"

"No. My sister and I were at our parents' wedding and we were at their divorce."

I knew, just as I'd known right away with Tina. Leon's alternating tentativeness and brashness, his desire to succeed and, at the same time, to remain on the outside, his playful seeking of approval, and willingness to submit to those, such as Emily, who

THREE

ON WEDNESDAY OF THE second week of Michaelmas Term, I checked my pigeonhole in the Lodge and found a letter from Camille. Next to it lay one of the squares of coloured construction paper that students used to send each other messages. On a purple square, a manicured hand had written: *We're going to the Eagle & Child tonight for Alex's b-day. See you there? Tina.* I waited until I got to my room to open Camille's letter. *Tu n'as pas de coeur,* she had written. *Je n'ai jamais pensé que tu t'en irais pour de vrai.* The openness with which Camille's feelings flowed startled me. I was taken aback by her claim that I was heartless and her admission that she hadn't expected me to really go away. Less than a month in England and I was forgetting the Québécois custom of never concealing an emotion, a habit I had half-internalized yet suppressed among fellow speakers of English.

After dinner in hall, I returned to my room and reread Camille's letter. Feet and voices went down the stairs and out the heavy front door of the graduate staircase. I waited half an hour, then set off on my own. I walked down cobbled pedestrian lanes that cut behind colleges, the gas lamps battling the mist-laden darkness. I crossed the four broad lanes of St. Giles by stages. The cream-coloured façade of The Eagle and Child, once the watering-hole of C.S. Lewis and J.R.R. Tolkien, glistened in the damp air. Inside the door, I found utilitarian high-sided booths where, improbably, Narnia and Middle Earth had been imagined. Coming upon a tall barman, I murmured that I was looking for friends.

"The Americans are in the back, sir. In the non-smoking section. Making a racket as you'd expect."

The back of the pub opened onto an outdoor patio of long tables. Cindy, who was being courted by Decibel Doug, was the only American present. Next to them stood Pia, an Italian lawyer with gold glasses. She wore a tweed jacket over a brown polo neck sweater. The donnish masculinity of her garb was in insouciant contrast to the femininity of her large breasts, accentuated by the tightness of her sweater. She fixed Cindy with a pout. "What are you studying?"

"American history," Cindy said.

"That won't take long."

"Huh?"

Pia met my eyes with a dazzling gaze. "My name's Kevin," I said, extending my hand. "I'm from Canada. Our history starts earlier than theirs. Maybe we can talk?"

Cindy, catching on, stormed away. Doug followed her. "I always laugh when Americans say they have a history," Pia said. She told me that in Italy her father had been a cabinet minister.

"On the right or on the left?" I asked.

"Social democratic. On the left, but not extreme."

"We might have something to talk about."

"It is good to meet a man who speaks like a man."

Sebastian, tall, blond, and red-cheeked, greeted Doug and Cindy. Farida came over and laid a hand on Pia's shoulder. The tall waiter asked Farida and me for our orders. Farida ordered tomato juice, I ginger ale. The waiter brought us the drinks with outraged speed. "Sebastian has a wonderful knowledge of German literature," Pia said, "but it is impossible to imagine him *fucking* a woman."

How could I describe this party to Camille? The Italians we knew in Montreal, the children of Sicilian or Calabrian immigrants, came from families that prolonged peasant customs in the name of cultural identity. Until tonight, I hadn't realized that emancipated urban Italians like Pia existed. Each new experience shredded the fabric of my life with Camille. I felt a pang of allegiance, vitiated by a flare of resentment at her ability to hobble me across the breadth of an ocean. I carried my ginger ale towards the back of the room, where Leon was talking to a very tall guy. As he had said, Alex lacked flesh on his bones. His shoulders were broad, his narrow face flowed over high cheekbones and ridged eyebrows. Christa, the tall German girl, stared at him, though another woman was standing at Alex's side.

"Kevin!" Leon said, hailing me. "Alex — meet another Canadian."

We shook hands. The dark, compact woman at his side extended her hand. "I'm Susan." In a tight-jawed southern Ontario accent, she explained that she was working in London. "I'm Alex's girlfriend. Alex is writing his thesis on Russian poetry."

"I love Russian novels. But since I can't read Russian, I haven't tried the poetry. I actually study politics, but I'm told my approach to politics is too literary."

"Politics is bullshit," Alex said. "It's just bullshit."

"It may be bullshit," Leon said, "but it's the bullshit that decides who's rich and who's poor, so if you're at all morally consequent, you engage with it."

"I didn't say I was ignoring it. I just said it was bullshit."

"Hey, guys," Susan said. "Is this really the time for this?"

"If you can't have a good wrangle over a pint," Leon said, "when can you?"

"Alex doesn't need to be in a pub to start an argument," Susan said in thin-lipped response. "What sort of politics are you studying, Kevin?"

I mumbled something about the fall of the Berlin Wall.

"The fall of the Berlin Wall is crucial, absolutely *crucial*, to us," Leon said. "We're the only generation that will have adult experience of life both before and after it fell. It's cut our lives in half."

"It's made Russians free," Alex said. Susan laid a hand on his elbow.

"Free to be exploited by the Mafia." Leon pushed forward. "Yeltsin —"

"Yeltsin's a drunk and the people around him are crooks. But it's better than Brezhnev and the fucking KGB!"

"Guys," Susan said.

Alex turned away, then, with Susan clamping his elbow, turned back. He looked down at Leon, and Leon looked up at him. I was aware of the whittled sharpness of Alex's features, the long-jawed roundedness of Leon's face, of their two differently slanted dark-eyed gazes. They were less two young men from opposite sides of the Atlantic than related offshoots of Russianness. Leon's mouth trembled. "Wait and see what Russia becomes without Marxism."

"Bullshit." Alex's tone was flat. I realized with a chill that he did not make jokes. In the silence, Christa asked Alex how much German he spoke. "*Ich komme aus Kanada*," Alex replied.

"Oh," Christa said, "with that accent a German girl will fall in love with you!"

Susan told me in a bright voice about her work in a public relations office. I saw that she understood that Christa was too inexperienced to be a threat.

The tall waiter returned. Leon, Alex, Susan and the German girl ordered more drinks. The waiter turned to me, I gestured with my glass. "Finish up, sir, and order your next round." He looked at Farida. "You, too, miss."

"I don't want another drink right now, thank you."

"Then you must leave, miss."

"All of our friends are drinking!" I said.

"I'm talking about you, sir. It's time for you to order another round."

"You shouldn't complain," Farida said, in her throaty southern African accent. "You're doing jolly well out of us."

"You're in England now, miss," the waiter said. "This is an English pub. You drink your pint or you leave."

He glanced over his shoulder and beckoned to another man, who set aside the tray in his hands and stepped towards us. "Got a spot of trouble here?"

"We're going to have to chuck these two out."

"Oh, come on!" I said.

"If you want to drink Coca-Cola, sir, go back to America!"

"I'm from –"

"Move along," the second man said. His raised hands hovered close to our shoulders.

I glanced at Farida as the men herded us towards the door. Her dark eyes widening behind her glasses, she looked like a school-girl who was about to receive a hideous punishment for a wrong she hadn't realized she had committed. I waved in the direction of Leon and Alex.

Christa emitted a feeble, high-pitched, "*Happy birthday, dear Alex —*"

Leon, whose voice resonated with the timbre of a trained singer, intoned a booming, "*We shall overcome ... We shall overcome ...!*"

As the waiters advanced, forcing Farida and me to retreat past the wooden booths, Alex glanced around as though suspecting this parody of workers' solidarity of being a joke at his expense. The singing grew louder.

The waiters pressed us through the door and out into the street. "If you do that again," the first waiter said, "you'll be banned."

The door shut behind us. We crossed the wide street. The castle-like walls of St. John's College reinforced the night's sepul-chral aura. After a short interval, Farida exclaimed, "Fuck!"

Guessing that she had not uttered this word many times before, I said, "Now you can tell your family that your drinking habits got you expelled from The Eagle and Child."

"I'd tell my father," Farida said, "if I were on speaking terms with him."

Her clotted voice, both emphatic and embarrassed, lapsed into silence. We walked back to Hamdaw College and made our way to the graduate staircase. Farida muttered a strangled "Good-night," and scampered up the stairs to the fishbowl quad.

I stood on the small landing outside the door of my room, wondering how I had ended up here.

The door opened at the bottom of the stairs. "I am hoping you are still awake," Pia said, the light glinting on her gold frames.

She came up the stairs with a smile which, though half-abashed, remained self-confident as Farida's smile had not been. She leaned against my chest. "What a ridiculous party. It is good to meet a man who is a man."

"It is good to meet a woman who is a woman." I closed my arms around her. We kissed, laughed again, heard our laughter amplified by the concrete staircase and shared a brief, nervous glance, uncertain whether we wanted to go through with this. Before the mood could change, I bundled her into my room. Once we were inside, with the door closed, she relaxed into a warmth and generosity I hadn't expected. I hadn't expected this at all. My mind remained loyal to Camille, but my body responded to Pia. Her English tweed jacket and tight polo neck sweater were obstacles that heightened my passion. It took us a long time to get naked. The last garment that Pia shed were her gold-framed glasses.

Even as I realized that this was a one-night stand, or, at most, the beginning of an intermittent hook-up, I was foolishly surprised to find that I could be intimate with a European woman. This possibility hadn't occurred to me. I had envisaged myself finishing my doctorate with one foot in Montreal, remaining Camille's lover, Joan's protegé, my mother's son, continuing to drift down to Boulevard St-Laurent and shoot the breeze with journalists like big Jake Mendelsson. Pia made me see that the world after the Berlin Wall was made of flesh as well as politics. I did not know who I would become, a thought that thrilled and unnerved me as the unfamiliarity of Pia's body excited me yet impeded me from satisfying her.

Stroking my hair afterwards, she said, "From the time I go into the pub I know what I want." She nudged me out of her, drew me against her side, my chin nestling near the top of her right breast. "In two weeks my boyfriend will visit me. I will not respect myself if I am not an independent woman until he comes." She sought out my eyes. "Where is your girlfriend?"

"In Montreal. But I don't think she's coming to visit me." As I murmured these words, I felt, for the first time in my life, that I was outside Montreal and looking back in. The Plateau Mont-Royal ethos of accepting with unruffled chic that one's partner had other lovers, as I had done with Camille, suddenly appeared less a proof of liberated progressivism than evidence of unhealthy passivity. I'd had to leave to begin to choose the experiences I wanted.

"I am not your girlfriend," Pia murmured. "We don't sit together at dinner, we don't tell anybody this happened. Tonight is something we both enjoy. Nobody needs to know."

I kissed her on the mouth. In the cold grey morning, sensing Pia stirring and fearing her departure, I entered her again with selfish greed. It was not the lovemaking of a feminist male. Camille, or any other Montreal woman of my acquaintance, might have given me a slap and thrown me off. Pia, though drowsy and unready, received this greedy rutting with a tolerant smile, as a homage of my masculinity to her femininity. I glimpsed in the glow of her golden earring the knowingness of old Europe, both more emancipated and more subjugated than provincial yet progressive Canada. The paradox troubled me long after Pia had returned to her room.

FOUR

MY NIGHT WITH PIA deterred me from drifting upstairs to the fishbowl quad. I didn't want her to think I was stalking her when I went to look for Alex and Leon. Staying away from the quad spared me from having to listen to Doug's desperate attempts to out-argue Sebastian on the subject of the arts versus the sciences.

One afternoon, having returned early from the Bodleian Library, I looked out the window and saw Alex approach the graduate staircase. I listened to his heavy stride go past my door, waited a few minutes, then climbed the staircase to the quad.

Alex stood outside his room on the upper tier, smoking a cigarette. When he saw me, he stubbed it out on the railing, stowed it in his shirt pocket and led me to his room. His tall body blotted out the light. The single bed looked too small for him. He had no computer; sheets of scrawled-on yellow notepad paper covered his desk. There were no souvenirs: no postcards taped to the wall, no photographs of his family or Susan, only a bag of tobacco and a box of rolling papers on the top shelf of the low bookcase. An ugly tartan suitcase that dangled an Air Canada luggage tag was stashed kitty-corner where the French window met the wall.

The only personal touch was his book collection. Alex's books were all in Russian, and they filled the long, low, regulation bookcase. More books stood stacked up in piles on the floor. He waved towards the shelves as though introducing me to his family. For the first time, I spied a glimmer of warmth in his smile. Realizing that he was inviting me to explore the shelves, that this was how Alex made friends, I ran my fingertips over the spines. I pulled a book out of the shelves and opened it, wondering at this indecipherable alphabet. I tried to envisage the worlds these books must summon up in Alex's imagination.

"The one good thing about the Communists," he said, stepping closer to me as I pored over pages I could not understand, "was that they produced fucking beautiful editions of Russian literature."

I returned the book to the shelf, looking at how it fit into a line of sturdy, compact volumes.

Alex waved me to the regulation armchair that we each had in our room, and sat down on his bed. Without preamble, he asked, "You like Russian novels, right? Have you read Andrei Bitov's *Pushkin House*?"

By a coincidence that made me feel roped into Alex's intensity, I had read this modern Russian novel over the summer. I hesitated, then wondered at my hesitation. I'd wanted to connect with someone from home and now that the opportunity was at hand, I was wary.

"The title's taken from a poem by Alexander Blok. Every page has lines from Russian literature. They're like ghosts! They're words you've heard before, then in Bitov you hear them again ..." I sensed him struggling to express in English emotions he'd experienced in Russian. The shared platform of our Canadian upbringings swung down beneath our feet like a trap door, plunging me into the depths of Alex's foreignness. Before my eyes, he metamorphosed into a man in a mitre, garbed in Russian cultural trappings. This surge of strangeness failed to dispel my fascination, or dull the emotive intellectual density that connected us. It occurred to me that Camille, who came from my city but had a different mother tongue, was both familiar and foreign, and that this merging of common reference points and unattainable strangeness might be the key to my attractions, whether of sexual love or of friendship.

"What was it like reading it in English?"

"It was lively. There were footnotes to explain the literary allusions."

"It's not the same! Reading a line from Pushkin in translation is like putting together shadows. It's like fucking with a condom."

I laughed, remembering my most recent experience in this realm, then wished I'd been able to quash my laughter. Alex must be eight or nine years younger than me – twenty-three or twenty-four – but his ancient Russian culture invested him with a ready-made intellectual self-confidence that anyone born on the North American continent struggled to acquire. Behind each statement lay the complete system of a civilization.

"There's a fucking contradiction," he went on. "When I write about Russian poetry in English, only Russians can understand me."

"Or people who've learned Russian."

He shook his head. "My supervisor knows Russian perfectly. When he visits Moscow there are articles in the newspapers. 'The great expert on Russian poetry is visiting Moscow.' But does he *feel* Russian poetry like a Russian does? The guy's a fucking syllable-counter! He writes about how long the lines are! That's all an Englishman can do with Russian poetry."

"It's unusual to meet someone who knows how much language means to him," I murmured.

"Language means everything to me! That's why I majored in Russian and Greek."

He had studied at Trinity, the most exclusive of the University of Toronto's colleges, whose stone spires and creepers identified it as a colonial imitation of Oxford. The thought of Alex rubbing shoulders with Toronto's Anglican elite, whose great-grandfathers had been pillars of the colony of Upper Canada, defeated my imaginative powers. I struggled to conceive how those coolly superior heirs to old money would have responded to Alex's irascibility.

"Tell me about your French girl."

I told him more than I'd planned. With Pia I was a listener, but with Alex, as with Leon, I confessed. In confessing my relationship, I made a passing reference to my job. Alex interrupted me. "That's cool," he said. "Hardly anybody in Oxford's had a job. They've just been students their whole fucking lives. What did you do?"

I'd been saving this for Leon. I had imagined consolidating our friendship as he strummed his guitar, earning his approval — why was this important to me? — by explaining my political work.

"I worked for a small left-wing think tank," I said. "My boss was a McGill professor who wrote a book about the spread of US multinational corporations into Canada after the Second World War. It was a research job. I did research then wrote up the results."

Alex looked at his hands. I'd never seen such long, strong

fingers. "Susan's parents always ask what the fuck I'm going to do with Russian poetry." He shook his head. "I met her at a poetry reading. She was reading a Russian book. Somebody told her I was Russian so she started talking to me. The next day I was crossing Queen's Park and I saw her. I'd forgotten her name. I shouted at her and we went for coffee. She was at Victoria College. A Vic chick. Her parents want her to marry a banker. When I got the Commonwealth Scholarship, they stopped hating me so much. They saw somebody was willing to give this piece of immigrant shit money to go to Oxford. Then she decided to follow me over here, so now they hate me for taking her away from them."

Alex's father, a professor in Moscow prior to his defection when Alex was seven, had been unemployed since they'd arrived in Canada; his mother, a physician in the Soviet Union, worked in a pharmacy. The helpless tone in his voice made me realize I'd tripped over a zone of desperate anger. Old-stock Canadians, he protested, divided jobs among themselves, cutting out immigrants. That was why immigrants were driven to illicit ways of making money! In a sheepish tone, I conceded that my boss was a friend of my mother's. Hastening to short-circuit accusations that I was a child of privilege, I told him how my father, browbeaten from an early age by his own brute of a father, had developed a mixture of working-class anger, intellectualism, and ineffectualness that had seen him fail to finish his MA thesis and be relegated to part-time teaching at a Cégep.

Alex didn't know what a Cégep was; our shared Canadianness seeped away. "It's a Quebec junior college," I said, "that you go to between high school and university ... My mother's background was more secure, though she may be the illegitimate daughter of Norman Bethune."

Bethune's name drew another blank. "Didn't you go to high school in Toronto?" I asked.

"For me, Toronto is a Ukrainian, a Russian, and a Belorussian sitting in a bar talking in Russian about politics and poetry. I don't know any of that Canadiana."

I felt thwarted, my impassioned confessions curdling in my throat. "Don't you want to know about the country where you grew up?"

"If the Canadians at my school had talked to me like you, maybe I would have cared." He shook his head. "It's fucking ridiculous that I had to come to England to have this conversation."

I saw that Alex was not a man who said sorry, and that this was as close as he came to an apology. I told him how my mother had been inspired by my father's struggle to escape Verdun. In later years she had grown disillusioned with his inability to heal the wounds of his childhood. She had been raised in a fringe culture of down-at-heel professionals who wrote poetry. Her father had been an unambitious lawyer, in a culture that produced too many lawyers, who had poured his energy into pamphleteering journalism, denouncing the conditions of the Great Depression to the point of neglecting his practice – and his wife, opening the door to the attentions of Dr. Bethune. My mother had opted for the security of working as an investment advisor in a bank, leaving her rebellious thoughts, reading, and petition-signing for evenings and weekends. My father, she said, was the part of herself that she had relinquished to attain stability. In the early years, he completed her; later, he was a reminder of why she had put that life behind her. To be with him, she moved to the most ragged section of the middle-class Anglo neighbourhood of Notre-Dame-de-Grâce, the rump below Sherbrooke Street, near the lip of the cliff overlooking the poor districts where my father had grown up. By the time I was in high school, those streets were riddled with crack houses. My parents, like other Anglo bohemians, responded to the shift in power from English to French by moving east to Mile End to immerse themselves in the rabble of Québécois radicalism and immigrant variety. The move was as much the product of economic necessity as political conviction. It was a choice of tattered lives; they felt better bringing up their children amid bohemianism than squalor –

"At least you got a job," Alex said. "If somebody gave my dad a job when he came to Canada, maybe I'd care about the country."

"Caring about Canada *was* my job. We fought against the Free Trade Agreement with the US! By the time I started working for Joan, people saw her as a relic from the sixties. She didn't pay me much, but I couldn't abandon her."

"That's cool." The trite phrase sharpened my awareness that the Alex I knew was filtered, diluted by the thinness of his English powers of expression. His gentleness felt more meaningful for being achieved with effort. "It's cool that things matter to you."

"But I didn't want to become Joan when she retired – especially without having her academic salary. That's why I'm doing the doctorate." As I uttered these words, I wondered whether they were true. Hadn't I come here in the hope of reaching Berlin? Leaving Montreal had freed me to invent stories about myself. Having spent my twenties assembling arrays of facts, I was unsettled by this veer into fable-spinning. Were expatriates condemned to be fibbers?

"I'm not sure why I'm doing a doctorate," Alex said.

"Because," I said, in an imitation of an Australian accent pretending to be an Oxford accent, "you have a place at Oxford!"

"Fucking Stan!" Alex's long arm looped towards a drawer. "You want to smoke some pot?"

He lighted up a vestige of a joint in which barely a thumbnail of grass remained. He sputtered and sucked and finally got it to burn, then passed it to me. I felt the moisture of his lips on the shred of rolling paper as I inhaled. Two quick tokes and the last buds were gone. The pot struck at my senses with unerring aim. In loud voices, we ridiculed Stan and Sebastian. We were laughing like fools when the glass door slid back.

"Oi, what have we here?" Leon said, stepping into the room holding a notebook under his arm. Struck by his casualness in entering Alex's room, I felt I'd trespassed on their friendship. "You lads having a natter?" He sniffed. "A little more than a natter, I'd say."

"He interrupted me when I was having a smoke." Alex's contrite tone surprised me. "I need to finish that cigarette." He ducked out the door onto the catwalk that encircled the upper tier of the quad. Leaning over the black wrought-iron railing, he snapped his lighter. "What a depressing view," he said, surveying the hub of concrete and glass. "If they had left an opening somewhere we'd have this great view of the skyline ..."

Leon and I stepped up on either side of Alex, neither of us equal to his height. Lined up in a row against the railing, we stood like three men pissing at adjoining urinals. The void in front of us amplified our words. Daring to speak aloud in the knowledge that the quad was empty, we laughed at the drinks parties held by Priscilla, the South African Rhodes Scholar. Very tall, young men in suits came up the winding staircase to sip cocktails and vow in loud voices that they would never return to Cape Town or Johannesburg if that scoundrel Nelson Mandela became president. Only Stan and Sebastian were invited to

Priscilla's parties. They dressed in their most expensive suits and hoisted their drinks with a will in the hope of looking as virile as the rugby players.

"Uptight bitch!" Alex said, taking a drag on his cigarette.

Leon's circumspect voice accentuated his Englishness, "The only woman in this quad who's halfway ... I'm at a loss as to how to put it ..."

"Fuckable?" I offered a translation of the evil French adjective *baisable*.

"Precisely," Leon said, completing his pronouncement with a wobbly, declarative certainty that made it sound as though he, too, had smoked pot. "The only woman on this quad who is *fuckable* — if I were in the market for fuckable women, which I'm decidedly not — is Pia."

"Right on, man," Alex said. "I figured that out."

I longed to spill my secret, certain that confession would seal our three-cornered friendship. Before I could open my mouth, Leon said, "You worked that out rather swiftly for a bloke who has a girlfriend in London."

Alex's stern mien cracked into an almost adolescent smirk. "Look, guys, nobody's perfect."

"What does that mean?" I asked.

"Look, I don't fool around on Susan. I just don't. But like I say, nobody's fucking perfect ..."

My chest clutched. I heard Leon say, "Are you saying, Alex ... ?"

"Like the second night I was here I was feeling so weird and abandoned. I went to the King's Arms with some people and the others left and Pia and I had a few pints and —"

"You filthy scoundrel." Beneath Leon's gibing tone, I heard an offended morality.

My throat was dry. I realized that when I'd first seen Pia at

The Eagle and Child, she had been standing with her back to Alex and Susan. It was clear why the urge to sleep with a man had gripped her when she entered the pub: the passion Pia had given me was her revenge on Alex.

"Come on, don't tell me you've never two-timed a woman!"

"Not since I met Emily. There's a marked difference between mindless shagging and a serious relationship."

"Don't be so fucking pious. How do you think Kevin sees it? This guy's been in a fucking open relationship for five years."

"That's fine. He chose that and so did his girlfriend. Did Susan choose an open relationship?"

"If you tell her, you fucking bastard —" Alex flung the butt of his cigarette down into the concrete quad.

"I'm not going to tell anyone," Leon murmured. "Not even Emily. I know how these things happen. I just don't think they're a very good idea."

I tried to distract myself from the confession I could not make. A moment later I decided I didn't want to confess; I didn't even want to be close to Leon and Alex. Yet, after this conversation I was finally bound to them. I had been longing for this moment for weeks and, now that it had arrived, I wished I could erase it.

FIVE

ON TUESDAY OF FIFTH week of Michaelmas Term, a note from my supervisor appeared in my pigeonhole, making an appointment for the next morning. Like me, Dr. Auberon Winslow had come to Oxford late. In contrast to most of the dons, who had been in Oxford their whole lives, first as students and then as tutors and Fellows, Auberon had received his appointment from Hamdaw College only eighteen months earlier. Having studied at the London School of Economics, he had worked in the Foreign Office, served in British Embassies in Poland and Brazil, then accepted a teaching position at a provincial university, where he had turned out three important books. His best-known book was on the impact of the economic integration of Western Europe on the politics of Eastern Europe. I had been honoured and intimidated when, shortly after being accepted by Hamdaw, I had received a letter informing me that Auberon had been appointed to supervise my dissertation. After taking his books out of the McGill University library, I realized that my impulsive flight from Montreal risked propelling me into a very severe discipline. Our first meetings had reassured me.

A lean, recently divorced man about ten years older than me with greying hair and the steady manner of a government official, offset by the mobile blue, approval-seeking eyes of the diplomat eager to curry favour, he had been affable and encouraging. Comparing notes with others, I saw that, in the context of an Oxford doctoral supervision, he had treated me with remarkable informality. I was in a relaxed mood as I ducked under an archway in the College's seventeenth-century front quad and climbed the stairs to Auberon's room. He ushered me in wearing a brown tweed jacket over a beige V-necked sweater. His relinquishment of his diplomat's blue serge made me think that he was trying to look like a don. As we sat in front of his fireplace, surrounded by walls packed with books, which emphasized the smallness of the loophole-like windows, the feeling of a man blending in with his environment became less forced. Over his shoulder, a door left ajar confided a glimpse of a small room containing a bed. As a result of his divorce, Auberon was living in College.

"This," he said, waving at the fifteen-page introduction to my thesis that I had dropped off the week before, "is journalism. A scholar gets to the root of things, Kevin. A scholar gets his facts right. A scholar presents an original contribution to knowledge." As though embarrassed by his own theatricality, he lapsed into a weak smile. The blue eyes darted, appeasing. "That's how they judge these things. A dissertation passes if it's 'an original contribution to knowledge.'" In a confessional tone, he murmured, "You're my first Oxford doctoral student, Kevin. I can't afford to have you be a damp squib."

Taken aback, I said, "I've written 200-page reports that were discussed in the media!"

"Journalism!" he scoffed. "I'm sure that outfit you worked for was jolly good in Canada, but you're in Oxford now."

I promised to write a revised introduction. By the time I reached the bottom of the stairs and stepped into the front quad, where the robed and bonneted statue of Hamdaw College's founder presided over the evenly-mown lawns from a niche high up in the wall, doubt swamped me. The lore surrounding the creation of Hamdaw — the only Oxford college founded by a woman, a single woman in the early seventeenth century, who had presided over the construction work herself and laid the foundation for the College's tradition of radicalism — only made me more certain that I'd never be able to claim Hamdaw's heritage as mine. The serrated spires that capped the battlements impaled my spirit. Doubt was a thug who lay in wait for us all; no foreigner pursuing a D.Phil. ever shed the coiled suspicion that the admissions officers had made a mistake. Only Rhodes Scholars were exempt from such doubts. No one expected a Rhodes Scholar to be an intellectual. They were jocks and class presidents, future management consultants and politicians; most of them came to Oxford to do a second undergraduate degree rather than a master's or a doctorate. If they barely scraped through an Oxford BA, after the BA they had completed at home, no one cared. Their purpose in being here was to meet other Rhodes Scholars. The Rhodies gave foreign graduate students a bad name, establishing North Americans, Australians, and South Africans as gladhanding dimwits.

To the tinkle of bicycle bells and the tang of chili and chips heating up for pub lunches, I made my way past whitewashed stucco and Tudor beams that yielded to the sand-coloured castle walls of the colleges packed together in the middle of town:

Jesus, Exeter, Lincoln. Dewy-faced British undergraduates thronged the streets. The twenty-four-week Oxford academic calendar was divided into three eight-week terms. Even the lives of graduate students were set to this frenetic, syncopated beat; seminars, speakers, library hours, and food service accommodated the undergraduate calendar. I felt like a dunce for not having produced a viable introduction by fifth week. I had been lured over here by visions of bricks falling from the Berlin Wall. I'd had only the vaguest idea of what Oxford was. Leon, by contrast, had known exactly what he was getting himself into; Alex lived and breathed Russian poetry. I turned a corner and heard an undergraduate woman tell a young man in an upper-class English accent, "Oh, you are a prat!"

In a cobbled alley off the High Street, I saw Alex looking at a shop window that displayed scarves and sweaters emblazoned with college logos.

"Kevin, help me!" He waved me over. "My supervisor asked me to go to dinner tonight." Alex's supervisor, like many of the Eastern European specialists, was at St. Antony's College. "I got a cigarette burn on my matriculation shirt and he wants me to wear fucking sub-fusc. Fucking Oxford!" He nodded towards the shop window. "I'm gonna get this shirt."

I followed him into the shop. A tall man with the bearing of a butler approached us. "May I help you, gentlemen?"

"I need a white shirt for sub-fusc."

"Certainly, sir." The clerk appraised Alex's build, went to a rack at the back of the shop and returned with a transparent package that contained a shirt. "Here you are, sir. That's forty-three pounds, sir."

"Forty-three pounds! That's over a hundred bucks! It's a shirt, not a suit."

"This is the Rolls Royce of shirts, sir," the clerk said.

"I think my friend's more of an Austin Mini man," I replied. We left the shop. "I know where you can get a shirt that looks just the same for nine pounds."

We walked to Cornmarket Street. Streams of buses pushed crowds of pedestrians onto the sidewalks in front of garish shops. We went into a shopping centre and found Alex the shirt I had bought for our matriculation photo.

"Thanks, man," he said, as we escaped up the narrow passage of Ship Street.

The din of Cornmarket Street receded. The squashed-together Tudor houses on our left looked as though they were inhabited by elves. We heard a piercing scream. There was no one else in the street, yet the scream came from nearby. A second scream. This time we traced it to a pane of glass on our left. Alex took two quick steps and peered in a window. I followed him. In a tiny, slope-roofed room built for people of seventeenth-century slightness, a naked young woman knelt on a narrow bed, only her face and long blond hair visible as a huge, whitely nude, male body pressed into her. The woman could have looked into our eyes at little more than arm's length, had she not been staring at the ceiling with her face clenched. We watched the crack of the man's meaty white ass narrow as he pushed in, then widen as he hauled his rump back for the next thrust. I was startled by the undiluted milkiness of English undergraduates; by comparison, the whitest Canadians and Americans looked stained. Alex's breath grazed my cheek. The boils on the young Brit's shoulders flooded with a deeper redness as he huffed, jolting the woman back against a Tudor beam. She screamed again, as though her back were being scored by seventeenth-century splinters. As she rose over his shoulder, we glimpsed her pinkish nipples. She screamed more loudly as the boy uttered an animal grunt; his pumping slowed. The woman opened her eyes, spotted us and screamed in a higher octave.

We fled down the street. "Fuck!" Alex said. "That girl just screaming and screaming, and the guy just fucking her and fucking her ...!"

"Her look when she saw us ...!" I flung my arm around his back. "You know that the night of your birthday I went to bed with Pia."

The words came out in a gasp. As soon as I'd spoken them, I wished I hadn't. Alex stopped, shrugging off my embrace. The plastic bag that contained his shirt crinkled in his hand. "Are you fucking kidding me? What did she say about me?"

"Nothing. If I'd known, I —"

We looked at each other in discomfort.

"Fuck," Alex said. "This never happened at U of T."

We reached the corner of Broad Street. He stood shaking his head. He stared out at the street, where blond young men on bicycles flashed past. "I'm sorry," he said. "It makes me feel fucking bizarre that we fucked the same woman."

"As we were saying, there aren't a lot of fuckable women available." I said this to make us both feel better, yet it only made the situation more uncomfortable. At length I asked, "Are you going back to College?"

Alex looked away. "No. I'm going to Blackwell's." He brandished the shirt. "Thanks for the help, man."

I watched him cross the wide street to the Blackwell's bookstore. My sour mood pursued me as I tried to improve my introduction. My attempt to write an intellectually respectable thesis had produced journalism, and my foray into sexual adventure had fallen into imitation of my new friend's one-night transgression. I had assumed myself to be unique, yet in England each of my acts was condemned to mimicry.

At dinner in hall, Christa's gangly form stooped over the table as she told me about the European Union's Erasmus program, which had brought her to Oxford. Doug and Sebastian's caustic voices, as they cudgelled each other over utility versus culture, beat down the chatter of four hundred undergraduates, making it difficult for me to hear Christa's soft voice. Tina, glancing in the direction of Doug and Sebastian, shook her head. "They've been at it for hours. It's pathological."

After dinner, I tried to work in my room, became restless and went upstairs to the fishbowl quad. On the upper tier, Doug's door was open. Tonight his voice, rather than his stereo, was pumping out decibels.

"*No way!* No friggin' way. Don't tell me that science is just a *branch* of your artsy-fartsiness! Science tells the truth!"

"It tells one truth."

Leon's room was lit up. I climbed the stairs and knocked on his door. He was sitting on his bed, unshaven, his guitar slung across his knee, an open packet of McVittie's biscuits on his pillow. Gesturing with his scoop-shaped chin in the direction of the night air behind me, he said, "They're going at it hammer and tongs."

"Doug has a Canadian inferiority complex and Sebastian has a Viennese superiority complex," I said. "It's a bad combination."

"If you ask me, they both need a spot of Viennese psychoanalysis." He strummed the opening chords of the Rolling Stones' "Angie." "I've been skiving."

I was learning to respect the ability to skive. At first, I'd disdained the habit British students had of slipping into neutral and doing no work for days. I regarded it as a symptom of a class-bound society where work was pointless because few people advanced beyond the niche into which they were born. As time passed, I saw more flexibility in the society and a necessary outlet from stress in skiving.

With a nod in the direction of Doug and Sebastian's voices, he asked, "Did your parents have lots of rows?" It was the first time we had returned to the subject of divorce.

"Yeah, mainly about money. They fought in the kitchen, shoving the kitchen table into each other's legs. She said she wouldn't have had children if she'd known he wasn't going to support them; he said he wouldn't have had them if he'd realized she was going to bring them up as bourgeois. My sister and I acted like clowns to distract them."

"You learned to please. I remember learning to please." He passed me a McVittie's biscuit. Doug and Sebastian's voices caromed off the glass like echoes of our parents' arguments.

"*I give up!*" Doug shrieked. The ruff of my neck bristled like that of a cornered dog. I shook my hair, which now fell past my ears, and got to my feet. As though he had despaired of words, Doug extended his final syllable into an ululating werewolf howl.

"What on earth ...?" Leon said.

I opened the glass door, stepping outside in time to see Doug burst from his room and run flat-out, white-faced, along the railing of the upper tier. He took a desperate glance down into the centre of the quad, as though about to hurl himself over the edge, then put his head down and kept running until I stepped in front of him, stopping him like a defenceman at the blue line. His big body staggered in a jumble of uncoordinated limbs. "I'm wrong and he's right!" He fixed me with a gleaming stare. "You lied, Kevin. It's a lie. We're coolies. We're nothing nothing *nothing* ..."

"Doug, get a grip on yourself."

He kept yelling. I grabbed his sleeve and shook him. Sebastian retreated from Doug's room, slipped next door to his own room and turned on the light. As Doug continued to blubber, a door on the upper tier opened and dark little Cindy slid out onto the balcony. "Doug, baby, what's wrong?" Cindy ran a long slinky stroke down his back. "Don't let that Sebastian get you down. Those Europeans ain't nothin' but a bunch of swells." She looked me in the eye, taking Doug's hand in hers. "I'll look after him now."

She led him away, meek and sputtering, to her room.

Leon came out and laid his hand on the railing. "What on earth was that about?"

"More aftermath from the fall of the Berlin Wall," I said.

"You could have fooled me."

Classical music boomed from the far side of the quad.

"Decibel Sebastian."

"Wagner's Ring Cycle," Leon said. "*Eine kleine Nazimusik* to give me sweet dreams." He stepped back into his room and slid his door shut behind him.

I stood on the balcony, listening to the chords of Sebastian's victory march. Doug's failure of nerve penetrated me, making his defeat mine as well.

SIX

AFTER DECIBEL DOUG'S HOWL, graduate life at Hamdaw College decamped from the fishbowl quad to the Middle Common Room. The MCR, which overlooked the front quad on the second floor, consisted of a long, narrow lounge full of sofas, armchairs and window seats, a small television room in the back, and, at the opposite end, a grimy kitchen. The title stood for both the organization that gave graduate students political representation in College, and for this suite of rooms, where first-year graduate students living in College mingled with upper-year graduates who lived out. British students read the newspapers and cooked sausages and spaghetti in the kitchen. A lanky guy from Toronto named Ron, who fulfilled almost too well my stereotype of the Ontario WASP, broadcast his plans to go home to work for the Liberal Party of Canada. A solitary, arrestingly long-legged Japanese woman, listened in silence.

In the MCR all conversations were public, stoked by the tinder of generous newspaper subscriptions. The lounge received *The Guardian, The Independent, The Times, The Financial Times, The International Herald-Tribune, The Economist, Le Monde*

Diplomatique, and *Der Spiegel*. Leon became a public figure, his dashing mien and socialist bravado thrilling women graduate students from the colonies. I listened to him regaling a pair of second-year Australian women Rhodes Scholars with his interpretation of the war in Yugoslavia.

"Bourgeois nationalism. That's all it is, pure and simple. Bourgeois nationalism ..."

I went down to the Lodge, where my pigeonhole held a letter from Camille and a note from Auberon inviting me to High Table dinner that night. Knowing that such invitations were usually planned in advance, I wondered why he'd summoned me on such short notice. I put Camille's letter in my pocket and went to the College gardens.

Each Oxford college opened up, like a reverse sequence of Chinese puzzle boxes, the narrow entrance telescoping into a symmetrical front quad, which foregrounded more irregular back quads, which unfolded into sprawling gardens insulated from the bustle of the street by high pale brown walls. The gardens were redoubts of contemplation and privilege. They sheltered a pastoral ideal in the bosom of the city; they were, above all, *private* places, a refutation of any suggestion that higher education should consort with society.

I sat on a bench, feeling cold and English as I absorbed the outpouring of Camille's emotions. *J'ai trente ans. Je me sens extrêmement sexy. Mais, à la fois, je commence à réaliser que ça ne sera pas toujours comme ça ...* Turning thirty was hitting her hard. The message that emerged from the letter's thicket of doubts was that if I didn't return soon, I would find her settled with someone else. I took a lover's cruel pleasure in her despair. For the first time the possibility that I might end up living on the wrong side of the Atlantic settled in my mind.

In the evening, I pulled on my black, two-thirds-length graduate gown over my suit jacket. As I entered the dining hall, I walked past the undergrads being brought their food by hurrying porters, to the fireplace, where Auberon awaited me. A double-breasted suit glinted beneath his billowing doctoral gown. Restored to diplomatic suavity, he was a striking figure: tall, fit, silver-templed. He introduced me to the Warden, Sir Peter, and the Warden's guests for the evening: a high-ranking civil servant and a nervous, jumpy man who, Auberon murmured, had donated more than half a million pounds to Hamdaw College. "Thank you for coming, Kevin," Auberon said. "I'm going to seat you next to Zed. He'd like to speak to you."

Zed, known to all in College by his nickname, was Mr. Cedric Robinson, Tutor for Graduates. As the final High Table diners congregated around the fireplace, Auberon leaned close to me. "Do tell me ... who is that appealing young woman over there?"

I saw Pia speaking to Dr. Dennock, a broad-shouldered, ample-bellied Fellow with the innocent face of an eternal schoolboy. "A cabinet minister's daughter," Auberon murmured, after I had identified her. "She does look Italian, in spite of that unexpected blond hair."

The Warden waved us towards the High Table. He sat at the head, with the civil servant — "Number two man in the National Health Service," Auberon whispered — and the millionaire on either side of him. Auberon sat next to the civil servant. I sat next to Auberon, and Zed sat next to me. Facing us, with their backs to the students, were the millionaire, Dennock, and Pia. Fellows and administrators filled in the rest of the table. On the menu card on my plate, beneath the Hamdaw College crest and the day's date, I read: *Riesling Burgreben Zellenberg (Bott-Geyl)*, 1986. As the Warden ran the wine over his palate and nodded his approval, I saw that our meal would start with *Watercress Soup*; this would be followed by *Crab & Gruyere Tartlet*. The main course was *Wild Sea Bass with Field Mushrooms, Parmentier Potatoes, Ratatouille, and Broccoli Florets*. For dessert, we would have *Exotic Fruit Salad & Cream*. Later, in the Old Library, there would be port and chocolates, followed by a savoury. The evening would conclude with coffee and biscuits in the Senior Common Room. Fellows like Dennock, who dined at High Table every night, were hefty. In contrast to the waddling ooze of cheeseburger-and-cola-fed North American obesity, the Fellows' bulk was a distended robustness, as though each cell of their bodies had expanded to occupy more than its allotted dimensions without losing its vitality. I wondered about the marriages of these men who dined in College, returning home at eleven o'clock every night, and about their wives, who accepted that family life was subordinate to the male camaraderie of the tutorial, the dining hall, and the Senior Common Room.

"You're the third man," Zed said. "Every third person at a High Table gets left out of the conversation." He leaned back in his chair, crossing his right leg over his left. The cuff of his grey dress slacks slid almost to his knee, exposing a bony shin and dark hair. Like every incoming graduate, I'd had an interview with Zed on the day of my arrival. "So, you've flown the Atlantic," he'd said. "I've never done that. It must be a fascinating experience."

Zed belonged to the waning generation of Oxford dons who had been appointed to a Fellowship on the strength of a good BA. For that reason, he was Mr. Robinson rather than a doctor or a professor. A specialist in the history of the church in England during the Dark Ages, Zed had written two substantial books on this subject. He had been at Hamdaw College since the age of seventeen, and cared about nothing more than the well-being of Hamdaw students. Graduate students, perpetually overlooked, had become his personal cause. His spare build and drooping suits — often worn with a ragged sweater — and his compulsive twitches and nervous giggles ensured that graduates from many cultures found him approachable.

"I won't be left out," I replied, "because Auberon tells me that you and I are going to talk."

"Jolly good." In a mystifying feint, Zed ducked towards the greying Fellow on his right and ignored me for the remainder of the first course. On my left, Auberon had buttonholed the man from the National Health Service. My attention snagged on the gold chain that glinted at Pia's throat. The table was just wide enough to make conversation with the person sitting opposite difficult. Against the background hubbub of the under-graduates eating dinner, Dennock was regaling Pia with his theories about Dante. The spell of warm gold and warmer flesh made me hot and restless. I waited for a lull in Dennock's dis-quisition, then called, in a voice loud enough to carry across the table, "I didn't realize you were going to be here."

"That's because you stopped visiting me."

As Pia smiled, Dennock's bonhomie faded. Zed swung around, his elbow sending his linen napkin to the floor. "Every-thing all right, Kevin?"

"Yes. I was listening to Dr. Dennock tell Pia about his book."

"Book by Dennock!" Zed said. "Extraordinary notion!"

The undergraduates had left the hall. As the graduates got up from their table near the stage, Dennock looked around. "Is that a *hunting jacket*?" he asked, staring at Sebastian. "I thought Hamdaw students were frightfully radical. Have we begun to attract fox hunters? It makes one wonder what sort of students our Tutor for Graduates is admitting these days."

Plates of wild sea bass were laid before us. Porters carrying the ubiquitous covered steel trays followed, arranging the vegetables one by one around the fish. "I need to talk to you about *your people*," Zed murmured. "I gather you're the senior incoming Canadian graduate. We're concerned about Douglas Landry. As you know, he came here to read for the D.Phil. in Physics. It's always a bit tight doing a D.Phil. on a Rhodes since they only fund three years, but now," he looked at me through his large glasses, "he's developed this peculiar notion that he wants to transfer to the BA in English literature. He won't take no for an answer." He leaned forward, spearing his sea bass. "He submitted two essays to the Tutor for English. The essays are tosh. He won't be offered a place. But he does have a place at Hamdaw so in theory he could sit in the graduate quad for the rest of the year and do nothing at all! Once Rhodes has committed for the year, that's the end of the story. They'll cut him off at the end of the year if his performance isn't satisfactory, but until then there's nothing we can do. We've never faced a case quite like this."

I glanced at Pia, who raised a playful eyebrow while continuing to display obedient fascination with Dennock's ideas about Dante. "Do keep an eye on Landry, will you?" Zed said as the fruit appeared. "Whatever the academic outcome, my main concern is to avoid a personal disaster."

A puck-shaped piece of wood in his right hand, the Warden looked up, clapped the table twice and barked out phrases in Latin. We picked up our napkins, filed out from behind the table, crossed the hall beneath the portraits of wigged Wardens, and walked through frozen stone passages to the staircase that led to the Old Library. As we reached the landing at the top of the stairs, Auberon greeted the Dean, Dr. Bessborough, a high-cheekboned man with narrow, cunning eyes, who wore very expensive Jermyn Street suits. We disrobed, hanging our gowns on hooks, before entering the Old Library.

Places set with silverware and glasses made small bright islands on the glistening surface of a long oak table. The Warden touched diners' elbows and dispatched them to points in the atmospheric semi-darkness, which was alleviated only by candle light. I spotted Pia standing near Sir Peter, her earrings glinting. I had stepped close enough to her to inhale the aroma of her perfume when Auberon materialized at my side. "Warden, would you give me the pleasure of this charming young lady's company during this stage of the evening?"

Sir Peter indicated two places near the end of the table, then waved me to a seat across from the Dean. Dennock was on my left; the young, side-burned Chaplain was on my right. Zed was close by, entertaining the man from the National Health Service.

Leaning towards me, the Chaplain said, "So where do you fit in, in all this God business?"

I didn't reply.

"They say you have influence over the new graduates. I'd like to know what you're telling them about God. Americans tend to have strong views on the subject."

"In the first place, I have no particular influence over other graduates. Second, I come from Canada, where we believe in multicultural tolerance and find it in poor taste to badger other people about their religious views."

"I suppose," Dennock said, "that you'll be going home for *Thanksgiving*." He pronounced the word as though it were of dubious origin.

"Canadian Thanksgiving was at the beginning of October."

Dennock squinted. "Toronto is where everyone wants to speak *French*, isn't it?"

THE WORLD OF AFTER | 57

"You may be thinking of Montreal." I could not help but extend my smirk into an invitation to others to join me in my ridicule.

Dean Bessborough pounced. "You are an extraordinarily immature man. Why else would a man your age become a student?"

"In my country it's common for graduate students to be in their thirties. One might as well ask why you wish to spend your time with undergraduates."

"It's my research," Bessborough said.

"What is your research?" I asked, reciting the statutory Oxford question.

"Edwardian pedophilia."

"Pardon?"

"You heard me." As the Chaplain looked at his plate, Bessborough said in a mild voice, "Discipline and punishment offer great rewards."

"I've heard that your parties are examples of that."

The silence hardened. At the close of each academic year, when the ban on playing music went into effect in the run-up to undergraduate final exams, Bessborough thumbed his nose at the regulations he himself enforced by holding a large, loud party, with a live band, in the College gardens. Some invitations were good only for admission to the gardens, others admitted the guest to a second phase in the Old Library, where the best of the Hamdaw wine cellar was on offer, while a few carefully chosen guests were invited to the party's third stage, which took place in Bessborough's rooms and revolved around whips, chains, leather, and anal sex. I'd scoffed at this last part the first few times I'd been told about it, but both students and Fellows insisted it was true. Bessborough, a wealthy man, financed these parties himself.

"You can hear whatever you wish. I've far too much couth to invite the likes of you."

The Warden looked relieved and sent the port around again, followed by a sheet on which the Fellows scribbled estimates of their consumption. This time when we rose from the table, we left our napkins on the polished oak.

I recovered my gown from the hook outside the door. As we went down the stairs and entered a subterranean stone passage that led to the Senior Common Room, Zed lolloped alongside me with his stiff-jointed gait. "Good to see you get the best of Good Queen Bess," he murmured out of the side of his mouth. "Just make certain you don't give him a pretext to get his own back. Otherwise you'll have to put on your flak jacket when you enter the front quad."

Dennock, Bessborough, and the older Fellows made the pilgrimage to the third stage of dinner in the Senior Common Room. The Warden excused himself, taking the millionaire by the elbow. As we sat down at a round leather-topped table in the brightly lighted, newspaper-strewn lounge, I realized that Auberon and Pia had vanished.

We cradled cups of espresso and munched cream-filled biscuits. Conversation was strained. We disbanded at eleven o'clock. I walked back to the graduate staircase through the dark. My mind was sectioned by thoughts of walls: the stone barricades of the College gardens, the Fellows' invincible parochialism, the cultural walls that divided the students in the fishbowl quad, the wall of blue and white advancing up Rue St-Denis, Leon saying that the fall of the Berlin Wall was *crucial* to our generation. I climbed past my room to the top of the staircase and entered the graduate quad. Pia's light was on. Doug's light was off, exonerating me from visiting him, though Cindy's room was bright behind her drawn curtain. In only one other room was the light on.

I walked up the stairs to the upper tier of the quad and knocked on Alex's door.

SEVEN

"DO YOU KNOW THIS?" Alex held up a cover with Cyrillic writing. "An early twentieth-century writer. That's such a great period! There's still creativity in the Revolution. There's this struggle between really revolutionary art, like fucking outrageous art, and these fucking commissars who want to send the artists to Siberia. I wish I could read this to you ... Let me read it!"

He stood up. The high-pitched syllables flowed, the dips and leaps of their inflections making palpable the passage's emotion. Listening to Alex's monk-like chanting, his reverential half-Asian recitation, I longed to communicate in his sighing syllables. It fell on me as a great gift, the friendship of this angry, impassioned young man who was from my country, but carried an ancient culture inside him.

When he finished, he reread the first two lines. "You hear that? It means 'a still stream.' It's from the end of Pushkin's *Eugene Onegin*, where Onegin realizes he's not going to get Tatiana. It's an image of everything drying up. You know that from now on, Onegin's life won't be worth shit. But then the next sentence is like a twist on a line from Stalinist propaganda. He's saying

Russia's going to be a still stream under Stalin, but he's saying it in such a poetic way ..." He caught his breath. "I met this Polish guy at dinner at St. Antony's. He's a lecturer in Warsaw. It's so great to talk to somebody who knows the books I'm studying."

"He doesn't mind that you're Russian?"

Alex shook his head. "He's not one of those crazy Catholic Poles. Slavs aren't that different from each other. The Ukrainians think they're different, but 'Ukraine' just means 'borders.' They're the people on the borders. The Belorussians say they're different, but they're not. Their language is just the same. There's hardly any fucking difference between Belorussian and Russian. I know because my mother's Belorussian. My uncle wants me to visit him in Minsk ... Fucking Minsk!"

"Maybe you will visit him one day." I sat down in the armchair.

"Maybe I'll go to hell. I want to visit my other uncle — my dad's brother. He's in Moscow."

I wandered over to his bookshelves. I, too, had grown up in apartments full of books. But my parents' reading had been disorderly: British and American bestsellers, Canadian poetry, radical political tracts, the existentialists and a few Québécois writers in French, some fat nineteenth-century novels, all of them paperbacks or book club hardcover editions. The orderly rows of Alex's books, the silver-grey covers with embossed gold Cyrillic lettering marching along the shelves with the precision of the walls of the Hermitage, made his culture feel solid and reassuring, even as it drew me in with its intensity, its promise of strangeness and engagement and avant-garde sensations.

Turning around, I told him about High Table. He laughed when I spoke of Zed's scorn at the idea of Dennock's having written a book. "This place is fucking perverse! These guys spend forty years eating together at High Table. Zed teaches, he writes, he helps the graduate students. Of course he's going to despise a creep like Dennock who never does anything but stuff himself and molest women –"

"Is it that different from the way you and Leon argue?"

"It's totally different! I don't despise Leon. He's my best ... one of my best friends here." His arms gave an abrupt thrash. "We're not fucking vicious to each other like Zed and Dennock." He placed the book from which he had read to me on his bed. "Hey, man, I didn't want to give you the wrong idea about me and Susan. I don't usually do that shit. From now on, Pia's all yours."

"She was at High Table," I said. "My supervisor was coming onto her. So was Dennock, but my supervisor won."

"You should go see her, man. Go to her room. Is her light on?"

Alex drew back the curtain. We looked down at the lower floor of the quad. In that moment, Pia's light snapped off.

"Too late," I said.

"Hey, man, now's the time to knock on her door. She just got into bed. She could use some company."

I gave him a smile and slipped out the door, carrying my graduate gown in my right hand. I was fed up with wearing a suit. Learning that Pia's body was a pleasure that Alex and I had shared had made my lust feel tainted. Even so, I remained lustful. When I got back to my room, I masturbated into the sink. For the first time since arriving in Oxford, I did not masturbate to the thought of Camille's body. The object of my desire was opaque, a blurred, welcoming warmth. By the time I woke in the morning, I wondered whether I had made a mistake by not acting on Alex's suggestion. I walked to the Lodge, tore a square of construction paper off the block, and wrote a quick note inviting Pia out for a drink. I scanned the alphabetized pigeonholes, searching for her surname. Her pigeonhole contained a sheet of Hamdaw College stationery written over in a tight-looped British hand. After glancing around to make sure I was alone, I withdrew the sheet and leaned forward to read it. *Dear Pia, It was such a delicious pleasure to meet you last night that I should count myself the luckiest man on earth if you were to consent to have dinner with me next week. I know a lovely little restaurant in North Oxford that I'm sure you would enjoy ...*

I slid the sheet back into the pigeonhole, crumpled my note, went to the Bodleian Library and tried, without success, to work. That evening, in hall, I sat with Leon and Tina, who had returned from a visit to her boyfriend in Paris. "Alex has been talking to some Pole," I said.

"I'm rather scundered about these Slavic enthusiasms. It's all bollocks, that Great Russian chauvinism. It's the worst part of Dostoevsky ... It's odd that Alex hasn't brought him to Hamdaw. Does he want to keep him to himself?"

"Have you seen Decibel Doug?" I asked Tina. When she responded with an expression of distaste, I said, "Zed asked me to look in on him. Will you come with me after supper?"

"You know he's seeing Cindy? He tiptoes across the balcony to her room at night."

After dinner, Tina and I walked to the graduate staircase. On the top tier of the quad Doug's light was on. We went up the stairs, walked around the balcony and rattled the glass.

Doug came to the door. His hair had grown out; he had pulled it into a tiny, strained ponytail ringed by a green elastic band. He was wearing a plain white t-shirt that emphasized his broad shoulders and deep chest. "My fellow Canucks!" He waved us in. Empty pizza containers were piled in the corner. Bruce Cockburn's "Mighty Trucks of Midnight" played on the stereo.

I listened to Cockburn singing that everything that existed in time, ran out of time someday.

"I don't get it. This is his anti-Free Trade song and he just accepts that Canada's toast. It's like: okay, we don't have a country any more, I'm out of here, man."

"The Free Trade Agreement is not in our national interest." Tina remained in the doorway. She wore a short, pleated navy blue skirt and the skin-hugging black leggings that were popular with young English women. The combination struck me as outlandish, yet her posture conveyed an air of tense authority.

"We got taken to the cleaners on that deal. We always get taken to the cleaners, eh? Kevin told me that people over here would respect us. I don't think so! They sure don't respect me. Except when they think I'm American. Then it's respect and despisal at the same time."

His staccato gestures irritated me. "I hear you've dropped out of physics."

"I dropped out of physics and I got kicked out of English literature." He picked up two typed, stapled essays. "I wrote these for a third-year English elective at Dalhousie."

I looked at the essays. The first was on Joseph Conrad's *Under Western Eyes*, the second on Thomas Hardy's *Jude the Obscure*. Doug had got an A- on Conrad and an A+ on Hardy.

"Now see what the Tutor in English wrote."

I flipped the pages and read the Fellow's pencilled comment. *These papers are far below the standard we would expect of a first-year undergraduate. I realize this will be a disappointment, given the marks you received on them, but Oxford is simply at a much higher level.*

"Why don't you go back to Physics?" Tina said.

"I ain't gonna be a coolie!"

His hand jerked, knocking the keyboard into the computer stand. The swirl of sympathy I had felt for him on reading the tutor's comments congealed into something harder. "We're not coolies," I said. "Maybe that's what the song is about. Whatever culture you belong to, there's a point where you just have to get on with your life."

Tina looked at me with an expression that was difficult to assess.

"I'm gonna use my Rhodes money to pay doctoral students to tutor me in English literature. Rhodes will kick me out at the end of the year. I won't get a degree, but I'll be cultured!" Doug's laughter set my teeth on edge. "I want more than a degree. I want something I can never have ... Hey, don't look at me like that. I just know I'm a coolie. Unlike you guys."

"Is that what Cindy's been teaching you?" Tina said.

Doug reached down and turned on his computer. "Sorry, guys. I gotta waste a few dudes."

We went down the stairs. "He may be a loser," Tina murmured, as we reached the door of her room, "but he's got a great body."

The next day Leon and Alex began to argue. They had been arguing since they had met, but never with this degree of bitterness. Their combat took place in the MCR, after lunch, when the graduates gathered to drink tea and peruse the newspapers. The prim young women who admired Leon were terrified of Alex. Yet it was Leon who got the worst of these arguments and became most emotional.

"Thanks to your free-market privatization, Russians can't afford bread —"

"It's not *my* fucking free-market privatization. It's the Congress of People's Deputies, which is full of Soviet apparatchiks.

They produced inflation by giving billions of rubles in credit to state enterprises that don't produce anything —"

"And who's in charge of the Congress? Yegor Gaidar, the boy wonder of the free market, who takes his orders from the Harvard Economics Department. If you want to know why Russians are starving, look to America!"

"That's bullshit. The chairman of the Congress is Khasbulatov. That guy's a maniac. He's not even Russian; he's a fucking Chechen —"

The MCR cleared. Their argument continued: Communism, capitalism, anti-Semitism, purges, wheat harvests, party politics, ethnic revanchism. They were both so passionate that once they began, no one else dared to utter a word. Only I felt bidden to watch. Finally, Alex, too, picked up his books. Leon wouldn't let him go. His short, deep-chested body worried at Alex like a terrier refusing to drop its prey. Alex pounded down the stairs. Leon followed him into the front quad, his dark hair falling over his forehead. "You have to admit it!" he shouted. "You have to admit that Yeltsin's ruining all that was built over seventy years!"

"I don't have to admit anything," Alex said, taking refuge in the niche below the overhanging plinth that supported the statue of Hamdaw's founder. Their argument petered out into bleats of emotion that did not attain the shape of words, their hostile, broken murmurs saturated by a troubled communion.

"Go talk to your bloody Pole," Leon said, finding his breath again. "He'll agree with you."

He put his head down and walked away. For over a week neither of them entered the MCR. Deprived of this bath of vicarious emotion, I was thrown back into the shallow waters of my thesis. I struggled to create a sequence of argumentation that my supervisor would find persuasive, a nest of congenial ideas in which I could take refuge. Returning early from the Bodleian, I ran into Tina in the Lodge. "I can't believe you stayed while they were arguing." She invited me to take a walk in the College gardens. We went under the arch towards immaculate lawns and sculpted shrubs that were retreating into the dusk. "Maybe they need you to facilitate their arguments. My parents always had their worst arguments in front of their children."

As long as Tina and I remained foreign students, with our personalities slimmed down to the fact of being Montrealers overseas, children of divorce, progressive Canadian nationalists, it did not matter that she breathed the pristine air of Upper Westmount while my dad had grown up in the pit of Verdun. "You're their Charles Ryder. You know *Brideshead Revisited*?"

"Of course. Charles Ryder: the innocent hanger-on, the passive foil."

"Except that Oxford isn't defined by upper-class Englishmen any more. Today's Charles Ryder is a mature foreign graduate student." We stopped in front of a statue of Hamdaw's Warden during the *Brideshead* era, who appeared as a character in Waugh's novel. He was famous for having announced at a wedding that he knew the new couple would be happy together because he had slept with both of them. "At least you're not all involved with each other sexually. You're spared that by your loyal long-distance girlfriends."

"Camille's not my girlfriend; she's my ex. And she was never loyal." I felt better after saying this out loud. "Anyway, you're in the same position, Tina. You're in a long-distance relationship, and you're not involved with anyone here in Oxford."

A smile pealed across her face. "Well, actually," she said. "I am." She glanced at her polished leather boots, then looked up. "I met a British guy. An undergraduate at another college – but he started late so we're the same age. He's the undergraduate president of his college, he's involved in the Labour Party —"

The young man's appeal became evident. "What about the Prince in Paris?"

"I'm going to give this two more weeks, then I'll break up with him. I'll tell him I met someone new. When a relationship ends it's always because one person meets someone new."

"That hasn't been my experience. Women have left me without having met anyone new."

"Poor Kevin! You must have been a terrible boyfriend."

Darkness had fallen. We walked under the arch into the front quad, then up the steps into the dining hall. Over the next few days, in the vain hope that I might run into Leon or Alex, I shuffled my routines, I carried my insomniac restlessness into the graduate lounge at seven in the morning, making myself tea there before breakfast. I found the long-legged Japanese girl sitting in a wine-dark window seat with a mug in her hand. She introduced herself as Kumiko. She was in the third year of a doctorate in history. If she completed it, she would be the first Japanese woman to earn this degree at Oxford. She spoke in a self-possessed, rather professional way that defused her beauty. I envied her independence. I felt more and more stretched, divided, and needy.

Next Monday I went into the MCR after lunch and found Leon and Alex sitting in a corner. They leaned together into the pages of *The International Herald-Tribune*, reading to each other from a poem by the exiled Russian poet Joseph Brodsky.

"After his Russian poetry," Alex said, "his English poems feel like prose. But it's good."

"I thought so, too, the first time I read it. But now I'm less certain. Listen to this –" Leon read a passage. "There's no real rhythm or progression of images. It's all statements."

I was eavesdropping on the reconstruction of a friendship. I did not intrude. The last ten days had made me realize how badly I needed our triumvirate. The force of this realization took me by surprise. I had never worried much about male friendship. For the last fifteen years my anxieties had clustered around women and sex. Yet the patriarchal culture of Oxford elevated male friendship, in its many forms, above those yearnings. Here, heterosexual relationships were conducted with furtiveness. A graduate man or Fellow required strong male friendships to secure his place among the libraries and common rooms. I listened to Leon and Alex murmuring to each other, taking their communion as an omen that tomorrow I, too, would be able to talk with them.

EIGHT

NOT EVEN AFTER THEIR reconciliation did Leon meet Alex's friend Jerzy. But I did. It happened the week that Miguel Sesteaga arrived in Oxford.

I had been introduced to Sesteaga's books by Camille. As a young Communist, and the author of denunciatory novels, Sesteaga had fled the fascist Spain of General Franco. He had settled in Paris in the heyday of Jean-Paul Sartre and Simone de Beauvoir, where he had lived with a Jewish woman writer prominent in Paris publishing circles, resisted Jean Genet's efforts to seduce him, and become a vocal supporter of Algeria's struggle for independence. After meeting Che Guevara at a conference in Algiers, he was lured to Cuba, where he embraced the Revolution and wrote an effusive book about Fidel Castro. In Paris, in May 1968, he took to the streets with the students, but shortly afterwards fell in love with a Moroccan construction worker, rejected socialism, and declared his devotion to freedom of thought and economic activity, explicated the impact of his growing support for Palestinian nationalism on his relationship with the Frenchwoman, whom he eventually married, while taking Arab men as lovers, and analyzed his youthful devotion to Castro as the homoerotic crush of a man who had been seeking the ultimate authoritarian father figure. His later novels stressed Spain's suppressed Islamic roots and, as Sesteaga came to terms with his Basque ancestry, demonstrated a disconcerting sympathy for separatist bombers. He had greeted the fall of the Berlin Wall as the advent of a great epoch of human liberty. When war broke out in former Yugoslavia, he was one of the first intellectuals to visit Sarajevo. The title of his first talk in Oxford was "We Are All Bosnians Now."

At dinner in hall the night before Sesteaga's talk, I invited Leon and Alex to come with me. Leon said he was going to London to see Emily.

"But you just got back!" Tina said.

"Emily finds this long-distance business terribly trying."

"I'll ask Jerzy if he wants to go," Alex said.

After dinner the others disappeared. Leon and I took the back route through the Ho Chi Minh Quad to the graduate staircase. "Alex goes to that Pole to get a sympathetic hearing on Yeltsin that he'll never get from me," he muttered. "Don't you think that otherwise he would have introduced me to him by now?"

The next evening, in the vault-like amphitheatre of the Ashmolean Museum, I found Alex in a top corner seat. He sat next to a wiry man in his mid-thirties with high, delicate cheekbones and fatigue smears beneath his dark brown eyes. The black thatch of his hair fretted at the tops of his ears. He met my eyes with an expression of calm yet severe watchfulness. The seats around Alex and Jerzy were occupied; I stood in the aisle making desultory conversation.

"You teach in Warsaw?" I asked.

"Yes, I teach history at university. Very small university."

"You're here for the year?"

"For one term only. Polish grant is small. In Poland I have many work. Here I read, I write. Nobody say you do this work. I like!" His smile faded into stony appraisal. "You are from Toronto? In Toronto many people speak Polish language."

"I'm from Montreal. There are Poles there, too."

On the stage, a portly Fellow approached the microphone. I descended half a dozen rows to find an empty seat. Sesteaga headed towards a seat in the front row. He was shorter than I'd expected. The brownness of his hair had deadened without going grey. The famous thick, scarred nose was as prominent as in the photographs on the backs of his books. He moved with a slightly hunched posture and a quick-shuffle stride. He was in his sixties, yet he seemed animated by a nervous, exploratory energy.

When the Fellow's introduction ended, Sesteaga sat down on stage. Without acknowledging the audience, he took out a sheaf of paper and began to read in his deliberate, accented English, the language he had learned after French and Arabic. The rigidity of his delivery stifled the nervous quickness of his movements. I reflected that the fall of the Berlin Wall had abolished the last vestiges of a nineteenth-century academic formality prolonged beyond its natural lifespan by the Cold War.

"... We trace the origins of the war in Bosnia to the collision of two empires, the Austro-Hungarian Empire which ruled middle Europe, and the Ottoman Empire, which ruled Serbia, Bosnia and Croatia. Like us, Bosnians are the survivors of empires. In this way, we are all Bosnians now ..."

This phrase repeated in each of Sesteaga's thudding perorations. The Latin symmetry of the paper's structure was evident

to the ear. The crescendo was: "Today hybridity has made trans-
gressors of us all. Our lives violate the boundaries taken for
granted by our forebears. In their multicultural heterodoxy,
the Bosnians are our forerunners. In this sense, too, *we are all
Bosnians now*."

He looked up, prompting restrained British applause. The Fellow returned to the microphone. His appreciation of Sesteaga's
talk having failed to elicit questions, he suggested that we move
on to the reception. Only a fraction of the audience followed.
By the time I turned around, Jerzy had left.

Alex thudded down the steps. "What fucking bullshit!" he
hissed to me, as the Fellow escorted Sesteaga to the reception.
"Croatia was ruled by Austria, not by the fucking Turks. When
he said that, I looked at Jerzy and said, 'That's wrong,' and he
said, 'I know it's wrong.' That's why he left. He thought it was
bullshit."

"But the larger points about former Yugoslavia as one of the
cradles of multicultural diversity —"

"Nobody wanted diversity. They wanted their own fucking
countries —"

"But they learned to live with diversity. It became part of
them."

We argued, as Alex argued with Leon. The heavy-set Fellow
approached us. "I say, we're taking our guest to dinner across
the street. We're a bit short on bums on seats. I don't suppose
you chaps would like to come along?"

"You're going to the Randolph?" I said. "It's a bit out of my
price range."

"If you order a coffee and a sweet, we'll treat you."

"That's very kind. I've actually read a couple of his books ..."
I turned around. "Alex!"

With a dismissive wave of his hand, Alex left the amphitheatre.

"How marvellous," the Fellow said, "to see his talk arouse such *passion*."

I accompanied a knot of Fellows and graduate students across Beaumont Street to the towering Randolph Hotel, which dominated the corner with St. Giles. Word among students was that ordering tea in the Randolph could lead to bankruptcy. In spite of the late hour, the dining room chandeliers glittered through the windows from behind the hotel's pale brown stone and dark blue trim. A long table had been reserved for us. I sat diagonally across from Sesteaga. As a Spaniard, comfortable eating at this late hour, he ordered a full meal. Three of the Fellows hastened to join him, even though they had almost certainly dined in their colleges. Following instructions, I ordered a black tea and a slice of cream pie. The other graduate students did the same.

Sesteaga asked the elegant, white-haired Fellow sitting next to him the identity of the robed figure in the portrait on the wall. "The Eighth Earl of Pembroke," the Professor replied. "He's wearing Garter robes." A meticulous explanation in Spanish followed. "A man can look wonderful in robes, can't he?"

"Beautiful men don't interest me," Sesteaga said. "I like rough men." Had I heard this correctly? "Last month I was on the coast of Turkey. There's no man like a Turkish sailor."

Sesteaga and the Professor discussed *los marineros*. I realized that everyone at the table was male.

The Fellow who had given the introduction restored the conversation to English. "The students have questions for you, Mr. Sesteaga."

The young man on my right asked about Bosnian identity.

His intricate syntax would have tripped up a native speaker of English. Sesteaga, as one would expect from a writer, responded by speaking from experience. He was in the midst of explaining the dynamics of the family he had lived with in Sarajevo when the food arrived. As he leaned back to make room for his plate, his gaze shifted to the waiter, a slender young man with light brown skin. Rich-sounding syllables uncoiled from deep in Sesteaga's throat. The waiter responded. The banter between them took on a playful quality that belied the high-pitched seriousness I associated with the Arabic language. The waiter looked welcomed, almost embarrassed. When he left, Sesteaga said with a smile, "He is from Morocco. Those are the best Arabs. They are *mongrelized*. The Berbers, the Arabs, the Jews, the French, the Spaniards, the Portuguese — many races have left their seed in Morocco!" He sipped his wine and wiped his mouth. "That is why I have an *appartement* in Marrakesh."

"I believe we have another question for you." The Fellow dealt me a purposeful gaze.

"*Moi, je viens de Montréal.*" Knowing that he lived in Paris, I couldn't help but continue in French. Everyone stared at me, but I knew their surprise would turn to scorn if I exposed my accent in English. Mentioning our constitutional crises, I evoked the possibility of the Balkanization of Canada —

"Canada will never break up like Yugoslavia," Sesteaga said in a clipped Parisian accent which itself sounded like a reprimand. "The history is different." He swivelled his head, inviting the next question.

I started to remonstrate, but the waiter returned. Sesteaga bantered with him in Arabic. The Professor of Spanish was fascinated. "Imagine talking to those chaps in their own language!"

I finished my cream pie. When the waiter returned, Sesteaga

got to his feet. "One minute, please." He hurried away. The young man next to me asked what part of America I came from. Surprised by the question, since he had heard me speaking French, I explained. On learning I was Canadian, he turned to talk to the man on his left.

"I wonder if our guest would like dessert," the Fellow said. "He seems to be taking rather a long time in the loo."

"I'll call the waiter." The Professor of Spanish waved his hand.

A blond, balding waiter appeared. "Sir?"

"Where's our other waiter gone? The Arab chap?"

"His shift's ended, sir. He's gone home."

"Could you bring us the dessert menu, please? One for me, one for my friend and one for this gentleman," he said, gesturing towards Sesteaga's plate.

"The foreign gentleman, sir? He's left."

"Left?"

"Yes, sir. He left with the other waiter."

The young man on my right uttered a single, alarming bark of laughter.

NINE

ON LEARNING OF SESTEAGA'S departure, the Fellow cancelled his dessert order and dismissed us. I walked up Broad Street in the dark, climbed the stairs to the second tier, went to Alex's room and rapped my knuckles on the glass.

He slid open the door. I told him what had happened.

"He fucked the waiter? Fucking faggot! I bet all he did in Sarajevo was fuck some Muslim boy up the ass!"

"So what? Does that make his experience less valid?" My neck and face felt hot. Alex and I weren't compatriots after all; the values of my bohemian Montreal and his Slavic immigrant Toronto could not be more different. "Does it threaten your sexuality if Sesteaga likes Arab boys? I didn't know you Russians were so uptight. I thought you left that to Catholic Poles —"

"Leave Jerzy alone!"

"Sure I'll leave him alone. He's all yours. I'll leave you alone, too."

I closed the door and thudded down the stairs to my room. Pacing, I sucked in angry breaths. My anger towards Alex was as wounded as that I might have felt towards a girl, not a woman, whom I would have dated as an adult, but one of the girls I had idealized as an eternal soulmate at fifteen, only to feel betrayed on getting to know her well enough to realize that we had nothing in common. The violent immaturity of my emotions only made me more upset. Why did I need Alex to be like me? In Montreal I'd revelled in diversity. In chauvinistic Oxford the coherence of my identity depended on asserting Canadianness as a unified bulwark against the crushing parochialism of upper-class British insularity and Yankee Rhodes Scholar arrogance. My compatriots could wound me merely by having different values.

Michaelmas Term was ending. Eight weeks on, six weeks off, that syncopated Oxford rhythm hurled us forward. One afternoon, fed up with writing trite opening sentences, I stepped out my door for a stroll on the balcony that overlooked the back of the dining hall. Pia was coming down the stairs. We could not avoid each other. Frustration stung me into flirtatiousness. I laid my hands on her shoulders and, with half-mocking bravado, kissed her on the lips. My breath quickened, my heart squeezed. She took a step back, her brown eyes observing me with fierce skepticism. To defuse the tension, I asked, "How did Giuseppe's visit go?"

"He respected me. He does not take me for granted after I tell him I have been with another man."

Two other men, I thought. Or more? Yet our banter relaxed me. Pia smiled, touched my shoulder and slipped away. Just before dinner, wandering out to the Lodge to check my mail, I ran into Tina. Rather than returning to Montreal for the holidays, she was staying in College until Christmas Day, which her new boyfriend, Simon, had invited her to spend with his family.

"Watch out," I said. "You'll become English."

"I'm considering it. When I think of what Canada will be like after Free Trade!" I must have grimaced because she said, "You're going to have to make the same decision, Kevin."

I asked Tina to accompany me on a visit to Decibel Doug. "Zed asked me to look after 'my people.'"

"Fortunately, in Canada we don't have 'a people.' You can be yourself. It's okay."

Her words brought back the Bruce Cockburn song. Still furious at Alex's homophobic scorn, I avoided him. I avoided everyone and their thrilling Christmas travel plans. Grinch-like, I sat in my room writing sentences like *The division of Berlin was the microcosm of a divided world* and then deleting them. The taste of Pia's mouth tormented me. On Friday night of eighth week – the end of Michaelmas Term – the vespers pealing from the chapel were interrupted by a loud knock on my door.

"*Ta-dah!*" Leon, resplendent in a natty black jacket, white silk shirt and shiny black slacks, flourished his hands like a magician pulling a rabbit out of a hat. "Kevin, I'd like to introduce you to my girlfriend Emily!"

Emily looked like anything but the working-class martinet I'd imagined. She was his height, lanky and thin-faced, with long tangled hair, a white blouse, a simple brown skirt, and an array of necklaces and scarves that spread out from her neck like ripples in a pool. Realizing that I had no idea what she did, I asked her. She seemed pleased that this should be my first question. In a voice that verged on Sloan Ranger London posh, she said that she was an artist who supported herself by working in an auction house in Knightsbridge.

"We're dining in hall," Leon said, "then we're going to Christmas service in the chapel."

"Christmas service? But you're Jewish!"

"Why should I allow that to exclude me from one of my society's essential rites?" Leon, basking in Emily's pleasure, was brimming with good will. I realized I'd never heard him mention the state of Israel, allegiance to which was the core of the identity of nearly every Jew I'd known in Montreal, even left-wingers like Jake Mendelsson.

"You're dressed up for chapel? Is this normal for a Jewish Marxist?"

"Kevin, you've obviously never seen men dressed in their finery at a working-class wedding."

"Commodity fetishism!" I objected. "The oppressed squandering their scarce resources to imitate their oppressors."

Leon appealed to Emily. "You see what I have to put up with?"

"He sounds like you, but with an American accent."

"Canadian," Leon said.

I saved the dross I'd been writing, turned off my computer and went to dinner with them. On the way down the stairs, Leon confided that he had submitted two chapters of his thesis to his supervisor, received favourable comments, and might be allowed to apply for confirmed D.Phil. status in Trinity Term. "Have you spoken to Alex? I tried to persuade him to come along, but he seemed terribly peeved and said he wasn't dining."

"We had a fight." I told him about the Sesteaga lecture. "He's decided that Jerzy is the fount of all wisdom."

"I do wish he'd introduce me to this marvellous Pole of his. It's awfully trying to perpetually face this insinuation that you're inferior to someone you haven't met."

We got to hall late. The graduate table was full. We sat at the corner of an undergraduate table. Emily made incisive comments about the hammerbeam ceiling and the portraits on the walls.

Leon invited me to accompany them to chapel. I shook my head, preferring to meet them in the MCR after the service. I went back to my room, turned on my Toshiba T1600 and wrote: *The ideological divisions that characterized the Cold War were reified into fixed concepts of identity, duty, and value.*

An hour later, when I walked to the MCR, the end-of-term party still hadn't started. Kumiko sat in the corner sipping coffee and flipping through *The Economist*. I asked, "Are you going back to Japan for the holidays?"

She shook her head. "When you have been away for two years, people in Japan think you are strange. It's better not to go back until you are ready to become Japanese again."

The graduates filtered in. Stan, his hair cut short, wore a black suit. He was talking to a similarly dressed British doctoral student. He imitated the Brit's phrases, pitching his voice as an echo that drew his accent closer and closer to that of his model. "I say, that *was* a fine service ..."

Leon and Emily arrived. Emily's radiance had wilted. "Rotten service," Leon murmured. "Our right-on young Chaplain sounded like an Old Testament prophet."

Sebastian arrived with Priscilla. As he praised the wonderful service, Leon touched my arm to indicate that he and Emily were leaving. I was left staring at Commonwealth students trying to masquerade as Brits.

"You have to respect the Chaplain," Stan murmured.

"People who don't respect authority deserve a hiding," Priscilla said. "In South Africa we have too many people like that."

A rough hand clapped me on the shoulder. "What a bunch of fucking wankers!"

Alex looked at his feet, then glanced up and peered over my shoulder. "This afternoon I was listening to the BBC. They interviewed Sesteaga. About his homosexuality ... about how that developed, how it fit into being a dissident against Franco and his idea of how Europe would be better if it was contaminated by the Arabs ... What a crazy guy!"

I had received an olive branch. I decided to grasp it. We walked back to the graduate staircase. When we said goodnight, he said, "I'll see you in January. I'm going to Moscow to visit my uncle. It'll be my first time in Russia since I was seven!" A sardonic clench that was as close as he came to a smile, "That's what the fall of the Berlin Wall means to me. I can go home!"

We shook hands. I saw Alex once more before I left. I was sitting at a corner table of the small, ornate two-storey main reading room of the Taylorian Institution Library, idly taking notes, when Alex came in with Jerzy. Alex walked in front, Jerzy behind. The Pole looked slight and compact in the shadow of Alex's careless, broad-shouldered height. Jerzy's gait was a shuffle and a dance; his shoulders bobbed. In an instant I understood the source of the softening of Alex's opinion of Sesteaga. My astonishment prevented me from getting up to greet them. I bowed my head and continued taking notes. When I looked up, they were gone.

TEN

AT FOUR O'CLOCK IN the afternoon I dragged my suitcase out of the Arrivals area of Dorval Airport and into the frigid blast of the Montreal winter. Camille, though I'd sent her a letter with my flight details, would have forgotten them, or felt obliged to demonstrate her independence by ignoring them. The dip of disappointment I felt hopped up into an unexpected gust of exhilaration at being under my own steam. I hauled my suitcase to the airport parking lot, made a quick connection by bus to a second parking lot, where I caught the bus to the Lionel Groulx Métro station, rode the Métro to Place des Arts, caught a number 80 bus up Avenue du Parc, got off in the darkness and dragged my suitcase over the packed-down snow that clogged its little wheels, to the duplex on the side street that my parents had bought together and my mother had paid off after their divorce.

My mother came to the door as though I'd stepped out for the afternoon. She had just come in from work and was wearing a blue blouse and a name tag: *Brigid Carmichael*. She had kept my father's name. After their divorce she had joked about adopting Bethune as her surname, although in her quieter moments she became despondent at the thought that her progenitor might have been a man whom she had never known.

In the shower my hand hesitated. Here the tap labelled "C" was hot, *chaud*, and the cold tap had an "F" for *froid*. As I changed in the room that had been mine until I got my own apartment at twenty-three, I imagined how surprised Auberon, Zed, Dennock and Bessborough would be by the discrepancy between the suburban mansions where "Americans" were imagined to reside and this creaking walk-up apartment.

When I returned to the kitchen my mother was wearing corduroy slacks and a black Irish wool sweater. Her long, thick hair, with licks of red still flickering through the silver, was pulled back into a ponytail. "Joan was asking for you. Marie says she'll come by tomorrow. I worry about your sister. She and that husband of hers drink like it was going out of style ... At my age," she said, "you wonder about the choices you've made. Imagine what you'll think of taking off for Oxford twenty years from now. You've changed the course of your life."

No city made its residents feel more guilty for abandoning it than Montreal. "You can't have it both ways, Mum. You can't get pissed off with Dad for not succeeding, then get pissed off with me because I try to succeed."

"Don't bring your father into this. Our conversations go downhill when you do that." She poured her daily ration of half a finger of whiskey into her coffee. "How are your studies going?"

"Fine." Before leaving, I had left Auberon an envelope. Rather than the two chapters I had promised him, it contained a rewritten introduction and half of an opening chapter.

"Have you been following the news?"

"Canada doesn't exist in the British papers."

"The Charlottetown Accord was defeated. Quebec's not in the constitution – anything could happen."

Conversations like this were my inheritance, the legacy of a time when my parents had been together and their friends had crowded into the walk-up to drink and argue. I calibrated my life by their debates: from dim recollections of exchanges about countries and their pavilions at the Expo 67 world's fair, to hushed, desperate talk of the tanks in the streets during the October Crisis in 1970, to my dad's hard-drinking journalist friend Nick's exuberant campaign for city council on the Maoist ticket in the early 1970s, to the outburst of Francophone euphoria and Anglophone dismay after the Parti Québécois election victory in 1976, with my now estranged parents and their friends unwilling to identify with either camp, a tension that only grew worse during the failed referendum on independence in 1980. My parents had separated, and their circle of friends dispersed, by the time that strangers were shouting at each other on buses on the way to work during the 1988 federal election over the Free Trade Agreement with the United States and, later, two and a half years ago, in 1990, when I had stood on my balcony and watched the crowds roar past after the death of the Meech Lake Accord.

I excused myself to use the phone in my mother's study. When Camille's answering machine clicked on, the sound of her recorded voice made me feel hot and embarrassed. In a breezy tone, I told her I would be on Boulevard St-Laurent that evening.

Two hours later, as I stepped out the door, the cold sapped my body. I felt like a sailor who had lost his sea legs. I walked through the side streets to Boulevard St-Laurent. This northern stretch of the Main, once lined with uninspired storefronts for the garment industry, was breaking out into small art galleries, cafés, and antique shops. I'd once glimpsed Leonard Cohen, dressed in black, walking down the street. Cohen stared straight ahead, his body almost rigid, terrified of being approached by strangers.

I walked south: old Jewish shops, new Latin American shops, staid Portuguese groceries, the porno cinema, the pool halls, former Slovenian delicatessens, and Polish travel agencies undergoing conversion into nightclubs with steel doors and neon-rimmed façades. Observing the Main with Oxford eyes, I perceived the provisional nature of these businesses. The absence of a monolithic culture enshrined in stone castles, the linguistic uncertainty of this multilingual borderland between French and English, generated the incessant provocation of a friction between cultures, the unending, unsatisfiable eroticism of glancing encounters.

As I entered La Cabane, I spotted big Jake Mendelsson, forty-five years old, sitting opposite a lithe young woman with features of dewy innocence. Jake's broad shoulders, sensitive, bearded face, and balding pate appeared on television whenever English Canada wanted a tongue-in-cheek take on life in Quebec.

"Kevin!" He waved me over. I shook hands with the young woman. Her name was Melissa or Melanie or Michelle. She was a demure English girl from the West Island, neither a Franco-phone, as I might have expected given Jake's tastes, nor a Jewish girl, as his parents might have wished.

Jake was in full flight. "Hey, Kev. You hear the latest? You're locked in a room with Saddam Hussein, Moammar Gaddafy, and Brian Mulroney. There's a gun in your hand, but there are only two bullets in it. What do you do?"

I sensed the girl's eyes assessing me. I felt jetlagged. "Ask them to let you out?"

"You shoot Mulroney twice!"

The girl laughed with surprising heartiness. The waitress came and we all switched to French to order. When the waitress left, Jake told his date, "Kev here works for the Independent Canada Institute. A reliable source for radical ideas."

The shrewdness with which Melissa or Melanie was sizing me up made me realize that though she looked sixteen years old and naive, she was neither. Jake's assumption that I was still working for Joan startled me. Hadn't anybody noticed that I'd left town?

Waving his fork, Jake said, "Tell Joan of Arc I might call her for a righteous quote." He shot a sly glance at Michelle or Melissa, who responded with an enthralled smile. In Oxford I'd felt nullified by sexual repression. I'd been in Montreal for three hours and already I was being upstaged by a man half a generation my senior.

I ate in silence, left my share of the bill on the table, and began my rounds of the bars, the cafés, the smoked meat shops. I thought of a Latin American novel that Camille and I had read — I in English and she in French — which opened in Paris with a couple who refused to make dates, preferring to drift around St-Germain-des-Près until chance allowed their paths to cross. I walked to Rue St-Denis, where the cafés and restaurants hewn out of the walk-up apartments created an arcade of light in the darkness. I stepped into a snow-drifted phone booth, called Camille again and was weak enough to leave a second message. After that, jetlag caught up with me, coating the long white tunnel of the street with a patina of unreality.

Camille phoned in the morning. Her voice was cautious, verging on reproachful. *"T'aurais dû me dire que t'arrivais hier ..."*

In the past I would have lashed back, pointing that I *had* told her. Now all I could manage was, *"J'ai hâte de te voir."*

"*Cette semaine c'est pas évident.*" Silence. She knew, of course, that I would know that, though I had just blurted out that I was eager to see her and she had demurred, the obstacle to our meeting was not work, but some man she needed to clear out of the way in order to make space for me in her bed – assuming we were going to bed together, which I did assume, or at least hoped for. Camille knew that this hope allowed her to buy time.

That afternoon I went to see Joan. She was as determined as ever, her long grey mane seemingly animated by a life of its own, her brown eyes scouring out society's contradictions. "I'm hanging on until you get back. Free trade deals and digital commerce have changed the issues we're fighting on. We need younger people who are capable of defining progressive policies after the Cold War." Joan's stare sank into my chest like a lepidopterist's needle, pinning me to the felt-draped walls of her private display case. Never having married, Joan regarded me as her spiritual son. I avoided promising to succeed her, left her office and got on the Métro to spend the evening with my father in the five-and-a-half room apartment in Verdun – poorly paid contract work had driven him back to the neighbourhood of his birth – that he shared with his old drinking buddy, Fred. After that, I marked time until Camille was ready to see me. At the end of my third day in Montreal, she phoned to say that I could come over the next evening.

"Why do you let her control you like that?"

My mother left the kitchen before I could reply. The next evening, I left with my backpack for Camille's apartment. Always ahead of the wave, Camille had moved to La Petite Patrie when everyone else was looking for apartments in the Plateau Mont-Royal. She enjoyed being hidden away a bus ride east of the Beaubien Métro station. She met me at the door with a smear of chocolate on her lip. She licked at it, her eyes testing me to see if I noticed. "*T'es écouerant, Kevin Carmichael. Tu m'abandonnes pis tu refuses de me lâcher.*"

Her second-floor apartment in a three-storey building drenched me in a cocktail of nostalgia, familiarity, foreboding. Much as I tried to wrap myself in memories of the love I'd experienced in this single large room, it was the silent moments, the painful discomfort of the final weeks prior to my departure, which filtered under my skin. The red stud of light on the answering machine next to Camille's bed flashed with messages she was ignoring. Life rolled on without me. Taking her declaration that I was disgusting as an affectionate gibe, I smiled and kissed the chocolate on her mouth. We had sex quickly, before we could establish who we were, or what we now meant to each other. Hungry for a woman's body, I ravaged her with a fury whose indiscriminate blindness I knew would be obvious to her. We had known each other too long for our words to be more than glistening foam on the ocean of our conversation. The leanness of Camille's thighs turned me back by contrast to the plushness of Pia's body. Camille's blue eyes made me want Pia's brown ones. Her dark, almost-black hair stoked my longing for the reflection of Pia's blond locks in her golden jewellery.

We shacked up over the holidays. I stayed in her large single room overloaded with memories of joy and betrayal. I cooked supper for her and completed my social rounds in Camille's company. This included the mistake of insisting that she accompany me to visit my sister Marie and her husband Dave, a unilingual Anglo who owned four *dépanneurs* in the West Island. Camille, who resented having to speak to a lifelong Montrealer in English, felt she was under attack. Marie protested that I'd invited Camille to provoke Dave, which was true. I couldn't help but taunt Marie for her husband's lack of integration. As we left their suburban monster home for a long bus ride back to the Métro, Camille murmured that if we settled down together, she would not be able to see my sister very often. Then, as New Year's approached, she said, "Do you have to go back, Kevin? Can't you stay in Montreal?"

I thought of Alex and Leon and Tina and Pia; this world that Camille could not imagine had grown into a palpable counterweight to the comforting, intricate, enclosure of Montreal life. My silences became a thick sludge. Snow swirled outside the windows and filled the streets. When I reached the departure lounge at Dorval Airport, I felt that a bracket had snapped shut on a particular segment of my experience. Whatever came next would make me too different to return.

ELEVEN

"THE SHORT TWENTIETH CENTURY has ended," Simon said. "It ended with the conclusion of the Cold War. We're still the best part of a decade away from the year 2000, but we're already living in a new millennium. It's incumbent on us to ensure that this millennium not become a time of even greater class divisions, and to ensure that Britain remains competitive by guaranteeing that our top students attend our top universities –"

Dean Bessborough's small mouth pursed. Tina's boyfriend had come to Hamdaw College to speak about undergraduate admissions. This was a debate that only the British understood. It was the only debate, I found, that converted phlegmatic upper-class English people into furious, red-faced ogres. I struggled to follow references to grammar schools, comprehensives, secondary moderns, state schools (which were public), public schools (which was what boorish upper-class people called private schools), independent schools (which was what clever upper-class people called private schools), fee-paying schools (which was what these schools were called by people who were insinuating that they were pernicious), Local Education Authorities, UCAS selectors, and a host of other acronyms, wielded with outraged irony and unfathomable cultural connotations. I regarded this debate as a spectator sport, little suspecting that it would administer a decisive blow to my future. The nub of the issue, so far as I could grasp, was that while only ten or eleven per cent of British students attended private schools, more than half of the undergraduate students at Oxford had studied at these institutions. In fact, Simon argued, of the forty-five per cent of Oxford undergraduates who came from state schools, nearly all had studied at a clutch of schools in wealthy neighbourhoods that were effectively private because parents had to be rich to buy a home in the school's "catchment area."

Tina had organized this talk by persuading the Warden that, since Simon had spoken at five other Oxford colleges, it would look bad if Hamdaw, with its progressive reputation, were omitted from his itinerary. Having found a scheduling conflict that spared him from attending, Sir Peter had sent Dean Bessborough in his place.

In addition to Bessborough and Zed, the audience consisted of Tina's friends from the graduate staircase and sixty or seventy undergraduates, all of whom supported Simon. Alex and I had come out of curiosity. Ron, the Torontonian Liberal, had invited us to a beginning-of-term Canadian party later in the evening. "Every Canadian graduate student of importance will be there."

"I guess we'd better go," I said, "or we won't be important."

Ron's tight-jawed non-laugh reminded me of why I didn't want to move to Toronto.

Tina brought Simon to dinner in hall. He was a tall, fit, poised, slope-featured young man who wore a dark blue designer shirt unbuttoned to the chest beneath the chunky collar of his menacingly proletarian steel-studded black leather jacket.

His posh voice husbanded a residue of north-of-England indus-trial raunch as though careful not to relinquish this vestige of working-class credibility. His parents, academics at the Univer-sity of Warwick, had sent him to an inner-city state school in the post-industrial decay of nearby Coventry to teach him the reality of class divisions.

"This is very interesting," Christa said. "I did not know that English students were political."

"How can you say that?" Alex said. "You know Leon."

The German girl looked crestfallen. Alex's capacity to wound her surprised me. "Where is Leon?" Tina asked.

No one replied. Alex looked at me from under his brows. We had gone to Leon's room to invite him to Simon's talk. "I'd be chuffed to meet Tina's boyfriend, but I'm so utterly fed up with this tiresome schools debate. It's simply the bourgeoisie's way of deflecting the working class's attention from problems that matter."

"No way," Alex said. "Nobody told me I couldn't apply to Trinity, which is worse than fucking Oxford, just because I went to my neighbourhood high school with all the other Rus-sian and Polish kids."

"I'd rather visit Emily."

"Of course you'd rather visit Emily. How many times a week do you have to fuck her?"

"You are a vulgar fellow." Leon's face was hot and red.

When Simon concluded his talk, the undergraduates cheered. "If we did as I propose," Simon added, by way of a coda, "lower-ing the minimum required marks for students who come from underprivileged schools, we would not only change the student body's class composition. We would also have more women and people of colour at Oxford. Why is the number of Black British undergraduates so low that the university refuses to release the figures?"

A fresh wave of undergraduate cheers carried Dean Bessborough to his feet. His grey suit, made of some rarified blend of wools, shimmered like a cloud; the gold buttons on his waistcoat gleamed. "I understand the idealism of the young. I was young myself once. But at some point, intelligence must intervene, and intelligence, I must say, has been singularly lacking this evening. In the first place, I don't know what anyone can possibly have against public school boys. Public school boys are a fine Oxford tradition! I should miss them terribly if they ceased to come here." His voice caught in his throat. "Furthermore, public school boys are what Oxford is *for*. They will become the men who run this country, so they must have the best education. *That's* how Britain will remain competitive. As for students who go to third-rate schools, it may sound harsh, but they're not at Oxford because they're not good enough. When it comes to coloured students, I agree that there may be a few of them who might cut it, but they don't apply, do they? And whose fault is that? It's the fault of right-on London teachers with chips on their shoulders who fill students' minds with hateful rubbish! If you are determined to have coloured undergraduates, there's a simple solution: sack the right-on teachers!"

Smiling, Bessborough sat down.

"You've obviously never seen a state school in Coventry or Birmingham or Bradford." Simon stared at Bessborough. "Well, have you? Have you seen the defaced property, the scrawls on the walls, the lockers that don't shut, the prison-fence around the school, the needles and shit in the alleys outside? And you have the gall to tell me that a student who scores twenty points at A-level under those conditions is inferior to a coddled public school boy, prepped for years in exam-writing, who scores twenty-four ...?"

"Tina should hold onto this guy," Alex whispered. "He's going places."

Bessborough and Simon traded exemplary scorn as only the English can. When it ended, a mob of young admirers surrounded Simon. Tina rushed to his side.

We were about to leave when Zed stumped over to us. "Pretty incendiary stuff, what?"

"I thought it made a lot of sense."

"There's some sense to the contradictions he points out. But you don't want to exclude anyone who ought to be here." Zed fixed me with an inquisitive look. "How's Landry doing?"

"He has tutors coming in."

"Becoming cultured like his Viennese friend." Zed clucked his tongue and scratched his shoulder. "Do pass along your impressions when next you see him. It's important for one to keep abreast of these things."

Alex and I left the Junior Common Room and skirted the front quad. As we turned into the misty street, Alex said, "I love Russian poetry, but nobody here understands what I'm doing. Good work in the humanities comes out of dialogue. Plato figured that out! There's nowhere I can go for intellectual community. I told my supervisor how I felt and he gave me an undergraduate to mentor —"

"A public school boy! In Oxford, the answer to every problem is a public school boy."

"This guy's really cool. Colin. He's nineteen and he taught himself Russian! It's amazing how much he knows. We meet in the King's Arms every week for a beer."

"You must miss Jerzy."

"I haven't heard from Jerzy since he went back to Warsaw."

A pair of undergraduates hurried past, college scarves draped around their necks like labels dangling from flora in an arboretum. The wooden front gates of the college where the party was taking place were shut for the night, but a smaller, swinging door remained open. We showed our university ID to the porter in the Lodge, and were directed to the Middle Common Room. We crossed a narrow side quad and went up an ancient staircase to a long, discreetly lighted room that was full of young men wearing flashy jackets over dress shirts open at the throat and women in shin-length dresses with brooches on their breasts. Ron waved at us. "Hey, guys, great you could make it. Hey, Heather — this is Alex from Toronto and Kevin from Montreal."

Heather assessed Alex's height. "Did you go to undergrad at Trinity? No way! You must know my friend —"

To my surprise, Alex did know Heather's friend, and put on a good show of exchanging pleasantries. Four years with the Anglican establishment had taught him a thing or two. "You're from Montreal, Kevin?" Heather said to me, as a patrician-looking young man in a blue suit came up beside her. "You must know Tina."

"I know her from here. We weren't acquainted in Montreal."

"You didn't go to McGill together?"

"No, I went to Concordia."

"No way! Concordia to Oxford, that's quite a jump!"

Ron, looking nervous, said, "Kevin had a really great job. He was principal researcher at the Independent Canada Institute."

Heather's friend smirked. "You worked for Joan of Arc? What are you going to do when you graduate? Revoke the Free Trade Agreement?"

"It might be an important battle," I said, "if we want to have a country."

"Forget countries! From now on, everywhere's going to be the same, same democratic process, same culture. The difference will be economic efficiency. That's how we'll make our future: cutting taxes, improving competitiveness, going global —"

"The only reason we're all in Oxford going global is that in the past, our leaders invested in our country. Competitiveness depends on comprehensive public services and strong national institutions —"

The young man gave me a sad smile. Heather shook her long body. "Is that right, eh? Why don't you guys get a drink?"

Heather and her friend fled. Ron ushered us to the drinks table. With an adroit sideways step, he vanished into a thicket of navy-blue jackets. I hefted a Pim's. The young woman reaching past me to spread pâté on her Ritz cracker wore a shorter dress than Heather's; she didn't have a brooch. Her hair was a little too long for her formal garb. Encouraged, I introduced myself. She was from Calgary. We exchanged flirtatious comments about how uptight everybody from Toronto was. Just as our eyes began to connect, she said, "Doesn't it just rile you rotten how people from Ontario look at you funny when you tell them you're a devout Christian and you're chompin' at the bit to vote for that Reform Party?"

Her gaze was firm. "Yeah," I said. "I have the same problem when I tell them that my last girlfriend was a Quebec separatist and my dad once campaigned for a Maoist."

Her consternation lasted only a second. "Hey, it's too bad we don't have a thing in common. It was just getting interesting!"

I found Alex arguing with two guys from Toronto about private schools. They took my approach as a pretext to disappear. "What jerks!" Alex said. "They're all jerks! Let's get out of here."

I followed him to the door. "The Canadian upper class is fucking retarded!" Alex said, as though he hoped the whole room would hear him. "At least English snobs make good arguments."

"Is that right, eh?" I said in a mocking voice. "I don't engage with arguments, I just say, 'Is that right, eh?'"

The door at the bottom of the staircase opened. A tall, rangy figure came in out of the mist. "My fellow Canucks!"

Doug had lost some muscle on his arms and shoulders. His ponytail had grown out. The teddy bear jock I'd met at the beginning of October had become a lanky hippie with silver-rimmed glasses perched on his nose.

"It's a great party if you're an uptight jerk who thinks that anybody who didn't go to Upper Canada College is a piece of shit," Alex said.

"You guys are way too negative." Doug's eyes darted. "Maybe I'll go back to my room and read *The Faerie Queen*. I've done *Beowulf* and Chaucer. Now I'm studying Edmund Spenser with a D.Phil. student from Magdalen. At the time Spenser was writing *The Faerie Queen*, he was in charge of slaughtering the Irish. I thought you studied literature because it was written by cultured people. I didn't expect to read a poem by a mass murderer."

"If Stalin had written great poetry, I'd read it even though it was by Stalin," Alex said.

Outside, the streets had grown damper. The heave-ho rhythms of drinking songs rolled out of the pubs. As we walked back to Hamdaw, Alex reminded me of a seminar on the unconscious that was being given that term by a famous Professor of French, Malcolm Bowie. "How about we go to it together?"

"Sure!" Our going to Bowie's seminar together, without Leon, would upset the widespread vision in the MCR that cast Leon and Alex as a pair – the two intimidating intellectuals, the two guys who had girlfriends in London, the two with Russian connections – and reserved for me the role of colonial third wheel.

We climbed the graduate staircase. Alex stopped and held his hand to his lips.

The staircase's only public telephone was on the landing above mine. A wheedling voice sashayed down the concrete stairs, "I just got back and I already miss you like crazy, honey … Oh, don't you worry none about him. He's nothing. It was just being over here by myself and he was right next door. I'm tellin' you God's truth straight down the line. Now don't you worry, honey, I'm done with him. I'm tellin' him tonight. You think I want to go freeze my ass off in Canada?"

"You figure she'll break up with him when he comes back from the party?" Alex whispered.

I nodded, wondering whether this was information I should pass along to Zed.

TWELVE

ON TUESDAY AFTERNOON OF first week of Hilary Term, Alex and I went to Malcolm Bowie's seminar. It was at All Souls, a college so exclusive that it had no students. Only researchers resided at All Souls. In a back quad we descended a staircase to a subterranean passage, watched over by statues of emperors and mythical beasts looted from Egypt, and found our way to a windowless underground vault. The doctoral students in French were affable. Professor Bowie, a square man with straight grey hair and large glasses that gave his eyes a sardonically enquiring air, was amused to find two Canadians at the table. He explained that this seminar was about the relationship between the psyche and the workings of language. He had a knack for making offhand remarks such as, "Rimbaud wrote that *je est un autre,*' yet the basis of Lacanian psychoanalysis is that *je pense donc je suis,*' is identical to Rimbaud's assertion." By the time Alex and I ambled back up Catte Street past the dome of the Radcliffe Camera in the seven o'clock gloom, I felt mentally wrung out in a wholesome way.

On his way back from the seminar, Alex stopped off for beer and curry in the King's Arms with Colin. "Do you want to meet him?"

I followed him into the pub. The young man who shook our hands was tall, though not as tall as Alex. Thick white-blond hair, parted in the centre, fell past the collar of his white dress shirt. The liquid blue of his eyes emphasized the freshness of his lips and cheeks. Nineteen, I thought. He looked fourteen until he spoke. "A seminar on the unconscious? Imagine how uncomfortable that would have made Dostoevsky! He was positively *driven* by the unconscious, yet his religiosity would have made him consider the whole idea immoral."

Alex smiled. Had I ever seen him smile before? The great syllable-counter had understood something about Alex that I, it seemed, had missed: more than a peer group with whom to thrash out the aesthetics of Russian poetry, what Alex had needed was a protegé. I wondered at the fact that his supervisor, whom I imagined as a chilly, cerebral British scholar, had perceived this need, or stumbled on it. In Colin's company, the gentleness that I had elicited from Alex on one or two occasions flowed in a steady, amiable stream.

He and Colin ordered pints and fell into a discussion of Dostoevsky. The angry, disparaging tone that ripped through most of Alex's intellectual discussions had vanished. I watched them for a few moments, lingering at the edge of their table and wondering whether I should sit down. This hitherto-concealed side of Alex was one that I, too, longed to get close to. Within a few minutes, though, it had become clear that they didn't want me there.

I left them, returning to Hamdaw for dinner.

I had returned from Montreal nursing the idea that I could belong here as well as there. Yet before I could belong in any other way, I must be writing an Oxford-level thesis that would earn me confirmed D.Phil. status. I started Chapter Two: *What is life after the Cold War? What is life after belief, after the disappearance of values that both restricted and defined us? Does tradition vanish, or does it return with a vengeance in the replacement of civil society with ethnic chauvinisms?*

Journalism, I feared.

On Tuesday evening of second week, I went up to the quad late at night and found Leon's light on. His desk was piled with books and scribbled-over pages. Like Alex, Leon wrote his thesis long-hand on yellow notepads. He used the typing up of his chapters as a pretext to escape to London, working on Emily's computer while she was at the auction house.

He held up a stack of printed pages. "The Wandering Jew returns with his wares. My supervisor says I can go up for con-firmed D.Phil. status in Trinity Term." He poured us each a dram of scotch. "Had a natter with me da' whilst I was in London. He'd had a visit from one of his mates who was in Spain with him ..." I leafed through his chapters. Each fact-nourished sentence was locked into that which followed it. By comparison, my work looked flimsy. "Have you met that lad Alex is teaching Russian to? You met his Pole, also, if I recall. Why does Alex never invite me to meet these boon companions?"

Before I could reply, the glass door slid back and Alex stepped inside. He shook hands with Leon. It was the first time they had seen each other since before Christmas.

"How's Colin?" I asked.

"Great. He's applying for summer language school in Moscow."

The word "Moscow" detonated like a bomb. Leon and Alex argued about Yegor Gaidar, Boris Yeltsin's Prime Minister, who had been dismissed by the Russian Parliament over the Christ-mas holidays. Leon defended the old Communists in Parliament.

"Leon! I was there! You don't know what it's like. You go to the markets and you see Asian people from Siberia buying and selling with blond guys from Estonia. This space and energy ... something's changed ... released."

Alex floundered on the thin soil of his English. I wished I could hear him describe his experiences in Russian.

For the next three days I avoided everyone and wrote. On the morning of the fourth day I reread my introduction and first two chapters, saved them onto a floppy disk and carried it to the Oxford Computing Centre. I printed the pages, put them in a manila envelope and left them for Auberon at the Lodge. Next morning there was a note in my pigeonhole inviting me to his rooms.

He sat by the fireplace, where a brace of spindly logs crackled. "It's better. There's still something that troubles me, Kevin, as though your work will gain ballast only when you go out and experience this post-Cold War world you're describing." His incisive eyes homed in on me. "Are you alone in Oxford, Kevin?" When I didn't reply, he said, "That charming Italian woman, for example, do you see much of her?"

"Not as much as I did last term."

"Nor I. It's curious how, in this community of scholars that we all inhabit, the different tiers live more separate lives than one admits." He got to his feet, signalling that I should do the same. "Makes you realize Oxford's a bloody hierarchical place, doesn't it?"

That evening, as we filed out of Hall, leaving the Fellows seated at High Table, I drew alongside Pia in the stone passage. "Did you have dinner with my supervisor?"

"You are jealous."

"I'm curious."

"I will satisfy you," she said. "Your supervisor is a gentleman.

He was very *galante* during dinner. After dinner he did not want to fuck me, but he could not act as if he was not interested in fucking me. He was too English."

We walked together to the graduate staircase and stopped on the landing outside my room. I laid my hand on her shoulder; my fingers got tangled in her fine, silky hair. I kissed her lips.

"Giuseppe visits me this weekend," she murmured.

She pulled back and disappeared up the stairs.

THIRTEEN

EIGHT WEEKS ON, SIX weeks off. Hilary Term rushed past. Since October, Oxford had been submerged in grey murk. One morning at the beginning of March, we saw the tepid English sun. People stood stunned, wondering at the fuzzy orb in the sky. Undergraduates flopped on the grass of the Ho Chi Minh Quad, barely able to drag themselves to tutorials. Pia and Farida were bowed together on a blanket in a corner of the quad; Sebastian and Stan sat on the concrete ledge next to the bar. I walked over to where Alex squatted on the grass with Colin, a book balanced between them, each with a pint of ale at hand.

"We're doing *Pushkin House*," Alex said. "You read that."

"Not in Russian." I was struck by how gentle Alex's voice sounded.

"It would be brilliant to read it in Russian!" Colin's blue eyes gleamed, his blond hair sparking in the sunlight.

"After you go to Moscow ..." Alex said. "Keep reading! You can't understand anything about Russia if you don't know the literature! Look at how in the opening section Bitov plays with how Chernyshevsky and Lenin both wrote books called *What*

Is to Be Done? The next section begins as a pastiche of *Fathers and Sons* ..."

The gift Colin was receiving was so wonderful that I couldn't bear to interrupt it. I left them, retreating to the edge of the grassy quad.

"Mr. Carmichael!" Dean Bessborough, standing in the shadow of the refectory, had responded to the warm weather by donning a beige suit, white dress shirt and red knit tie. Shuffling a pair of gleaming chestnut-coloured shoes, he said, "Who is that rather good-looking young man sitting with your Russian compatriot? He's not one of ours, is he?"

"I think he's from LMH," I muttered, referring to Lady Margaret Hall, a college that lay north of the University Parks.

"What's his name?"

"Colin. I don't know his surname."

"Colin from LMH. That's sufficient. Thank you, Carmichael."

He strutted away. Out of the corner of my eye, I glimpsed a small hand waving. Farida had disappeared; Pia was alone on her blanket. I went and lay down beside her. She showed me the book she was reading: Thackery's *Vanity Fair*. "I cannot always read competition law, and this book is about an independent woman. You seem solitary, Kevin. Solitary men can be attractive if they know when to stop being solitary." Lying on her stomach, she lifted her head. Her hair had curled at the ends as it had grown out. The eyes that took my measure were dark behind her glasses' gold rims. "I mean, when they kiss a woman on the stairs."

"You didn't like that kiss —"

"When I thought about it afterwards, I felt more for you than I expected."

My bad mood washed away. "That kiss can be repeated."

"It is good to meet a man who talks like a man." Pia smiled. "We do not go together. Go to your room, then I will come."

I tried to walk out of the quad at a sedate pace. The sunlight felt warmer now, baking me under my sweater. When I got to my room, I took off my sweater and paced the floor as I had paced the balcony of my apartment on Rue St-Denis, blue and white banners and flags in the street, on the day that had been the end of my Before, my personal fall of the Berlin Wall.

Pia opened the door without knocking and came in with the blanket folded under her arm. Rough, and scattered with stalks of grass, it got caught between us as we began to kiss. We ravaged each other in a thrilling balance of confident familiarity with the dangerous discovery of a stranger. The blanket fell to the floor. We ended up on top of it. We didn't draw the curtains, baring our nakedness to the restrained sunlight of the English spring. As I traced the camber of her leg with my tongue, weeks of loneliness were deflated into a sighing ease of affection and gratitude and warm, wrestling body heat. The solidity of Pia's curves, the upturned roundedness of her full breasts, drove me mad. "Do it now, fuck me now," she gasped. I complied, in slippery, firm, wincing delight. We held each other poised like a pair of goblets hoisted high until they spilled at once. I remained wedged inside her, reluctant to withdraw, as she nibbled my ear.

"You are a nice man. I can tell you now the first time with you was not very good." She tilted my head to give me a long kiss. A piece of grass clung to her eyebrow. "I don't want to go yet. Close the curtain. Let's get into the bed."

We squeezed into the narrow bed and murmured and dozed.

"This is nice," she said, "but in two weeks Hilary Term is over and I am in Rome with Giuseppe."

"But you can come back tonight ... tomorrow night?"

"It will get complicated."

My years with Camille had taught me to embrace such frustrations as a kind of bounty. I drew a breath, my arms wrapped around Pia's shoulders to hold us both on the bed.

"It is hard for me, too. I want to do it with you again." Her small, thick-lipped mouth, which closed into a natural pout, opened as it ran down the front of my body and snagged me. I breathed from the soles of my feet. Pia sat up with a smile. "He is big now."

A dam inside me broke. "I bet Alex's was bigger."

Pia's arms contracted around me, then withdrew. "What did he say to you?"

I regretted my words.

"I will tell you what we did. We went to the King's Arms, we got drunk, we went to his room and took our clothes off and nothing happened. He was not interested. I do not know how big he is. He did not get big." She looked at me with the nakedness of eyes innocent of glasses. "I am not bourgeois, Kevin. If I fuck somebody, I say so. But I did not fuck Alex. He didn't care —"

"I guess he was thinking about Susan."

"If he was thinking about Susan, he should get big."

I held her in my arms. At five p.m. she folded her blanket in a neat pile and left my room. At dinner in Hall we sat at opposite ends of the graduate table.

On the last Tuesday of Hilary Term, Malcolm Bowie devoted his seminar to the question of the future. "Linguistifying the temporal," he concluded, "is a way of inhabiting the forward-flung dimension of human existence. Could it be that the psychoanalytic picture will remain incomplete until the prospective and the anticipatory are added to the retrospective dimension?"

There was silence in the subterranean vault. "So by exploring the world of before," I ventured, conscious of the attention my accent drew, "we also carry within us the world of after?"

"We must," Bowie said, with a tiny smile that extended to his enormous eyes.

As we drifted over the lamplight-washed cobblestones of Catte Street, Alex said, "I wasn't convinced by what he said, but he was trying to explore an area most academics don't touch." He smiled. "Guess where I'm going over spring break? Warsaw."

"You're visiting Jerzy." I stumbled. "Is Susan going with you?"

He shook his head. "She likes the literature, but she doesn't want to travel in Eastern Europe. She goes to countries like France. When I come back, Susan and I are going to Normandy or some fucking place."

The graduate staircase cleared out. I went to the Lodge and paid to stay in my room for two more weeks. With painful deliberation, I struggled to rewrite my introduction and first two chapters. One night I climbed to the top of the graduate staircase. The music of Spirit of the West blasted from the fishbowl quad. I walked under the arch into the quad, where every room was closed up, beige curtains drawn – with one exception.

"*I am the face of my country, expressionless and small ...!*" John Mann's falsetto shook the glass.

I climbed to the upper tier. Doug sat with his back to me, his big shoulders narrowed as he zapped carbine-wielding hulks in tunnels. He turned around. His beard was spreading over his cheeks and creeping up his jawline towards his fine, high cheekbones. His glasses had slipped forward. "Hey, hoser! Is it cold enough for yuh? Eh?" When I let his parody pass, he said, "Nobody here but me and a bunch of killers." A helmeted he-man on the screen blew him away. Numbers flickered on a score chart, itemizing the cost of Doug's inattention. He clicked his mouse;

the screen went dark. "When you lose a game, you turn it off. Not like life, eh? You've got to look in the mirror every morning and face being a loser."

"You're not a loser."

"What's the matter, Kevin? You think I need to improve my self-image? Don't sweat it. Look at my *spotless* room." He waved his hand. "The scout reported me to Good Dean Bess for having an unhygienic room. They impounded my personal collection of pizza boxes."

"Are things okay between you and Cindy?"

"Jesus, Kevin!"

Spirit of the West's "Far Too Canadian" began again. He had the song on repeat.

"*I kiss the hand that slaps me senseless. I'm so accepting, so defence-less ... I am faar tooo Canaaaadian ...*"

"Despised by Europe, rejected by America," Doug said, taking a step forward. "Sorry, Kevin, but you're just the same. We're both fakers from Canuckville who got into the world's most famous university by mistake. At least I faced up to it and decided to get out with some cultural enrichment. You hang around Leon and Alex like you really understand what they're saying –"

"Fuck you. What do you know?"

I backed out his door onto the catwalk until the cross-struts of the steel railing pressed into my back. He advanced on me, tall and thin-faced, his long arms corded with muscle in spite of his lost weight.

"Back up a little more and you'll go over the edge. Not that any-body would notice if one of us jumped. That's about a nine-foot drop. 'The drop given was fourteen feet.' That's what Mrs. Verloc thinks in *The Secret Agent* when she's afraid they're going to hang her for murdering her husband." His face leered over me;

the railing pressed harder into my back. "Then she commits suicide by jumping off the ferry. She gives herself a drop!"

I pushed him in the chest with both hands and twisted away. We faced each other against the railing. "You're losing it, Doug."

"No, I'm lucid. You're deluded."

Furious, I returned to my room.

FOURTEEN

I HAD TO GET to Berlin. Only then would my thesis take shape. In the second week of the vacation, I walked to Gloucester Green and asked about flights at the STA travel office.

"Nothing cheap to Berlin right now," the girl behind the counter said. "How about Ljubljana?" Since the Yugoslav Army's assault on the city two years earlier, in response to Slovenia's declaration of independence, demand had gone soft. She could offer me a bargain.

Three days later, I landed at the Ljubljana Aerodrome – not even an airport – promising myself I would act like a doctoral student and research Europe after the fall of the Berlin Wall. Rather than the besieged freedom fighters I'd expected, I found a tranquil provincial city in the mountains, where the morning fog burned off to reveal a devotion to ecology, and the most popular book in the countless bookstores was the Slovenian translation of a fey hippie favourite, *Jonathan Livingston Seagull*. Having come in search of history, I felt that I had landed in a place that had slipped the noose of time. Hobbled by my ignorance of Slavic languages, and my mere phrasebook acquaintance with

German, which Slovenes used to address foreigners, I ordered pizza every night because it was the only dish on the menu I recognized. Seeking clues to the ideology of the new nationalism, I followed a map to the university, where I located three students who spoke English. When I asked them about the attacks of the Serb-dominated Yugoslav Army, they looked at me as though this had happened decades ago. I scribbled down their murmured replies, hoping that I might persuade Auberon that these uncoordinated conversations counted as in-country research. The students told me that to appreciate Slovenia I must go to the mountains. All ideologies were secondary to hiking. I checked out of my cheap hotel and rode a bus past alpine meadows populated by sturdy Swiss-looking lodges into regions of stark peaks and arid, rock-jutted paths that led to vast, jagged views. I hiked for three days in the Julian Alps, then returned to Hamdaw College.

Trinity Term, Ron warned me as he packed up to return to Canada and a job with the Liberal Party, was when you realized that Oxford was run for undergraduates. The final term of the academic year was dominated by undergraduate exams. During the last four weeks, all activity ceased in order to permit senior undergraduates to study for the exams whose results were the only lasting evaluation they would receive in their degrees. Graduate seminars closed down after fourth week so that the Fellows could concentrate on prepping senior undergraduates for this ordeal. During first week of Trinity Term, I ran into Auberon in the front quad and started to tell him about Slovenia. "Kevin," he said, "I am an *examiner*. We can discuss your work when exams are over."

On Monday of second week, Leon invited us to meet him at the King's Arms after his progression viva. Alex, Tina, Simon, and I went to the pub to order our pints. "Warsaw's a great city," Alex said, spume on his lips, "except for the fucking Poles. You wouldn't believe the nationalism! If I said I was Canadian they loved me; if I said I was Russian they hated me." He lowered his voice, turning his broad shoulders to screen us from the others. "It's fucking hard to be the way Jerzy is there ... But I feel like I've got a friend now."

I observed him, sensing that one angry chord inside him had been calmed. I clapped him on the shoulder.

Leon entered the pub in a tailored black suit and a silk waistcoat. His viva had been a roaring success. He was now a confirmed D.Phil. student. "I can't stay long. I promised Emily I'd get on the CityLink by seven." After ordering a Newcastle Brown, he said, "They asked me how a Marxist class analysis could be relevant after the fall of the Berlin Wall. Ha! I told them exactly what I thought. Finally, one of the boffins said, 'That's quite all right, Mr. Zamenhof, I believe you've answered the question in sufficient detail.'"

Tina and Simon smiled as Leon recounted his exchanges with his examiners. Undergraduates crowded into the pub. As soon as Leon left for London, awkwardness descended on our group. The hollering undergraduates reduced us to silence. As well as Tina and I got along here in Oxford – in Montreal, I suspected, our camaraderie would have shredded – I was finding that in Simon's company she become a more restrained, cautious, dutiful person whose reactions remained opaque. I could sense her feeling out the contours of Englishness, learning by rote, in a kind of contrite silence, the rules that would enable her to become a respectable English solicitor, an acceptable English wife.

Simon ordered a second round. I hesitated, remembering how Farida and I had been expelled from The Eagle and Child for failing to consume. Alex shook his head. "No, thanks, mate," he told the waiter. "I'm leaving."

Nodding to Tina and Simon, who suddenly struck me as at home and in their element in a way in which I would never be in an English pub, I followed Alex out the door. The damp, muggy air of spring in the Thames Valley clogged my lungs. Leaning over as we returned to Hamdaw College, Alex said, "Hey, man, Colin and I are going to London tomorrow. Do you want to come with us?"

"Yes!" I was unable to contain my elation. Still uncertain how I fit into Alex's friendship with Leon, I was filled with an infantile delight at the thought of being able to share a day with him and the young man to whom Leon hadn't been introduced.

"Okay," he said, terse and distant in a transition that made me wonder whether he was already regretting his offer. "Meet us at Gloucester Green at eight-thirty tomorrow morning."

The cloud and the damp returned the next morning. I sprinted up the winding staircase to the fishbowl quad. When I reached the second level, Alex's curtain was pulled back, his room empty. The embossed gold lettering on the spines of his Russian books winked at me in the dim glow. A dash of panic cut through my chest. Had Alex taken off without me? I turned and walked down the stairs. All the way to the Gloucester Green bus station I scoured the sidewalk ahead of me. The streets were nearly empty, as they often were on mornings in Trinity Term. I felt a flare of resentment against the undergraduates, whom I found so foreign – virtually all of them English and upper class, a disproportionate number of them male – and whose programs fixed the conditions in which I lived. In some obscure way, I blamed Colin for my failure to make better progress on my thesis, though I knew that deep down my real worry was that he might have absconded to London with Alex on an earlier bus, leaving me alone to face another day of being unable to write anything worth submitting.

When I reached Gloucester Green, I was relieved to find Alex smoking on the platform. Before we could greet each other, a bicycle swung into the bus yard and Colin hopped off. Leggy and impossibly lean, his blond hair dangling down on either side of his centre part, he wheeled his bike around the back of the shops that faced onto the platform. He returned, having locked up the bike, bounding towards us with bright blue eyes. "It's brilliant of you to invite me along!" he said, shaking hands with each of us.

His expression made me realize that Alex had gained an advantage from being an Oxford D.Phil. student — matriculated, though, like me and unlike Leon, not yet confirmed — that I had not. His social status had changed. From an immigrant in Toronto, he had become an Oxford tutor, a figure an upper-class young Englishman, like Colin, regarded with respect. The realization made me jealous, instilling a feeling that Leon and Alex had made their marks in Oxford, while I had not. Having thrilled at the thought of spending a day with Alex, I found my curiosity shifting towards Colin. He was the one I wanted to know more about because he had made Alex into someone more substantial than he had been before.

We bought our cheap day-return tickets from a uniformed man standing behind a lectern-like mobile podium on the platform and waited for the bus to roll in.

"Are you going to stay in London to see Susan?" I asked Alex.

He rebuffed me with a sharp look. "She's coming to the MCR party," he said. "I'll see her there."

When we boarded the bus, Colin sat next to the window and Alex next to him. I sat across the aisle from Alex. The bus left

Gloucester Green with only half a dozen passengers, but as we rolled out of Oxford, it made many stops and eventually filled up. Alex and Colin hunched together in conversation. I couldn't decipher the low grumble of Alex's voice, which was more restrained, and far freer of four-letter words, than usual. My inability to hear what they were saying made me feel excluded and irritated. Why had they invited me along? Did they regard me as being as much of an intellectual irrelevance as Decibel Doug? My anger crested, then faded, as the bus pulled out onto the highway. I dozed off. When I woke up, we were on Marylebone Road in London. Now it was Alex who was asleep. Colin, alert and avid, was drinking down the London street life as though it were he, not Alex or me, who was the foreign student.

We got off the bus at Marble Arch and walked down Oxford Street past the name-brand clothing stores, the wide sidewalks overflowing with tourists and shoppers. The greyness was denser here than it had been in Oxford. I inhaled a thick *fug*, as the Brits called it, the texture of which was distinct from the speck-of-dust-in-the-eye acridness of a cloudy day in Montreal. The murk lent the flashing lights of the Oxford Street shops a surreal fuzziness. England, a country I had been reading about since I was five years old, whose institutions and history I had studied in school, felt alien.

Alex looked intimidating in a black leather jacket, Colin suave in an exquisitely tailored brown corduroy blazer. I kept getting marooned behind them, separated from them by large South Asian and Middle Eastern families lingering in the doorways of the shops. I finally caught up with them, perspiring slightly in a sweater that was one grade too heavy for the mild English spring. "Where are we going, Alex?"

"To this Russian bookstore Colin knows."

Why had I come? I didn't belong here. As Auberon would be certain to tell me, I wasn't in a position to take a day off from writing my thesis.

We walked and walked, covering the length of Oxford Street, then turning north on Tottenham Court Road, then east in the direction of the British Museum. The long hike rankled me. We could have covered the same ground much more quickly by underground or bus. "You've really never been here before?" I heard Colin ask Alex.

"I usually just go to Susan's place, then follow her around. Most of the time when I'm in London, I don't even know where I am."

"London's massive! You have to suss it out."

"Wait till you go to Moscow this summer."

"You teach me about Moscow and I'll teach you about London."

Alex draped an arm across Colin's shoulders. I didn't know how to interpret Colin's smile. His effusiveness surprised me. As he led us towards the Russian book store, I glimpsed a confidence in him that I hadn't seen before. He was in his element here. Catching up to them, I said, "Are you from London, Colin?"

"Surrey," he said.

Alex shook his head. "I don't know where the fuck Surrey is."

"South of London," I replied, shaken into an awareness that, as disoriented as I had felt on Oxford Street, my kind of Canadian was less out of place in England than Alex's kind of Canadian. Though I would have struggled to locate Surrey on the map, I knew, at least, that it was a millionaire suburb where Eric Clapton and Mick Jagger had lived.

Turning into a side street, where the sound of the traffic fell away, we were able to hear each other's voices. Colin led us past University of London residences in the direction of the

British Museum. In front of the venerable red brick buildings of Bloomsbury, we passed East Asian students joking with each other in ripsaw bursts of languages we didn't understand, African-American students asking each other where their brothers were at. Even among the other Londoners, Colin's whiteness stood out. The population of London had been mongrelized for centuries. The unearthly pallor of many Oxford undergraduates was the pallor of an unmixed provincial elite. Or was I imagining these differences? I didn't know England well enough to be sure. Leon, the only Englishman I knew well, was an East London Jew, and not representative. As Alex asked Colin how far we were from the bookstore, I envied him his access to a native informant.

The bookstore was on Great Russell Street, in front of the British Museum. Behind the museum's wrought-iron gates, enormous crowds were lining up. Tourist buses nudged down the street. Touts in beefeater uniforms offered us guided tours. A single syllable of Colin's refined accent sufficed to turn them away. Stepping past a display window, where volumes with titles in the Cyrillic alphabet gazed out at the street, we entered the shop, an oasis of silence. Alex hesitated, then began to prowl the shelves with a poised concentration, his broad-shouldered body almost too large for the shop's confined spaces. Colin followed in his wake; I lingered by the door. A small, rumpled man came out of the back. Alex spoke to him in a rich, curdling Russian. Colin stared. Alex and the bookseller fell into an elaborate conversation − about literature? Colin might be able to catch enough to identify the subject of the conversation. Unable to understand a word, I let my attention drift, scrutinizing the books in some of the other Eastern European languages. Even here, I was lost. I couldn't tell the Polish books from the Czech ones. I assumed that the other Cyrillic collection was of Bulgarian literature, though it might have been Serbian.

The bookseller went into the back and returned with a book in Russian. "*Spasiba!*" I heard Alex say. He turned to Colin. "Here it is. Pilnyak. *The Naked Year*. It's a great novel, but it's not long or difficult. When you come back from Moscow, you'll be able to read it."

"You are teaching him Russian?" the bookseller said in accented English. "He is your little brother?"

Alex looked troubled. Without smiling, he said, "He's like my little brother *because* I'm teaching him Russian."

He slid his arm around Colin's waist. I expected the young Englishman to react with discomfort, but he looked soothed and fulfilled. "Thanks awfully, Alex. That's brilliant of you."

Alex paid for the book. He and the bookseller spoke in Russian. As he explained after we had stepped back out onto Great Russell Street, he had promised the man that he would return to the store. "His poetry collection is really good. He's got some stuff I'd love to add to my Russian library. When you start reading Russian, you'll have a Russian library, too."

Colin beamed. "I'm chuffed you told him I was like your little brother."

"Do you have brothers and sisters, Alex?" I'd intended the question to be offhand, but it snapped out in a demanding tone that exposed a competitiveness I hadn't realized I was feeling.

"N– no."

I'd seen Alex's hesitation. He saw that I'd seen it. When I tried to meet his eyes, he lowered his gaze. I attempted to salvage the situation by saying, in a voice that resounded fatuously in my own ears, "So Leon's a confirmed D.Phil. My supervisor hasn't even suggested I go up for confirmation. How about yours, Alex?"

As Alex shook his head, Colin, responding to my earlier question, asked, "Do you have siblings, Kevin?"

"A sister. We don't have much in common."

"I'd love to have a sibling. I'm an only child."

Colin's bright eyes offered up his enthusiasm as a balm to the tension that had gripped us, yet Alex only grew more gloomy. Another difficult triangle, I thought. Were my British friendships doomed to fall into this pattern?

To cheer us up, Colin led us south to Covent Garden. We looked for snacks, and were deterred by astronomical prices. "Isn't there anywhere we can get Russian food?" Alex said, as we stood in the middle of a cobblestoned pedestrian street surrounded by Americans wielding Nikon cameras. "I haven't had Russian food since I was in Moscow."

"I know there are Russian restaurants in northeast London ... I went to one once with my father and a friend of his."

"Let's go. I'm not paying these prices for tourist shit!"

Colin hesitated. "That area's off the Tube line. You have to take the Tube to a bus."

"Who cares? Let's fucking *go*."

This rougher, more uncensored Alex, no longer making an effort to speak like an Oxford tutor, flooded the unearthly pallor of Colin's face with a blush. "I've never gone on the bus ..."

I responded to the quaver in his voice by trying to prompt him. "You went in a car?"

"With my father's driver," he whispered, embarrassment or discretion nearly extinguishing his voice. "You don't notice where you're going when you're being driven," he added, as though he had only just realized that neither Alex nor I would be familiar with this experience.

"But you know where it is, right?"

Alex's apparent failure to grasp just how rich Colin had confessed to being puzzled me. Surely his undergraduate years at Trinity College had attuned him to the fact that, even among the very rich, there were discrete levels of wealth? Colin's confession of touring northeast London with his father's driver placed him much higher up the social scale than either of us had imagined. Or had Alex conserved his poor immigrant's view that all rich people were equally different from you and me? Something in his imperviousness to the implicit confession Colin had just made harried me with the need to soothe Colin.

"It's all right," I murmured. "Just take us to East London. I'm sure we'll find something."

Colin led us to an underground station where we struggled with a cumbersome machine to buy day passes that cost more than our return bus tickets from Oxford to London. As we rode east on the Central Line, Alex looked as confused as I felt. We surfaced at a station in East London, transferred to a red double-decker bus, and headed aimlessly northwards. I didn't have a clue where we were; neither, I feared, did Colin.

Intimidating blocks of faceless flats broke the symmetry of old buildings of tarnished brick.

"It looks like fucking socialist housing," Alex said.

"Council flats," Colin murmured. "Built after the War ... When the original buildings were bombed ..." He might have been reciting information learned in school about a foreign country.

Around us, cockney voices discussed the fate of the Arsenal football club, bearded men in turbans and clean-shaven Hindus huddled in separate groups, speaking in different South Asian languages. The Black people who boarded the bus spoke with West African accents. We rode and rode. It was mid-afternoon now and I was starving. My hunger turned me against this grim precinct I'd had no desire to visit, and which did not meet any foreigner's expectations of "London." There were no tourists. Normally, I would have been happy to escape them, but the pangs of my hunger, hardening into a vice that gave me a headache, made their absence perversely irritating.

It was hard to believe this was the same country that I'd become acclimatized to in Oxford. I was consoled to see that Colin's blazer caught the attention of the locals in a way that Alex's black leather jacket and my grungy sweater did not. As long as we kept our mouths shut, Alex and I were anonymous while every manicured centimetre of Colin's being screamed that he did not belong.

He led us off the bus in a bleak area of garish little shops, awash in the fragrance of stale oil wafting from vats in which fish and chips were fried. The street ran alongside the embankment of an overland train line. "I seem to recall it being somewhere around here."

"You don't remember? This is your city, man!"

Alex's cheeks clenched. I detected the effort he was making to stifle his anger, as well as his habitual torrent of swear words. "Hey," I said, "Canada's your country, and there's lots *you* don't know about ..."

"Okay, Mr. Canadiana. Wouldn't you know where to find a fucking Russian restaurant in Montreal?"

"I know the Polish sausage place on Prince Arthur."

"Right now, I'd settle for Polish."

Colin headed up the street with anxious steps. He turned down a side street, which opened into another large, commercial avenue. My hunger became a veil which drenched this drab street in an aura as distorted and surreal as that cast by the lights of Oxford Street in the mist. The air had grown less damp. I was thirsty as well as hungry by the time Colin, with a gush of relief, shouted, "Here it is!"

Glancing at a doorway in a row of single-storey businesses, I glimpsed the glint of a samovar crowning a polished mahogany dresser behind a dim display window. The writing on the window was in three different alphabets. *Tbilisi Road House* it said in English; below was the restaurant's Russian name in Cyrillic; below that, another, even more ornately arabesqued, alphabet unfurled.

"It's Georgian!" Alex said in disgust. "They're not Russians, they're fucking Georgians."

"My father's friend said they spoke Russian," Colin squeaked hopefully.

Alex swayed his broad shoulders around to face us. "Stalin was a Georgian!"

"Yes," Colin said, taking refuge in the mien of the diligent schoolboy. "At Politburo meetings he and Beria, the head of the secret police, would stare at other members of the Politburo and talk in Georgian about which of their comrades they were going to liquidate."

"Fucking monsters. Why should I eat in a Georgian restaurant?"

"You said you'd settle for Polish," I muttered a little sharply, aggravated by a wave of the enticing yet sickening odour of fish and chips cooked in grease that had been refried too many times. We continued wrangling; passersby turned their heads at the sound of our accents. In East London, we all sounded foreign. The British and their accent obsession! The South Asian Londoners gazed at us just as pryingly as the cockneys. How I longed to get off the street. "If I don't eat soon," I said, "I'm going to keel over."

"Okay, okay," Alex said, "we can go to the Georgian place." In a tone of gruff concession, which reasserted his role as tutor, he told Colin, "When you go to Moscow, you'll find that a lot of the best restaurants are Kazakh ... and some are Georgian."

As we went in the door, an ancient grandfather clock next to the counter informed me that it was almost four p.m. We had been wandering for hours. I was relieved to sit down and have toilets within reach. My head spun with hunger and I was parched with thirst. Still unaccustomed to the fact that restaurants in England didn't bring glasses of water as soon as one sat down, I turned to the drinks menu. The waiter urged us to order the house's finest Chacha brandy. Alex cautioned us against this. "If you haven't eaten anything, it'll knock you unconscious."

The middle-aged waiter smiled. "You are American," he said, his accented English ripe with condescension.

Like a Soviet commissar asserting suzerainty over far-flung republics, Alex reprimanded him with a burst of vehement Russian. The waiter grew huddled and rigid inside his embroidered waistcoat. Having put the man in his place, Alex interrogated him about drinks. "Okay," he announced to us, "I'm having Argo beer."

Colin essayed a phrase or two in Russian, asserting that he, too, would be drinking Argo. I nodded my confirmation of the order. As the waiter turned away, leaving us to peruse the trilingual menu, Alex slapped Colin's arm. "Your Russian's great. Keep practising!"

We ate like Eurasian despots. For starters we ordered *khinkali*, which looked like Chinese dumplings that had sprouted twirled spires. In spite of his derision of the Georgians, Alex was able to show us how to hold the *khinkali* aloft, bite into the side and suck out the potatoes or mushrooms they contained, then discard the doughy spire. We ordered *khachapuri*, eyedrop-shaped pastries with cheese and a fried egg baked onto their surfaces. By the time we finished the *khachapuri*, I had started my third Argo beer. I paid less attention to the food that came after that. There was a grainy substance that resembled rice, delicately spiced meats, stewed vegetables. The waiter's hostility yielded to biddable obedience, then expanded into extravagant hospitality. He called other waiters, middle-aged men like him, to the table to help serve, or simply to speak to Alex. They all revelled in speaking Russian and initiating Colin into the Russian-speaking world. The boy's eyes gleamed an unearthly blue. His white-blond hair slid down the collar of his blazer as he tossed back his head and called out Russian phrases. Observing him audition new words, and answer questions about his family, I discerned a daring in him that hadn't been visible before. The deference that Oxford's hierarchies had bred into Colin's relationship with Alex relaxed. I grasped how, for the young Englishman – as for many upper-class Englishmen before him – mastery of a foreign language and culture provided an outlet for spontaneities, sexualities, emotional openness, that proper English behaviour repressed. Colin was teetering on the brink of varieties of self-knowledge he couldn't have imagined before he began to study Russian. Alex was his guide and initiator into these realms of language, literature, and history which would excavate previously unsounded depths of his being.

Alex loved it. I don't think he perceived Colin's dawning liberation quite as I did. My reading in Victorian novels – not to mention *Brideshead Revisited* – had attuned me to aspects of the British class system. Alex's tone-deafness to this institution prevented him from grasping certain nuances of Colin's growth. Yet, in a way that would never be true in Hamdaw College, Alex was in his element in the restaurant, effortlessly fluent, with every cultural reference at his grasp. He knew exactly how to behave, what to say, how to elicit the reactions he sought. Though I didn't know Russian, I sensed that Alex's sentences had lost their flailing quality, their incessant resort to profanity to compensate for the deficiencies of his vocabulary. After my third beer, I stumbled off to the basement washroom, where the lettering was exclusively in the Georgian alphabet. When I came back upstairs, I saw it was dark outside. I was ready to leave, but Alex and Colin had decided to sample the Chacha brandy. I asked for a glass of water to clear my head. I tried the dessert of grape pudding that Alex had ordered. Thesis anxieties began to suck away at my enjoyment of this experience. If we came back late and drunk, I would have lost not one day, but two.

Another hour passed before Alex and Colin were ready to leave. I nibbled the grape pudding until I felt bloated. Our leave-taking was interminable. There were elaborate thank-yous and farewells to the waiters. The bill, when it came, was monumental. Alex and I desperately counted out pound notes from our wallets without being able to scrape together enough cash to cover the tab. Colin brushed our money aside. "This one's on me." He handed the waiter a bank card.

The waiter scrutinized the card. "What is this?" he said in English. "I do not know this card. This card is good?"

"It's very good!" Colin said, still caught up in the ebullience of the dinner. In a muted voice, though with flushed cheeks, he said, "It's a private bank in the City. My father wouldn't have any truck or trade with an ordinary bank."

"Yes, sir," the waiter said.

The festive mood dissolved. Colin had become a public school boy again and it was time for us to leave.

We stumbled through the dark streets. There were fewer people out now. For the first time in England I sensed a whiff of caution, even fear, in the pedestrians around me, a sensation that Camille and I had experienced one night during a weekend in Boston. We came to a bus stop, waited a judicious distance from four guys with crewcuts and black leather jackets, and boarded the first bus that arrived.

"Is this the right one?" Alex asked.

Colin nodded. I was fairly certain that he didn't know where the bus went and was operating on the principle that most buses stopped at an underground station sooner or later.

We sat down in the crowded bus. The silence stifled me. There were no sparring matches about the Arsenal football club, no animated conversations in Hindi or Bengali. The passengers sat still and watched the streets out the window as they had not done during the day. The bus ran down an alley between blank-faced blocks of poorly lighted council flats. It ground to a stop. Craning forward, I saw a police cruiser parked across the road. The driver leaned out the window to talk to a police officer who had approached. "Please, Constable."

"Road closed," the policeman said, then something else I didn't catch.

The bus backed up until it reached a side street. The driver turned the bus down the street.

"We won't be making the next stop!" he shouted.

"What the fuck was that?" Alex said in a whisper.

"Likely a murder," Colin said. "We're near Murder Mile here."

"Murder Mile?"

Colin did not reply. The bus picked up speed as it returned to larger, better lighted streets where many of the pre-Second World War buildings were intact.

A few minutes later Colin said, "Next stop's the Tube." We got out in a rush of people. I imagined I felt small exhalations of relief. My own relief disappeared as we went down onto the platform. The muggy air and low ceiling stifled my senses. The wariness I'd felt on the bus returned. There were skinheads in black leather jackets, punks with quiffs dyed pink or green poking up from the smooth terrain of their crewcuts, young people with metal in their faces, older Hindu women sticking together and keeping a firm grip on their plastic shopping bags, a lesbian couple with bright blond hair shrinking to the back of the platform, brown women in hijabs, women who were almost white and also wore hijabs, a group of Black guys thrusting their hips forward in brash stances even as they kept a safe distance between themselves and the skinheads. We were all packed in too closely together. I smelled waves of beery breath, heard a shout, an exchange of insults in cockney slang too thick to decipher. A young Black British man in a black leather jacket said, "Oi, mate! You don't call me that name!"

"I'll call you whatever fucking name I please. It's my fucking country and you don't belong."

The punk gave the young man a shove, then rammed his palm into his face. Young Black British men rushed in on one side, punks and skinheads on the other. The punk lashed out again, his fist colliding with his victim's brow. The young man leaped forward, struggling against the punk. His right hand latched onto the metal ring threaded through the punk's eyebrow. He twisted and pulled. The punk screamed. A stream of blood spattered over the punk's leather jacket and drooled onto the platform. Seized up in pain, a flap of skin falling over his eye, the punk was unable to defend himself. The Black guy grabbed the ring in the punk's other eyebrow and hauled on it with a twist of his wrist, drawing out a wave of blood that hung in the air for an instant, striking everyone motionless, before falling to the platform with an audible splat.

"Fuck!" Alex said.

Colin, at my side, stared with eyes that grew rounder and paler.

People shrieked and ran. The train rushed in. The young Black man wriggled away. Two punks grabbed him and tried to throw him in front of the train. They were too late. The young man bounced off one of the train's front cars with a hollow thunk and sat down on the platform not far from the spreading pool of blood. A skinhead dived forward, aimed a kick at his face and missed. His next kick caught the sitting man in the shoulder. The punk fled as Black men rushed forward to defend their mate. The white guy with the gaping gashes in his eyebrows looked stunned, as though two spare eye sockets had been gouged out of his skull. Punks and skinheads hoisted him to his feet and rushed him back up the stairs in the direction of the street.

A middle-aged white lady, picking her way towards the train as the doors opened, stepped in the blood. With a scream, she slipped and fell, bathing her pink jacket in a redness that turned almost black.

I heard a soft gurgling sound. At my side Colin's blue eyes rolled up, revealing a milky whiteness. Every muscle and joint in his body gave way. I lunged forward as he collapsed, catching him by the shoulders and preventing his head from hitting the floor.

He sprawled senseless on his back.

"What the —?" Alex knelt at my side.

The passengers entered the train. The white woman climbed heavily to her feet and looked down in disgust at her smeared jacket and dress. Lamenting her fate in a cockney voice, the woman dragged herself onto the train before the doors could close. The few passengers who disembarked picked their ways around the blood stains. The train pulled away. The brawl was over, the combatants had fled; the only casualty remaining on the platform was Colin.

FIFTEEN

IN THE MORNING, OUR pigeonholes contained Dean Bessborough's missive warning that the playing of music was banned after fourth week. Bessborough's enforcers, two universally despised graduate students known as the Sub-Dean and the Sub-Sub-Dean, threaded up and down the residence staircases, wire clippers in hand. A trickle of music sufficed for them to enter the offending room with a pass key and clip the stereo's wires. As stereos fell silent across Hamdaw College, the MCR Committee announced the final graduate student party of the year for Saturday of fourth week. I planned to attend, but, as I nursed a rare coffee over breakfast in the refectory on Tuesday morning, more pressing thoughts enveloped my mind. The Dean's sheet warning about music during the run-up to exams, which I had picked up before coming to breakfast, reminded me of how I had betrayed Colin by divulging his name to Bessborough. *Colin from LMH. That's sufficient. Thank you, Carmichael.* If the Dean could find Colin, so could I. The softness and vulnerability of his face in the seconds before he had fainted on the underground platform called out to me. Colin's camaraderie with Alex in the Georgian restaurant had prevented me from posing the questions I had wanted to ask him. He was the only public school boy, the sole traditional Oxford undergraduate – of the sort that Zed and Bessborough approved – of my acquaintance.

Once the underground train had pulled out of the station, Alex and I had dragged Colin to his feet. As he was a couple of inches taller than me, I found myself perched on my tiptoes as I propped him up. He remained senseless for an alarmingly long time. At last he moaned and turned his head.

"He needs water," Alex murmured. We settled Colin on a bench. Alex went back up the stairs. He returned with a water bottle he had bought from one of the kiosks inside the door of the station. Passengers began to filter down the stairs. Colin, though still groggy, was sitting up. I caught a man staring at the bloodstains on the platform. He took in Colin's elegant clothes and sprawled limbs, and shook his head. Another snotty-nosed, upper-class schoolboy sparing his debauchery for the poor part of the city, I imagined him thinking. Yet, though Colin looked drunk, and had undeniably downed two or three Argo beers, as well as a small tumbler of Chacha brandy, he hadn't collapsed from drink; he had fainted, like a Victorian maiden, at the sight of blood. That was what stuck in my mind over my breakfast coffee in the refectory the next morning: Colin's sensitivity, his unworldliness, his lack of a tough outer shell, even as he drenched his imagination in the language, literature, and history of brutal, epically miserable Russia. His vulnerability was what made me want to see him again.

After a few sips of the water Colin had begun to revive. "Excuse me," he said, sounding decades older than his actual age. "That was a rather poor show ..."

"It's okay," Alex said, tipping up the water bottle in front of his mouth as though it were a baby bottle. "That fight was fucking insane. Susan always says she wants to stay in London. I bet she's never seen anything like that."

"It's quite likely that she's never been to this part of London."

Having succeeded in uttering this sentence, Colin let his head droop. His chest seemed to fold forward. His head lolled. "He's going to faint again," Alex murmured. An underground train whooshed in, passengers boarded. The few who disembarked looked from the three of us to the stained platform, and gave us a wide berth.

By the time the next train came in, we had hauled Colin to his feet. We found him a seat and stood protectively in front of him. Colin was far from being the only passenger in this nighttime crowd who looked bleary. As the train hurtled westward into more prosperous districts, the roughness was leavened by the entrance of people in business garb. Some of these people would have studied at Oxford or Cambridge. Finding myself among them might have made me feel more at home, yet the accumulation of the day's events had undermined my illusion that I understood anything at all about this country. I wondered how Tina would integrate here. Though I continued to cherish the thought that I had become that elusive and fashionable being, a transatlantic person, I began to associate this veneer of cosmopolitanism with not being at home anywhere.

We got off the Tube at Marble Arch and, standing on either side of Colin and holding his arms in case he keeled over again, swayed through the network of pedestrian tunnels, eventually finding the tunnel that led up to the bus stop on the edge of Hyde Park. We only had to wait a few minutes before the CityLink arrived. Colin was still groggy as we helped him up the steps. The bus was crowded. Colin and I ended up across the aisle from each other; Alex was stranded next to a window one row behind. In a state of restive alertness, I followed the bus's route out of London, glancing across at Colin and waiting for him to wake up so that I could talk to him. He slept all the way back to Oxford. When we reached Gloucester Green, around midnight, he snapped awake. As bright-eyed and dewy-faced as he had been that morning, he joined Alex and me on the platform with a crooked smile. "Thanks ever so much for getting me out of that scrape. And thank you, Alex, for the Pilnyak. It's brilliant. Once I come back from Moscow ..."

Alex slapped him on the shoulder. "Hey, man, let's get you a taxi home. LMH is in the middle of nowhere."

"My bike's locked just around the corner." Colin led us around the barrier of shops into the square that filled with stalls on market day. The square was deserted. Two bikes remained in the bike stand.

Alex said, "You can't ride a bike ..."

"I'm fine, Alex. I took a kip on the bus. I'm completely lucid now."

"... at night. It's dangerous."

"I ride around Oxford at night all the time."

Quickening his pace, he walked towards his bike and clipped the copy of *The Naked Year*, which Alex had returned to him, into the rear rack. He unlocked his bike chain, gave us a bright, boyish smile, and shook hands with each of us, thanking Alex profusely for inviting him. He swung his right leg over the bike, glided across the square and disappeared onto George Street.

"I hope he's fucking all right," Alex said.

"He'll be fine," I said, the pang of unasked questions lingering in my chest. "He slept the whole way back."

The unasked questions were still there as I finished my coffee in the refectory the next morning. I drifted towards the front quad. The founder stared at me from her plinth. The morning post would have come in by now; I risked another glance at my pigeonhole. Nothing. Camille's letters had petered out. My empty pigeonhole was a reminder that Tina was right: at some point I must choose on which side of the Atlantic I was going to live.

I walked north through a tentative spring day that did not quite dare to own up to its name. A clinging grey drenched the buildings and trees in spite of the thinning cloud, the air was saturated with a dankness that made me shiver until I had walked two blocks, at which point I began to sweat. I skirted the University Parks, then continued north to Lady Margaret Hall.

At the LMH Lodge, I found a block of coloured construction paper identical to the one we used at Hamdaw. Tearing off the top square, I wrote: *Can we meet for a pint? Tomorrow or the next day? Kevin Carmichael (Hamdaw) (Alex's friend).*

I folded the square of construction paper. As I approached the porter, I remembered that I didn't know Colin's last name. The porter looked me over carefully, assessing, as Oxford porters usually did, whether he could afford to inflict a verbal mauling on me, or whether I was someone before whom he must bow and scrape. Porters, who were often retired police officers or army sergeants supplementing their pensions with part-time work, were bullies or sycophants, rarely anything in between. This porter, a burly man with thick white eyebrows, sized me up as I stepped to the counter. For once I sensed my advantage in being older than the common run of graduate students — an advantage, I knew, which would vanish the second I opened my mouth. Porters loved nothing more than to ridicule any student they perceived as a "Yank." Attempting to coil my vowels deep

in my throat, I said, "I'd like to leave a message for Colin, a first
-year undergraduate. It's about his Russian tutorials."

At the mention of the tutorial the porter, who had begun
to open his mouth in gruff rebuke, paused. If I was leaving a
message about a tutorial, I might be here on behalf of a Fellow.
I might even be a Junior Research Fellow. With a cautious nod,
he murmured, "You can leave it here."

I passed him the folded square of paper and walked out of
the Lodge with a queasy feeling at having failed to elicit Colin's
surname. Would the porter really put my message in his pigeonhole? Or would he open it, see it was simply about meeting in a
pub, and toss it away? At least I had known, on entering the
Lodge, to look for the block of construction paper, to approach
the porter with deference, to minimize my accent. The habits I'd
acquired at Hamdaw were as universally transferable to other
Oxford colleges as they were utterly useless in helping me to
navigate East London. It comforted me to think that I was not
an outsider in Oxford, even though I remained one in the rest of
England.

I walked back to Hamdaw and ran into Leon in the front
quad. He wore an open-necked dress shirt; his hair was damp
from the shower. "Glad to see you're still here," I said.

"I'd far rather not be here. I have an appointment with Zed.
Apparently it falls to him as Tutor for Graduates to decide
whether I've completed my D.Phil. residence requirement now
that I've got confirmed status. Emily's very eager for me to move
back to London. There's bugger-all to do here in Trinity Term
with everyone obsessed by finals."

"Some of us," I said, "feel we still have quite a lot of work to do."

"Where is it you're working? I came round to knock you up
yesterday and you were nowhere to be found. Alex was gone, too,

though I suppose he's in London with Susan."

I hesitated. "Alex is here. He's probably not up yet because he had a lot to drink yesterday. We went to London with Colin, Alex's —"

"His public school boy."

I gave him a succinct summary of our day. Though I related the events in a muted, matter-of-fact way, I was aware of the perverse, suppressed pleasure I took in asserting experiences that Alex and I had shared. The bruised look in his eyes made me feel more firmly anchored in the front quad of Hamdaw College.

When I finished, he shook his head. "I don't know why Alex doesn't introduce *me* to these mates of his."

His words swept my moment of victory out from under my feet. He didn't care that I had met Colin. The central axis of our triangular friendship was his bond with Alex; it was what transpired between the two of them that mattered. "I'm sure you'll meet Colin soon," I said.

"Must go. Zed's waiting."

"If Zed makes you stay here, come and see me," I said. "I'm usually around."

"You're coming to the end-of-term party? I'll see you there."

Feeling that something had soured between us, I returned to my room, turned on the Toshiba T1600 and wrote in spidery letters: *After the fall of the Berlin Wall, East and West comingle.* I struggled for the rest of the afternoon to assemble quotes I'd scribbled down during my trip to Ljubljana as support for this statement. At the end of the next day, lost in a blur of introverted concentration, I wandered out to the Lodge, checked my pigeon-hole and found a square of folded purple construction paper. A precise hand had written: *White Horse tonight at 8:30. Colin.*

At dinner in Hall that night, I was too distracted to follow

Farida and Stan's argument about the collapse of U.N. Safe Areas in Yugoslavia. I left quickly when the meal ended, went to my room, put on a jacket against the damp evening, then walked to the White Horse. A Tudorish-looking pub squeezed in between larger buildings, it had a low roof and heavy beams. I ordered the beer on tap and sat down in the gloom, in a niche of a seat which afforded me a limited view of Broad Street. A few minutes later I saw Colin wheel his bicycle past the window. He came in the door, ordered his pint and folded his long legs, clad in beige corduroy slacks, into the seat across the low table from me. A whiff of foam on his lips from his first swig, he said, "Alex isn't here yet?"

"Alex isn't coming. This is just me."

"Oh, I thought –" He looked disconcerted.

"I hope you don't mind. I don't know many English undergraduates –" The feebleness of my pretext for this meeting dangled awkwardly between us. Like Leon, I wanted to get to know Alex's new friends.

"Quite all right. Any excuse for a pint ..." In this shift to briskness, I glimpsed the diffident middle-aged Brit Colin might one day become. Relaxing again into a less focused mode, he said, "I can't tell you how surprised I was when the Professor of Russian told me the graduate who would be giving me extra tutoring was from Canada. Are there a lot of Russians in Canada?"

"There's lots of everything in Canada. But no, in general, the Russians are a fairly small minority. We have more Ukrainians."

"It must be wonderful to be writing a thesis on Russian poetry like Alex."

As Colin displayed his admiration, it occurred to me that, though I had glimpsed long yellow sheets covered with a dark scrawl and interspersed with set-off citations in the Cyrillic alphabet stacked on top of the books on the top shelf of Alex's Russian library, I had not spoken to him about the grind and discipline demanded to churn out the three good chapters required to secure confirmed D.Phil. status. Leon had done it effortlessly. My first attempt had produced journalism. Since then, I had wrestled and written and rewritten and deleted, advancing at an infinitesimal crawl in my attempt to forge the vaunted "contribution to knowledge" that would earn me an Oxford doctorate. And Alex? Though he spoke often about Russian poetry, I never heard him talk about the act of writing his thesis. I supposed it must come as naturally to him as it did to Leon. They had both grown up in older, more erudite cultures. I was the misfit, the uncouth colonial who didn't belong at Oxford.

As Colin paused to take a sip from his pint, I said, "And how did *you* become interested in Russian? It seems unexpected ..."

"It's true. I was admitted to read history. But a couple of years ago I began to develop this peculiar interest in Russia —"

"Who was responsible for that?"

"My father, I suppose." Another long pause. "I don't see him often. I grew up with my mother. I was sent away to school. When I was fourteen, my father began to take an interest in me. He would take me with him on business trips. A car would come to Eton, and I'd be whisked away to Heathrow and handed over to my father. Suddenly I would find myself in Paris or Frankfurt or Zurich. My father would set me the task of learning something about the city whilst he was in his meetings. At the end of the trip, I had to give him a report on what I'd learned. He's very demanding."

"And your school ...?"

"Eton didn't take kindly to my disappearances. I was a fag and there were expectations ..." His voice trailed away in response to what was likely a startled look on my face. "Oh," he said, his translucent cheeks exposing a flood of red, "that means something different for you, doesn't it? Fagging is doing chores for older students. It teaches you to respect authority." I waited for him to attenuate this comment with an ironic smile; none was forthcoming. "As I became older, my disappearances grew to be less of a problem."

"You had your own fags."

"Well, yes, rather. Life is easier when there's someone to do your chores. That's a point my father always makes. He tells me I must make certain to be in a position in life where others look after chores and leave me to concentrate on the important matters. For him the important matter is money." A smile, tight with English irony, appeared for the first time. "I'm not sure that's the case for me."

Two lads with accents like Colin's strolled into the pub, ordered pints, and began to play a rowdy game of pinball at a machine in the corner. As people raised their voices to be heard over the racket, an auditory illusion gave me the impression that Colin's voice was dropping. I leaned closer to him across the small table of varnished ancient wood. "What interests you?" I asked.

"Well, my father *did* set me the task of learning about all of those cities' cultures ..."

"Did you enjoy that?"

"I wanted to please him." His voice caught. "I see now that he was preparing me for Oxford tutorial papers. He wanted me to succeed; he didn't necessarily want to spend time with me. I did as he asked. But the trips were an agony. I went on them because I knew they were the only way I'd see him. But I didn't — I hardly saw him at all. He spent the whole time in meetings. Half the time

I presented my report to him in the airport restaurant as we were leaving." He shook his lank blond hair. "It was terribly trying."

His yearning for male approval radiated across the tiny table in a wave. The gulf between our ages – thirteen years? – charged me with a responsibility to reassure him. Emotion was the last thing I'd expected from an English public school boy. Watching him sip his pint in consolation, I eventually said, "My parents divorced when I was a teenager. It sounds as though yours split up when you were younger."

"Very young," he murmured, tight-lipped. For a second, the shadow cast by the overhanging beams caught his cheek at an angle that made him look as old as I was. "My father is rather a lad. My mother divorced him when I was three, after he was arrested for curb crawling in his Bentley."

"Curb crawling?" I wasn't familiar with the term.

"Soliciting prostitutes from an automobile."

He spoke with clinical distance. Eager to change the subject, I said, "And what about Russian? How did that happen?"

"When I was sixteen my father became frightfully excited about Eastern Europe. The markets opening up within easy reach of London ... Suddenly the trips we took weren't to Frankfurt or Geneva, they were to Prague and Warsaw. It's impossible to go to those places, even for two or three days, without becoming aware of Russia as this tremendous, looming presence on the horizon, both horrifying and magnificent. I read Dostoevsky and that made me want to read Russian. I bought one of those self-teaching books and copied out the alphabet and worked my way through all the exercises that most people are too slipshod to actually do." A harsh derision cut his voice: an echo of his father? "By that time, I'd been given a place at LMH to read history. When I arrived here, I spoke to my tutor about my passion for Russian, and he sent me to see the Professor of Russian ..."

"The great syllable-counter," I murmured.

Colin smiled. "That's what Alex calls him. I say, I'd like another pint. Do you —?"

"No, thanks," I said, as he scampered away to the bar. I had been expecting him to reciprocate by asking me questions once I had mentioned that my parents were also divorced. Yet, observing him banter with the barman in a patronizing vein, as though the man were one of his father's employees, I remembered that he was a nineteen-year-old upper-class male; his world was himself. He might have developed a curiosity for academic subjects, but his reactions to other people were couched in terms of personal needs, not human empathy.

When he squeezed back into the niche of a table, I asked him, "How long did these trips with your father go on?"

"Right up to the time I came up to Oxford. A few months ago, my father and I were in Warsaw when I suddenly realized that studying Russian allowed me to understand lots of Polish words."

"Have you ever been to Russia?"

"Well, that's rather a secret."

"What do you mean?" Having finished my pint, I suddenly craved a second one.

Colin looked muddled, his voice quavering. "Alex ... Alex assumed I'd never been. It seemed important to him, as though my not having been there was what made him eager to tutor me ... So I never let on ..."

"But you have been?"

"Please don't tell him, Kevin. You simply mustn't. It would spoil everything. You understand how important it is ..."

"How long were you there?"

"I've been to Moscow twice with my father. He began to make deals with a Russian businessman who's a mate of Boris Yeltsin's. The same man who went with us to that restaurant that I was too dim to realize was Georgian ... We stayed about three days each time. It's an utterly awe-inspiring place. I know I'll have a terribly different impression once I've been there for a whole summer and really sussed it out and studied the language properly ..." His voice stumbled to a halt. "My father was so proud the last night we were there, when I was able to say a few words to the waiter in Russian ... I can't wait to speak to Alex in Russian when I come back! I want him to think it was all his doing, because basically it has been his doing, I never would have got the summer bursary if Alex hadn't encouraged me to apply and helped me cram for it ... I don't want him to think I already knew about Moscow."

"You've been there twice," I murmured.

"You mustn't tell him! You absolutely mustn't." His almost transparent blue eyes nearly vanished in the darkness of the low-roofed pub. "It would ruin everything." An insight slithered, in a nearly palpable way, from the back of Colin's mind to the front. "You and I are mates now, right, Kevin? We'll have a pint here every couple of weeks, and you won't say a word to Alex. I promise you I'll turn up. As long as you don't tell Alex I've been to Moscow."

I was breathless. Colin had detected a neediness in me that no one else had seen. I felt more troubled and exposed than at any point since my arrival in Oxford. I nodded, tacitly promising to keep our secret. Colin's beseeching, half-opened mouth, his super-naturally soft cheeks, could not be denied. As he had understood my yearning for inclusion, and possibly also other yearnings I preferred not to recognize, I, in turn, had grasped a fact about

Colin. It came to me unexpectedly, with irrefutable clarity. Somewhere, at Eton, or when he was wandering alone around a European city, someone, possibly an older boy, conceivably a master or an older man met by chance, had seduced Colin. It was obvious in the way he cadged me to do his bidding, offering himself with a practised, enticing skill. "Colin," I said. "Do you often speak to men like this?"

Our intimacy had become so precipitously close that the question didn't even sound shocking. Through a light blush, he said, "Only men I fancy."

Now I felt as though I were blushing. "Does Alex know that you're —?" In spite of my years among Plateau Mont-Royal bohemians, I was unable to pronounce the word "gay." Before Colin could answer, I approached the subject from a different angle recounting how Jerzy had softened Alex's views on gay men. I was breathless by the time I finished the story.

"I think Alex knows, though I haven't told him in so many words. The first time I went to meet him, a pal of mine came along ... What will bother him is if he finds out I've been to Moscow. It's very important to him to be the man who introduced me to Russia." He fixed me with a suddenly icy stare. "I simply couldn't deprive him of that. He *mustn't* know."

"That's fine. My lips are sealed."

As Colin leaned back from the table with an angelic smile, I realized I had promised to keep two secrets at once.

SIXTEEN

ON FRIDAY NIGHT, THE music of Oasis was keening down the staircase outside the MCR. Opening the door, I was nearly squashed by Priscilla's date, a gigantic white South African in a Savile Row suit. In the corner, Christa had unfurled a rubber Twister board. She, Farida, and Cindy were contorting themselves to plant their feet on the dots. Dressed in jeans and sweaters, they looked like pre-teen girls on a play date. British doctoral students in dress slacks and blue blazers crowded around the bar, where dark pints of Guinness were on sale. The wine-coloured armchairs, varnished oak tables, newspapers and magazines had been cleared away to create a dance floor. A few couples bobbed with self-conscious introversion, dancing like intellectuals.

Alex wore a dark brown jacket over a white shirt. Susan, standing at his side, was garbed in a black dress. I asked her about the trip she and Alex had taken to Normandy a month earlier, at the end of the holiday between Hilary and Trinity Terms.

"We stayed in our *gîte* most of the week because something we ate disagreed with us."

"Susan was vomiting for two days," Alex said.

"It came out the other end with you."

Alex shifted his feet like a workhorse in a paddock. I reminded myself that this was what being in a relationship was like: permitting a woman to enter your entrails and announce her findings to the world. I was surprised to see that these same rules applied to Alex.

Christa came up, her dirty blond hair curling on the nape of her neck. With an affable, blue-eyed smile, she said, "*Bitte*, Alex. Come and play Twister with us?"

Alex nodded at Susan and slipped away. As the music intensified, Paul Weller strumming fierce chords on his guitar, the dance area grew more crowded. Kumiko, a Guinness in her right hand, kicked up her heels. The height of the man she was dancing with had the paradoxical effect of extending her long-legged elegance. It would take her many months, I saw, to become Japanese again. As Alex spun the spinner, then stepped over Farida's splayed body to plant his left foot on the appropriate dot, I told Susan, "Most of the women here are innocent."

She looked at me, small and bright-faced, her eyes almost black in their polished brilliance. "Poor you, if the women are innocent."

"Are you and Alex looking forward to living in London next year?"

"If that's what we do."

Her tone reminded me of the women at the Canadian party: *Is that right?* In spite of my discomfort with her evasiveness, I was unable to quash a flare of hope. Might Alex be in Oxford next year? I imagined myself accompanying him and Colin on outings to Georgian restaurants.

As Alex returned from the Twister board, Priscilla's date squired her to the centre of the room, set his hands on her hips as though he owned them, and began to dance. Priscilla blushed in scarlet fury, sashaying with robotic stiffness.

"Look at that guy," Alex said. "He's a real M.Stud."

The Master of Studies was a second-string graduate degree designed to keep South African rowers, Australian swimmers, and American tennis players at Oxford. Real master's students did M.Phil.'s. Those who failed their doctoral exams were sometimes charitably downgraded to an M.Litt. But even an M.Litt. was superior to the low-browed M.Stud. "That guy's definitely a stud," I said.

Alex caught my arm. "Hey, Kevin. You know what that pervert Bessborough did? He invited Colin to his fucking party — all three stages."

I felt a shaft of guilt pre-empted by jealousy at the thought that, in the twenty-four hours since I had seen him, Colin had been in touch with Alex again. "I'm sorry, Alex," I said, in a state of confusion as to what I was apologizing for.

"I told him not to go." Alex ducked his head. "Bessborough sent me an invitation, too. Just for the first part, in the College gardens. When Colin got his invitation there was a note inside saying that I was going to be there, and it would be 'a delightful opportunity to enjoy conviviality in the company of your tutor' or some fucking shit. Can you believe that fucking pervert?"

I was about to leave the party when Leon and Emily made their entrance. Leon wore a white jacket with diabolical pointed tails, a lime-coloured silk tie, white loafers; Emily was a festival of necklaces, scarves, headband, and earrings that revolved around a patchwork peasant skirt and a taut black blouse that hugged her large breasts. They dived into the centre of the dance floor. Their hips shuttled like pistons; they bopped around each other with a rapid-fire coordination that gave the impression that they had rehearsed this routine. The intellectual dancers, their limbs going limp, conceded them the spotlight. When the song ended, Leon and Emily glided to the edge of the dance floor, their faces shining with sweat. "Oi, mate," Leon said, flinging an arm around my shoulder, "are you going to be around? Zed gave me the thumbs-down. 'In all consciousness, I cannot yet regard you as having fulfilled your residence requirement,' he told me. I have to be seen in Hamdaw until the end of Trinity Term. They won't let me scarper off to London quite yet ... You'll be here, won't you?"

Leon turned to Alex. "You'll be here, too, won't you, mate? Or will you be off with your charming public school boy?"

"Your Dean has his eye on Alex's public school boy," Susan said.

"Does he now? What an utter wanker. Well, if Good Queen Bess gets to see him, why don't I? Why haven't *I* met the delightful Colin?"

"Hey, man. You're always in London."

We all left the party early. Over the next two weeks I worked and worked. Much of the time my efforts felt futile. My withdrawal coincided with the closing down of Hamdaw social life. Alex, who had taken me by surprise by confiding to me that he was trying to patch some of his handwritten essays about Russian poets into chapters, spent his days in the Taylorian Modern Languages Library and the Oxford Computing Centre. Leon, by contrast, spent all of his time in his room. His guitar slung across his knee, a dram of whiskey on his bedside table, he strummed mournful ballads from Ireland and the US Deep South and mouthed the words in a barely audible voice. Having sought his company for months, I now wanted to get rid of him. My puritanical Canadian soul failed to grasp how a guy who was capable of brilliant academic work could also be capable of such self-indulgence. "I'm skiving, mate," he'd say, proffering a third dram of whiskey that I knew would obliterate my concentration.

I immersed myself in books about Slovenian history and Marshall Tito's Yugoslavia, trying to create a context for the quotes I'd scribbled down in Ljubljana. The more I struggled to put these parts together, the more artificial my writing felt. I was still wrestling with this when Hamdaw College's studious silence was shattered.

All over Oxford, tranquility reigned as undergraduates prepared for exams. Yet at Hamdaw College, the sound of hammering pummelled the silence as stages and scaffolding took shape. Dean Bessborough, flaunting his power to defy his own regulations, was mounting his annual party.

The afternoon of the party, Leon came to my room. Brandishing a bottle of Glenfiddich, he said, "Natter, mate?"

Unable to pretend that I was getting any work done, I pushed back my chair and accepted a dram. Leon sat down in my armchair. "Queen Bess must have loads of money! Think of the sheer cost of hiring the gardens and the workmen and the band and the wine!"

"It's quite a message he's sending to the undergraduates: if you play your music, I clip your wires, but I can make as much noise as I like."

"He's teaching them how privilege works. That's a vital part of an Oxford education."

We drank. "You must be looking forward to moving back to London," I said.

Leon hesitated. "You know, as dreary as Oxford's been, I've never had such good conversations as I've had with Alex ... and you." He poured us each a fresh dram. "Alex has been so busy with that lad of his recently I've barely had time for a really good row with him!"

I was going to ask what he knew about Alex's thesis when instead I said something that may make me responsible for what happened next. "So you still haven't met Colin?"

"No!" He leaned back in the chair. "I was rather hoping that lad would come to Bessborough's shindig so that I could catch a glimpse of him."

"He'd come if Alex told him to come."

Leon's Jagger-wide, big-toothed smile unfurled into its full carnivorous savouring of life. "I suppose Alex could ask him, even now."

"You said he was working."

"Precisely my point. He doesn't have to know. And the school-boy can't check up on it. There's no way they can communicate between now and the party."

"What are you suggesting, Leon?"

"I'm suggesting you come with me. We'll teach Alex not to hide his protegés!"

I followed him out the door and up the stairs to the big steel pay phone. Pumped up with whiskey, I felt good about myself and glad to be at Leon's side.

He pulled out his wallet and sifted brassy one-pound coins and hexagonal silver fifty-pence pieces. He slid coins into the slot, dialled directory assistance and asked for the phone number of Lady Margaret Hall. More coins fell down the slot. He dialled again. Adjusting his accent to a refined register, he said, "I say, can you do me a favour? I need to leave a message for an undergraduate. Colin – oh, dash, his surname's slipped my mind ... That's right, interested in Russian. *Blake*. Of course – Colin Blake. How could I be so absent-minded? The message is from Alex. Yes, he knows who I am. Now I'm afraid I mistakenly gave him the impression I wouldn't be going to the Dean's party in the Hamdaw College gardens this evening. If you could leave a message in his pigeonhole, please, telling him Alex *will* be at the Dean's party and *very much* hopes to see him –"

By the time he hung up, he could barely contain his laughter. We hurried back to my room and drank another whiskey. I hadn't felt this silly since the day Alex and I had smoked pot – an activity that had come to a halt since an undergraduate had been rusticated for marijuana usage. When the punishment was announced, Alex and I were mystified. Leon had to explain to us that "rustication" meant being banned from the city limits of Oxford for a year.

"I had no idea you could sound so upper-class," I said.

"It was a sight easier than imitating Alex's real accent."

At some point he staggered back up the stairs to the quad. I lay down on my bed. I woke up with a headache in the dark. Cool evening air flowed in the window. I sneezed. The echo of my sneeze made me realize that the banging in the gardens had ceased; the stage, marquee, and gazebos of Bessborough's fantasy land were in place. The College lay in silence, awaiting its guests. I looked at the time and realized that I had missed dinner in hall. Gripped by anxiety, I went to my washbasin and splashed water on my face, then scrambled up the stairs to the fishbowl quad. Lights were on in many of the rooms. Alex's room was dark, but Leon's was bright. I knocked. "I took a kip," he whispered. "When I woke up, Alex had left."

"Colin might turn up at the party. We should be there."

Starving, we walked to the kebab van on Cornmarket Street. Ten minutes later, as we stood on the sidewalk munching our kebabs, Leon said, "I don't know what possessed me to leave that message. This environment has infantilized me."

"I'm sure Colin will enjoy the party. He doesn't have to go to the third stage."

"We need to spot him on the way in to warn him —"

We returned to Hamdaw, our mission having become an altruistic one. The guests were arriving: willowy young men in fine suits, stately Fellows from neighbouring colleges, London high-society couples in gowns and dinner jackets who asked the porters in the Lodge to find a man to park the Rolls Royce. They entered the front gate, skirted the quad, stopped at the arch over the passage that led to the gardens to show their invitations, then disappeared inside. The first live band of the evening took the stage. The music began to crank up. The volume was excruciatingly loud; reverberations trammelled through the seventeenth-century stone. Guests continued to flow in, giving us unpleasant looks. Leon and I didn't match the guests' image of Oxford students: older than the undergraduates, the worse for wear as a result of our afternoon debauchery, we were dressed in blue jeans and open-necked shirts. My hair, falling over my collar, was longer than it had been in years. Leon's chin was a sheen of blue-black stubble. The finely-garbed folk who sailed in the front gate, paused, affronted at the sight of two ruffians. We stared back. I gave each young man a hard look, trying to imagine what Colin would look like in a dinner jacket.

As nine o'clock approached, the stream of incoming guests grew thicker. We saw no sign of Colin.

"I wonder if he didn't check his pigeonhole," Leon said. "He could be sitting in his room.'

I looked up and saw the young man I was looking for — except that it wasn't the young man I was looking for. My mind had made a subliminal association.

It wasn't Colin coming in the front gate. It was Alex.

"What are you guys doing here?" When we failed to reply, Alex said, "I just spent an hour in a café on Little Clarendon Street waiting for Colin. We were supposed to meet – I'm going to check my pigeonhole to see if he left me a message."

He disappeared into the Lodge.

"I feel utterly foolish ..." Leon said.

"But if Colin wasn't there, he should be here."

The rollicking music rode down the diaphanous night air.

Alex returned from the Lodge, his face blanched.

"... supervisor just phoned. Colin was hit by a fucking truck. The porter told me as soon as I went into the Lodge. He's at the corner of Parks Road and Banbury –"

We rushed out the gate and ran northwards. We sweated in the incipient warmth, shivered in the residual chill. The street was empty and very dark beneath spreading branches and long shadows that hugged the stone walls. After half a block, our sprinting fumbled into a hurried, disarrayed run-walking. Alex wheezed, "I can't fucking believe it. He's got to be okay ..."

I glimpsed Leon's face, his long jaw clenched. Caught up in the effort of running, in the strange companionship of the three of us joining forces to do something in a physical way, I avoided the thought, until I took in Leon's desolate expression, that we were responsible for this accident.

Sweating like the out-of-shape layabouts we were, desperation in our voices, we saw a large truck lodged with its tail end in Parks Road and its front end crossing most of a lane on Banbury. We ran past the hedges that climbed the black wrought-iron fence of the University Parks. How had word of the accident reached Hamdaw College so quickly?

Before we could get to the truck, a tall, bald man with large glasses, wearing a pale trench coat, intercepted us. Alex stepped towards him. "I saw it happen," the man said. "I was out for my evening constitutional. It's quite the most dreadful thing I've seen in twenty-five years in Oxford ... I ran to LMH to tell them to ring emergency services and inform Colin's family. I told them to ring Hamdaw and leave you a message —"

He gasped for breath. Like us, he was an intellectual unaccustomed to running.

Though his influence would haunt me in later years, this was the only time I saw the great syllable-counter in person.

"Where is he?" Alex said, brushing past his supervisor.

We followed him onto the hook of pavement where Parks Road fed into Banbury. Only then did I see the bicycle lying on its side in the near lane of Banbury Road. Dazed, Leon and I trailed in Alex's wake. My heart gave a single, demolishing thump as I saw Colin lying in the road. His legs were under the truck; his blond head lay on the pavement where Parks Road and Banbury met. I remembered a dead doe I had stumbled over in the woods as a high school student, hiking from a friend's cottage in the Laurentians. Colin's limp body had the same soft vulnerability, the same gentleness. Having perceived Colin as an ethereal presence, I saw him for the first time as a warm, heavy body.

"Fuck! Is he dead?" Alex asked.

"Concussed, I should imagine," his supervisor said. "We should stand back. The police and ambulance will be here any minute."

Alex ignored him, stepping forward and crouching down next to Colin. The syllable-counter uttered another murmur of warning, then said, "I wonder what's happened to the driver? Is he still in the lorry?"

While his supervisor went to look in the truck's cab, Alex bent over Colin's head. His large hand, its fingers spread, hovered in the air in a motion somewhere between floating and trembling. It was as though an invisible force field prevented him from lowering his palm and caressing Colin's shoulder. In compensation for his inability to make physical contact, he began to chant in Russian. I heard the sloshing richness of his vowels, the half-Asian reverence he poured into his words. He was reciting poetry. His supervisor, returning from the cab, stared at Alex through his glasses with a humbled, respectful expression. Leon gazed at the pavement beneath the truck, where Colin's legs disappeared. Just as I had decided that what Alex was reciting must be a funeral dirge, or would have to serve as one, Colin's head jerked. My body clenched as though I'd seen a ghost. Behind me, I heard Leon murmur, "My word, he's brought him back from the dead ..."

"Ugh ... ugh ..."

"Colin!"

"My head hurts." As he opened his eyes, his body convulsed. "What am I doing here?" He sat up in alarm and dragged his legs out from under the truck. Life shot through him, animating his limbs. "I'm dreadfully sorry, Alex ..."

Pressing down on the elbow Alex offered him, Colin levered himself upright. Once he was standing up, he looked fine. He didn't even waver on his feet. The only signs of his accident were the smears on the knees of his pressed black trousers. He wore a black dinner jacket and a small black bowtie; evidence, I realized, that he had received our message and had been on his way to Dean Bessborough's party. In his formal clothes, he looked like an overgrown, half-abashed little boy who had crept off to roughhouse in the backyard after being dressed up in his finery for his aunt's wedding.

"It's a bloody miracle!" Leon said.

"I'll tell the driver," Alex's supervisor said. "He's a Muslim. He's been sitting at the wheel praying for you, Colin ..."

As though physically animated by his jubilation, Leon bounded out into Banbury Road, held up a hand to halt an oncoming car, gripped Colin's bicycle by the handlebars and wheeled it across Parks Road and onto the sidewalk.

We all joined him in the shadow of the hedges of the University Parks. The driver got down out of the cab. He shook Colin's hand. "I am so glad you are alive! *Shukran lakoom!* God is great! He hears our prayers!"

"Or Alex's prayers," Leon murmured, "if that's what he was chanting."

"At least we're off the hook," I whispered for his ears only. "Imagine how we would have felt if it had been serious."

Leon's face stiffened. "It doesn't bear thinking about."

Colin relieved Leon of his bicycle. "Poor thing," he said, regarding its twisted front forks. "It's done me sterling service ... Look here, I'll have to leave this in the LMH bike shed then see whether someone can mend it —"

"We'll come with you," Alex said. "Then we'll all go out for a pint to celebrate!"

"I can leave?" the driver said. "You are all right?"

Alex's supervisor stepped forward. "I think we should all stay right where we are until the police and ambulance arrive. They'll want to make a report —"

Colin shivered. "My father would disapprove awfully of my name appearing in a police report."

"It's the right thing to do," the syllable-counter said, looking askance at this response.

"I'd never hear the end of it." Colin's defiance of the Professor of Russian took me aback. Whether curb crawling or pavement falling, it seemed, Colin's family had a marked antipathy to the police. He nodded at the driver, who lingered next to his cab. Speaking to him as though he were a butler, he said, "You can be on your way. No hard feelings, mate."

"Thank you. *Shukran*. Thank God for protecting you."

Braving the Professor of Russian's reproachful glare, the driver climbed back into the cab. The truck coughed, then eased its way out onto Banbury. His lips pressed into a thin line, the professor said, "You should wait for the ambulance, Colin. You need to get yourself checked out. Even a minor concussion can be a serious matter."

"If it's all right with you, sir, I'll go to emergency at the John Radcliffe tomorrow morning. Ambulances are in short supply. There's no justification for my taking up a place when I'm feeling as right as rain." His voice quavered as he uttered the final words. I sensed the depth of the fright he had received. Like a skittish fawn, he was eager to scamper away from the place where death had nearly ambushed him lest the menace strike again.

"If you insist. I shall remain here to speak to the police when they arrive ... If they ask for names, I shall be compelled to supply them."

"I understand," Colin said. "Thank you very much, sir."

As we hurried away, forming a circle around Colin, who was wheeling his wounded bicycle in front of him, I remembered Leon's complaint that the Oxford environment had infantilized him. I felt the same. I tried to imagine a similar situation in Montreal, in which I and my friends would *not* have waited for the ambulance. Flouting the authorities was childish; it was also a sign of class privilege. As Leon and I fell behind Colin and Alex on the walk to LMH, I glanced across at Leon with what I hoped was a meaningful, look. He rolled his head in affable response. "Well, I must say I'm chuffed to finally meet one of Alex's boon companions. He seems a likely lad."

We waited outside LMH as Colin went to lock up his wrecked bike in the College's bicycle shed. Alex stamped his feet. He rolled and lighted a cigarette, inhaled, exhaled and met our eyes. "It's a fucking miracle he's okay. I don't usually say this," he went on, glancing at Leon in jest, "but we all need a fucking pint."

Leon laughed. Colin returned from the bike shed, still garbed in his tuxedo. It occurred to me that in his shoes I would have taken five minutes to go to my room and change into ordinary clothes. Oxford undergraduates were uniquely comfortable in formal dress, more relaxed in ties or dinner jackets than they were when wearing blue jeans.

We set off into the dark, a rabble of lads out for a pint, little different from other gangs of young men who were roaming around Oxford that night. Colin's recovery filled us with the elation of the immortals. We made the leaves of the greenery on Norham Gardens shudder with our gibes. We followed Banbury Road back into the city centre, where it dovetailed with Woodstock Road to form St. Giles. We crossed the extra-wide confluence of the two streets in front of St. John's College, making our way to The Eagle and Child.

"I do hope they've got room for us," Colin said. "It's sure to be chock-a-block."

"The real question," Leon said, "is whether they're going to let Kevin in. The last time we were here, he nearly got himself banned."

"For not drinking enough!" Alex laughed.

As we dodged the minibuses heading north on St. Giles, Alex and Leon told him how Farida and I had been expelled from Oxford's most famous pub.

Inside, we found that a party had taken over the back patio, where I had met Alex on his birthday at the beginning of Michaelmas Term. One of the high-sided booths in the front had just come free. Smoking wasn't allowed in the front section of the pub; Alex said he didn't mind. "I don't have to smoke. I'm just happy to be here with Colin."

He draped his arm around his protegé's shoulder.

The demanding waiters appeared. We each ordered a pint. This seemed to placate them.

"The Bird and Baby," Leon said, surveying the hard-drinking undergraduates. "I can never quite believe that *The Lord of the Rings* and *The Chronicles of Narnia* started here. It all seems somehow too coarse — not the place for fantasy. More like a spot for upper-class wankers to get drunk before losing their virginity."

Leon's allusion to "upper-class wankers" delivered in his most cutting East London twang, made Colin wince.

Our pints arrived. We hoisted them and drank. Borne along by the euphoric mood, I caught Colin's eye. My glare lingered in a reminder of our pact to meet in a pub on a regular basis. His blue eyes were translucent. He was staring through me as though to avoid thinking about the secrets he had divulged to me. Even so, I discerned a tightening of his smile, the ghost of a nod of recognition. His reluctance to acknowledge the bond that now linked us in front of the others turned me back on the secret that Leon and I might be obliged to reveal to him and Alex.

Setting down his glass on the table, Alex said, "What are you doing in that fucking tux, Colin? Did you dress like that to meet me on Little Clarendon Street?"

Colin looked startled. "But, Alex, you left a message telling me to meet you at your Dean's garden party!"

I glared at Leon. He avoided my stare. Realizing we were going to have to confess to our prank, I leaned forward, swallowed my gulp of bitter. I cleared my throat. Leon laid a hand on my forearm as though ready to physically restrain me.

Before I could open my mouth, Alex said, "I never left you any fucking message. I was waiting for you on Little Clarendon Street!"

"But the porter said –"

I said, "I have something to –" I was hot and nervous. Our phone call had changed Colin's plans, redirecting his bicycle onto a collision course with a truck. Leon and I could have been responsible for a disaster.

As I faltered, Alex roared, "Bessborough! That fucking pervert! I bet he called your Lodge to tell you I was going to be there. That guy's fucking twisted!"

Leon leaned back in relief.

"He sounds utterly diabolical," Colin said. "Do you think he actually did it?"

"How else did that message get there? The guy should be locked up! Half the Fellows in Oxford are perverts. They fuck any student they like and nobody can touch them. Hey Kevin, who's that other Fellow at Hamdaw – the one who's always hassling graduate women?"

A Fellow who hassled women. A number of options presented themselves. "You mean Dennock?"

"Yeah, Dennock, the guy who Zed says has never written a book." He turned to Colin. "You should hear what that guy does."

"What does he do?" Colin asked.

They were the last words he spoke. Before Alex could reply, Colin dropped forward like a marionette whose strings had been cut. His head hit the table with a crack that squeezed my heart. The roar of the pub receded from my senses even as it seemed to grow louder. I heard Alex shouting for a waiter, for an ambulance. I saw Leon's eyes glaze over, then, very slowly, harden into some sort of absorption, which I could barely grasp, of the fact of death. Because Colin had been dead before his head had hit the table. The suddenness of it left me breathless and sweating. As the waiters forged forward, I tried to get out of the way to let them past, as though they would be able to do any good. My legs refused to respond to my urge to rise to my feet. I wished in vain that I could escape from this booth, flee the pub, distance myself from all that I had done.

"Move it, mate! Make way! Make way!"

The waiter's voice resounded through a pub that had become utterly silent. Colin remained crumpled on the table. Leon, Alex, and I stood next to the booth. For a long time, none of us opened our mouths.

The Eagle and Child's manager slid into the booth alongside Colin, as though inviting him to a pint. He gripped Colin's wrist, turned it over and felt for a pulse. At length he shook his head. "He's gone," he said, his voice overwhelmed by sadness as though he had known Colin for years.

Leon, Alex, and I continued to stand in silence. Alex's mute inability to react alarmed me, pressing the reality of Colin's death into my unwilling mind. One of us had to break this awful silence. I was counting on Alex. I didn't understand why he had nothing to say. He looked younger and more vulnerable than usual. I remembered that he had turned twenty-four in Michaelmas Term. At the same time, it almost seemed to me as though he'd had a premonition of this horror. I stared into his face. He failed to respond. I looked away.

The paramedics came in the door in green uniforms that resembled combat fatigues. Blue NHS flashes on their chests, they hurried through the crowd, which pulled back to let them pass. In clear accents that hovered somewhere in the lower middle-class — more refined than the accent of an Oxford porter, far less posh than that of an Oxford undergraduate — they urged us to stay out of the way. It took them only seconds to confirm that Colin was dead. I heard a bang behind me as a stretcher cracked against a booth. A paramedic tried, without success, to squeeze it through. The first two paramedics eased his body — his floppiness made me aware, with a jab of horror, that it was no longer him — out of the booth and carried it to the stretcher. I heard a young woman cry out and burst into sobs. People began to filter out of the pub. In a dazed, zombie-like gait, we followed them. The pub's owner stepped in front of us, "You lot need to wait for the police."

The next hour was a daze. The Eagle and Child grew quiet. We settled our bill and were allowed to sit in a booth, not drinking, without being expelled. The police came and checked our student cards. They interviewed us one by one: name, nationality, date of birth, our account of what had happened. Each time I tried to explain the events in detail, to get to the core of what had occurred, the constable, a young Black British man with curved sideburns, said, "I'm not allowed to report supposition. Tell me what happened, please."

The interview layered frustration over the top of emotional devastation. I shuffled out into the street. Leon and Alex were waiting for me. Seeing only two of them there felt wrong. Where was Colin? It was impossible to suppress the feeling that someone was missing.

We crossed St. Giles and cut down a gloomy pedestrian alley that ran alongside St. John's College. Beneath the lamps casting pale shadows through the branches of untamed shrubbery, Alex said, in a doleful voice, "I should've listened to my supervisor. We should've taken Colin to the hospital."

We walked in silence. At last Leon said, "I'm absolutely scundered by what's happened, but you know it wouldn't have made the slightest bit of difference if he'd gone to the hospital. If you have a cerebral hemorrhage, it's going to kill you even if there's a pack of doctors sitting right in front of you."

"But if he'd been in the hospital ... If a doctor had been examining him when it happened ..."

"It's quite likely he would have died in the waiting room at the John Radcliffe. Better to spend your last moments in a pub, I say ..."

"That's what all you fucking Englishmen think. The best place in life is a pub. That's why you have such a fucking anti-intellectual culture." Alex shook his head.

We turned onto Parks Road, walking through a wider space, beneath larger trees.

"Fuck!" Alex said. "I hate this fucking place!" He shook his head. "I'm leaving."

Sunken in despair, and a kind of stupefied unreality, I ignored his final words. When he said nothing more, I heard Leon ask, "You're taking up your offer at Harvard?"

"What offer at Harvard?" I asked.

"... I always thought you might do that in the end."

Leon's knowing tone outraged me.

Alex said, "I'll have seminars, I'll meet people I can talk to about Russian literature ..."

"What are you talking about?" I asked.

"I got into Harvard as well as Oxford. I deferred Harvard to take up the Commonwealth Scholarship because Susan likes London more than Boston."

"You always were uncertain about staying here," Leon said.

"No, you weren't!" I said. "You never even mentioned Harvard. You didn't say a word! We spent a whole day together in London ...! How come you told him and not me?"

"I don't know, it never came up." His dismissive tone wounded me. "Fucking Oxford. God – Colin! He was so young, so *alive*."

I understood why Susan had not responded to my comments about Leon and Alex both being in London next year. The friendship I had taken to be flexible and triangular had left me alone in more ways than I had understood. Leon and Alex's departures from Oxford would not make me more alone; they would confirm what should have been obvious from the start. I had been a dupe, a blind man, a dumb Canuck. Decibel Doug, in his self-laceration, had been more aware of his position.

Alex stopped, gazed up at the dark branches of the trees and resumed the poetry recitation he had begun at the site of Colin's accident. With his chanting pursuing me, I left them. My legs were trembling. The alcohol-tainted smell of my sweat stank in my nostrils and my mouth. Our fateful triangle had collapsed, a stage of my life had ended, and I was alone.

PART TWO

CONFIRMATION

SEVENTEEN

IN THE MORNING, I remembered the companionship that I had felt flourishing between Leon and me as we hatched our prank, and how utterly it had vanished when I'd realized that Leon and Alex had secrets from which I was excluded. Leon, not Alex, stood at our fateful friendship's core, sharing secrets with both of us. By consenting to remain silent, I confirmed him in this role. I loathed him for his power, yet I was loyal to him because I feared that if I spilled the beans I would lose both his friendship and Alex's.

Two nights later, Alex packed up and left Oxford. He didn't say goodbye or leave me his address. I climbed to the upper tier of the graduate quad. Through the glass wall of his room, I stared at the empty bookshelves where, until a few days earlier, the spines of his Russian library had glowed like bullion. I had no way to reach him. We were the final year of entering Oxford graduate students not to use email. Our friendship, anchored in literary essays written by hand, was not transferrable to the zapping lightness of the screen. Leon remained in Oxford for another ten days, at Zed's behest, but was rarely in his room. He knocked on my door as he was moving out. I asked him about Alex. He was in London, he said. Alex and Susan were "trying to make a go of it." Susan, who was the kind of Canadian who was allergic to the United States, would not be accompanying Alex to Harvard. Disappointing both him and her parents, she had decided to stay in London.

Leon and I looked at each other as though we had more to say. He shook my hand and turned away.

One night, struggling to finish my third chapter, I turned off the Toshiba and climbed the staircase to the graduate quad. Trinity Term was nearly over. The fishbowl rooms had been cleared out. Only Decibel Doug's door was open. The sound coming from inside was not music, but the shriek of Scotch tape being stretched across a cardboard box.

I climbed the steps to the upper tier of the quad. Doug saw me coming along the walkway. "I'm done," he said. "I've done all of English literature. Last week I did Toni Morrison, Thomas Pynchon, and Angela Carter. I'm as up-to-date as you can get."

"Do you feel cultured now?" My mood was foul.

"Fuck you." He waved the tape gun at me. "You're a coolie just like me ... Kevin Carmichael! Your ancestors were starved Irish peasants and mine were Acadians kicked off their land. We were both booted in the ass by the English, and now we're here begging for their approval. Don't act like you're something big."

His Maritime twang became sharper. His hair had begun to curl at the ends since reaching the nape of his neck. "You wanted to be like Leon and Alex, and I wanted to be like Sebastian, but we're really like each other. Coo—"

"Don't say that word. It's racist." I scrutinized him. "Are you going home for good?"

"You mean am I a total failure?" He took a step forward. "You get a Rhodes, you get two years at Oxford. Nobody can take that away from you. They'll never give me the third year, but they can't stop me from coming back for the second one. As long as I can find a one-year degree." He laughed. "I'll be an M.Stud.!" He shook his head, his long hair snaking like a prehensile tail. "Take off, hoser. I've got to finish packing. The truck's coming in the morning to take my stuff to the docks." When I didn't reply, he said, "Tilbury. I'm going back by ship. I paid for it out of my Rhodes allowance. After reading Joseph Conrad, I want to cross the Atlantic on a boat."

"But you read *Under Western Eyes* and *The Secret Agent*. Those aren't sea stories!"

He looked abashed. "My ancestors crossed the Atlantic when they came over from France. Hah! My ancestors spoke French, but I don't; yours spoke Gaelic from the bog and didn't know English or French, and you know both."

I didn't see Doug again. My hours in front of the Toshiba translated into the arduously rewritten and documented pages of three tentative chapters. Auberon took a long, deep breath and said, "All right, Kevin, you may put yourself up for confirmation. We shall see what happens."

The Faculty of Politics complied with Auberon's request to squeeze in my progression viva before the university emptied out for the summer. On the day that would decide my fate as a doctoral student, I suited up in my sub-fusc, dark suit and graduate gown and walked through a sunny afternoon to Hertford College. In a shadowy room decorated with a Welsh flag, two Fellows in Politics from other Oxford colleges examined me.

"The methodology of this work isn't clear," the younger Fellow said. "Is it a work of political theory, or is it a work of comparative politics? If it's the latter, you need to make clear from the start which countries you are researching and why they are appropriate case studies."

The white bow tie of my sub-fusc pinching my Adam's apple, I said, "It's possible that just as divisions between East and West have begun to melt since the fall of the Berlin Wall, so the boundaries between analytical approaches may need to be reconceived in order to capture the new reality."

"Postmodern rubbish!" the older Fellow grumbled.

The younger Fellow shot his colleague a sharp look. "Stripped of its jargon, it may be a viable proposition. But one needs to make a robust case for such procedures. If you wish us to accept your argument, you must present it with conviction."

He was offering me the chance to save my skin. I thought of Leon berating his examiners. I felt saturated with invincible sloth. Before I could muster my defence, the older Fellow said, "You need to spend more time in an *ar-chive*."

The younger Fellow stopped just short of rolling his eyes. As their disagreement grew, I talked about the dissolution of the nation-state.

"Generalizations are all very well," the younger Fellow said, "but we need to get down to specifics. In your second chapter, you mention Yugoslavia —"

"Yes, I suspect the rest of my thesis, building on my research in Slovenia, may extend in that direction. I mean in a southward direction, towards Croatia, Bosnia, and Serbia —" As I spoke, I tried to knit together the calamitous events in Yugoslavia, where three weeks earlier open warfare had broken out between Bosnia's multi-ethnic government and Serb forces, with my observations about the erosion of national cultures. I regurgitated editorials from *The Independent* and *The International Herald-Tribune*. I cribbed opinion columns written by the intimidating

St. Antony's lecturer Timothy Garton Ash, who, to my relief, had not been assigned to examine me. I had soon committed myself to writing my thesis on former Yugoslavia.

"A frightful mess. A complete dog's breakfast," the older Fellow said. I was uncertain whether he was referring to Yugoslavia or my thesis. "Yugoslavia is where Waugh's *Sword of Honour* trilogy ends. A far more pertinent work than that tiresome *Brideshead*. Do you speak Serbo-Croatian?" He pronounced the word as though it were a species of exotic beetle.

"I speak French."

"Quite. With a ghastly Canadian accent, no doubt. That's not good enough. I shall make it a recommendation that you learn a hard Eastern European language."

"You must clarify your methodology," the younger Fellow said.

"Quite. You won't know what's what until you've spent a good long while in an archive."

A muted sun emerged as I reached the bottom of the stairs and crossed the Hertford quad that Evelyn Waugh used to negotiate in a drunken stupor. I had passed from decadent skiving to Balkan politics, from *Brideshead Revisited* to *Sword of Honour*. I walked past the Bridge of Sighs. On the other side of the street, a man in a Cleveland Indians baseball cap, spotting my sub-fusc and gown, said, "Look, honey — a real Oxford student!" His wife lifted a Nikon with a huge lens that clicked like rolling tumblers.

The morning after Trinity Term ended, I walked to the Lodge to pay to stay in my room. "Carmichael, yah?" the porter said. "Tutor for Graduates wants to see you."

"He's in his rooms?" I pocketed my receipt and passed through the front quad and the Ho Chi Minh Quad to a row of squat, whitewashed Tudor houses that looked as though a large hand had pressed down on them from above. Built side-by-side with their backs to the street, the houses formed a section of Hamdaw College's outer wall. I bent over to pass beneath the heavy lintel of a low doorway tailored to the stature of seventeenth-century Englishmen. I walked down a short hallway, knocked, and found Zed sitting in the middle of three large desks awash in books and papers. A small Anglepoise lamp illumined a sheet of letterhead notepaper on which he was writing with a black fountain pen.

"I'm afraid it's bad news, Kevin."

My confirmation viva. "The Canadians haven't done well this year."

He pushed back his armchair and crossed one spindly leg over the other in a gesture that made his trouser leg ride up his shin until thick hair snarled over the drooping cuff of his sock.

"I really thought I'd scraped through!"

"You're referring to your viva? You passed. Not a particularly distinguished pass, I must say. The graduate equivalent of a gentleman's third. I'm talking about Landry. It took rather a long time for the news to reach us, but it seems he jumped off his ship."

"What? In the middle of the Atlantic?" *The drop given was fourteen feet.* Of all of Conrad's characters, why had Doug imitated Mrs. Verloc? During his year at Oxford, he had stuck a knife in no one but himself.

"No, foolishly, he waited until they were coming into harbour. He hit the side of the pier. It seems one of his legs is in fairly ghastly shape. He may not walk again."

"I don't know what I could have done to stop him." It began to sink in that Zed's characterization of my viva result was a form of acceptance. Unlike my compatriots Doug and Alex, I had earned my membership in a club for English gentlemen.

Where I had failed was in looking after "my people." Acceptance beneath the dreaming spires had sapped me of my reliability as a native informant. The management of foreign graduate students at Oxford, like the administration of British colonies before it, depended on collaboration with go-betweens from the colonized tribes. Doug's catastrophe dashed my credibility. "He was very bitter about being a Canadian overseas."

"Quite. A colonial chip on his shoulder. I shall be writing to the family tomorrow, asking them to keep us up to date."

Clearing my throat, I said, "Have you heard anything more about Colin?"

"That would be an LMH matter. They're unlikely to inform me."

"It's just ... I was surprised we weren't invited to the funeral ... Those of us who knew him here."

"They're a very esteemed family. I imagine they would guard their privacy at a time like this."

A very esteemed family, I thought. Esteemed English families wouldn't want second-rate colonials besmirching a ceremony as sombre as a funeral. I didn't say what I was thinking for fear that Zed would accuse me, too, of having a colonial chip on my shoulder.

His narrow frame squeezing out the solicitous generosity that never failed to surprise me, Zed looked me in the eye. "You must think about yourself, Kevin. What are your plans for the summer?"

I told him I planned to work on my thesis, then go on a research trip. I left his rooms feeling that I had failed him. In the morning, as I passed through the Lodge, the morning porter gave me a startled look over the lapels of his blue blazer. "They told me you jumped off a ship."

"No," I said, "that was a different Canadian."

EIGHTEEN

BENEATH A HOT SUMMER sun, I rounded a corner on Broad Street and glimpsed a tall, blond lad bent forward over his handlebars. Uttering a cry, I started after him. As the bicycle skimmed away through the crowd, I realized I was burned out. Finishing my three chapters, the abrupt, perhaps permanent, withdrawal of Alex and Leon's company, Doug's leap, Colin's death; I needed to get away. Since Hamdaw offered graduate students only one year in College, I also needed a new home. A petition I had made to move to the multi-college graduate student residence building in Wellington Square, in central Oxford, had elicited a letter telling me that in August I would be allowed to "decant" from Hamdaw College and "migrate" to my new room. If I stayed here. If I were continuing. In this emotionally dishevelled state, I went to my pigeonhole and found a letter from Camille. Her loopy handwriting spilled out humanity, intensity, misery, loneliness, recriminations, tenderness, nostalgia, sensuality, and an invitation that struck my eyes — acclimatized to the muted ironies of Oxford social interaction — as shockingly unguarded.

I phoned her that night. A week later, having left my belongings in a Hamdaw storeroom, I boarded Air Transat. Almost too quickly, I was off the plane, onto a bus, then down into the Métro. I felt like a revenant. Strung out by the endless day of an east-to-west transatlantic flight, I rang the buzzer of Camille's apartment in La Petite Patrie. When I got to the second floor, the door was open. She was speaking on the phone. Her hair fell straight and unusually long from a centre part. When I tried to hug her, she turned her back and continued talking. I realized she was arranging to see a man. I felt as though I had died and was levitating above Camille's head, spying on how her life continued after I was gone. She put down the receiver. "*J'en reviens pas*," she said. "I didn't think you'd actually come. Crossing the Atlantic is unimaginable to me."

Having delivered this jab at my privileges — privileges that I scraped out of a scholarship — she gave me a kiss and shook her head. She poured us each a glass of red wine and looked me in the eyes. "I think I wrote you that letter for the wrong reasons. I was breaking up with someone. In fact, I'd been dumped. I needed to know that someone loved me. When you phoned, it made me feel so much better that I ignored the guy who dumped me, and of course my ignoring him brought him back." She reached out and took my hand. "I'm sorry I made you come all this way, Kevin. I didn't think you'd really cross the Atlantic."

We knew each other too well to overlook the significance of this misunderstanding. It was not something that would have happened before. I had stayed away too long.

Squeezing my hand, Camille said, "*Chuis désolée, Kevin. Vraiment ...*" I started to cry. She hugged me. "I feel terrible that I brought you all this way.

She asked me to wait and went to the washroom. I ambled around the single big room that had contained most of my emotional life for more than five years. A recent issue of a literary journal lay on Camille's desk. The table of contents directed me to one of her poems. *Toi la neige qui fond/ vide dans le fond/ homme sans fondation* ... "You the melting snow/ empty at the core/ man without a foundation." The resonances Camille had pulled out of the verbs *fondre*, to melt, and *fonder*, to found, were untranslatable. In order to have been published now, the poem must have been written months ago. I had underestimated how long Camille had been grappling with her Kevin Carmichael problem.

When she emerged from the washroom, her eyes red, but her face composed, I hoisted my backpack. Down down down I went. Down the stairs to the lobby, down the street to the Beaubien Métro station, and down into the earth and onto a train that rushed down off the Plateau as my disturbed, abandoned emotions plunged into the pit of my stomach. I changed lines at Lionel Groulx and rode down into the city's depths, feeling, in a wash of vestigial Catholicism, as though I were descending into hell. I got out in Verdun, where, even when I was standing up, I felt as though I were lying on my back staring up at the rest of the city. Here the redbrick low-rises were older, sadder, and packed more tightly together than in La Petite Patrie. The wrought -iron spiral staircases were rusted; the procession of uninspiring buildings was punctured by the abandoned hulks of factories that used to employ the people who lived here. I found the building and clanged up the outdoor spiral staircase to the narrow second-floor balcony that gave access to three doors. I knocked on the middle door. Fred came down, a Molson Canadian in his hand. "Hey, Shawn," he called over his shoulder, "Kevin's here."

I climbed the stairs and crossed the parquet floor to the kitchen where my father was frying bacon. He cooked breakfasts at all hours of the day. His thick, grey hair fell to his shoulders; the surprising black bolts of his sideburns stitched his cheeks. "I thought you were in England? How come you aren't staying with Brigid?"

I dropped my backpack to the floor. "I was going to stay with Camille."

He prodded his greasy fry-up. "I notice you said 'was.'"

"On again, off again, eh?" Fred said, cuffing me on the shoulder

"Fred, why don't you get Kevin a beer?" My father slid his bacon, and a conglomeration of fried eggs, tomatoes, and cheese, onto a plate. He buttered his Wonder Bread and carried his plate to the table. "The living room sofa's all yours. Just bring in some groceries. Fred and I are on pogey until Cégep starts in the fall ... Christ, did you just fly across the Atlantic? We can't even afford to go up to the Plateau! We're both trying to get some creative thinking done this summer. Did I tell you about my book on the working-class tradition in Canadian poetry ...?"

Fred brought me a Molson. In my late teens, with my own intellectual enthusiasms bursting open like buds on a prickly bush, I used to treat these book projects, which vanished without a word having been written, with enraged scorn. Now, humbled by my faltering thesis, I listened. As I watched him chew, I reminded myself that this man with the thick, grey hair and the sleeveless T-shirt used to decide my bedtime. "I assume you can't face Brigid because she told you not to go back to Camille," he said. "Don't fight with your mother, son."

"Why not? You did."

My father looked startled. This was the kind of thing I used to say to him when I was sixteen. Seeing the colour rise into his grey cheeks, I said, "I'm sorry, Dad." My voice caught. "It's hard for me to talk about Camille with Mum."

"She fooled around on you," my father grumbled. Fred looked at him in barely discernible reproach, in the unobtrusive way that one half of an old married couple communicates with the other. "Your mother's liberal views don't extend to sexual morality. That's the one place where she's a square — that and being a slave of the goddamned banks."

I sat in silence as my father finished his fry-up, got to his feet and began to wash dishes. When he had finished, he tossed a damp dish rag over an inverted colander and said, "Bring your pack in here."

I followed him down the hall: two bedrooms, a washroom and a living room. The living room had a big sofa, crammed bookshelves, piles of books on the floor, with the dog-eared appearance of having been foraged in second-hand stores or yard sales. There were milk crates full of LPs, and a Formica-topped brown coffee table that supported a turntable I remembered from the apartments where I'd grown up. A pair of two-by-fours extended across three inverted milk crates made a platform for the fourteen-inch black-and-white television. Behind the television, through a sliding glass door, was a black wrought-iron balcony that looked out at other, identical balconies.

My father turned on the television. He and Fred sat down on the couch. *The National* came on. Peter Mansbridge read the CBC news.

"Look at how much friggin' hair the guy's lost," Fred said.

"He's not going to hold down the anchor unless he gets a rug," my father muttered.

They'd had the same conversation when I visited them at Christmas. In their late fifties, grey-haired and trundling bellies in front of them, my father and Fred were content to live like undergraduate roommates. My mother claimed that my father's living arrangements confirmed his immaturity. Yet their settled air suggested premature old age as much as they did prolonged adolescence. My father had let life go. His revolutions had failed, his marriage had fizzled, his plans to be a radical intellectual had dissolved without a book or article having been published. His primary achievement, for a couple of decades, was to have escaped from Verdun – and now he was back. Fred, who was from rural eastern Ontario and called the couch a chesterfield and the *dépanneur* on the corner a "confectionary," seemed content with having made the move to the city. In the winter, when they were each teaching a couple of courses at the Cégep – my father in English composition and Canadian Literature, Fred in bookkeeping – the drinking extended beyond Labatt's Blue and Molson Canadian to French and Italian wines. On cold winter nights there were parties and outings to other districts of the city. Sometimes there were women, a fact that I found embarrassing, sordid and, at the same time, a relief, since these affairs disproved my mother's murmured insinuations that Dad and Fred were a secret gay couple.

Their friendship had started in the 1970s, when they were both married men from working-class backgrounds who were nurturing intellectual ambitions while raising young families. They had met working together when Nick, who was friends with both of them, had run for city council on the Maoist ticket. Their bond had been strengthened by their divorces and consolidated by their years as roommates. They had spent the late 1980s watching as *The National* followed the Cold War to its conclusion and had infected me with their enthusiasm for these events. The Berlin Wall was gone, but my father and Fred remained together, their friendship enduring long after the era that had shaped their beliefs had passed.

In the morning, I bought them a load of groceries. I'd intended to spruce up their fridge with fruit and vegetables, but the Provigo catered to neighbourhood tastes and budgets, stocking low-priced carbs and grease. I settled for orange juice as my contribution to good health. Having done my duty, I started on my rounds. I was conscious of doing rounds, conscious, as I made one phone call after another, of the whiff of desperation that underlay my need to remain present in people's lives.

"Jake Mendelsson saw you at La Cabane," Joan said, ensconced behind her period colonial desk in her office on the edge of the McGill campus. "He thought you were still working for me."

"That was at Christmas. He was paying too much attention to a certain young woman to notice what I was saying."

Joan had trimmed the unruly grey mane that had been her visual signature on television. When I spoke of Eastern Europe, she said, "Ever since the Solidarity movement emerged in Poland, with all those right-wing Catholics behind it, the Americans have been rebuilding Eastern Europe in order to destroy the European Union."

"Do they really have the power to do that?" I disagreed with Joan's underestimation of Europe's strength. I knew it was I, not she, who had changed. Our conversation foundered. I left her office and walked east. The turrets of the Royal Victoria Hospital, where my dad's father had worked as a technician under Norman Bethune, twirled skyward like the battlements of Dracula's castle. I crossed Avenue du Parc with the Mountain at my back and entered the Plateau Mont-Royal. At the intersection with Boulevard St-Laurent, with gas lamp lighting fixtures stretching before me above the red paving stones of Avenue Duluth, I observed Montreal as an outsider feasting on its visual delights.

Reverting to insider status, I walked to Mile End and let myself into my mother's apartment. I went to my old room, fell asleep and was woken by her coming in from work.

"Kevin, you could have stayed here." The flesh around her eyes looked tired. "Were you so ashamed at having made a fool of yourself?"

I pressed my lips shut. "Each time I come back, I have less to say to people."

She changed the topic. "The situation in Eastern Europe must be so different than it is in China, where the Communist Party is still in power. Thanks, in part, to the man who sired me."

The archaic verb felt shamefully intimate. "Do you really think Bethune might be your father?" Was I the grandson of a certified international saint and scoundrel, the possessor of a revolutionary pedigree even more dramatic than Leon's?

"Bethune came back to Canada between the Spanish Civil War and the revolution in China," she said, as I followed her into the kitchen. "They say he had a passion for the wife of a law professor at McGill, but I'm sure he would have visited Mother as well. That's all it would have taken. Mother was very self-centred. She felt she had the right to certain things, and she didn't think twice about the consequences of taking them." She looked at me across the sink. "It would be such a relief to blame my problems on an aberrant gene."

Her words upset my assumption that my mother was fine and only my father's descent into Verdun merited my concern. I sat down. Misjudging my movement, I jarred the edge of the table with my palms. My mother pushed it back towards me with a hostile shove. It was an instinctive reaction. I froze, my face growing hot.

I got up and ran us each a glass of water.

"You'll patch things up with Camille, won't you?"

The sound of Camille's name plunged a dull spike into my back. "I don't think that's possible this time."

When I returned to Verdun, I told my father of my mother's theories about her parentage. "Is that even possible, Dad? I mean, Spain, China – do the dates add up?"

Fred got to his feet. "I'll take care of it, Kevin." He waved his hand at the piles of second-hand paperbacks. "I'll bet yuh any money the answer's right here in this room."

All that Fred had unearthed by the time I went to bed was a Hugh MacLennan novel in which Bethune survives the revolution in China and returns to disrupt the grey flannel life of 1950s Anglo Montreal. "This is cool, Kevin! You and me both doing research!"

I looked into his enthusiastic face. Who was I to claim distinctions between my research and his? His research didn't introduce him to new people. I'd barely mentioned Leon and Alex to my parents. I'd told no one about Colin's death. Being in Montreal, where someone like Colin was imaginable only as a creation of *Masterpiece Theatre*, scoured him out of my system for a few days. The day before my return flight to London, remorse flooded me. Why had Leon and I made that stupid call? I needed to talk to someone about it. I lifted the receiver, intending to phone Camille. Feeling the plastic turn cold in my palm, I realized that Camille had become an obligation, like Joan or my sister. Or maybe I did want to see her again, but was terrified of being rejected. It was too soon for me to distinguish between fear and indifference. I stared out the window at the sparse cirrus clouds, marvelling that the next evening I would fly away into endless space.

I put down the receiver.

NINETEEN

I DECANTED FROM HAMDAW College and migrated to Wellington Square. I went to an office, paid my rent and was given a
key. There were no moving trucks, and no fellow graduates
to help me. I picked up my suitcase from the storeroom, made
the twenty-minute walk, then returned for more belongings.
In three ambling relays, I had moved. My new home was one
of dozens of tiny, bright rooms, grouped in clusters of four
around a washroom and a kitchen, in a faceless concrete building
that had replaced the demolished north side of a Georgian
square. At the back of the building, Little Clarendon Street ran
past small shops with a narrow, shaded, passage-like busy-ness
that mimicked life in a larger city. The residents of my building,
affiliated with every college in the university, resembled big-city
people in their scant regard for their neighbours. I felt not
bereft, but sprung loose, adventurously adrift. At a stroke, my life
had been pared down to me and my thesis. I was no longer in
a long-distance relationship, nor was I constrained by the contradictions of being an Anglo-Montrealer. My history had sunk

into the ocean, while I had levitated into a diaphanous ambience of bright, warm air.

When I went out in search of groceries, I ran into Kumiko. Not yet ready to become Japanese again, she was staying in Oxford for the summer. Listening to her, I decided that there was no point in chaining myself to a desk until I had more material. Later that day, I walked to the STA travel office and asked about cheap flights to Berlin. "Berlin's awfully full," the girl who had sent me to Ljubljana said. "I can get you a deal to Budapest."

I gave myself three weeks, bought a backpacker travel guide, and began to fill my pack. On the evening preceding my early-morning flight, I went out to Little Clarendon Street and spotted Kumiko in the crowd. Her smile was reticent, as though running into me had become part of a routine she must tolerate. When I told her I was on my way to get an ice cream, and asked her if she would join me, I sensed a door opening in the evening sunlight. She rewarded me with her smile and I felt daunted by her company. We sat across from each other on high stools with a green-painted bar running between us and chipped at the ice cream in our cups with tiny, square-headed plastic spoons. My awareness of the un-Japanese length of her legs, twisted around her stool, kept my eyes trained on her face.

"Do you have a girlfriend in Oxford?" she asked, surprising me.

"No." I hesitated. "I had a girlfriend in Canada, but that is over."

She carved a slice of cookies-and-cream from above the lip of her cup. "I had a boyfriend in Oxford. Last year."

She mumbled the last two words, as though she had pushed beyond the limits of Japanese discretion. Not to respond would be to disdain her courage, I sensed, yet I was wary of prying. "Do a lot of Japanese girls in Oxford have boyfriends?"

"Most of them talk to lots of men. But they do not have boyfriends. They giggle."

Kumiko was writing her thesis on Victorian England. To her supervisor's approval, she had spent six months in a London archive. I told her about my trip. She gave me a look of fresh appraisal. "It will be an adventure."

Outside, darkness had fallen; the streetlights came on. The wine bar across the street had opened its doors. "Would you like a glass of wine?" She paused, then nodded. In the wine bar, I watched the candlelight crackling in her dark hair. She asked me how old I was and seemed pleased by the answer. She was twenty-eight. She had grown up in the Tokyo-Yokohama magma. By sacrificing her adolescence to study, she had earned admission to a university for the Japanese "super-elite." After graduation, she had worked as a researcher for a famous history professor and taken night courses to improve her English. Arriving in Oxford at twenty-five, she had felt "always separate" yet eager to learn about Englishness. At first, dutiful and studious, she stayed in the archive every day until closing time. Once her archival research was done, she began to feel restless. "I started to drink and do other things. If my father know I am drinking wine with a man I meet in the street ..."

"We didn't meet in the street. We met in the MCR."

"I will tell him we meet in the street. To make him angry!" Her eyes gleamed as her cheeks flushed. She knocked back her Sauvignon as though it were ginger ale. "Now you will think I am one of those Japanese girls who giggle."

"You're not giggling, you're laughing." I reached across the table and took her hand in mine.

"Good! My English is good enough to understand this

188 | STEPHEN HENIGHAN

difference." She squared her shoulders as though making a speech. "It is a triumph of international understanding."

My throat dry, I invited her back to my room. She accepted, then avoided my eyes. I paid the bill. We slipped across Little Clarendon Street and sprinted up the stairs. As we entered my room, the glare of light on the striped plastic curtains and the whitewashed cinder block walls was harsh and uninviting. As quickly as I had turned on the light, I snapped it off. I turned to Kumiko in the darkness and, without having laid a finger on her body, kissed her mouth. The gap between the curtains gave us all the light we needed. As though deterred by the narrowness of the bed, we remained on our feet as we undressed. I ran my gaze up the length of her nakedness before I essayed my first caress. She had been wearing shoes with unobtrusive heels; without them, she was less tall, her body more delicate than I had anticipated; a delicacy wrapped in a self-possessed solitude.

We lay down on my bed. I kissed Kumiko's belly. She arched and winced. I bent forward, kissed the tendons in her neck, spread her legs as far as the narrow bed allowed and tried to enter her.

"No," she said.

Bruised by the threshold of her warmth, my erection pulsed like the primeval beast it was. "I'll get a condom."

"No." She turned on her side. The supernatural smoothness of her back, descending to her round bottom, made my desire swell. Kumiko lifted her head and gestured in the direction of the backpack in the corner. "You go away."

She relapsed onto the bed, drew a long breath, then sat up and kissed me on the mouth. The kiss contained a formality, a seal of recognition, that felt elaborately Japanese. "You're the most beautiful woman I've ever been naked with," I murmured.

"I am not ready to give all of me to you," Kumiko said.

The simplicity of this observation both exonerated and crushed me. We got under the sheets. Murmuring about our families, we confused each other with details of unfamiliar societies. I woke at two a.m. and started to kiss her again. She took me in her hand, her fingertips like silk on my flesh. I pulled away, stumbled towards the washbasin, touched myself once and came. She smiled, kissed me, then said she would go; I persuaded her to leave with me. At twenty to four I called her a taxi, even though she said she could walk home. We stumbled out the door, Kumiko having left her phone number on a scrap of paper on my desk. Little Clarendon Street was sepulchral. The taxi crawled over the speed bumps. I insisted on paying. Kumiko pushed the money away, then accepted it with a distressed smile that left an uneasy feeling in my stomach. Our farewell kiss was off-target, my lips brushing the corner of her mouth.

I hoisted my backpack and walked through the dark to Gloucester Green to get on the bus to Heathrow. Having remained comatose through most of the journey, I revelled in the heat of noon in Budapest. I got a bus in from Ferihégy Airport. The drabness of the decaying apartment blocks rose before me in a greying wave, yet once I reached downtown the huge Habsburg avenues thrilled me. Here was the history I had been seeking! My intoxication was tempered by the feeling of having arrived too late. Budapest was gloriously overloaded with history, dynamic in the energy of its street life, but few vestiges of the political somersault of 1989 were discernible to the untutored eye. The language was a barrier more impregnable than the Berlin Wall. Even words that were the same in every other language were different in Hungarian: "police" was *rendőrség*, "restaurant" was *vendéglő* or *étterem*, "hotel" was *szálloda*. Although what I was looking for, it turned out, was *fizetővendégszolgálat*: an affordable private room in someone's apartment. This system was a vestige of Communist accommodation policies. Those things that were convenient and affordable in Hungary – tram tickets, train fares, books, lunches in workers' cafés – were holdovers from Communism, while those that were garish or expensive – tawdry night clubs, plush downtown restaurants, luxury boat tours on the Danube – were creations of the first four years of capitalism. All other insights were thwarted by the wall of the language. The girls at the office in the Keleti Pu train station, who allotted me my *fizetővendégszolgálat*, spoke English; most other people responded to me in broken German. The sun came out, elevating me as though I were water evaporating into the atmosphere. The hot wind glossed everything I looked at with the sheen of Kumiko's beauty as it might have been seen through the translucence of Colin's pale eyes. If his eyes could still see. If he were still alive.

Before leaving for Prague, I mailed Kumiko a postcard. In the Czech capital, the feeling of having arrived too late deepened. Compact, exquisite Prague was so inundated with tourists that the Cold War felt irretrievable. Research was out of the question; a tourist was all I could be. The realization made me impatient, even though Czech was less indecipherable than Hungarian, a few of the words resembling words I knew. People addressed me in German, but also in English. There were young Americans everywhere. I feared that, not having known these countries before, I would be unable to take the measure of the world of after. I sat in the sun, reading an old black Penguin Classics edition of Ivan Goncharov's *Oblomov*. The life of overcrowded boarding houses and overwrought feelings, the spiritual depths of nineteenth-century Russia, made me long for conversations with Leon and Alex and Colin, even as my longing was tainted with embittered sadness.

I pushed on to Poland. Coming from Canada, I saw European countries as small. In the case of Poland, this was a mistake. Hour after hour of swooping plains and glimmering golden rape seed passed outside the window of the train. Farmers forged across vast fields, thrashing wheat with sickles or bent over horse-drawn ploughs, as though resuscitated from the novels of Tolstoy. The wide expanse made me think of Central Europe as a sun-struck plain where I floated above the history I knew, above history altogether. Yet once I had arrived in Krákow and found my way to a dormitory-like residence left over from Communism, I discovered that this city provided access to the past. It was not the past of Cold War Eastern Europe, but rather an invented, imaginary past of a nation enshrined in the Catholic Church. Squads of aggressively asexual young men patrolled Krákow's streets, each with his pious chin lifted to bare the white flash of his clerical collar as though it were a fist.

The first day in Krákow I wrote Kumiko a postcard: *Every time I close my eyes, my head fills with your beauty.* I added a postcard to Auberon in which I referred to this journey as a "research trip." The fib exacerbated my bad conscience. I had no questions formulated about Poland, and no method for getting answers. In Krákow, as in Prague, the banishment of the actual recent past had fed an ersatz reinvention of a past that was either romanticized (Catholic Poland) or had been brutally extirpated (Jewish Prague). Sitting in Krákow's central square, the Rynek Glówny, I wrote in my notebook: *The elaboration of these fictitious histories is a response to a present that cannot accept or engage with the history from which it has sprung.*

The guild hall, Sukiennice, was awash in souvenirs. I shook my head. Someone said something in German. "The Poles are learning to be capitalist," the voice repeated in English.

A woman in three-quarter-length trousers in alpine style — *Lederhosen* — stood before a table of glossy statuettes. I noticed her remarkably thick dirty-blond hair and owlish glasses. She looked like a dishevelled, cerebral version of Heidi. "I think they have learned already," I said. We drifted out into the sunlight. "They repress the past by letting the church run the country." I pointed towards an enormous poster of Pope John Paul II. "His face is everywhere. As though he were the new Stalin."

A second too late, it struck me that, like many tourists to Krákow, Heidi might be an ardent Catholic. A sneaky smirk crept across her face. "In Bavaria they *want* the Pope to be Stalin."

"You're from Bavaria?"

"I hope you enjoy Krákow," she said, and walked away.

Two days later, as I was boarding the train to Warsaw, I spotted Heidi climbing up the steps ahead of me. She wore blue jeans; her mane was pulled back into a ponytail that made wings of hair bulge on either side of her head. Inside the train, I found a narrow passage running past six-seat compartments. Ignoring my reservation number, I looked for Heidi, entered her compartment, stashed my backpack on top of hers on the overhead rack and sat down opposite her.

She regarded me with an untrustworthy expression. "I don't like Americans."

"Neither do I —"

"But —"

"I'm Canadian."

"Ah, you have no culture."

As the train pulled out of the station, a ravel of low hills giving way by stages to the flattest, drabbest plain I'd seen, Heidi, having introduced herself as Leonie, argued with me.

"You are insular," I said.

"And you are not? We are speaking your language. You only speak English."

"I also speak French. Your country has only one language, mine has two."

"I speak Italian," she murmured in retaliation. "I had an Italian boyfriend for five years."

"I had a French-Canadian girlfriend for five years."

"Europe will always have its culture. It will never be ignorant like America."

"But now you must integrate the east. Are you really interested —?"

"We are in Poland and you ask me if I'm interested in the east?"

"Are Germans willing to see their tax money spent on East Germany and Poland?"

"We are not like you. We do not destroy society to have low taxes."

Everything each of us said grated on the other. My culture was an assemblage of shards, hers was integrated. She knew classical music, she read Greek and Latin, and took for granted that everyone lived and breathed the differences between the ideas of Kant and those of Hegel. By the time the train pulled into the vast, echoing Warsaw station, we had established that we were both planning to stay at the Youth Hostel. In the station we chuckled at the exterior-frame backpacks with cheap vinyl pockets that betrayed the Polish young people who tried to pass as Westerners. I pulled out a five-złoty coin, explaining to Leonie that my guide book listed the phone number of the Youth Hostel.

We lined up at the pay phone. I dialled the number, waited for a reply and began to speak in slow, clear English. "*Sprechen Sie Deutsch?*" a voice replied.

I passed the receiver to Leonie. I saw her wide mouth spread into a smile. She replaced the receiver, a glint in her eye.

"Your book is *wrong*. That poor woman receives many phone calls from stupid Americans because *your* book says the Youth Hostel number ends in 32 when it is really 23." Her face shining, she dialled the correct number and, speaking in German, booked us each a bed.

The hostel was spartan. Men and women were separated at the reception desk and dispatched to dormitories on opposite sides of the building. The showers didn't work, there was no breakfast room, the front doors were locked at eleven p.m. and the dormitory lights snapped on at seven a.m. As we went our separate ways at the reception desk, Leonie asked if I would like to walk around the city that evening.

The broad avenues of central Warsaw looked barren in the shadow of the thirty-storey Palace of Culture. There were fewer priests than in Krákow, and more drunks. From early evening onward, the police raided the street corners to round up the staggering hordes. Leonie and I wandered into a nineteenth-century district. A restaurant beckoned. After observing the tuxedoed doorman and exchanging comments about how we would never eat in a restaurant this expensive in our own countries, we were greeted with candles and water in tall glasses and white bread under a cloth, brought by the four different men who were waiting on our table. We were given a six-page menu in Polish and badly translated French. When the head waiter came, Leonie ordered her meal.

"*Ne pas,*" the waiter said. Leonie, grasping that the dish was not available, suggested an alternative. "*Ne pas,*" the waiter repeated.

Leonie looked angry. "You order."

I ordered.

"*Ne pas!*" the waiter exclaimed, as though this fact were a revelation to him. I suggested two other dishes from pages five and six of the menu. I received the same response.

I scrutinized the tall waiter and his immaculate tuxedo. Echoing his pidgin French, I said, "*Qu'est-ce qu'il y a?*"

"*Hünchen und Reis!*" he said, mysteriously switching to German. Leonie translated for me: chicken and rice. I said in French that we would both have that. The three sub-waiters smiled to indicate that we had chosen wisely. The head waiter leaned over our table. "*Polonais,*" he whispered, as though divulging a secret. "*Kultur gut. Literatur très gut ... Mais l'économie —bah!*"

Not daring to order drinks, Leonie and I sipped our water. Fixing me with an accusatory look, Leonie said, "You do not make research. You are a tourist."

"Shh," I said. "Don't tell my thesis supervisor."

Leonie did not laugh. "You must have a plan to make research! You must write to the *Archiven* you wish to visit, you must organize. I am sure you do not know anyone in Warsaw!"

"Yes, I do!" As I wondered how to extricate myself from this lie, I realized I knew Jerzy. "I'm visiting a professor tomorrow. Will you come with me?"

"You want me to come to your interview?"

"Yes, I think he will say more if we both go." In fact, I feared the opposite might be true.

The chicken and rice arrived. The bird had been boiled until it fell off the bone. The rice was not rice but a harsh grain that stuck between my teeth. The sub-waiters replenished our bread and water each time they were on the verge of running out. As we ate, Leonie told me that she was a doctoral student in comparative linguistics at the University of Bonn. We talked about languages and filled our stomachs for less than the cost of a sandwich at an Oxford sandwich shop.

We walked back to the Youth Hostel through poorly lighted streets. When we emerged onto the broad Aleje Jerozolimskie, where a spotlight shined on a gargantuan portrait of Pope John Paul II, I confronted the ignominious necessity of confessing to Leonie that I did not know the name of the university where Jerzy taught. She looked at me in triumph. When we reached the reception desk, I unfolded my map of Warsaw. Leonie asked the two young women at the desk about small universities. They asked her a question. She looked at me, "Is it a very Catholic university?"

I struggled to imagine a Polish entity which was not very Catholic. But yes, I seemed to recall Jerzy mentioning something of the sort. The woman who was in charge of handing out locker keys made a mark on the map in an older part of town, near the Vistula River.

At seven o'clock the next morning, the fluorescent lights came on. A crewcut man strolled between the dormitory beds, smacking a spoon against a frying pan. I got up, shaved, and washed my torso at the sink. I choked down the breakfast of acrid coffee and a dry bun while sitting on my bed. Later, Leonie and I trailed through the grounds of royal palaces near the river, then fell asleep on the grass. Waking, she said, "I used to sleep in parks in Italy with Salvatore ..."

Giuseppe, Salvatore, the echo of Pia went beyond blond hair and haughty Eurocentrism. The distant Italian boyfriend, exercising control though no longer present, was both a warning and a challenge.

At ten o'clock we walked to an older district and found the university in a small courtyard with a church steeple at one end. Staircases led up into a venerable building. Long-haired students trundling shoddy daypacks passed us going down the stairs. We emerged into a broad, gloomy hall with high ceilings. Oak doors bore small brass frames, inside which instructors' names were scrawled on threadbare slips of paper. A peeling red-on-white *Solidarność* decal covered one door; on another I saw the light-haloed face of Ronald Reagan. "What is your friend's name?" Leonie asked. When I told her, she said, "No, his family name."

In a crushed voice, I admitted I didn't know.

"You don't know? For you, this is research? You are a doctoral student at Oxford University?"

"I'm a bohemian who ended up in a doctoral program by mistake."

"You are not a bohemian. Salvatore is a bohemian. You are bourgeois, with no intellectual culture!"

Before I could reply, I spotted Jerzy. His face didn't look quite as my mind recalled it, but I knew it was him. The man at the end of the corridor was of slight build, his dark hair tousled, with deep bags beneath his eyes. He wore a blue sweater and walked with a shuffling gait.

"Jerzy!"

His head turned. Determined not to look ridiculous in front of Leonie, I walked down the hall, extended my hand, and said, "Jerzy, I'm Kevin. Alexander Spokoynov's friend. We met in Oxford."

He hesitated. He shook my hand. "Also from Canada, yes? I remember. That bad lecture. It is good to see you. Welcome to

Poland." His smile contained a whiff of irony. "Where do you stay?"

"We're at the Youth Hostel." I gestured towards Leonie.

The pale flesh over Jerzy's high cheekbones flushed. "She is your wife?"

"No, Leonie is from Germany. We met on the train from Kráków."

This unsettled him even more. "You must come to my apartment," he murmured. "For tea. You would like?"

"Yes, yes," I said. "Are you teaching?"

"I already teach for three hours. My lesson begin at seven o'clock."

I understood where the Youth Hostel got its schedule. We waited for Jerzy to pick up his satchel from his office, then followed him down the stairs and into the courtyard. When two students stopped him to ask a question, Leonie murmured, "I leave. He does not want me here."

"I want you here," I said, then wondered where this had come from. We were standing very close, our blue-jeaned hips grazing each other. As though to recover her balance, Leonie hooked her arm around my waist, then withdrew it as Jerzy turned to point the way to the tram. I asked him whether he knew that Alex was going to Harvard. Heads turned at our English, yet the stares felt warm and curious.

I wondered whether Alex had told Jerzy about Colin.

"Alex tell me about Harvard when he come to Warsaw." Jerzy, too, had known before I did. He produced three tickets, punched them at both ends, then handed one each to Leonie and me. The tram carried us past buildings with crumbling stonework. We crossed a broad avenue and entered a district of pollution-smeared high-rise apartment blocks with exteriors of stippled grey stucco. "Alex make mistake," Jerzy said. "He must stay close to Russia." He lowered his voice. "In Poland we do not like Russian people, but I must say that Russian language have very great literature."

We got off on a main street and walked down a side street where children played in bald, dusty yards between the high rises. Tinny little grey Trabants, and the occasional more ample Lada or Škoda, were parked along the streets and on the sidewalks. Laundry hung from grey balconies, drip-dripping onto the dust below, where men in tank-topped T-shirts sat on concrete picnic tables, sipping vodka from the flask. Jerzy led us into the fourth high rise on the right. We climbed to the seventh floor. There was no elevator. I was puffing by the time we reached his door. Leonie, reverting to her Heidi image, looked as spry as a young fräulein waltzing up alpine meadows. I sweated, cursing the showerless Youth Hostel.

Jerzy opened the door. The modest dimensions of his living room were encroached upon by two head-high wall units made of beige pressboard lacquered to look like varnished wood. The unit that stood against the longer wall contained clothing closets and a recessed mirror; the unit that lined the wall perpendicular to it offered countertops and bookshelves. The phalanx of books in Polish was interrupted by dictionaries of Russian, English and German. The lone English title was *A Single Man* by Christopher Isherwood. I spotted a black-and-white photograph of a severe-looking couple, flanked by a crucifix and a loudly ticking gold-hulled clock. Next to it stood a photograph of Pope John Paul II wearing a scarlet robe. The third wall of the apartment contained a window that offered a view of the adjacent high rise. At the back of the apartment was a dark niche of a kitchen, a small bathroom and a bedroom whose ajar door revealed that it was barely broader than the narrow, cot-like bed within. The living room had two upright armchairs with wide armrests; a small television sat in the corner; on the table there was a manual typewriter and two piles of paper. Little within these walls had changed since 1989. I had reached the world of before. Alex had stayed here. Possibly he had slept on the floor between the two armchairs where Jerzy invited Leonie and me to sit down.

"I make tea," Jerzy said. "I learn to drink tea in Oxford."

He disappeared into the kitchen. Feeling the pressure of Leonie's owlish stare, I waited for Jerzy to return, then asked, "How has life in Poland changed since 1989?"

"It is easier for me to travel," Jerzy said, "but it is harder for me to live. Before everything was cheap. Now food costs thousands of złoty. A train ticket – five hundred thousand złoty. They say this is transition. But many changes are bad."

"What are the bad changes?"

"There is pornography. You see it everywhere. Naked woman in magazine, naked woman in movie. This is bad. Young people forget how it was before. They act like people in movies. And there is feminism. Now some girls at university are feminists. This must stop. With feminism, family does not survive. If family does not survive, Poland does not survive. We live between Germany and Russia. We need strong family to have strong Poland."

Leonie gazed into her tea, her expression inscrutable. I longed to ask Jerzy the one question I could not ask him. "So you support the intervention of the Catholic Church in politics to make laws that will encourage morality?"

"No, this is not good. Abortion must be illegal because it is wrong, not because priest tell us. It is not good if politicians listen to priests. I support democracy. Not Communists, not army, not priests. Just people vote."

Keeping my tone gentle, I said, "No liberal democratic society in history has been moral." Seeing his discomfort, I said, "I'm sorry to interrogate you, Jerzy. It's good to see you. It reminds me of Alex —"

"You and Alex talk with Jewish friend about literature and politics. This is very good. To have a group of men who are intelligent and talk all night!"

Leonie stirred in her chair.

"Do you have a group of men like that, Jerzy?" I asked.

"When I am a student, yes. We argue about writers, about how is best for fight Russians, fight Communism. It very sweet time. Later, change come, and it is good, but now we do not talk. Our government say we do not talk about past. We do not arrest torturers. Today torturer work in shop, work in business. It is difficult to talk about history. And my friends married now. They must stay home with wife and children. Married man cannot talk all night."

Seeing Leonie hunched into a ball of tension, I got to my feet to explore Jerzy's bookshelves. The hardbound spines of Polish classics, promising riches beyond my understanding, made me feel a nostalgic ache for Alex's Russian library. I picked up the Isherwood novel. Inside the front cover, a jagged hand had written: *To Jerzy, from Alex.* A couple of words in Russian followed. Again, Alex had surprised me.

"I sad for Alex," Jerzy's voice said over my shoulder. "He find no place in world. Not Russia, not Canada, not England, not America."

"His home is the Russian language, Russian literature. He'll have that wherever he goes."

"His brother write poetry. It not enough for him."

"What are you talking about? Alex doesn't have a brother." I turned around.

Perched on his chair, Jerzy said, "Brother is dead."

"What?" I took a step forward. "What brother?" Did he mean Colin? Had Alex told Jerzy about Colin? Did Jerzy know that Alex had regarded Colin as a little brother? "What are you talking about, Jerzy?"

Jerzy hesitated. "Maybe it is not right for me to say. Alex have older brother. Both boys love poetry. Brother write poetry. But he not like life in Canada. He not like English language, only Russian language. Alex follow, do everything like him. Except Alex is younger, he speak English language like Canadian. Brother join Russian men that sell drugs and girls from Mafia. He need Russian friends, he happy with Russian men. Then there is a business problem. Mafia kill Alex brother."

I stared at him. I was about to dismiss his words, until I remembered our conversation in East London and Alex's hesitant denial when I had asked him whether he had a brother. "Are you sure about this, Jerzy?"

"Yes. In Oxford you and Jewish friend are like his brothers. Boy he teach is like little brother. Boy who die." He stared at me from beneath his unkempt eyebrows, as though to assure me that he and Alex remained in close contact.

"I was there when that boy died," I said, my need to assert an equal closeness with Alex overriding my caution before Leonie. I saw her stare at my words.

"It is terrible. Nothing is enough." Jerzy shook his head. "Alex need more. He need ... something. That is what he look for now."

TWENTY

IN THE MORNING, LEONIE and I were kicked out of the Youth Hostel.

At seven a.m. the guy who banged the frying pan told me to go to the reception desk. The girl who was behind the desk that morning spoke some English. "You go now. August. Two night limit."

"And my friend? The German girl?"

"Two night. No space."

I retrieved my backpack from the men's dormitory and sat on a wobbly bench next to the reception desk. A poster of the Beatles, in their clean-cut, early 1960s incarnation, hung next to the statutory portrait of Pope John Paul II. Leonie, when she appeared, put up a better fight in German than I had put up in English. The outcome was the same. An hour later we were sitting on the rim of a concrete fountain, our backpacks between our knees, I immersed in *Oblomov*, she in a daunting German volume of linguistic theory.

A young Pole bounded up to us. "Change money? Dollar? Big złoty!"

I waved him away.

"You are a bad researcher," Leonie said. "Yesterday you could ask Jerzy more questions. When he talked about the Polish family, you could ask him why he does not have a family. You must think about the contradictions. But of course you are American so everything must be simple."

"I didn't ask Jerzy why he doesn't have a family because he's gay. Is that simple enough for you?"

"For you it is not bad that he is gay?"

"Leonie! You sound like the Pope."

"Do not try to tell me that I am conservative. You are Ameri—"

"You know nothing about where I come from. If you visited Montreal —"

"I will never leave Europe."

We returned to our reading. Water splattered in the fountain at our backs; trams clanked on the edge of the square. My mind strayed from *Oblomov*, trying to work out how old Alex would have been when his brother was murdered.

"That is the book about the man who does not get out of bed?" Leonie wanted to talk.

"Yes. The final part has the most beautiful love story. You really believe the characters are in love."

She regarded me with an appraising stare. "That is special," she murmured.

"*Geldwechsel!*" a man shouted. He opened his jacket to reveal a massive bolt of multiple-zeroed złoty.

"Leonie, we need to find somewhere to stay."

"I can sleep in a park."

"I don't think I want to sleep in a park," I said, risking an accusation of bourgeois conservatism. "I haven't had a shower for three days. We could get rooms in apartments."

"You don't want a hotel room?"

From a park to a hotel room. Worried about my budget, I agreed to give it a try. Hoisting our backpacks, we walked to a Communist-era concrete tombstone hotel. The clerk didn't speak English, or even much German, but after long division of the zeroes on the end of the złoty price, we calculated that we could share a room for less than ten dollars each.

Our room was on the top floor. The decor reflected a commissar's conception of finery; bulky 1950s furniture, a television the breadth of whose screen was in inverse proportion to the clarity of the images that appeared there, a wall-unit identical to those in Jerzy's apartment, a sentimental painting of a young man wielding a sickle in a glimmering field and a young woman trailing behind him. On the wall above the bed was a discoloured rectangle where a portrait-sized frame had been removed. I wondered how many leaders' faces had hung in that spot.

"*Sozialistischer Realismus!*" Leonie sat down on the wide bed. "Take your shower. Men always smell."

I foraged in my pack for a pair of shorts and a T-shirt, then shut myself in the bathroom. The tub was dingy, but I felt a burst of relief when the water poured over me. I got an erection and told myself to calm down. I would soon be back in Oxford ... with Kumiko?

When I stepped out of the bathroom, the carpet tickled my heels. Leonie took her shower. I looked out across the flat-roofed city, imagining Leonie's body in the steam. I lay down on my side of the bed and stared at the ceiling. When I woke up, Leonie, dressed in startling red corduroy shorts and a yellow T-shirt, lay across from me. Without her glasses, she was brown-eyed and inquisitive looking. She gave me a playful push. "A good researcher does not fall asleep."

Her wide mouth fascinated me. Swinging myself up on my elbow, I gave her a long, slow kiss. Our tongues became the centre of the world. I began to stroke her body. At the first touch of my hand she sat up, crossed her arms behind her neck and pulled her T-shirt over her head. She was not wearing a bra. She leaned back, her mouth twisting into a smile. I grasped that she lived amid a thicket of rules and derived her pleasure by breaking them. I caressed her breasts: two platters, very wide and perfectly circular, yet rather flat. Her nipples, the largest I had seen, spilled a dark stain over her pallid flesh.

"Suck them. That is what you want to do."

Exploring Leonie's body released an unexpected wave of gratitude towards Kumiko for having liberated me. Kumiko had cranked me up into the sky, where I floated in the hot air and pillaged the landscape below. As I mauled Leonie's breasts, her smile became joyous with illicit pleasure. I returned to her mouth and kissed her until my hands craved her shoulders, the curve of her stomach. My fingers delved beneath the buckle of her corduroy shorts.

She brushed my hand away. "No."

I came down to earth; my buoyancy cushioned the descent. "You inspired me."

"That is what men always say. 'Women are so inspiring!' The woman has her romantic dreams, but the man has his big thing he wants to put inside her." She looked me in the eyes. "I was ready for a little fun, that is all."

We rolled over onto our backs. Leonie glanced at my shorts and laughed. "Oh, poor man!" She laid her hand on my hip, agonizingly close to the flesh that cried out for her attentions. "Go to the bathroom and take care of your problem. I cannot talk to you when you are like that."

She dispatched me with an affectionate nuzzle in the ear that pushed me out of bed and to the brink of orgasm. In the bathroom, I shucked off my shorts and underwear in warm, moist air laden with the scent of Leonie's flesh. Spurred on by the thought that Leonie would enjoy the performance, I moaned with pleasure as I spurted into the rectangular Stalinist sink.

I washed and dressed. Opening the door, I surprised Leonie, virtually naked, tugging her red shorts over her wide, flat hips. I glimpsed a twist of caramel-coloured pubic hair. She stood up, showing me her breasts with pride, then pulled the yellow T-shirt over her head and lay down on the bed. "I did what you did," she said. "We came at the same time. Few men have come at the same time as me." She sat up. "Now we do not need to make love tonight."

I protested. Leonie said, "At Jerzy's apartment, when you talked about your friend Alex, I saw your emotions. If I had not seen that, I would not go to a hotel with you."

"So it's thanks to Alex that we're sharing a bed?"

Her smile twisted into a more serious expression. "Who was this boy? The boy you saw die?"

"Yes," I murmured. "I was there when he died. So were my friends Alex and Leon. What I didn't tell Jerzy," I said, my throat dry, "is that Leon and I were responsible for the boy's death." I hadn't told him, I realized, out of fear that he would tell Alex.

I told Leonie the story. As soon as I finished, I wished that I had refrained from sharing this experience with a woman who was essentially a stranger.

"I don't think you're responsible," she said. "You were irresponsible to make that phone call. It is the kind of stupid thing Americans do —"

"I'm Canadian and Leon is English."

"– but you didn't make the truck hit him. He could also have been killed going to the first meeting, the one he made with your friend Alex. Would Alex be responsible if that happened?"

"Yes, if the prank call was all we had done I might be able to think that way ... Maybe. It's the fact that we didn't let him go to the hospital. We made him go to a pub instead ..."

"I have heard about these pubs. The English love them, don't they?"

"If he'd been in a hospital when he had the hemorrhage –"

"A brain hemorrhage is very serious," Leonie said. "Maybe if you are in a hospital when it happens there is something they can do ... But even when you are in a hospital –"

"He would have had a better chance in a hospital," I said, gripped by a remorse that I hadn't felt this explicitly before. I felt grateful to Leonie for helping me to clarify my emotions. I laid my hand on her wrist, hoping I had made a new friend.

That evening, we went out for a pizza on Aleje Jerozolimskie. Without warning, Leonie grew tense, her shoulders ridging high. As we ate our pizza, she replied to my attempts at conversation with withering stares. By the time we returned to the hotel, the thought of sharing even a very large bed with her made me uncomfortable. We took turns changing in the washroom, avoiding each other's eyes.

In the morning, we both awoke in high spirits. The prospect of travel made Leonie loose-limbed and irreverent. We put on our backpacks and made our way to the station. My train to Prague left an hour before Leonie's train to western Poland. On the platform, when I asked for her address, she wrote a funny code in my notebook; she was the first person to give me an email address. In the sunny, windswept day, I imagined our words flying through space on bright air threaded with electrical currents. Only then did I realize that I had forgotten to send Kumiko a postcard from Warsaw. I met Leonie's eyes and laid my hands on her shoulders. The gesture caught the attention of the women with wrinkled faces who wore headscarves, the red-faced men in grey jackets and cloth caps who were piling hemp sacks on the platform. Leonie's mouth twisted. "Let's show them a Western farewell kiss. Like in the movies!"

She flattened herself against me and gave me a lascivious, full-tongued kiss that clubbed my mind with the spreading perfection of her hips. Withdrawing her mouth from mine, she murmured, "Now I have felt your big thing."

I reached for her again. Leonie gave me a playful shove, warning me that I would miss my train. I entered the carriage and found my compartment. The train rolled out of Warsaw and entered the countryside. Young boys forked late-summer hay onto wagons drawn by mules. The summer had brought two new women into my life, as my arrival in Oxford last fall had brought me two male friends. This time, I was at the apex of a sexual triangle. As I made this claim to myself, a voice, which I heard as Camille speaking in Québécois, pointed out that my romantic tally for the summer amounted to two instances of masturbation, one of them separated from the object of my lust by a bathroom door.

Two nights later, I climbed out of the CityLink from Heathrow at Gloucester Green. I walked up John Street in the Oxford dampness, crossed Wellington Square, and returned to my room. The digital clock on my desk read 11:48. Next to it, the scrap of paper with Kumiko's phone number was gathering dust. I dialled the number, fearing I would wake up an irate landlady, but it was Kumiko's voice that answered. Her accent, accentuated by the telephone, reminded me that we did not know each other well. "Three weeks is a long time. Thank you for your post cards ..."

"Would you like to come to dinner tomorrow night?" I said.

Kumiko accepted, her voice devoid of enthusiasm. I turned on the BBC in time for the midnight news. The Red Army had withdrawn from Lithuania after an occupation of more than fifty years. The withdrawal seemed to have taken place while I was in Poland, yet I had remained unaware of this milestone.

The telephone rang. Startled, I turned off the radio. The phone rang again.

"What do you do now?" Kumiko asked.

"I'm still unpacking."

"You did not go to bed?"

"No, I'm still awake from my trip."

In a very soft voice, she said, "Can I come to see you now?"

"Yes!" I caught my breath.

"I come." She hung up.

I set down the receiver, plunged once more into the midnight silence. I breathed in the odour of my body, stale from the plane. I wanted to shower, yet didn't dare in case the buzzer rang while I was out of the room. I paced in the lamplight, too agitated to continue unpacking. I dug my condoms out of my shaving bag. The night crept past. Had Kumiko's phone call been a figment of my imagination?

The buzzer sounded.

Kumiko wore old blue jeans, a polo-neck sweater with bright horizontal stripes, the running shoes that Oxford had taught me to call trainers. I didn't have time to think what to say because without a word being spoken our hug of greeting became a kiss and the kiss became lovemaking, and Kumiko spread her long legs as wide as the narrow bed permitted, a restriction that heightened the rage with which our bodies thrashed together.

The bed slipped on the floor, its metal wheels squeaking.

I rolled to the side, still gripping her in order not to tumble off, gripping her because I did not wish ever to release her. "I don't think I've ever felt such desire," I whispered. "All lovers should be forced to interrupt their first night together and think about each other for three weeks."

"If you think about me, I am happy."

"This isn't just for tonight, is it? Do you have anybody else?"

"No, not now. I will be your girlfriend. But we must be discreet ..."

"You mean at Hamdaw, in the MCR?"

"Yes, in public. Only in private we are together."

In private, we were very together. I was buffeted by recollections of the early days with Camille, when we had been young enough to talk about loving each other forever. No such illusions were possible here. My love with Kumiko was an expatriate passion, undergirded by a latent emotional restraint. Having entered into contact with Europe through Pia, I had failed to seal this union; I had failed again with Leonie. In the end it was Kumiko, my fellow observer of Europe, to whom I was able to relate with an intimacy that stabilized my life. The feelings we shared were more powerful than either of us wished to admit. Beneath Kumiko's discretion, I detected the glistening of her eyes, the catch of her lips, emotions that felt stronger than those she voiced. This guardedness of speech and gesture decanted a reservoir of unarticulated emotion into our lovemaking. Being old enough to dismiss love as an adolescent disorder, we sought fulfilment in sex. We were not a Hamdaw couple. Our visits to College rarely coincided. She preferred to come to Wellington Square late in the evening and teach me to cook squid in a black cast iron skillet in the deserted kitchen, or simply to enter my room and test how many times I could come inside her in the space of a long, gloomy Oxford night. Yet a distance persisted, emerging not only in a lack of common reference points, or in linguistic obstacles, but also in the Japanese austerity of her behaviour and the Canadian deference of mine. I rarely visited her house in Kidlington. The landlady lived on the ground floor. Kumiko and a Chinese girl shared the upper floor, which had a separate entrance via a modified fire escape. The landlady had made clear, when the two young women came looking for accommodation after meeting at an Asian Studies Club party, that she liked renting to Asian girls because, "You don't get legless and you don't pull." Kumiko said that neither she nor Mengyin had understood these idioms; they had nodded and assured the landlady that they neither got legless nor pulled. "And it was true then. It is still true for Mengyin. But then I began to get legless and sometimes I pulled," she said, reaching up to kiss me.

We were sitting in her small, windowless kitchen when Kumiko explained this to me. We never made love in her sagging bed with the high headboard carved with the coat of arms of an obscure English family. Piles of library books and notebooks sat on the desk where she wrote by hand; a plastic box contained the floppy disks on which she saved her chapters after typing them up at the Oxford Computing Centre. The only personal touches were a few books in Japanese, a photograph of a very serious young couple – "My parents after wedding" – and a second framed photograph of an elderly man with long white hair. "My professor. He help me come to Oxford."

I was so wrapped up in Kumiko that time stopped. On a September morning, over a breakfast of Rice Krispies and the seaweed that Kumiko bought at an Asian shop off Charing Cross

Road, we heard the BBC announcer say, "In Moscow, the Ministry of the Interior has barricaded the White House after bloody clashes between special forces units of the police and anti-Yeltsin demonstrators —"

If only Leon and Alex were here! I went into Hamdaw and left a note in Leon's pigeonhole, urging him to phone me when he came to Oxford. I learned from the porters that Alex had left a forwarding address care of something called the "Department of Slavic" at Harvard. I longed to write to him, yet was stymied by my impasse over whether I should reveal my role in Colin's accident and the deeper conundrum that this revelation was not mine alone to make.

One morning, just before Michaelmas Term began, I accepted Kumiko's invitation to accompany her to the Oxford Computing Centre. Normally eager to reclaim her independence in the mornings, she suggested I follow her onto the little traffic island with the tiny cemetery where St. Giles divided into Woodstock Road and Banbury Road. In the Computing Centre, she waved me to the seat next to hers. As she began typing from yellow sheets covered with her handwriting, I opened my email account.

I had received my first two email messages. When I realized they were from Leonie, my cheeks grew hot. Her first message dated from shortly after her departure from Warsaw:

In Berlin an American guy got on the train. He talked about himself in English in a loud voice. He sounded just like you. I felt embarrassed. It made me happy that I have always had European men for my lovers.

The second message, sent two weeks after the first, noted that I had not responded: perhaps I was illiterate? She had always been attracted to half-educated brutes. I wrote back in a frenzy, trying to correct each offence. As I signed off, I glanced over to check that Kumiko was looking the other way, then typed very fast to Leonie that I relished the taste of her nipples.

Kumiko inserted a footnote at the end of a paragraph. "You feel better! You must use email more often."

TWENTY-ONE

"TECHNICALLY, YOU'RE NOT CHEATING on Kumiko," Tina said, "but technically isn't what matters. Even with the women my dad only flirted with, my mum suffered terribly."

We were drinking tea in Simon's room, in the nondescript 1960s building that formed the south side of the Ho Chi Minh Quad. Having finished his undergraduate degree, Simon had migrated to Hamdaw College for graduate work in cancer research. It was November 1993, Michaelmas Term of a new academic year, and I was struggling with my fourth chapter. Many of my first-year neighbours had left, not only Alex, but also Pia, who was working for a bank in Rome, and Christa, who was finishing her teacher training in Berlin. Stan and Sebastian, perfecting their Oxford accents, ruled the MCR. The war in Yugoslavia having exposed the Greek behind Stan's colonial mask, he argued in favour of his Orthodox co-religionists, the Serbs. Farida supported the Bosnian Muslims. Stripped of their post-colonial nationalities, the Australian and the Zimbabwean clashed as adherents of ancestral ethnic monotheisms, arguing about massacres, mass rapes, concentration camps, and the destruction of the beautiful bridge at Mostar, which they both blamed on the Croats.

"I'm introducing a motion at the Hamdaw Student Union," Simon told me, as the conversation about my email exchanges with Leonie lapsed. The motion would propose banning students from fee-paying schools from Oxford. With a broad grin, he said, "If Oxford colleges accept only students from state schools, then well-off people will see it as their duty to improve the state school system."

Removed though I felt from the schools debate, I couldn't resist the opportunity to watch Simon infuriate the upper class. To my surprise, Kumiko said she would go with me. Two-thirds of Hamdaw's four hundred fifty undergraduate and graduate students packed into the JCR. As Simon began to speak, grey-jacketed toffs uttered tight-lipped jeers. He repelled each objection with a reply of premeditated completeness, delivered in accents of mild disdain made more potent by their residual north-of-England bite. The left voted for Simon in a block, his cool rationalism won over the uneasy centre; the right, where Stan, Sebastian, and Priscilla stood among undergraduates from Eton or Winchester, raised their hands for the Nay vote in the sullen knowledge that they had lost.

Back in Wellington Square, Kumiko and I made love, then listened to the BBC at low volume.

"In Japan, my professor say if I want to study in England I must listen to BBC. Sometimes we listen together. Like this."

"Not exactly like this, I bet." I slid my palms over her nipples.

"Yes, exactly like this." As I sat up, she said, "We listen like this. Now you know. I thought I am too Japanese to tell you."

I didn't know what to say. Her body leaned back into mine. "In Japan, this is very complicated because I must respect him.

When I arrive in England, I am angry. But now I am peaceful. If he would not do this, I would be a good Japanese girl until I marry a boring man. He make me free to travel, to get legless and to pull."

"You think he realized you would be a more liberated woman? That's why you have his photograph on your wall?"

"No." She shook her head. "His photograph is on wall because he is my professor."

In the morning, Kumiko asked me if I would edit her next chapter, a task for which she usually hired graduate students in English literature. Sensing that her decision was less about saving her scholarship money than about offering me another avenue to understand her, I accepted. I spent two mornings in the Upper Reading Room of the Bodleian Library correcting Kumiko's prepositions. Her thesis narrated the history of a nineteenth-century London trading company that had done business in Asia. The chapter I read used letters Kumiko had found in the archives to trace the company's decision to stop importing tea from India and begin to import it from Ceylon. The story was surprisingly compelling, as different directors "argued their cor-ner," as one of them wrote, in rotund Victorian prose. Why couldn't my thesis be like this?

I left the Bodleian at noon, bought a chicken masala bap, and went to eat it in the MCR. In addition to the usual newspapers, two copies of the *Oxford Mail* lay on the tables; Simon's motion to outlaw public school boys had made the local news. The next day, Tina and I were standing near the Lodge when a porter told us that gentlemen from *The Independent* and *The Daily Telegraph* were looking for Simon. I heard Tina's voice growing more English as she led two middle-aged reporters in baggy suits around the front quad, a pair of rough-and-ready photographers trailing in their wake. The reporters regarded Tina with uncertainty. Neither her elegance nor her barely concealed foreignness fulfilled their expectations. One of them leaned towards me, "Are you one of the conspirators, then?"

I looked like a more credible character in this drama. My hair fell to my shoulders. I had lost weight on my seaweed diet. Kumiko liked my gaunt, disreputable appearance; it certified her rebellion against Japanese conformism. Yet I spoiled my usefulness as soon as I opened my mouth.

"What's a Yank doing mixed up in this?" the *Telegraph* man asked.

"Actually, I'm Cana—"

He turned away.

When we reached Simon's room, the journalists looked dismayed by the tall, clean-cut figure in a navy blue shirt who met them at the door. They grew more disgruntled as we stepped outside for the photo shoot. The low-rise modern dormitory was not "Oxford." We returned to the front quad. Squatting, the photographers lined up Simon's stolid jawline against the backdrop of Hamdaw's crenellated battlements. The *Telegraph* reporter shook his head. "This is bloody pointless. The only one who looks bolshy is the Yank."

He left. The man from *The Independent* asked Simon questions, took notes, then turned to me. "Would you mind terribly," he asked Simon, "if we took his picture rather than yours? I need an image that says 'Rebellion at Oxford.'"

"Do you mind, Kevin?" Simon asked.

I complied, mugging a pose as the photographer went down on one knee to capture the Tudor spires above and behind me. "Brilliant!" he said.

The next morning, as Kumiko and I were sipping Japanese

tea, the telephone rang. "You'd best put on your flak jacket before you venture into the front quad," Zed said. "Good Queen Bess is livid ... I take it you've seen this morning's *Independent*? You look like a positive menace to civilization."

We went to the off-licence to buy the paper. *Oxford College to Ban Public School Boys*, read a headline on an inside page. The black-and-white photograph projected my feral profile against the serrated spires in a wash of dramatic lighting. *At Hamdaw College Oxford*, the caption read, *radical students have passed a motion that would ban the admission of "pompous twits" from fee-paying schools*. The article mentioned Simon's name three times, leaving the reader to infer that the mangy figure in the photograph was the campaign's promoter.

When I crept back into College at the end of the week, a sheet of A4 letterhead stationery protruded from my pigeonhole. As I withdrew it, scanning the tight-looped handwriting that covered it, a sickly sense of déjà vu made my head swim. *Dear Kevin, You have got yourself into a proper mess. Through your rashness, surprising in a man of your age, you risk tarring me with the same brush. Zed reminds me that it's my duty to put my neck on the block by reintroducing you into the fold. Since we're due for a meeting, I suggest you come to my rooms next Wednesday at six, dressed for dinner —*

The next week, as I came in the door, Auberon waved me towards his fireplace. "The next time you make a research trip, you must plan it properly. If you are going to Poland, where I was first secretary of the British Embassy, then we shall decide beforehand to whom it is useful for you to speak. Who did you talk to in Warsaw?"

I told him about Jerzy, making my visit sound like a formal interview.

"Did you speak to −? Surely you must have seen −? *Everyone* has coffee with −" Unknown Polish names concluded each sentence. He shook his head. "What a waste of resources! I suppose it's a North American habit to be profligate." He stared into the ebbing fire. His rooms were freezing. "Still, your third chapter felt more grounded than the first two."

"My life is more grounded now."

"Well, good for you, Kevin." His blue eyes became shrewd. "This groundedness of yours, does it involve that charming young Italian lady?"

"No, she went back to Rome." The urge to protect Kumiko enveloped me. I shook out my graduate gown and pulled it on over my navy blue suit. Auberon robed himself in his flowing, pleated, high-collared doctoral gown. The moment of sharing robing muted the awkward note on which the supervisor session had concluded. As we straightened our gowns, I was conscious of our enforced intimacy. We crossed the darkened front quad looking like master and protegé, entered the hall and joined the High Table guests assembled at the fireplace. Dean Bessborough and Dr. Dennock exuded joyous hostility.

The Warden led the diners onto the stage. I was seated with my back to the hall. Auberon was on my right, Zed on my left. "I had a letter from Landry's family," Zed muttered. "Very gracious, I must say. He's in a wheelchair. Doesn't seem to be much likelihood of his getting out of it."

The hall porters poured ten-year-old Tokay Pinot Gris d'Alsace and brought us the Thai squid salad that was to precede the pan-seared loin of venison, dauphinoise potatoes, red cabbage, and sugar snaps that was tonight's main course. I felt roiled by impatience, in spite of the soothing tang of venison in my mouth. At last, the Warden clapped his wooden puck on the table, bringing the first stage of the meal to a close. When we went upstairs to the Old Library, Bessborough and Dennock kept their distance. I left the dinner as soon as I was able.

Two mornings later, when I accompanied Kumiko to the Oxford Computing Centre, I found a new email message.

There is, from what I can see, something inauthentic in your life; maybe that's the right word.

Okay, I'll stop it now. I'll go home and work on my thesis. If you're reading this, you're not at home working on your thesis, so you should do the same. I wanted to write to you about masturbation — our masturbation in Warsawa — but there are too many people looking over my shoulder so it'll have to wait. Take care, Leonie.

P.S. Are you really intelligent? Or are you like the stupid American boy on the train?

"You write to Russian friend?" Kumiko said. Whenever I read email, she insisted that I was writing to Alex. I loved her for her blithe disregard. Unlike Tina's relationship with Simon, my entente with Kumiko did not demand that either of us absorb the other's culture. Just when I had decided that we could go on in expatriate companionship forever, she said, "When I finish thesis, I must become Japanese again."

That night, I told her about Colin's accident, minimizing the role that Leon and I had played in it. "Colin remind Alex of brother death," she said.

"Yes." Brother Death was stalking Alex. I should have seen that more clearly.

As Kumiko raced towards the finish line of her thesis, writing her conclusions and double-checking her bibliography, my

analysis of Poland withered because I had not done the inter-
views Auberon could have arranged for me. At Hamdaw, Simon's
motion had reached the College's Governing Body. The Fellows
referred it to a committee. My moment of notoriety faded. Yet,
as my second year at Oxford cranked past – eight weeks on,
six weeks off – I produced nothing. I decided not to go back to
Montreal for Christmas. Relieved not to have to negotiate the
appropriate distance from Joan or Marie or Camille, I suggested
to Kumiko that we explore England's sunny south. We found a
decaying village hotel on a beach in Devon, where we took long
walks between bouts of reading, eating, and lovemaking. In the
first months of 1994, I produced nothing. Kumiko was a model
of industriousness. Near the end of Hilary Term, when the
March cloud was sinking into darkness, I ran into Leon in the
Lodge. I hadn't seen him in such a long time that I hesitated
before approaching him. He looked at me with blurry eyes. "Oi,
mate. Fancy seeing you. Got time for a natter?"

I was by myself this evening. I invited him to dinner in
Wellington Square. He accepted.

I made spaghetti in the kitchen, grilling sausages – "bangers,"
Leon called them – and tomatoes on a blackened communal
frying pan, then tossing them in with the sauce. We carried the
meal to my room and sat on the two chairs, balancing the plates
on our laps. I clicked a Van Morrison cassette into my ghetto
blaster. Side one of the cassette ended with the desperate singer
revealing that the object of his unrequited desire was a fourteen-
year-old girl. "Hopeless passion," Leon murmured, as I flipped
the cassette over. "Did I tell you I had a chat with Alex?"

I sat down, suspecting that this was the reason for his visit.

The tone of the budding historian blending with that of the

East London lad, Leon said that Alex had told Susan he was fed up with living apart. She refused to leave London. Their relationship now depended on a routine of his phoning her from Massachusetts at six p.m., when long-distance rates went down, in order to catch her at home at eleven p.m., before she went to bed. Now, even on weekdays, she was often out. "I'm not seeing anyone," she said. "It's movies in Leicester Square and plays in the West End with girlfriends and dinners with clients."

Susan sensed the repressed energy that was building in Alex. She told Emily, who told Leon, that she wanted Alex's energy to be vented on her, not some Boston debutante. She was referring not only to his sexual energy, but she also to a more deep-seated malaise. She arranged to meet Alex in Toronto for Christmas, "to make sense of things," Leon said.

The visit hadn't gone well. Alex's mother was battling depression; Susan's parents, far from being proud of their daughter's rise in the London public relations world, berated her for not settling down at home. She and Alex parted at Pearson Airport three days into 1994. Alex's flight landed in Boston before Susan had cleared Canadian airspace. She was still high over the Atlantic, by Leon's reckoning, when Alex got back to his room in Somerville, Massachusetts, where one of his housemates invited him to a post-New Year's party. He got drunk with a woman and spent the night with her. He had just returned to his room the next morning when Susan phoned to tell him that she had arrived in London. He did not tell her about the one-night stand, but three weeks later, he phoned Susan at six p.m. Boston time, eleven p.m. in London. "I've got something to tell you," he said.

"I've got something to tell *you*."

Leon said that all he knew about Susan's new boyfriend was that Emily called him the Toothpick. "It seems he's very tall and needs some flesh on his bones."

"Like Alex."

"There's no escaping one's patterns, is there? This business with Alex and Susan gives me the willies. Emily and me, we reckoned we'd got this couple business sorted —"

"Are you having problems?"

"I thought we'd got it sussed." I was aware of his English restraint. "Living together has been terribly trying. She's out all day. When she comes home, I'm famished for conversation and she's fed up with talking and wants to be alone to do her art."

He finished his spaghetti. Van Morrison, reaching the end of side two, moaned that his unattainable nymphet was a heroin addict. "What happened to Alex's Russian library?" I asked, remembering the embossed lettering on the spines gleaming in his room in the graduate quad. "Did he ship it to Boston?"

"No, the whole Russian library is in Susan's flat in London."

"He'll have to come back to pick it up, won't he? We'll see him then, right? If we see him, we'll have to tell him."

Leon concentrated with blurry eyes. I realized he'd had a couple of pints before I'd run into him. "Tell him what? That we're his mates?"

Puzzled, as I often was by the British category of matehood, I said, "If we're his fucking mates, we should tell him the truth —"

"What truth? That it's dangerous to cycle around Oxford at night? Quite likely that boy was going to get clobbered anyway. If he hadn't got our message, he would have ridden to meet Alex in the wine bar, they would have got sloshed together, and he would have wobbled home in the dark and been run over by a different lorry. All our little prank changed was the name of the poor sod of a driver who ran him over."

"For Christ's sake, Leon! You're a historian. Acts have consequences."

"Not all acts! Every day we do scads of things that have no influence on history."

"This act had consequences."

"You say that as though you had no part in it. Who egged me on?" He jabbed an accusing finger at me. "You think you're the pure, unsullied observer from the New World, but it's not like that, not now. Don't try to absolve yourself of fucking responsibility."

We frowned at each other in silence as the fluorescent light glared off the cold, whitewashed walls. "That doesn't answer the question of what we tell him when he turns up."

"We tell him we're his mates and we take him out for a pint –"

"Yes, that's the British way, isn't it? Drink a pint and avoid the issue."

He got to his feet. "I must scarper. Emily gets cross when I come back in the middle of the night." He shook my hand with a formality that confused me. In a minute he was gone. I washed dishes in the kitchen across the hall, returned to my room and phoned Kumiko. "Can I come over?"

She hesitated. "Mengyin here."

Or did she mean "Mengyin hear"? Mengyin was there and would hear our lovemaking, particularly in Kumiko's sagging bed. The night pressed down, heightening my need to confirm our union. "Can you come here?"

Another silence. "Kevin, I almost go to bed."

I offered to pay her taxi fare. She hesitated, then agreed. I went down to Little Clarendon Street, ambling back and forth until the taxi rode over the speed bumps. I paid the cabby and ushered

Kumiko upstairs. In the lamplight of my barren room, haunted by the tang of spaghetti sauce, I undressed her with a relentlessness that brought a tremor of uncertainty to her eyes. I kissed her body until her distracted air contracted into a harsh concentration. After we made love there were tears in the corners of her eyes. "I'm sorry ..."

"Couldn't you stay in England ...?"

"English university not hire Japanese woman to teach English history."

I never again made love to Kumiko with the passion of that night. We continued to cook fish together and have sex in my bed. I did not ask again to sleep in her bed. I tried to delay the inevitable to the point where it might no longer be inevitable. The morning after Leon's visit, gripped by a wild premonition of loneliness, I wrote a letter to Leonie by hand, inserted a photocopy of the *Independent*'s article on Simon's motion, and mailed it to her address in Bonn. Three days later I sneaked off to the Computing Centre on my own.

> I was surprised by how long your hair is now. But as I read the article, my doubts returned. There is something too coldly rational about the way you have made this action. A vote, a motion, instead of students in the streets, as in Europe. The English must always be conservative even in their way of being radical. And your letter was the same. There is something cold about it, even though I can see that you are trying to get closer to me, and I admit that sometimes I think about what it would be like to be close to you. What if we would become lovers and I would find you are cold?

The day of her viva, Kumiko emerged from her house in subfusc. She looked ravishing, though I could see she was nervous.

Other Japanese graduate students in the humanities had seen their doctoral theses demoted to M.Phil.'s, M.Litt.'s, or even ignominious M.Stud.'s, for not being able to defend their ideas in top-flight English. Kumiko's trim black skirt, black cardigan and curled white tie made her look not so much slimmer as slighter, an impression that was accentuated by her black high-heeled shoes. As she shrugged into her black graduate gown and perched her mortar board on her head, she blushed. Mengyin took photographs. The English landlady, miffed at my presence, took photos of Kumiko and Mengyin together, then of the three of us. We called a taxi and rode to University College. The examination took place in a meeting room off the front quad. The examiners were seated behind a long table. Kumiko, as docile as a schoolgirl, sat down in the chair facing them. The guests — I, Mengyin and two D.Phil. students in Victorian history — sat off to one side. The internal examiner was from Merton College, the external was from Cambridge University. The Oxford examiner noted that as there was an audience, "permission to disrobe will be withheld." Kumiko was allowed to remove her mortar board, but not her gown. As the examination began, the realization hit me that Kumiko had written three hundred twenty-five pages of cogent, copiously documented argumentation in a foreign language. Even as she blushed in response to the questions growled by the Cambridge professor, who was determined to display merciless brilliance on the opposition's home turf, I felt her determination. Her phrases faltered, her English grew more accented, she delved for a word with an almost palpable lunge, but no one could deprive her of her self-discipline. The Cambridge don thought she had not theorized British colonialism sufficiently; the Oxford don retorted that theory was balderdash and she had cluttered her pages with too much of it. Kumiko

the airport, but she had been adamant that we would say goodbye in Oxford.

We couldn't look at each other.

Gloucester Green! Why did it have to end there, in the most heartless, denuded, unromantic corner of Oxford? Gloucester Green, which was devoid of the tiniest speck of green. We stood under the overhang of the station platform. The CityLink and Oxford Tube ticket sellers, positioned behind podiums like proletarian lecturers, competed for passengers. Tourists got off buses and stumbled around the narrow platform, asking where the university was. Behind us, people were shouting in Chinese and Russian and Brazilian Portuguese. A whiff of sausage from a nearby stand, the jostling of British commuters brandishing tabloid newspapers, the stench of burnt petrol, prevented us from looking into each other's eyes. Kumiko consented to a move to the edge of the platform. I kissed her on the mouth. "If it's impossible to become Japanese again, promise you'll come back."

"I promise," she said with the smile of a woman charmed by a man's incorrigible immaturity. "I must try very hard. I have duty to my parents and my professor."

What was her duty to the old professor now?

"Kevin, I am glad we share —" Glimpsing a hint of weakness, I crushed her in a hug, almost lifting her dainty black shoes off the ground. I kissed her neck; my tears slicked her cheek. She emerged from our embrace with her eyes glistening. "Japanese man no kiss me like that," she sobbed, and ran for the bus.

I thrust my hands into the pockets of my jeans. I saw Kumiko sit down next to the window. The driver swung the bus into gear; the interior light went out. The bus backed out of its bay.

Far down the platform, I detected a pair of dark eyes watching me from behind black-rimmed glasses. Farida had got off the CityLink in time to witness our farewell. In hideous need of a friend, I stepped forward. Colonial propriety clicking into place, Farida dodged away into the crowd. Having learned my lesson, I let her go.

TWENTY-TWO

It is not easy to become Japanese again. But this is not for
reason I expected. Japan is less certain than before. Even
economy is not good. Tradition is weaker, too. My girl students
plan to travel in Europe alone! When I am young, Japanese
travel in groups …

Kumiko and Leonie awaited me in successive lines in the
inbox of my email program. Just up Woodstock Road from
the Computing Centre lay the Language Teaching Centre. The
introductory German course I took there three days a week in
Trinity Term filled the spaces vacated by my thesis. Accepting
that Kumiko would not return, I concentrated my energy on
Leonie's language. In class, I sat between a serious British woman
who was completing a D.Phil. in medieval history, and a super-
naturally quiet girl with short legs sheathed in faded blue jeans
who answered the instructor's questions in a neutral voice of
unruffled composure.

The rhythm of my communication with Leonie accelerated.

One night we spoke on the phone. "All right," she said. "You should come and see me."

In the morning, I walked to the STA travel office in Gloucester Green and bought my first ticket to Germany. "Berlin?" the girl behind the counter said with a smile.

"No," I replied, reciting the name of the airport whose name Leonie had given me. "Köln-Bonn."

A week later, as the plane took off from Heathrow, I realized how little I knew of this continent with which I was presuming to form an attachment. As Germany unfurled beneath the wing of the plane – greener than I had expected, hillier in its irregular rise and fall than I had imagined of a territory next door to Holland – I tried to perceive in the long brown hook of the Rhine the answer to questions I could barely formulate.

Leonie was waiting for me in the airport in a lustrous purple waistcoat, her bohemian equivalent of dressing up. She kissed me with her whole body, picking up where our farewell embrace in Warsaw had left off. When we reached her apartment in a Jugenstil building in Beuel Mitte, across the Rhine from the old city and the university, I set down my backpack in the hall. Leonie led me to her bedroom. My flesh grew hot, as though it were a superfluous skin. At first, I tried to suppress comparisons with Kumiko; then I held and savoured them, revelling in the awareness of moving from one lover to the next. Leonie was slender yet broad-chested; the circumference of the twin pancakes of her breasts was startling. Her strong, lean legs held her body taut beneath the mass of her unruly hair. She set her glasses on the window ledge and looked at me through serious brown eyes.

The next few minutes revealed something I didn't like about my sexual needs, making plain that as needs, they were sexual and separate from my emotional requirements. Cynical old Europe had exposed my colonial romanticism as an illusion. My feelings were in tumult. I resented Leonie for depriving me of the belief that what I had felt for Kumiko was love. At three a.m. we walked naked into Leonie's narrow kitchen, ate *Schwarzbrot* with Gouda cheese and ham, and washed it down with Italian white wine, then romped back to her bed.

For the next four days Leonie was my guide, in her bed and in her small town in Germany. Bonn, like Oxford, was a city on a river. Here, civil servants, of all people, were staging a revolt to preserve the contours of the Cold War by campaigning for Bonn to remain Germany's capital. For the moment, only the upper echelons of the civil service were to be moved to Berlin, the former centre of the Cold War world and now the once and future capital of Germany. The assumption that the world of after could be out-argued endeared Germany to me. I had found a country where intelligence had a chance of prevailing. On my third day, Leonie and I rode a series of trams to Cologne, a larger, rougher city, where we drank beer in a seedy dive and listened to throaty singers huffing out songs in Kölsch dialect. Between harsh Cologne and stately Bonn, I found a unified world. Yet I was cautious. "Are you sure you want a long-distance relationship?" I asked Leonie on the last morning. "There must be lots of men in Bonn."

"In Bonn, all the men are good guys. Nice, simple guys with no depth. You are a difficult man. You want things, but you don't know what they are. You remind me of Salvatore. But I think you are an intellectual. When I am happy with you, I think this. When you disappoint me, you are like the stupid American boy on the train."

"You'll come to Oxford to visit me?"

"I do not want to go to England." She frowned. "You will come to see me."

I visited her for a week every month or two. My relationship with Kumiko, though discreet, had filled my life. Leonie and I shared an escape from life. When I came to visit, she cleared her agenda. Once again, I was in a relationship with a woman who was efficiently producing a doctoral dissertation; once again, her assiduousness failed to rub off on me. The brief flight from Heathrow to Köln-Bonn, bearing me up into the sky in an arc that whisked me through a realm of glaring light, restored me to the heat of my Polish summer. I tried to imbibe Leonie's example, yet when I returned to my room in Wellington Square and turned on the computer, my legs shuffled beneath my desk as though I were riding a bicycle. I slept late, sometimes not getting out of bed until eleven a.m. At a subliminal level, I realized I was experiencing some sort of depression.

I spent Christmas of 1994 in my room in Wellington Square. Nowhere was as depressing as England during a holiday. The streets were vacant. Every shop and service was locked, even the ATM machines closed down. Devious planning, and expeditions to insurgent Islamic kebab vans, were necessary to avoid starvation. My isolation forced me to confront the fact that I had blown the greatest opportunity of my life: two scholarships to Oxford, which were now running out. I must either finish and move on, or drop out and move on. Either way, I must move.

Early in the new year, I walked to Gloucester Green and bought a day return ticket to London on the CityLink. As I relaxed in a window seat, a voice behind me said, "Oi, mate, what brings you to London?"

I jumped up and went to sit with him. He pulled himself upright as I sat down. I was aware of a rivulet of discomfort, an edging away from our sudden closeness. As he laid a palm flat against the window in the chill of the updraft from the vent, I felt trapped in the monkey-suit of the exuberant colonial who was doomed to say all the wrong things. "What brought you to Oxford?"

"Supervisor meeting. I'm in the last lap." Leon sighed. "There is rather a chasm that yawns when one doesn't know what comes next." He tossed back his head. His hair had grown longer; I spotted a lick of grey above his ear. He sighed. "Emily and me, we're done for."

His voice as soft as ash, he murmured that Emily had begun to count months and weeks, calculating the date of Leon's viva, the likely start date of his first academic job. "All leading to a calculation of the date on which a regular pay packet might support a little nipper." They had quarrelled in front of her family at a relative's mansion. An uncle had made a remark that sounded anti-Semitic. Leon moved his belongings out of Emily's flat.

"Where are you living?"

"Not in bloody Notting Hill Gate, I'll tell you that." His scoop-jawed face tightened. "I've gone back to me roots." He gave me an appraising look. "Are you doing something important in London, or are you just skiving? Because if you're skiving, you might as well come and see my digs."

We stayed on the CityLink all the way down to Victoria Station, where we descended into the Underground. We rode the District Line to a southbound spur of the Northern Line, then got off at an overland rail station. We sat in silence as a clanking commuter train carried us past an infinity of drab, stone row houses — terraced cottages, the British called them — that made London seem vast and bleak. We got off the commuter train and walked through streets of ratcheted-together row houses. "We've got a progressive council in this borough. This whole street is co-op housing. As long as I'm a student, my digs cost a pittance."

We entered his house. The radiator in the front hall dripped onto a fluffy grey carpet, the kitchen was a battery of notices about dish-washing rotas and rubbish-disposal schedules. Leon opened the door of a room on the ground floor. "Bung your stuff in there." I glimpsed a bed, bookshelf and desk, a tangle of unsorted washing on the sheets. Leon led me to the kitchen. As he was making tea, a shy, large-boned blond man came in. "This is Archie. Archie and me, we've got the place to ourselves for the moment."

When Archie had retreated to the living room and turned on the television, Leon led me to his room. Shadowed by the garble of television voices, Leon sat on the edge of the bed. I sat in the chair that went with his small desk. "I'll be spending my life in tips like this." His energy felt harsher and flatter than in the old days. I envisaged Leon at fifty, a reflection of my father's life in the mirror of the Atlantic Ocean. I was about to pursue this thought when I noticed an offprint of a scholarly article on class analysis lying in the corner of the bed. I assumed it was part of his research until I spotted the author's name: *Leon Zamenhof, Hamdaw College Oxford.* "Leon!" I said. "You've got an academic publication. You *won't* be spending your life in tips like this."

"Forgetting about Oxford helps me to write."

In a cautious voice, I said, "Of the three of us, you're the only one who's going to finish."

"I'll likely end up working with Archie and his mates. Intellectuals on the factory floor, that's when revolutions start! Or they'll fob me off with a research assistantship that will grind me down. My father would say that was worse."

"Is your father still alive?" I grasped the opportunity to change the subject. "I sometimes imagine your father and my grand-father together in Spain."

"It was easier for their generation. They knew where to find the enemy." He set down his tea on the offprint. "I may be the one who's going to finish, but you're the one who pulls these days. First that Japanese bird and now your German damsel. What's her name? Gretchen?"

"Leonie."

"You don't say? Is that a name in German?"

"Is Alex alone, too?" I asked, hurrying on.

"I'm afraid our Alex is rather adrift. He rings me whenever he's thinking of crossing the pond to reclaim his Russian library. It was on the bookshelves in Susan's front hall until she and Alex split up. Then she bunged them in a cupboard. They're stacked up absolutely chock-a-block. Now Susan's threatening to buy a flat with the Toothpick —"

"Leon, we've got to tell him! He's our best friend."

"I don't believe you, Kevin! It's meaningless bloody postur-ing. You don't want to tell Alex any more than I do."

I stood up and stared at a poster of a soccer player. How many references I failed to recognize here! "It's easy for you ... You're writing. I haven't written a word in over a year —," I drew a deep breath. "It would be so liberating!"

"It wouldn't change a thing. Alex wouldn't give a toss. He's past all that now."

Our conversation wound down into mutual discomfort. I found my way back to the overland train line. I caught the City-Link at Victoria, got off in Gloucester Green and walked through Oxford with my head down, ignoring students, tourists, and bicycles. A week later I left for Bonn, and stayed for two weeks, trying to write there. I produced a few pages of subpar scribbles, written by hand on a long yellow notepad like the ones that Kumiko, Leon, and Alex had used. I begged Leonie to visit me in Oxford. She demurred. In Oxford, Hilary Term of 1995 was beginning. The thought of another year terrified me. I went to the Computing Centre to write her a long email thrashing out all of my feelings about our relationship. When I opened my email program, a message was waiting for me.

> I write to say I am all right. Here we felt only aftershock of earthquake. It does not seem real that the earth open in peaceful Kobe. Japan does not feel so safe now. I never thought this would be the difficult part of becoming Japanese again. I think of what I say to you before I leave Oxford, that you and I have different problems. I want to say I am wrong. Our problems are similar. I did not see that then. Now I see more, but now it is too late.

That night, as I walked back across Oxford with my graduate gown rolled up in my right hand, facing down the sallow-faced undergraduates who spilled out of the pubs, I felt a surge of energy scour away the despondence that had been miring me in bed until eleven o'clock every morning. I closed the door of my room and, for the first time in longer than I could remember, turned on my computer. I turned it on with gusto, impatient to hear the inane ditty it emitted as it booted up. I loosened my tie, crouched over my laptop in my navy blue suit like a policy wonk and, concentrating a lifetime's assimilated information, wrote until one-thirty a.m. I got up at nine a.m., throwing off months of lethargy, and continued writing.

I was taking the easy road to a doctorate. Countless glib slackers had achieved the vaunted "contribution to knowledge" by writing about subjects related to their countries of origin. When I went to the MCR that afternoon, the newspapers had burst out in a fresh round of referendum stories. Everyone was abusing the example of Quebec, demonstrating an ignorance of the facts that made me hunger to return to my Toshiba. I realized that in my writing, I was returning not to Canada, but to Quebec, just as Leon had returned not to the Ireland his father had inhabited as a child — which was the subject of his thesis — but to his own mental corner of left-wing Jewish London. Like proper denizens of the world of after, we had abandoned the nation for the ethnic enclave. Beneath the deluge of Canadian detail that I poured into my screen, I felt myself writing my way towards Berlin. I was now in an intermediate German class at the Language Teaching Centre. In a burst of enthusiasm, I told Leonie that I wanted to talk to her in German and rattled off a couple of mangled sentences. There was a long pause. "Sometimes," she said, "I think you are not very intelligent."

Undeterred, I kept talking about my class, skirting the referendum because I knew she would regard a Canadian crisis as irrelevant. My ebullience buoyed her up. "Maybe I will come to visit you."

The woman who sat on my right in German class rarely spoke. Her slight plumpness investing her with a robust sense of presence, she would look down at my hiking boots as she absorbed the declensions required by particular combinations of prepositions. She learned German grammar faster than anyone. If I learned as fast as she, Leonie might regard me as intelligent.

Leonie decided to visit me on October thirtieth. I had failed to find the right moment to explain that this was the day of the Quebec referendum. A week before her arrival, the possessor of two new chapters whose existence I hadn't divulged to Auberon, I decided to go to the Computing Centre to write a message to Leonie about the referendum. As I reached for my jacket, the phone rang.

"*On va l'avoir, not' pays!*" The torrent of Québécois French continued, "Why are you still over there? We're building a country here!" The referendum was too close to call; among Francophones, support for independence was over sixty per cent. "*C'est un miracle!*"

"It's not a miracle," I said. "It's a consequence of the fall of the Berlin Wall."

"You belong here, Kevin. When we make our nation, I want the people I love to be in it!"

England had bred out of me the ability to respond to deep emotion expressed with raw candour. After a second, I said, "*Tu me manques.*" I was startled to hear myself tell her that I missed her. French revealed feelings to which my English-speaking self lacked access. Outside my window, Wellington Square subsided into the mingled mist, smog and early darkness of the English autumn. "I don't just want to hear about Quebec, I want to hear about Camille."

"*Ça va bien chez Camille. Je ne peux pas me plaindre.*"

If she couldn't complain, there was a man in her life. Our conversation returned to the referendum. She was effervescent at the prospect of independence. I left my room twenty minutes later than planned. On Little Clarendon Street a square-framed old wreck of a bicycle, its rusty handlebars ridged high, rolled towards me through the late-afternoon gloom. The woman who sat next to me in German rode upright in the saddle, her arms spread a little too wide, her feet pushing the pedals. She concentrated on me for a second with an inert yet tranquil grey-faced stillness. I gave her a half-nod as she passed.

In the Computing Centre, I tried to compose a message to warn Leonie that she would be arriving on the day my country's fate was decided. With Camille's words resounding in my ear, I felt the burden of four hundred fifty years of history. If I tried to lay this out in the blunt idiom of email, she would be offended, as Europeans were always offended by the fact that Sir John A. Macdonald had preceded Bismarck, Samuel de Champlain had preceded the Peace of Westphalia, and John Cabot had preceded Henry VIII.

I wrote her a brief, flirtatious message, then returned to my room.

On Tuesday evening the phone rang. "Hey ... Is this the right number?" As I struggled to identify the rustic Canadian on the other end of the line, the voice said, "You should see what's happening here. Holy liftin', this city's going haywire." It was Fred. "A hundred thousand people came here. They're giving away plane tickets to anybody who'll come to Montreal to tell the French Canadians to stay. You should see all the hosers out there! They can't even figure out how to use the Métro!"

I imagined how Camille would respond to thousands of Anglo outsiders telling her what to think.

"Listen, Kevin, I should get off the phone before I bankrupt us, but I've been reading about Norman Bethune. Every book I read, I write down the dates. I'm not sure yet, but I'd say there's a window."

"A window?"

"A window when Bethune could have become your mum's dad. Don't get me wrong, I'm not saying it's a sure thing. I just hope your research is as much of a ball as mine is."

I assured him it was. For the first time, my enthusiasm was genuine.

On Wednesday, at the end of the German class, we all said, "*Bis Freitag.*" On the way out of the classroom, I fell into stride with my right-hand neighbour. "Do you always ride around Oxford on that old bicycle?"

"Do you always walk around in those old hiking boots?" As she turned to face me, I saw her features, both square and round, as having been carved like a presidential bust, erased, then sketched in again in an inchoate form. Her eyes, of an indefinable hue between grey and hazel, were playful. Her short-legged firmness on her feet raised her large breasts towards me like a trophy. I perceived that she was aware of this provocation and was gauging with a cool mind how much bait to offer me. "I apologize for not having introduced myself." Her English was inscrutable: native, yet not obviously British, American, Australian, or Canadian. "I'm Catherine."

"Kevin, from Canada." In the cushioned stillness of the Language Teaching Centre's wall-to-wall carpets, I said, "You haven't told me where you're from."

A dart of colour appeared in her cheeks. "That is the question I can never answer."

Her idiom-free correctness of diction made her sentences verge on sounding as though they had been lifted from an advanced English textbook. Her obstinate silence continued until I said, "Are you Globalized Woman?"

"Actually, I'm American."

"I suppose that's one way of being globalized."

Sensing my coolness, she said, "I grew up in the Soviet Union and Yugoslavia. I live in Yugoslavia — and East Germany. As I am certain you can hear, I grew up speaking English to people who did not speak English as their first language."

"But there is no East Germany anymore —"

"We keep those places the way they were!" As I watched her, something in her face slipped. "I will see you on Friday, Kevin. *Bis Freitag.*"

We left the building. Catherine unlocked her bicycle with a key that hung around her neck and wobbled up Woodstock Road.

On Friday morning, photographs of Lucien Bouchard and Jacques Parizeau appeared on the front pages of the newspapers that I read in the MCR before walking to Gloucester Green to catch the CityLink to Heathrow. With the difference between the two sides smaller than the margin of error, no one knew what Canada's map would look like by the end of the day. And I was on a bus between Oxford and Heathrow!

As Leonie strolled into the arrivals lounge, her easy gait reassured me. An hour and a half later we were making love in my room. An unexpected ray of sunlight fell between the curtains. It laid a bar of warmth across my back, and a molten glow on Leonie's wide face which, after the removal of her glasses, looked even more naked than the rest of her body. As we stole into the shower at the end of the hall to soap each other under the hot jets, our complicity felt unbreakable. When we returned to the room it was seven o'clock. We dressed and set out for dinner at an Indian restaurant. I told her about the referendum.

"But this is only in Canada," she said.

"It's an emotional issue. Didn't you feel emotional when the Berlin Wall fell?"

"When the Wall fell, I was drunk in a squat in Palermo. I didn't find out for weeks."

"Well, this is like that. It's important for the world — that's why it's been on the front page of the newspapers for the last week."

"You are exaggerating. In Germany the newspapers say nothing about this vote you talk about."

I led her into a Broad Street off-licence and pointed at the photographs of fleurs-de-lys flags that flourished above the fold on the front pages of the British quality dailies. She shook her head. "The English always want to talk about things that are not important."

Her smile became tolerant. I knew this tolerance, remembered how it was capable of congealing her flesh into a scaly, hostile surface that repelled my touch. As we opened our menus in the restaurant, I turned the conversation to naan bread versus pappadams, korma versus biriyani. We drank a bottle of cheap red wine, went back to Wellington Square and made slow, deliberate love, falling asleep on the narrow bed in a rumpled, naked clasp.

I woke with a jolt. The curtains were splayed and the room was full of light. Leonie stirred, her arm flung across my side. I twisted my stiff neck and glimpsed the time on the digital clock: 7:58. "I'm turning on the radio," I said.

I waited for the signature tune for the eight o'clock news. Instead I heard a hollow background of static. I thought I'd lost the signal until I realized that within the static were shouts in Québécois French, a language that I doubted BBC Radio Four had ever transmitted before. I heard a contesting yell, a ripple of chants, a faltering rendition of "O Canada," with everyone singing different words, beaten down by the thud of "*Le Québec aux Québécois!*"

"*Those were the sounds of the streets of Montreal last night ...*" the announcer said.

Most of the broadcast was devoted to the referendum. The *Non* side had received 50.58% of the vote, the *Oui* 49.42%. Both sides were claiming electoral irregularities. Jacques Parizeau had made a belligerent speech, blaming the defeat on "money and certain ethnic votes." When the initial returns came in, predicting a *Oui* victory, the reporter said, Québécois pilots at Canadian Forces Base Bagotville had headed to their fighters and prepared to fly them away for service in a future Quebec Army.

That night, my relationship with Leonie ended, though I did not accept this fact at the time. My restlessness over the referendum enraged her. Being obliged to take seriously an event in Canada struck her as humiliating. She curled up as though the hide of her flesh were contracting, tightening her body into an inert larva. To break the tension, I put on a Leonard Cohen cassette.

"You are a typical man. You can't talk. You just put on loud music."

"It's not loud. Leonard Cohen is —"

"Yes, we know him in Europe. He is different from other American singers."

"That's because he's not American. He's Canadian."

"I do not believe you." She stared at me through her glasses.

Cohen droned into "Suzanne." "Listen. He's singing about Our Lady of the Harbour. It's a statue on top of Notre-Dame-de-Bonsecours chapel on Rue St-Paul —"

She shook her mass of hair. "You tell me he is singing about Canada and you expect me to think this is true? You are very stupid."

The tension in her body pulled her head closer to her shoulders, as though her neck had retracted. That night she slept in the bed and I slept on the floor. In the morning I accompanied her to Gloucester Green to catch the bus to Heathrow. The realization that this might be her only visit to Oxford made me seize her shoulders and rain tearful kisses on her mouth and cheeks. Mustering a fatigued smile, she kissed me back. "You should not blame yourself if this does not work," she said. She squeezed my arm, then turned away and climbed onto the CityLink. I waved goodbye, though I did not see her wave back. Gripped by a premonition that someone was watching me, I turned around. At the bay where the bus from London had just arrived, stood Farida.

I walked towards her. "You must think I'm a disreputable fellow. Every time you get off a bus from London, I'm kissing a different woman."

"Kevin," she said, as I accompanied her across the market square behind the platform, "has it occurred to you to wonder why I'm taking the bus to London?" We came to a halt on the far side of the square, where black taxi cabs queued in front of little shops. Farida no longer dressed in the navy blue slacks and white blouses of the Commonwealth schoolgirl. Her suede shoes, black skirt over tight black leggings, discreetly checkered jacket and stylish glasses emanated London chic. Like me, she had abandoned her plans to study European civilizations in favour of a thesis on the area she knew best. She was writing about urban planning in southern Africa. This was not the only change in her life. A year ago, she said, she had accompanied a group of graduate students to a gallery opening in Islington and started chatting with the painter. "When he asked me to have a drink, I didn't even think about the fact that I shouldn't be doing this. In a funny way, though, intimate contact with the infidel has made me more of a Muslim. The *other* thing I do when I go to London is volunteer for a charity that sends clothes and food to Bosnia. We're collecting funds to rebuild the beautiful bridge they destroyed in Mostar. I feel like I've become myself, but it hasn't been easy."

Touched by this confidence and still in emotional turmoil over Leonie, I said, "Do you remember the night they chucked us out of The Eagle and Child for not drinking?"

"You know, I was in there for a drink the other night and it never crossed my mind."

"That was the night I met Alex."

"Alex?" She looked puzzled. "Oh, the mad Russian. He left ages ago."

A hostile impulse flushed through me. As I walked back to Wellington Square, I realized that the sight of tall, fair youths bent over handlebars no longer bored into my mind.

My thesis now consisted of four theoretical chapters and two on Canada and Quebec. Trying not to think about Leonie, I slipped into the mien of the asexual Oxford scholar. On Monday, the seat on my right in German class was empty. My medievalist colleague explained that during the class I had missed, Catherine had announced that she was returning to eastern Germany. I imagined her secluding herself behind a barrier where the Berlin Wall had stood. I remembered Clawdia Chauchat in *The Magic Mountain*, who returned "behind the wall of the Urals," a phrase Thomas Mann used to define the borders of Europe. Catherine had disappeared into Europe, a revanchist deep Europe, a chronologically delayed, richly textured terrain.

In November, Auberon sent me a note asking whether I had work to show him. It was Michaelmas Term 1995 and I had entered the fourth year of my D.Phil. It was time to think about a completion date. The tone of Auberon's missive — typed on letterhead stationery rather than jotted in his usual loops — suggested that he was formally acquitting himself of his duties. He had given up on my ever finishing. The note's condescension made me angry. I hurled myself into my thesis for hours every day until I had melted down the four theoretical chapters into three tighter ones, and sowed references to Canada and Yugoslavia through the theoretical discussions to prepare the ground for the case studies in the second half of the thesis. I had never been to the former Yugoslavia, except for my hiking trip to Slovenia, and had no idea what I would look for if I went, but it was safer to stick to the plan I had on record.

By early December, as the end of Michaelmas Term approached, I had a revised thesis of five chapters and one hundred sixty-eight pages. Two chapters on Yugoslavia, plus conclusions, footnotes, and bibliography, would bring me close to the three-hundred-page figure cited as the standard for an Oxford D.Phil. thesis. I might be a second-rate slacker, but this draft would show Auberon that I was not a lost cause. After avoiding him for over a year,

TWENTY-FOUR

WHEN THE AIR TRANSAT flight came in to land in Montreal, the scabs of snow on the damp green ground startled me. Back in Oxford, mid-April meant rain. I was so attuned to England that as the plane dropped out of the clouds, I mistook the snow for chalk marks, the residue of Stone Age mining ... Snow! I hadn't recognized snow.

The city looked grimy as the snowbanks disgorged their winter cargo of twigs, half-rotten leaves, and dog turds. I rode the bus and Métro to my mother's apartment. As I unlocked the front door and eased my backpack-broadened profile through the narrow entrance hall, my mother's voice whispered, "It's him."

A robust middle-aged man with a soft face and steel-wool curls emerged from the kitchen. My mother stepped past him. "It's so wonderful to see you, dear." She hugged and kissed me.

The man offered his hand. "Kevin, I'm Paul."

"I guess I've been away for a while."

"I'm going to take a walk," Paul said.

The unending day of a transatlantic flight made my perceptions thin and unreal. I carried my pack to my teenage room.

When I returned to the kitchen, my mother was making hot chocolate. "I meant to mention Paul during our phone calls, but was afraid of making the situation sound like more than it was. Not that it isn't anything. But we're both cautious."

"He's divorced, too?"

"His separation is more recent. Poor Paul. It's the reverse of the usual story. He invited his attractive female research assistant home for dinner and she ran away with his wife!" She shook her head. "We're not living together yet, but we're not ruling it out either." She changed the topic to my thesis. "If you finish –"

"I'll finish. I'm not going to be like Dad, if that's what's bothering you." I looked at the cocoa dregs in my mug. "Where does Paul live?

"In an apartment downtown. His wife and the student are in his house in N.D.G. All that has to be straightened out. His children went to university in Ontario and won't be coming back."

When Paul returned, I tried to reconcile the thought that my mother looked older than the last time I'd seen her with her coy, rejuvenated air in his company. I detected a vein of insecurity in Paul's manner, an excessive self-deprecation that he masked with bonhomie; yet he also had a no-nonsense quality that complemented my mother's practical side. He was not an old-stock Quebec Anglo, but a Manitoban who had come to Montreal to take an academic job twenty-five years earlier. He called the Québécois "French Canadians"; his pronunciation of place names confirmed that he had not learned the language. "But now I feel like a native. I never thought I'd get to know the unacknowledged daughter of Norman Bethune!"

My visit, which I had decided to make simply because it was

now the spring of 1996 and I had not been home in almost two years, acquired a perfunctory air. My father and Fred, buoyed up by Cégep teaching contracts, felt flush enough to take me out for smoked meat at Reuben's on Rue Ste-Catherine. They arrived in the company of a middle-aged woman with the air of an aging hippie. The four of us squeezed into an upholstered booth. I sensed that they had met her recently and our lunch was an opportunity to court her. "Hey, Kevin," Fred said, "I found new books about Bethune. I'm writing down all the dates."

I realized that the longer I stayed away, the fewer people I had to visit. Joan was at a conference; I could not imagine phoning Camille. At my mother's request, I met my sister Marie for lunch in the food court in Alexis Nihon Plaza, overlooking a convent that had been converted into a Cégep. Even in dress slacks, the blouse she wore to the office, and a brown suit jacket, my sister looked far too young to have been married for fifteen years. Her brown hair had turned an ashier shade. Her features, like mine, had an Irish symmetry marred by a small nose. She dealt me a brisk peck on the cheek and waved me towards the Lebanese pita stall, where she addressed the servers in English. The last time I'd been in this predominantly Anglo mall, they would have accepted the English order; now, they verified her request in French, "*Laitue et tomates, madame? Des oignons? Champignons? Pamplemousse ...?*"

"*Oui, j'prends tout,*" Marie said, her mouth tight. "*De la sauce tzatziki, mais pas trop, là.*" She paid for my lunch. As we bussed our trays to a table, she said, "The worst thing about the referendum is how fucking mean it's made everybody."

"It won't kill you to order tomatoes in French. You speak the language perfectly well."

"*Perfectly well.* Listen to his fancy English accent." She sucked root beer through a straw. "I have the right to speak English. It's a bilingual country."

We looked at each other across our trays like circling dogs spoiling for a fight. One challenging word and lunch would be over. Marie and I disagreed on many subjects, but none cut deeper than language. Dave, who ran his business in English in defiance of Quebec's language law, was an Angryphone who lived in a state of perpetual rage against the French language. His best friend had chained himself to a flagpole in front of the United Nations building in New York, draped in a sandwich board demanding that the UN recognize Quebec Anglophones as victims of cultural genocide.

"In Europe, nobody thinks twice about speaking two or three languages."

"You don't say?" The Cégep students poured in for lunch. "Why couldn't you move to Toronto like everybody else's brother?"

"I have a German girlfriend."

"Yeah, that's about your speed. You can't even date someone normal."

"Only Europe has the political will to hold globalization at bay —"

"I hate it when you talk like that! Every time I hear that crap, I think of the craziness we grew up with." Frowning at me as she chewed her pita bread, she said, "Don't you think it's a little immature to imitate our parents?"

"It's not about living their lives; it's about appreciating their values. They were right to encourage us to pay attention to who's rich and who's poor, and why."

Impasse. "You notice I'm not having booze for lunch," Marie said. "Dave and I are off the sauce. You hit thirty-five and alcohol goes to your hips. Dave's packed on a few pounds recently."

"But you haven't. You look great, Marie."

"Moi? I'm the product of mucho self-sacrifice in the gym. As long as I keep fit, I have the option of leaving Dave for a younger man. Hey – doesn't Mum look great? Paul's really good for her."

"I haven't seen them together much."

"Don't be ungracious. She's happy."

"He's another intellectual."

"An employed intellectual with tenure."

"She's decided she's Norman Bethune's daughter."

Marie looked irritated. "Maybe she is. What do I know? As long as she's happy."

We parted in Québécois style, with a *bec* on each cheek. Two days later, convinced I no longer had any ties that mattered in Montreal, I flew back to England.

When I checked my pigeonhole, I found a note from Leon. He had passed his viva and was now Dr. Zamenhof. We should have a natter, he'd scribbled, because Alex was coming over to pack up his Russian library. The note's offhand tone obscured an imperative. The word "natter" rubbed me the wrong way, feeling loaded with the evasiveness that the English disguised with irony. That night, I phoned Leonie.

"Your accent has changed. You sound like the American boy on the train."

"It's not an American accent, it's a Canadian accent. As a linguist, you should –"

"I have decided that this summer I will go to Italy." She paused, as though anticipating an objection. "I will go by myself." Another pause. "The question is ... if I see Salvatore." When I refrained from replying, she said, "One of my friends told him I had a new boyfriend who was a doctoral student at Oxford University. He told her, 'I knew I was not good enough for her.' It tore my heart. That is a strange thing for me to say. It is an Italian thing to say. You see, he made me feel as an Italian feels. But you — you just make me *think*."

Telling myself that I could conserve the relationship by not placing too much pressure on it, I did not ask to visit her. As Trinity Term began, I continued studying German. I set my mind to memorizing *trennbar* and *untrennbar* verbs — those that remained a single word when conjugated and those that separated into a stem and a preposition. The instructor gave the example of the verb "to begin," *anfangen*. "I begin" was *Ich fange an*. I raised my hand. "So it takes two to begin?"

There were only six students in the class; the laughter was friendly. The instructor gave us our homework. As the class ended, Catherine came in the door. She was trimmer than I remembered, a glowing, pallid presence. "I have been in the east," she told the instructor. "May I rejoin the class?"

I left the room and lingered outside the door. A soft voice behind me said, "When I heard your voice through the door, I remembered your hiking boots."

The breadth of her smile surprised me. We walked as far as the double doors that gave onto Woodstock Road. Catherine was a doctoral student in Russian at St. Antony's College. She was working on a poet who had been a member of the Romanov family, a man whose desire for an artistic life had been hampered by social privilege. Konstantin Konstantinovich Romanov had published as K.R. to downplay his position as the czar's grandson. "He is very creative, yet he seeks modesty and simplicity. He preferred to conceal his privileges and talk about art with his best friend, Sergei."

"Do you have privileges to conceal?" I asked.

She held her breath like a schoolgirl about to make an embarrassing confession. "My father is an ambassador." When I remained silent, she said, "To Yugoslavia. He was once ambassador to East Germany, after East Germany ceased to exist."

Catherine had been born in Czechoslovakia, soon after the crushing of the Prague Spring. A year later, her family moved to a military base in southern West Germany where the US government trained spies and diplomats in Russian. Catherine's first memories were of the Alps; her first auditory recollections were of the voice of her German nanny. "I feel so contented when I speak German. The structure of those sentences comforts me." The landscape of her infant memories was Belgrade, where she lived from the ages of four to seven. *Beograd*, in Serbo-Croatian, the second music of her childhood: White City, an impossible name for a place shadowed by hills and valleys, glowering with the moss-like shadow of abundant greenery on ranks of dour apartment blocks. Her father's first posting to Moscow confirmed her eternal apartness. Other diplomatic families lived a rhythm of three years out then three years back; the years when the father worked at a desk job in Washington, D.C., and the children became Americans. But once Catherine's father had established himself as a man who lowered the temperature of every Cold War crisis, they stopped going home. Her parents, whose American ambition perplexed the languid long view of their Eastern European daughter, sent her to a Soviet school for two years until a note from the State Department suggested that the American School would be more appropriate. Perpetually busy and rarely at home, her mother and father left her in the care of a Russian nanny. By the time Catherine began to play in the Moscow snowbanks with other American girls, she spoke

Russian better than English. From Moscow, they moved to Leningrad. Life fell into three-year slices. Each time Catherine made
friends, she knew that the friendship would last three years;
only her striving parents, with their raw southern accents, were
eternal. Years of diplomatic dinners made them fat. Her mother
got bored, overate, drank too much. Undaunted, they popped
pills and waded into the next crisis. Her older brother, who had
been three at the time of their departure for Prague, absorbed
her parents' Americanness; Catherine drank down her surroundings. She spent her teenage years back in Belgrade, travelling to a boarding school in Austria. She was "sent home for
college," but succeeded in graduating from Bryn Mawr College
while spending two semesters as an exchange student in Leningrad and a third in Berlin. For a year after the fall of the Berlin
Wall, the United States maintained its embassy in East Berlin.
Catherine's father's first posting at ambassador level was to a
country that no longer existed. After this, there was a return
to Moscow, as the number two man at an embassy where the
ambassador was a political appointee. When the Soviet Union
broke up, Catherine became clinically depressed and was flown
to an American military hospital in Germany. President George
H. W. Bush awarded her father a presidential citation for his
handling of the disintegration of the Soviet Union; the Repub-
lican president conferred this honour on a diplomat who was a
registered Democrat. By then, Catherine's father and his striving friends from the bad old South that they had all worked to
reform were supporting the smooth-talking young governor of
Arkansas in his campaign to unseat Bush in 1992.

"Everywhere my parents go, I find streets or attitudes or
languages that are as they were before." She met my eyes. "Sometimes I feel as though the universe has been annihilated. I grew

up learning every detail of the world — *that* world — and now it's gone!"

For the third time in their careers, her parents were in Belgrade, where another war had ended and new wars threatened; she lived in East Germany. "But I go to see them in Yugoslavia. My father's driver, Janko, gives me tennis lessons. I like to support my parents. There is honour in representing America."

If a graduate student in the MCR had uttered such a phrase, I would have pounced. *Ost-Nostalgie* and US triumphalism locked in the same spirit? It made no sense. Yet Catherine's palpable anguish, the heart-shaking vulnerability that surfaced in a personality that had seemed remote, gave me pause.

It was dark outside. We had been standing in the doorway for an hour and a half.

We both smiled in embarrassment. *"Bis Freitag,"* we murmured. As I ambled away, I stole a backward glance at Catherine's bicycle, as obsolete as a Trabant, wobbling up Woodstock Road.

On Friday, Catherine came late to class, glanced at my hiking boots, and confided me a conspiratorial smile. After the class, I asked her to have a sandwich with me. She shook her head, saying she had errands to run. On Monday, when she didn't come to class, I feared she had returned to East Germany and felt sore with envy that she had a home in that world.

TWENTY-FIVE

A BLACK-BORDERED, STIFF-BACKED envelope in my pigeonhole. Who would send me such a thing? I opened it and found an invitation to Leon's graduation ceremony. I sent my RSVP and circled the date in my agenda. On the day, I reached the Sheldonian Theatre early and saw Leon arrive with a tall, elderly man who hauled an elongated version of Leon's stocky body across the floor. The old man's long, sparse, white hair, plastered across his skull, converged in a feathery ruff at the nape of his neck.

The first twenty minutes of the ceremony were in untranslated Latin. Mr. Zamenhof absorbed the proceedings with a watchful stare. At the end of the ceremony, the crowd spilled onto a patio between the Sheldonian and the Bodleian. Dressed in my navy blue suit, I eased my way through a throng of upperclass English families. Having cut my hair short for the first time in three years, I passed unnoticed.

"Canadian, are you?" Mr. Zamenhof said in an accent that surprised me with its Celtic lilt. "I knew Canadians in Spain. Mac-Paps, we called them."

"Did you know Norman Bethune? He may have been my mother's father."

"Norman Bethune might have been any number of people's fathers! I knew Bethune. I knew Hemingway and Orwell, too. Internationalism was a small world, you know. It was Kasja Rothman I knew particularly well."

The elegant crowd jostled us. "She was an old flame of Dad's," Leon said. "His Trotskyite transgression."

"She may have been a Trot, but I was a young man and she was damned good-looking." Mr. Zamenhof said. "No one seemed to mind when I was with her. But her affair with Bethune was so notorious that the Party feared he was feeding information to undesirable elements. That's why Bethune left Spain, you know. The Party kicked him out. They no longer trusted him."

Mr. Zamenhof's eyes focused on the 1930s. I imagined a chain of interlocked flesh: Isaac Zamenhof and Kasja Rothman, Kasja Rothman and Norman Bethune, Norman Bethune and my grandmother. "It's almost as though we're related," I murmured.

"I'd rather not think about that." Leon's mouth grew as tight as those of the upper-class people who surrounded us. "Not my cup of tea."

"Kasja escaped to Mexico when the fascists took over." The old man's gaze ambled over the gaudy, babbling crowd. "She's dead now. When you're my age, most people you know are dead."

I thought of the resilience of this man's principles, which had endured so many defeats. "Do you believe history has ended, sir?"

"No, that's rubbish. But a certain way of living in history has become more difficult."

"I have to get Dad home." Leon took a step forward. He gave his father his arm, dealing me a parting nod with his head.

The old man and the young man made their way through the crowd, unsuspected and deadly among the class enemies who surrounded them.

I returned to my room to write high-school-level truisms about Marshall Tito's Yugoslavia and tick off the days until the end of my lease. One night, as summer warmth was creeping into the Oxford stone, the phone rang. For a moment I heard only silence. Then a rambling voice said, "Your grandad and me da' 'ad it off with the same bird. I could be your uncle, ha-ha. But since she didn't spawn, what's that make us, mate? Spaniards in the works?"

"Are you all right, Leon?"

"Of course I'm not all right. Emily told me to shove off. She told me that a year ago so I rang her to see if she still felt that way ... And she told me to shove off again ..."

"Find someone else."

"... And now me da's in hospital and who knows how long he has to live, and there's nothing anyone can say, is there?"

"I'm sorry, Leon. Your father's an amazing man."

"You're just interested in him for academic reasons. You're too fucking —"

"Canadian?" I wondered what Decibel Doug was doing in Nova Scotia.

"How can you expect anyone to be close to you when you're so morally pure? I'm not going along with it. When Alex comes back here, I don't want any fucking moral purity. No colonial holier-than-thou. We're going to treat Alex like our mate and buy him a pint and let bygones be bygones. Ashes to ashes. That's what they'll say about the lot of us. Kasja, me da', that lad of Alex's ... Ashes to ashes. History's not a moral science. Marx understood that."

The line went dead. As I replaced the receiver, I realized I didn't have his phone number. To my surprise, he called me two days later, sober and solicitous and joking about women. His father had come home from hospital. When I told him that my lease in Wellington Square was about to expire, he said, "You could bung your stuff in my storage bin here at the co-op." I accepted his offer with relief. I took down his address and phone number, delighted by our renewed connection. The next day, in the middle of my German class, I felt a soft touch through stiff leather. Catherine's running shoe was grazing my boot. She raised her hand and gave the instructor the conjugation of the *trennbar* verb *ausmachen*. "*Ich mache aus.*"

"Can anyone give me a sentence with *ausmachen*?" the instructor asked.

"I make out?"

Startled to hear Catherine, who used few idioms, utter this one, I laughed. The medievalist gave me a stern look. I remembered that this expression did not have the same connotations in British English as it did in North America. I rarely thought of myself in North American terms. Yet "North America," the assimilationist illusion that had destroyed Doug, did not prevent me from feeling drawn to Catherine's wide-mouthed smile.

"It doesn't mean to make out?" Catherine asked. "Doesn't it take two to begin?"

Her coquettishness banished the greyness from her face. "Not to make out, but to put out," the instructor said. "*Ich mache aus das Licht.* I turn out the light."

At the end of the class, Catherine said, "Weren't we going to have a sandwich?"

Her deftness both comforted and unsettled me. We walked to a sandwich shop on St. Giles, then back to Little Clarendon

Street, and through the black, wrought-iron gate that enclosed the circular park in the centre of Wellington Square. We sat down on the green grass and talked like D.Phil. students. I told Catherine I was having difficulty finishing my thesis. She regarded me with a keener gaze. "Of course, I love poor K.R. But I do not want to finish because I do not want to hurt my parents by leaving them. It keeps them young for me to be a student."

"What do *you* want?"

Catherine looked startled. "I want to live in the world I know. But that world is gone."

I finished my mango chutney sandwich. Making a joke about losing my home also, I told her about the end of my lease and Leon's offer to store my belongings in South London. I might still get enough odd jobs to remain in Oxford, but I would be more versatile if I had fewer belongings. I told Catherine that I had spotted a notice on a billboard that said *Bloke With Bedford*. I'd phoned the bloke. He had offered to move my stuff in his Bedford van for fifty pounds.

"When are you moving?"

"My stuff goes into London the day after tomorrow."

"You and I should take a walk together." She stopped on the edge of Wellington Square. "One o'clock tomorrow."

"It doesn't have to be tomorrow. I'll be here until the end of June."

"I won't be." The expression of a schoolgirl abashed by her transgressions returned. "I'm going back at the end of the week."

"To Yugoslavia?"

"To East Germany."

I didn't dare tell her East Germany didn't exist. When I failed to reply, she repeated, "One o'clock. You can take a break from your packing."

"Make it three-thirty," I said.

She stepped forward, her face thrust up in front of me. She was not letting me off the hook!

"If it's one o'clock, I'll only be able to spend half an hour with you. By three-thirty I should be finished and we can take a real walk."

Some treaty, some procedure for accommodating each other's needs, was forged in that flash of sunlight. She turned away, her diplomacy concluded. As in any good compromise, I felt that I, too, had got what I wanted. I spent the next day hearing Spice Girls tunes playing on the radio as I threw out plastic bags, took old T-shirts to the Salvation Army, piled books and paper in cardboard boxes. Dust motes floated in the bright air. I opened the window and felt caressed by spring warmth. My arms sore from stacking, I borrowed the caretaker's Hoover and vacuumed the floor. After a day's physical activity, I felt clear-eyed and pleasantly gritty. At three o'clock, having got everything ready for Bloke With Bedford, I took a shower. I was rubbing my short hair dry with a towel when Catherine rang the buzzer.

Closing the door behind me, I went downstairs. "Port Meadow?" Catherine said.

We walked up Walton Street, past Jericho's pubs and cinema, and the best hamburger shop in Oxford. By asking if she had eaten there, I learned that she was a vegetarian and a Quaker. As we crossed the bridge over the canal that led to the meadow, we stopped and looked back at Oxford's spires.

Port Meadow, an ancient common, was a rough plain with the mud-banked squiggle of the Isis River curling down its side. Left fallow for a thousand years, it was infinitely changeable. Sometimes, when I walked there, I felt as though I were descending into a prehistoric world. Herds of horses and cattle roamed untended, as though at the dawn of time. In the spring, the meadow vanished beneath the Isis's flood waters; on summer days, it attracted kite flyers, sprawled lovers concealed by thatch-like grass, or young dogs racing at full tilt. Today, the meadow was dotted with buttercups. Thousands of delicate yellow goblets, each no larger than the nub of my thumb, rode the tufted grass like fairies' washtubs. Catherine ran her fingers through them. "They have come out to greet us."

A herd of horses was watering at a bend in the Isis, half savage-looking beasts with tufted hair over their withers.

"Look at the buttercups!" Catherine said. "They're like little suns ... they bring the earth and the sky together."

"The union of up and down," I said. "I feel I've entered this world where I'm up in the air and nothing is tied down."

"It takes two to begin," Catherine murmured. We trailed our hands through the buttercups. "The sun!" Catherine said. "How I need the sun!"

She swung close to me. "I had a depression this winter. I was in hospital with tubes in my arms." She shook her head. "Now I'm feeling better. My face is less grey. These buttercups are my cure. Everything inside me is waking up."

The shaggy, primeval-looking horses tramped along the muddy river bank. They came up the slope onto the rough plain, rocking on their haunches. One of them pitched forward and began to run. Their blond manes flew, thrashing their shoulders like natural reins. They cut in front of us three arms' lengths away. The rhythm of their hooves thudded into the soles of our feet. I caught Catherine's arm; for a thumping moment, she, I, and the horses trembled to the pulse of the earth.

We walked to the end of the meadow. At the pub, where the water ran through the weir, there were Rolls Royces and

Jaguars pulled in on the roadside and upper-class English people drinking wine and spirits. Abandoning our plan to sit down, we cut around the pub and walked back across the meadow. We returned to Oxford feeling lost, yet together. As we drifted through North Oxford, I told her about Leon and Alex and our first year at Hamdaw. She looked at me as though evaluating my Russian credentials. I cut the story short before I got to the end. We ate a sandwich at a shop in Summertown. In the sunlight, the flesh of Catherine's cheeks and bare arms was of a greyness that had been rubbed with the yellow of buttercups. She glowed with an immanence that heightened the firmness with which her rounded body was planted on its feet.

The large brick houses of North Oxford, surrounded by tall trees, became a maze. Catherine led me down the side of a three-storey house and unlocked a basement door. Like other colleges, St. Antony's had bought North Oxford houses and divided them up for students. Catherine was sharing the basement of this house with an English girl. Her room was at the back, half below ground level, with a broad window that opened out onto the garden. She made tea in a samovar. We sat on the floor and talked about the East, about my parents and hers. "When my parents go back to America, their brothers and sisters ask them, 'So yous guys talk to them Commie-nists?' They don't care that my dad's an ambassador. They just can't believe we talk to Russians." Her father was poor white trash from Arkansas, her mother the product of an Irish-American's one-night stand with a Cherokee woman in Nebraska. Both parents had grown up moving houses as their parents abandoned homes where they couldn't pay the rent. "They've passed that heritage on to me."

I felt an anxiety at my rootedness. I was a multiple-generation Montrealer, denizen of an island city that had a culture unique in the world, someone who had lived his whole life in one place. How could I match Catherine's insights?

We drank tea and ate biscuits. When darkness fell, crickets trilled in the garden. I saw the lights go out on the top floors of the house on the other side of the hedge. Suddenly it was three-thirty a.m. We had been talking for twelve hours.

Catherine got to her feet. "Oh, what is to be done?"

"Chernyshevsky," I said, thinking of Alex teaching Colin in the Ho Chi Minh Quad.

"I meant Lenin's *What Is to Be Done?* A more radical version. A call to action."

I walked to the back of the large room and picked up the long-sleeved shirt that I had discarded on the floor. The flare of Catherine's hips in her faded blue jeans caught the light. I saw her watching me observing her and felt caught out in a camouflaged stab of desire.

"I think you should stay."

"All right, I'll stay." My voice was hoarse. I discarded the long-sleeved shirt and approached her in my T-shirt. We kissed. When we subsided onto the single bed next to the wall, the springs screeched. Our kissing grew fiercer. Catherine lifted her hand. "This bed's too noisy. Help me put the mattress on the floor. No, next to the window. I want to be close to the garden. It will remind me of Port Meadow."

"Shouldn't we draw the curtain?"

"There's no one out there."

She turned off all the lights except for a small lamp, which she placed on the floor. She dropped to her knees and slid her blouse over her head. The lamplight catching the bra-clip on her shoulder, she looked at me sideways. "I'm just coming out of a relationship."

"So am I."

The shared confession of infidelity heightened our excitement. Catherine switched off the lamp. Her body glimmered under pale moonlight. As I closed my arms around her, I felt how raptly my muscles were trained to Leonie's lean frame. The swell of Catherine's hips, the globe-like ampleness of her breasts, sent my caresses astray.

"I want you on top of me," Catherine whispered. "And inside me." Once I had complied, she giggled. "The union of up and down."

"The union of in and out."

"I like that. No, don't slow down."

"I'm getting too excited."

"Do you know the novel *Catch-22*?"

"Yes. I mean I haven't read it ..."

"I'm seeing a therapist. She asked me what I was reading. I said *Catch-22* and she said, 'Oh, the book with the blue cover.' Think about that. Think about a book with a blue cover."

I thought about a blue cover, suppressing the thought that my naked body was thrashing under the moonlight with a woman who was not my girlfriend. Catherine did not come, but she seemed happy with my homage, ebullient at having possessed me. Afterwards, all I dared to ask was, "Is your boyfriend German?"

"Ye-es."

"So's my girlfriend. That class was bad news for the Germans."

She laughed and kissed me. We fell asleep on the mattress on the floor with a raspy blanket flung over us. As dim light crept over the garden amid the tweeting of birds, we woke and made love again. Later, I got dressed and, not knowing where I was, wandered among North Oxford mansions until I came out onto Banbury Road and found my way back to Wellington Square.

I fell asleep in my room and woke up, realizing it was time for Bloke With Bedford. We loaded up the van and drove into the desolation of south London. We could have been in Moscow for all that I knew, yet the bloke found the house. Archie met us at the door. We carried my belongings out of the Bedford and into one of five head-high Bristol board containers in the storeroom at the back of the house. I piled up boxes of books and flung rolled posters and garbage bags full of clothes into the bin, then shut it with a huge padlock.

"This 'ere's the key," Archie said. "You won't want to lose that."

I slipped the key into the change pocket of my wallet. I wondered whether I would see this stuff again.

That evening the telephone rang.

"You left me this number because you wanted to see me again, right?'

"Yes. There's a party here at eight o'clock tonight. You can lock your bike downstairs."

The party had been announced on a billboard in the entrance hall. A D.Phil. student in French history was celebrating his viva. Another one who had finished. At quarter past eight Catherine rang the buzzer. I went downstairs to open the door. We hesitated, then kissed. She asked to see my room. I took her upstairs, waved at the bare shelves, the laptop on the desk, the backpack propped up in the corner. "My home for three years," I murmured.

We went to the party in the lounge on the top floor. Wall-to-wall carpet and worn 1970s furniture in shades of garish orange and yellow had been spruced up with balloons; crisps, cheesies, and boxed juices sat on the table. "This reminds me of parties in Eastern Europe," Catherine said, "where people show off the products they buy on the black market."

I nodded my congratulations to the new doctor of French history. Catherine and I left the party early. Once we were out in the hall, she took off. I ran after her and caught her. Laughing, we descended two flights of stairs and plunged in the door of my room. "My depression is gone," she said, during a pause in our kisses. "I'm alive again." We undressed. Catherine flung herself naked on her back on my narrow bed. I thought of Kumiko, of Leonie. The vision of three naked women on the same bed choked me with excitement. I reached down to the outlet in the wall and unplugged the phone. "Go slowly," Catherine said. "I take forever. Especially after I've been depressed." As naked as my shelves and drawers, I approached her, confident in the knowledge that tonight I could dispense with the blue book. We buckled and moaned and came. We clung to each other and continued kissing. I *was* Catherine, an itinerant wanderer in the world of after, an alien in search of past cultural coherence, a pilgrim whose religion was *Ostalgie*, nostalgia for the vanished East. I was an English-speaking European, a North American not in the slavish way that Decibel Doug had been, but in the active sense of looking on Europe from a transatlantic vantage point. Catherine and I awoke naked in the bare, whitewashed room like newborns in a hospital ward. This time it was she who had to pack. I had forgotten that she was leaving. I followed her downstairs. Her bicycle lay on the steps beneath the building. She had locked it to a grate where bicycles weren't supposed to be locked. The caretaker, the clippers still in his hands, had cut the chain. "It doesn't matter," she said. "I'll leave it in the St. Antony's bicycle shed for the summer."

"I have to see you again," I whispered.

"I promised Andreas I would spend the summer with him."

It was the first time she had spoken her boyfriend's name. She

TWENTY-SIX

TWO NIGHTS LATER, WHEN the telephone rang, my hopes soared that the call would be from Germany. And it was. "I am back from Italy," Leonie said. There was an aching pause. "I did not see Salvatore! My friends told me I must give Salvatore another chance." The realization that she was fighting back tears stifled my rebuttal. "The last day I was in Milano, he phoned me and said, 'I am coming.' He spoke like a man who wanted a woman. Salvatore is a man! He stole a motorcycle to follow me to the airport, he begged me to miss my flight for him. But no, I am a stupid bourgeois girl who cannot miss her flight. That is why I have a boyfriend who is Canadian ..."

I gave her time. I wanted Leonie *and* I wanted Catherine. Everything I wanted was something I couldn't have. I wanted to stay in Wellington Square, yet my lease was about to expire. In the morning, when I walked to the Computing Centre, planning to send Leonie soothing words, a message was waiting for me.

Please do not write to me again. I am Japanese woman now,
with Japanese husband. Life makes us different. You will see
when you finish D.Phil.! Please finish soon.

I blundered back to Wellington Square, threw myself on my bed and sobbed. Leonie was wedded to the allure of southern Europe, Catherine had returned behind the wall of the old East, Kumiko had reverted to being a woman of the unreachable Far East. I stayed in my room, avoiding Hamdaw, where tents and gazebos were being set up in the gardens for Dean Bessborough's annual party. The mere thought of that party made me furious. If Leon and I had been the active agents of Colin's accident, the intellectual author of his death was Bessborough, with his flouting of rules and his flaunting of his privileges. And Bessborough remained impervious, untouched by Colin's fate or that of anyone else.

Late that night, when the phone rang, I hesitated before answering.

"Where the fuck are you?" The voice, male and British, hit me like a truck. "You're always moaning for me to post things to your pigeonhole, then I do, and you don't fucking respond. Alex is here, mate. We're at Susan's flat, packing up his Russian library."

"I haven't been into College ..."

"Why don't you pop over to Gloucester Green and hop on the CityLink?" He paused for effect, as though cocking an eyebrow at the other people in the room. "You have the key for the bin, right? The storage bin in my digs? Bring that along, will you? We need it."

He gave me the address and directions. I hung up, looked at my vacant mien in the mirror, grabbed my wallet and left.

Alex ...! I arrived at Gloucester Green just as a CityLink was about to depart. The highway was dark all the way into London. I was adrift in a darkness that expelled lightness and buoyancy. The glare of Oxford Street's shops fatigued me. I got off at Marble Arch, rode the Central Line west to Shepherd's Bush and came up out of the underground among dark side streets. Cars were parked bumper-to-bumper. Up ahead, at the end of a block, an Austin Mini, denied a full space, was lodged at an oblique angle. Though it was a small car, the way it protruded into the street reminded me of a truck.

"I don't know when the fuck I'm going to pick up ..."

The tall figure bent over the two-door car and hefted cardboard boxes into the back seat. "Hey, hoser!" I said. No response. I remembered that Alex did not know Canadian slang. His aquiline features had settled into wedges, as though the eyes of the Alex I'd known had been walled up in someone else's face. I noted the thickness of his neck, the hint of a belly that pulled at the front of his red dress shirt. "Alex," I murmured.

Leon circled around and gave me a slap on the back as Alex and I shook hands. "Well, well, look who's here! Did you bring the key, mate?" He continued talking, derailing my attempt to speak to Alex by telling me that tonight they were getting the Russian library out of Susan's flat and into the storage bin in the co-op where it would share space with the belongings of someone else he knew, that's right, exactly the same bin, and someday when Alex had a place of his own he would send for his books, we all liked to think that we'd eventually have a place of our own, didn't we ...?

Silenced by Leon's garrulousness, I followed them along an unevenly lighted sidewalk and into an apartment building. We rode up five floors in a tiny elevator that squeezed us together, then entered a flat where empty cardboard boxes were stacked in the entrance hall and books were piled in the closet. At the end of the hall, Alex's tartan suitcase lay flat on the floor. Susan came out of the kitchen wearing a long, belted dress and smart black shoes, her dark eyes alert. She shook my hand. Alex resumed pulling books out of the closet and packing them into boxes.

Leon asked me for the key. I gave it to him. He kept talking, wittering on, as the English said. His verbosity made me wonder what he had been drinking. As I tried to ask Alex about Harvard, Leon said, "Our Kevin's not 'alf a lad. Rumours from Hamdaw say he's got a new bird."

"You sleazy bastard!" Alex paused with a Russian volume in his hand.

"In fact, I think I've lost her. She went to eastern Germany, or maybe Yugoslavia."

"She went east?" Alex said. "You should go look for her. If you don't, maybe I will!"

"You should go back to Harvard," Susan said in a reproving Torontonian voice. "Do you know what Alex has done, Kevin? He did two years of brilliant course work at Harvard. He got the highest marks in years on the Russian literature comps. The committee invited him to tell them what he was going to write his thesis on, and rather than talking about the poetry he loves, Alex denounced the doctoral program and said he'd taken a job as an investment banker in Moscow!"

"Investment banking?" I said.

"Don't you start! Leon's already told me I've sold out to capitalism. Man, I've been broke my whole life. I'm storing my books in some hole I can't even pay for. I want to be able to afford a place where I have my own study —"

He held up a book with Cyrillic lettering, opened it and began to read. As though lifted by the ringing inflections of the Russian language, he grew taller. The long, word-full trunk of his body yoked heaven to earth. His wide chest vibrated, an infinitely sensitive instrument.

"A still stream," I said. "It's that 1920s writer – Pilnyak? – alluding to the image from the end of *Eugene Onegin* when Onegin realizes he's not going to get Tatiana and the rest of his life will be meaningless." I turned to Leon, "Alex taught me that in first year."

"It's all Russian to me." Leon bent over and picked up a box. "Come on, lads. Time to bung this stuff in the Mini."

We pulled books out of the closet and stacked them in cardboard boxes. When we had finished, there were five boxes. We picked up one each, leaving two on the floor. Susan opened the door to let us out. In the elevator, Leon wittered on: the Austin Mini belonged to his da', who was out of hospital but no longer drove, he had been applying for jobs but there was bugger-all on offer, such was the logic of capitalism –

We stepped into the darkness, hearing the sound of traffic out on the main streets. Leon put down his box on the sidewalk, opened the Mini, and swung the front passenger seat forward. One by one, we placed our boxes on top of those which were already stacked there. Leon was about to close the door when Alex, who was staring down at the back seat, said, "That's it. That's my fucking life."

"Your home is the Russian language. That's what Jerzy told me."

"It's weird to think about you and Jerzy talking –"

"Alex, the passage you read, is that what you were reciting the night –?"

"Oi, Kevin, we're finished here. Alex and I can fetch the last two boxes."

"So my service to the Party is terminated?"

"The night Colin died, you mean?"

"You just needed me because I had the key? That's the reason you called me?"

"No, it wasn't that."

"I sent you a letter, mate. If you'd checked your fucking pigeonhole, you could have spent the whole evening in our glorious company –"

"No, that was Pushkin. I needed Pushkin that night –"

"After Alex and I drop off the books, I'll take the Mini back to me da's flat."

"Which Pushkin?"

"Did I tell you I'm living with me da' now? I've still got the spot in the co-op –"

"Fuck – Colin! It's painful just to think of him. He was so young!"

"– and the storage bin, of course."

"Which Pushkin?" I asked again.

"Oh, push off, mate," Leon said. "We can't stay here all night. Alex has a morning flight."

I was about to object, or try to find a way to tell Alex that Colin had seen Moscow, that he hadn't died without that vital experience, when he took a step forward and smothered me in a bear-hug of Russian devoutness. "Good luck, man. I hope you finish your fucking thesis. I hope you find that girl."

Leon and I hugged with an embrace stiffened by Anglo restraint. He slammed shut the door of the Mini. They turned their backs on me and disappeared into the apartment building.

I wound through the streets until I found the Central Line Shepherd's Bush Tube station. I rode standing up, gripping the bar over my head. Fury at how they had treated me tensed my muscles. I was one and none, a voice from the attic with a key to the bin. I hadn't had time to remind them of how angry I had been to discover that Leon had known about Alex's Harvard plans. By talking incessantly, Leon had prevented me from raising the question of Colin's death.

I got off at Marble Arch and dodged through the maze of tunnels where homeless men in grimy sleeping bags taunted the passersby as though we, not they, were the social outcasts. I came up out of the tunnels and had to wait only a few minutes before the blue, white, and gold bus roared out of the darkness. I imagined Leon and Alex driving to South London in the Mini, piling Alex's Russian library on top of my belongings in Leon's storage bin, then Leon driving Alex back to Susan's flat, and finally driving home to his dad. What would they talk about all that way? Leon, at least, would be able to relax now that I had left. The thought made me restless and upset.

The closer the CityLink came to Oxford, the angrier I felt. I was angry with myself for not having told Alex about the call Leon and I had made. I was angry at my failure to challenge Leon on our decision to take Colin to The Eagle and Child instead of the John Radcliffe Hospital. The more I thought about it, the more likely it seemed that doing the right thing would have made all the difference. I felt only sympathy for Alex — *It's painful just to think of him* — but the thought of Leon made me angry, and the thought of Bessborough had me boiling. I wished I could go to Bessborough's rooms and beat him with one of the whips he was rumoured to collect. But tonight he would not be in his rooms. He would be admiring the stately young men of Oxford at his goddamned party.

Bessborough. He was the one who needed to have a few home

truths delivered to him — preferably by the full force of a fist. Leon skated around the issue of our responsibility, yet he knew what I thought. Bessborough knew only his own self-indulgence. He was oblivious to the fact that his party had caused a fatality. He might not even care.

His lack of caring drilled into my brain.

I burned to hurt him. Hurt him physically by punching him in the face, or wound his esteem by destroying his party.

Feeling that the anger I had sometimes experienced, yet never allowed myself to express, at Oxford's snobberies and oppressive conventions had congealed around the image of Bessborough's odious smile, I got off the bus on the High Street and walked towards Hamdaw College. Light, danceable, pop music played at mind-numbing volume made the night shudder. It was the third anniversary of Colin's death. Breathing faster, I entered the Lodge and, with a cursory nod at the porter, scrabbled at my pigeonhole. Sheets of paper that announced desultory deadlines crinkled between my fingers. There was no letter from Leon, no fucking letter at all.

Everything was a lie. No relationship was authentic; nothing had meaning beyond the shimmer of gowns and jackets. At the core of that trivialization of experience stood Bessborough. And Bessborough did his worst damage through his party.

I threw the junk mail into the bin.

"Quite a racket the Dean's making," the porter said.

"You'd never know he was in charge of discipline."

"On the contrary, it's being in charge that gives him the right."

The abject complaisance of the English working class pushed me over the edge. I rushed out of the Lodge and skirted the front quad, keeping close to the ancient walls. At the arch that led into the Hamdaw Gardens a pair of tuxedo-clad undergraduates at a table were checking tickets. Behind them I saw balloons floating over the lawns. The music vibrated through the ancient stone until the band brought its set to a close. "Thank you," a voice said into a microphone. The two lads turned around, craning to watch the band leave the stage.

I put my head down and ran. A young woman in a ladder-backed white dress gave a lady-like shriek as I sprinted past her. I was aware of my vagabond look, my unshaven, blue-jeaned, T-shirted affront to dozens of ball gowns and dinner jackets. Standing out like a member of an alien species, I kept running. My anger drove me on, supercharging me like a high-octane fuel. Where was Bessborough? I would step up to him and give him the surprise of his life: an unexpected punch in the face. Scouring the crowd at full tilt, I was unable to locate the Dean. I tore a futile circle around the grass.

A big-bellied security guard came lumbering after me. With a leap of outraged joy, I tore away from him in the direction of the stage. If I couldn't hurt Bessborough with my fists, I would wound him with my words. Sweating, delighting in my grunginess in this wax museum of manicured toffs, I found the stairs to the stage and reached the microphone in time to spot Dr. Dennock, hoisting a drink, staring at me in disgust. He was enjoying his disapproval as much as I was enjoying outraging him. A cool midnight breeze blew in my face. I slid my hand around the stem of the microphone and pulled the grate close to my lips as I had learned to do when leading chants at anti-Free Trade rallies. "Ladies and gentlemen," I said, "if there are any ladies or gentlemen here, if you aren't all as vapid as you appear. Three years ago tonight a young man died as a result of Dean Bessborough's party. A brilliant young scholar diverted from his studies by the false promise of glamour, by values that were not his, took the risk of riding his bicycle across Oxford at night to get to this ersatz occasion, simply because he wanted to meet a friend. That young man died a horrible death –"

"Sod him!"

Upper-class young men waved their fists, reviling me as proletarian scum and a barmy Yank. No feeling was more exhilarating than being greeted with cries of execration. Dean Bessborough – I had spotted him now – had interrupted his conversation with a willowy young man. Stan and Sebastian rushed forward, garbed in their finery. They overtook the wheezing security guard, pounded up the stairs behind me, and grabbed my shoulders. I kept a firm grip on the microphone. "We are all responsible. *You* are responsible for the death of Colin Blake! Queen Bess and his whips and chains are responsible ..." A roar of applause. As I shouted my final words, I felt their hollowness. I had not known Colin well; his death was not mine to grieve. Yet, as no one else would assume the anger that his death deserved, I had taken it on myself. Looking out at the dinner jackets and ball gowns and appalled white faces, I saw that the enduring casualty of our prank had been Alex. Colin's death had resuscitated Alex's trauma at the death of his brother. By sending our most emotional friend, the most sensitive literary intelligence either of us was likely to be personally acquainted with, careering off the rails – leaving Harvard! becoming an investment banker! – Leon and I had relegated the literariness in our own lives. My awareness of the true source of my outrage, and the actual object of my grief, struck me just as Sebastian tried to tear the microphone away from my mouth. I stamped my foot on his shoe, my trainers making little impact on his black leather, and lunged forward, empty of words yet still furious.

Stan brought me down with an Australian rugby tackle.

Winded, I hit the stage. A jeering roar flailed up from the crowd. "You get a place at Oxford," Stan said, in his squeaky little voice, "and you act like a wanker."

"You're an exceptionally immature man." Bessborough leaned over me. In the glare of the stage lights above, he spoke from hooded shadow. "As Dean, and Fellow responsible for discipline, it gives me extraordinary pleasure to tell you, Carmichael, that your days at Hamdaw College are over!"

PART THREE

RUSTICATION

TWENTY-SEVEN

STAN AND THE SECURITY guard frog-marched me out of Hamdaw Gardens and around the front quad, where I felt the founder, in her long gown, surveying my removal in stony silence. Dean Bessborough stood with his arms crossed as they pitched me out the front gate to the vibrations of the next band breaking into an Abba cover. By the time I returned to Wellington Square, I was ecstatic and perturbed. I fell asleep in an instant.

The phone rang. I stirred. It kept ringing. It was a bright morning. I answered. "It seems a chat is in order," Zed said.

"What time should I come to your rooms?"

"My rooms are off limits. It's not official yet, of course, but there's no point in making matters worse by flouting your rustication until it goes into effect. At this point you need all the allies you can get." The asperity in his voice suggested that he included himself in the roster of those whom I must win over. "King's Arms at eleven," he said, and hung up.

Rustication! A wave of mutinous energy ran up my sore arms. I showered, put on some of the better clothes that I had spared from Leon's storage bin, and ate breakfast. I had assumed that I would remain in Oxford next year, picking up enough tutoring or research chores to pay the rent on a far-flung room, as other fifth-year D.Phil. students did. Unreality enveloped the shadowed shops as I grasped that my eternal-student life was being legislated away from me.

At eleven o'clock, I found Zed at a corner table of the King's Arms. The half-pint of bitter gathering condensation in front of him looked more ample in girth than the man who proposed to drink it.

"What are you having?" Zed murmured. "More to the point, what were you having last night?"

"Last night I didn't touch a drop. I was carrying boxes of books at Alexander Spokoynov's ex-girlfriend's flat in Shepherd's Bush."

"Spokoynov," Zed muttered. "Another Canadian graduate who didn't work out."

"He transferred to Harvard."

"Where, I gather, he's now withdrawn."

I should have known better than to mislead Mr. Cedric Robinson on the subject of Hamdaw graduate students. The casual omniscience with which Zed uttered his correction made me feel I was in safe hands. I let him order me a ginger beer. I looked down at the circular pressboard coaster on which he set my glass. The pub's front door was open; the room was full of light. "I want to hear your side of the story."

I reminded him of Colin's death, sidestepping the issue of precisely why Colin had changed his plans and tried to reach Hamdaw College. "I think this event is responsible for the changes in Alex's behaviour."

"One would expect a man of your age to know better than to allow such feelings to result in a public display. The crux of your self-justification comes down to Good Queen Bess holding a party when everyone's meant to be swotting for finals, and that's not going to fly. Not that you're not right. There are members of Governing Body who would like to see Bessborough move his shindigs out of College, but the manner of your protest was wholly inappropriate."

"I'm going to be rusticated for interrupting a party? How can they justify that?"

"There, I'm afraid, you've been dealt a rather poor hand. Nothing's official, of course, until Governing Body's had its say, but on the basis of an informal poll in the SCR this morning, I'd say your chances of wriggling out of this are nil. All that many members of the SCR know of you is that dreadful photograph that cast you as the scourge of public school boys. For most of them, that alone would warrant rustication. To make matters worse, Bessborough's out for your blood. Ray Dennock can't forgive you for making him look like an ass at High Table —"

"What does it mean to be rusticated?"

"You're banned from setting foot on College property. To respect the terms of the rustication, you must leave Oxford. Traditionally it meant being sent to the countryside. Cambridge rusticated John Milton and John Dryden!" He smirked at the foolishness of the competition. His Tutor for Graduates mien slipping back into place, he said, "You must return and finish your dissertation! Too many people simply drift off after rustication. Auberon Waugh, the son of the chap who wrote *Brideshead*, never graduated after being rusticated —"

"Speaking of Auberon, *my* Auberon, can't he —?"

"Hasn't been here long enough. If he were a Big Beast of the SCR, like Bessborough or Dennock, he might get the punishment reduced — because, frankly, the case for rustication isn't compelling. There's meant to be an element of academic failure.

Though your dissertation is progressing too slowly, your supervisor believes you will finish."

He had phoned Auberon, I saw, who had been fair about my work. Boisterous end-of-term students and early-season American tourists came in the open doorway and ordered pints and ploughman's lunches. "So he won't stand up for me."

"The last thing you need, Kevin, is to make matters worse by having a spat with your supervisor. Auberon is an experienced diplomat. He understands the limits of his influence as a relative newcomer to the SCR. It will have more weight if I'm the one who tells Governing Body that your dissertation is of acceptable quality." Under his breath he murmured, "It doesn't help that you both fancied that Italian girl." As I looked up, he smiled. "Nor that you had more luck with her than Auberon did."

I stared in astonishment. On my left, a pair of undergraduate men pumped coins into video display terminals, making them flash and ping. Oxford belonged to no one; Zed was one of the tiny minority who had chiselled a lifelong niche here. "You owe it to yourself to come back and finish, Kevin. Send me a forwarding address so that I can post you the letter laying out the terms of your rustication. You may resume your studies next Michaelmas Term. If you continue writing in the meantime and return with a completed draft, that will move matters along. The Lodge will forward your post. I cleared out your pigeonhole this morning. All I found was this."

He dropped a pale blue envelope onto the table. I saw my name in squiggly letters, a return address in London. I tore the letter open. It had been written a week earlier. *Dear Kevin, I'm taking a moment to let you know that Alex is crossing the pond —*

For the first time since bursting into the party, I felt that I was in the wrong.

Leaving his half-pint untouched, Zed stood up. His long-fingered hands fluttered in front of his narrow waist without coalescing into a handshake. "Do come back to finish your dissertation. We'll talk then."

A video display terminal squawked. How I had disappointed Zed! I, his native informant, the local chief of the Canuck tribe, had proved to be as much of a failure as any of "my people." In rusticating me, Oxford had relieved me of the burden of colonial responsibilities. Leon's letter crinkled in my pocket. I tried to quash the thought that if it had been delivered a day earlier, I would remain an active D.Phil. student. I returned to Wellington Square, where I opened the door on my bare room: heaped clothes, Toshiba T1600, a couple of paperbacks, and dustballs in the corners. My lease was about to expire, I had £600 of scholarship money in my Oxford Barclay's account, $500 in a Royal Bank account in Montreal, no other assets, no credit card, a shaky unfinished doctoral thesis and no job prospects. My girlfriend seemed to be breaking up with me; I had glimpsed love in an affair with no future. I was thirty-five years old and had just been rusticated from Oxford, an indignity conceived for spoiled English nineteen-year-olds.

Gazing at the brown Georgian houses of Wellington Square, I remembered the wonder of my first days at Oxford, when I would wake to Hamdaw's seventeenth-century architecture and think, *How did this happen? What's going to happen next?* That sense of possibility had dwindled. What had Zed just demonstrated, if not his inability to see beyond Oxford's rules to protest an injustice wreaked by insecure middle-aged men? Any firmly defined society curtailed perspective. The only liberated outlook was one that sprang from the spaces between societies. The world after the fall of the Berlin Wall homogenized local particularities, diminishing the possibility of gaining perspective by comparing differences.

The more I thought about this, the more clearly I realized that my thesis was not dead.

In the morning, I rode the CityLink into London and walked through the residential neighbourhoods I'd heard mentioned by people at Oxford. I looked in the windows of estate agents' offices and saw that my £600 wouldn't get me in the door. Even Earl's Court, where Australian and Russian accents echoed from the off-licences, was out of my price range. London rents were five times those of Montreal and salaries were lower. In Oxford I had never taken time to observe the job ads posted in the windows of the employment agencies. *Secretary £11,000. Bookkeeper £16,000.* How could such meagre wages pay for London housing? Being an Oxford student had shielded me from the contradictions of British society, its class divisions amplified by an overblown real estate market.

Life would be easier in Montreal, yet I had no desire to return. My longings were for Leonie, Catherine, Alex, Yugoslavia and Berlin, and a post-Cold War condition whose Central European heart seemed to offer a kind of hope. I could not allow the Atlantic Ocean to slip between me and my desires. Next morning, opening my eyes to the realization that Oxford would not be mine for much longer, I walked to Gloucester Green and bought a ticket to London to try again to find somewhere to live.

"At least this time I haven't caught you kissing a woman," a hearty voice said.

Farida wore a low-cut yellow blouse that enhanced the warmth of her brown skin. Her rumpled, glowing appearance betrayed her early-morning return from a night in London. "I'm being rusticated," I blurted.

"I heard. It's unfair, but it wasn't terribly clever of you to provoke those dinosaurs."

"I'm going to work in London and save my money to travel to Eastern Europe to research the last two chapters of my thesis," I replied in a defensive rush.

"I take it you'll be living in East London? About a decade ago the artists moved out there and began to pioneer civilization in the wilderness."

I pulled out my thick A-to-Z. Farida pointed out the neighbourhoods where I should look for housing. I realized they were the same districts I had stumbled through with Alex and Colin. The thought gave me a kind of comfort. I looked up from the A-to-Z. In a vestigial D.Phil. student impulse, I asked Farida about her thesis.

"I submitted last week! I'm waiting for my viva and working with a Bosnia solidarity group in London. There are thousands of women and girls who are helpless because the men they depended on were murdered at Srebrenica."

Her intimacy with the world about which I aspired to be an expert silenced me. In the summer, when the Srebrenica massacre had taken place, I had been mired in my room by inertia. I left Farida to her swirl of activity, a paragon of the colonial who had acquired knowledge of every sort by moving to the imperial centre. When I got off the CityLink at Marble Arch, I rode the Central Line east to Bethnal Green. I came up out of the Tube amid robed, bearded South Asian men who crossed the streets in busy formation. I found an estate agent, went in and, softening my voice to mute my accent, asked about flats. "A flat in Befnaw Green cost you ninety quid a week, mate," a young man said. "But we ain't got nuffin' now. Try further north, in Hackney."

I left "Befnaw Green," where the cockneys who pronounced

the neighbourhood's name in this way lived among throngs of Bangladeshis and Pakistanis, Nigerians and Ghanians, Cypriots both Greek and Turkish, Turks from Turkey and now refugees from Bosnia, Kosovo, and Sierra Leone. I walked up Mare Street. A British Rail line ensconced on top of a three-storey-high embankment of sooted Victorian brick ran parallel to the street. I turned left and walked down the middle of the street that ran under the embankment, keeping clear of the raised, railed, piss-smelling sidewalks. On the other side of the embankment, I entered a secret corner of a neighbourhood, bounded by Regent's Canal to the south, London Fields Park to the north, the elevated railway line to the east and, to the west, by council flats of Soviet grimness. The main street, Broadway Market, was lined by older, lower businesses, most of them boarded up. I found an estate agent, went in and was told that a flat was available. It cost eighty-five pounds a week.

I followed the agent, a shambling, blond, balding man, into the street. By contrast with the boarded-up shops, it was Oxford that was unreal. I was being rusticated to reality.

The agent inserted a key into a hole in a blank wooden board next to an off-licence. The board swung back, revealing a dark corridor barely wider than my shoulders. The agent slapped at the wall until a pale light came on. I followed him down the corridor. At the back of the building he pushed another blank board. It opened and we stepped onto a fire escape-like wrought iron catwalk that twisted down into a subterranean yard: dozens of paint cans, lengths of frayed wood, a junked stove, shattered furniture. Weaving through the debris, the agent unlocked a door. I stepped into a low-roofed basement paved with all-weather carpeting. A kitchenette, a fridge, and a table occupied one corner, there was a sofa and two chairs and, behind a curtain, a double bed. The bathroom was next to the bed. The sole window, grated and curtained, looked out at the littered yard.

"It'll be gone before the end of the day."

"I'll take it," I said.

"Then I need to see your money."

We went back up to the street. The agent stepped into the off-licence to introduce me to Husain, who would be my landlord. "You want a big fridge, you tell me. The Turkish people want a big fridge so they can put in a whole sheep."

Back in his office, the estate agent explained that though prices were announced by the week, contracts were drawn up by the month, on the marginally extortionate assumption of four and a half weeks to the month. Sundry other charges brought my monthly rent to £390. To secure the flat, I must provide a void cheque to set up a direct debit, and pay the first and last month's rent in cash before the end of the day. I needed £780. Leaving the agent the void cheque, I followed his directions and rode a bus to a Barclay's machine in Whitechapel, where I withdrew £600. In desperation, I put my Canadian banking card in the machine. It worked. Taking this unexpected technological collaboration as a positive omen, I withdrew £200 from my Canadian account, cleaning out most of my $500 balance. When I returned to the estate agent's office, a young South Asian couple was sitting at his desk. "I'm sorry, the gentleman's returned," the agent said as I came in the door. "The flat's taken."

The couple looked disconsolate as I counted out £780 in cash.

We signed the lease. The agent handed me a large key for the door to the street and a small one for the flat. In place of the surrendered key to the storage bin in Leon's co-op, I now had a London key of my own.

The hours ticked down towards next month's rent. I must find a job.

Employment agencies had vanished since I had reached Bethnal Green. Feeling dazed, as though this day were stretching out into the distorted duration of a transatlantic flight, I took the Central Line west to Notting Hill Gate, then scoured this prosperous district until I found an employment agency. I was glad that I had cut my hair and was wearing a sports shirt with a collar. A brown-skinned young woman dressed in a formal blue blouse spoke to me in an English accent that was less posh than an Oxford accent yet more middle-class than the estate agent's cockney. "Are we looking for something clerical, then?" She typed at a desktop computer. "Got a spot of education? Fancy data entry? Paddington Health Authority needs data entry clerks." She pronounced the position as "clark." "Start tomorrow morning, can we?"

This was too sudden. "I have to get my accommodation straightened out. Could I start the day after?"

"Let's see." She made a phone call. Yes, I could start the day after. My breath went short. I was not ready for this. Yet as the cheerful young woman went over the agency contract, assuring me that my lack of legal permission to work in the United Kingdom was no obstacle, I saw that I would need every working day I could get. Jobs were easy to find in London, but the job you found might not pay your rent. This was the reverse of Montreal, where rent was negligible and jobs were scarce. By the time the agency had deducted its fee from my hourly wage, I would make £750 a month. My rent would consume half my income. The advantage of being sent in by an agency was that I got paid weekly; by Friday I would have a few pounds to pad my depleted wallet.

When I returned to Oxford it was dark. I saw no one I knew, as though decades had spun by and my time there belonged to the remote past. I walked to my room and packed my belongings in the suitcase I used for transatlantic flights. With the suitcase in one hand and my Toshiba case in the other, I would walk to Gloucester Green in the morning and leave Oxford. Short of cutlery for my new flat, I slipped into the kitchen and stole knives and forks, two plastic plates and a pair of mugs. Salvatore steals motorcycles, I thought, and I steal cutlery. That was how far I had fallen.

TWENTY-EIGHT

HAVING DREAMED OF BERLIN, I resigned myself to London. By the time I came up out of the Tube at Bethnal Green at the end of the day, the streets were dark and empty. The pinnacle of the distant, pyramid-capped spire of Canary Wharf emitted its pulsing flash. I headed north, turned off Mare Street and walked down the middle of the underpass beneath the railway embankment. As I emerged from the tunnel, two figures who looked nearly as tall as the tower blocks that reared up on the horizon crowded in on me. They grabbed me and rammed me against a brick wall. "Oi, gimme your wallet, mate."

"Oi, this toff thinks he can barge into our local. What you lookin' for, mate?"

"He's lookin' for his wallet, to give to us. Ha!"

I couldn't give them my wallet because one of them had thrown a tackle on me that pinned my arms against my sides. I heard the rising intonation of West African accents cut through laid-on London slang. I was too stunned to struggle or speak. We rocked against the brick like a necking couple while the second man told me to hand over my money. "I haven't got any money ..."

The slow-motion wrestling continued. "I'm not going to the pub. I live here!"

"You expect us to belief a cockamamie like that?"

"Who's your landlord, then?" The hug tightened one intimidating notch.

"Husain," I gasped. "From the off-licence."

The second man straightened up to his full height. "You're not English. Where you from?"

"Canada."

"Is that so? Oi, that's a good place, in't? Me da' brother in Toronto says they're not as rude as English people. They're polite about their prejudices."

"We're very polite racists," I laughed, startled by the turn this mugging had taken.

"You live here, you pay us a pound. I need a quid for me meter. Gimme a quid for the meter. You our neighbour. That make us mates, don't it?"

I covered my remaining cash with my left hand while I shook out a coin. When I handed him the pound, the man in front shrugged his shoulders.

"Aw, you didn't have to do that, neighbour. That's very kind. A good evening to you."

I fled into the darkness.

In the mornings, I made a long commute on foot and two different underground trains to reach my computer terminal at the Paddington Health Authority by eight-thirty. My job was to vet hospital requisitions and print them for pick-up by the warehouse. I had to check items requested by different health institutions as they appeared on my screen. If a hospital ordered thirty-five surgical masks, and they came in packages of twenty, an order that said "35" would dispatch seven hundred masks to the hospital. I had to check the packaging and change the "35" to "2." The potential for confusion was multiplied by the possibility of sending an order to the wrong institution. My first morning at work, a young woman from Nova Scotia with a bleached-blond crewcut, who had arrived in London too late to savour the punk scene, was bawled out by the supervisor for sending the Grey Nuns Nursing Home two thousand condoms. "What the hell do you expect the Grey Nuns to do with two thousand condoms? Bloody Yanks! Always mucking things up."

A stocky man in a suit worn askew, who spoke with a north-of-England accent, the supervisor was incapable of stepping into our room — where twenty computer terminals sat in five rows — without making a derogatory comment about my accent or that of the girl from Nova Scotia. He made no comment on the accents of the Australians, New Zealanders, Irishmen, middle-aged Indian or Pakistani women, or young Croats and Poles, who sat at other terminals. Their various musics twined around each other unmolested, mingling with that of the Grenadian mail boy, and the Scottish warehouse foreman who came in to pick up the requisitions. My Oxford colleagues had refuted national stereotypes; they had been Russian Canadians or Jewish Englishmen or Greek Australians or Muslim Zimbabweans, Japanese women who were independent, Americans who had grown up under Communism. In the Health Authority, everybody conformed to type. The Aussies and Kiwis were fair-haired and muscular and talked about rugby, the Irishmen were drunks, the Scotsman was dour, the Indians were all named Mehta or Patel, the Poles and Croats were fire-breathing Catholic nationalists, the other Canadian was subservient to the styles of a more powerful culture. Two chapters short of holding a degree from an institution of educational privilege — a fact I revealed to no one — I had cast myself, in Leon's terms, as an intellectual on the factory floor, or at least in the clerical pool. Yet social class, as was brought home to me by daily interaction with Brits who lived their lives in council flats, applied to people who were born in a society. I was simply one more colonial who had found temporary work in London.

I had been in Hackney for two weeks when the pub down the street lowered the Union Jack and replaced it with a flag that consisted of a thin red cross on a white background. I asked about the change at the Hackney Hookers Club, a cockney hangout whose members fished in Regent's Canal. "That's the flag of England. Seeing we're English, it don't make sense to have a flag that's for the friggin' Scots and Welshmen. They can go fuck themselves, that's what we say."

For the first time since the Quebec Referendum, I felt my thesis nudge at my mind. But I wasn't ready to resume writing. I wrote letters to Zed and Leon, and carefully worded letters to my parents in which I explained that I had moved to London to work in the public health system while completing my thesis. I bought a long-distance phone card from Husain and walked to the pay phone down the street.

"Why do you phone me?"

"You're my girlfriend. I love you."

"You don't love me. And it is obvious I do not want to be your girlfriend." Then, as though she had said more than she had intended, "What are you doing in London?"

"I have a job in the health sys—"

"One of those stupid temporary jobs." As though compensating for her own harshness, she said in a teasing voice, "Give me your phone number. If I am bored you can come to Bonn for a weekend."

On Friday afternoons, the temps received our cheques from the mail boy, who sang, "Save it for a rainy day ..." as he placed the envelopes on our desks. My third Friday, I rode the Central Line to Tottenham Court Road, walked to the British Museum and stumbled on the British Library Reading Room. There was a desk where one could apply to be a reader. I asked about this; a prickly woman told me that the Reading Room was for serious scholars. I opened my wallet and produced the University of Oxford photo card that identified me as *Graduate / Hamdaw College / Politics*. "Well that's rather different, then," the woman said.

In five minutes, I had a reading card. Stowing my pack in a wooden locker, I edged into the area beneath the dome. A tension drained out of my body, the library's acceptance inoculating me against Oxford's rejection. The dome opened up like a flower of possibility. I filled in a slip, ordered a history of Yugoslavia, and sat down at one of the flat tables bunched in arcs around the circulation desk, aware that beneath this dome Karl Marx had written *Das Kapital*. My reading in Oxford's libraries had been enforced; in London, reading restored me to myself. The next week, I was at the lockers on my way out of the reading room when a small woman hissed at me. I saw that it was Susan.

"I was just talking about you with Alex," Susan said, gripping my wrist. "Let's go for coffee."

We walked past the white Doric columns of the museum façade and down the marble steps. The touts who recruited tourists for bus tours of London were ambling homeward. Beyond the wrought iron gate, on the other side of Great Russell Street, was the Russian and Eastern European bookstore. "I came here with Alex and Colin," I said.

"I came here with Alex after that. He bought all sorts of Russian poetry."

"Which is now stored on top of my stuff in Leon's co-op."

"Isn't it funny how you're all still mixed up together?" She led me into a redbrick café three doors over from the bookstore. Susan wore a navy blue silk blouse. Beneath her gleaming energy, she was a demure presence. She had gone to the British Library to research Victorian costumes for an advertising campaign. When our tea arrived, I observed the taut curve of her shoulder as she poured her milk. My mind clogged with a vision of Alex's huge hands closing over her small breasts, which telescoped into Pia's more ample breasts, then into the couple whose screams Alex and I had witnessed on Ship Street.

"Alex phones me every month or so." She bit her lip. "He gets driven to work by a chauffeur who's also his bodyguard."

I struggled to imagine Alex in a suit, in Moscow, with a chauffeur. What cloverleaf of fate had spiralled him up to such heights while I scraped by in a basement? Why did the thought of his success make me feel guilty? "My mother works in a bank," I murmured, "but not like that."

Susan's smile was pitying, reminding me that back in Canada she was a Rosedale girl who wouldn't have wasted a second having coffee with me. Only here in England did we share a nationality. "You know he phoned Hamdaw to look for you? Can you give me your phone number? He needs to talk to his mates. The women he's seeing are rubbish. He was always flirting with women. Like that German girl at Hamdaw."

"Christa? That was utterly innocent —"

"Sometimes, it's not about infidelity destroying a relation-ship, but about flirting wearing it down." She straightened up. "What are you doing in London, Kevin?"

I let her drag it out of me.

"Oh, you're a temp." Her mouth closed in a small line,

reminding me that for the Canadian elite London was a playground. The silver tower of Canary Wharf, taunting me with its winks each time I came up out of the Tube at Bethnal Green, had been built by Canadians. Susan's parents may not have wanted her to leave Toronto, yet her choice of rebellion had confirmed the patterns of her class. "I asked Alex if he wanted me to ship him his Russian library and he said, 'What for? I'm in Moscow, I can get all the Russian books I want.' I'm sure that's true, but when he got this job the first thing he said was that he wanted a place for his books. I wish you guys were in touch! Why don't you use email?"

She took out her agenda. She copied Leon and Alex's phone numbers from a list of numbers that covered the front pages onto a page at the back, which she tore off and handed to me. She opened the agenda to today's date so that I could write my phone number. When we left the café, I realized that the only number that had not been divulged was Susan's own.

TWENTY-NINE

MY MAIL WAS PUSHED through a slot in the door to the street and lay on the floor of the passage until I picked it up. Most of my correspondence was unwelcome: telephone bills or formal confirmation of my rustication (*Rustication is one of the most serious sanctions Oxford administers ...*). Then one morning I trod on a brown A4 envelope addressed in a cramped British hand. Inside was a postcard of a square in Central Europe: *Where ARE you?* I read on the back. *I'm at Hamdaw and you don't have a pigeonhole. The porters say that if I leave you this card, they'll forward it. What's going on? Are you in Siberia? Love, Catherine.*

I took the postcard to work. All day I thought about it sitting inside my daypack. That evening, I dialled the number Catherine had written at the bottom. The phone was answered by a young man with a posh accent. I had called a North Oxford graduate house. When Catherine came to the phone, we asked each other questions at the same time. "I can't come to Oxford. I've been rusticated. Will you come to London?"

"Of course I'll come to London, Kevin!" Her voice, which I remembered as neutral, sounded audibly American. "You've been what?"

That Friday after work, I waited at Marble Arch for the City-Link to come in. A poised, discreetly rounded figure, trimmer than I remembered, bobbed down from the bus. Her pale brown hair was short, barely covering her ears. Her face had an inchoate appearance, as though it were taking on a new shape; her skin, purged of its greyness, looked diaphanous by contrast with her wide, rubicund mouth. She reached up, demanding a full snog, as the young people in the data entry room said. "Kevin Carmichael," she said, in a low voice that penetrated the din of buses and black taxi cabs that raced past on Park Lane, "you are a dangerous man! My housemates say you must have done something truly evil to be rusticated."

Uncertain where to go, we wandered down Park Lane. The embassy of the Republic of Angola looked out over eight lanes of traffic; a red star and an enormous machete-and-half-cog-wheel blazed from the building's façade. Catherine looked startled. "Sometimes I think my world is too limited. All I know is Eastern Europe. I worry I'll be boring for you." She bit her lip. "It's obvious I've just been dumped, isn't it?"

"You told me you were coming out of a relationship."

"I couldn't believe I was saying that! Now that I'm completely out of it, I think I need to be single for a while."

Unsure of our boundaries, I suggested that we walk through Grosvenor Square into Soho. She didn't know London well, and was charmed by the narrow streets. Over dinner — fish and a potato for me, vegetarian soup and salad for Catherine — I gave her an imprecise account of my rustication, then told her about East London. "Would you like to come and see it?"

"I'll come and see it, then I'll take the bus back to Oxford."

We got on the Central Line at Tottenham Court Road. From the moment Catherine's feet struck the wooden cross-struts of the antique escalator that carried us up to the street at Bethnal Green, she smiled in a way that made me feel her happiness as a rekindling which banished the threat of greyness. We walked north into Hackney. "This seems nicer than the rest of England. Nicer because it's not nice." Looking through Catherine's eyes, I noticed the shuttered factories of sooty brick, the yellow double-decker D6 bus whose destination panel read *Isle of Dogs*, the groups of robed Bengali men, the interracial couples. I pointed to the passage beneath the railway embankment.

"That's where you live, Kevin?" Catherine gambolled ahead of me. She walked down the middle of the sunken street with the raised sidewalks on either side.

She disappeared into the darkness. A scream tore the night.

I ran, fear smacking down like a hammer. I came up the far side of the underpass to see Catherine's running shoes being dragged into the darkness by two very large men.

"We ain't going to hurt you, miss. Just give us your money ..."

"Hey, mates!" I shouted, my voice hoarse. "It's me, from Husain's basement. That's my girlfriend!"

They straightened up. "Oi! It's the Canadian bloke!"

"She's your girlfriend? Why dint you tell us, mate?"

"Here, neighbour," I said, dipping into my wallet. "Take a quid for the meter."

I handed the coin to the man on the left.

"Next time, miss, just tell us who you are. You won't haf no trouble from the likes of us."

I reached for Catherine, waiting for her to fall into my arms in a heap. She turned on her heel and promenaded with me hand-in-hand. When we had reached the corner of my street, she murmured, "You *are* a dangerous man, Kevin. Nobody in Oxford is friends with muggers."

Her expression became dubious when I opened the battered door and remained so as she surveyed the junk-strewn yard. We went down the metal stairs, across the yard and into the basement. "This feels safer," Catherine said, taking in the single large room. "Hold me!"

I hugged her. A tremor ran through her body. I looked down; she stared at me with a desolate expression. "That was a little frightening. Though in a strange way, in all my adventures, I'm never frightened. I always know I'll survive." She took a step back. "This summer I was so happy to go back to Leipzig and find I still had a home in the East. I decided to stay there as long as Andreas wanted me. I got an old bicycle, I cleaned flats for money and didn't depend on my parents." She looked away. "Andreas finally kicked me out. He wanted to finish his Magister —"

"I haven't seen Leonie in months." My voice was hoarse. "She went to Italy by herself."

"She's still your girlfriend?" Before I could reply, she said, "Do you want to sleep with me?"

"Yes."

We made love on the bed behind the curtain at the back of the flat. We stayed in bed for most of the weekend. Catherine's pleasure filled me with joy. Her slowness in rising to orgasm, which felt like teasing even though it wasn't, refashioned my body as her accomplice. We thrashed together for longer than I remembered thrashing with anyone. As though it were the product of her Quakerism or her vegetarianism, or the antidote to the geographical arabesques that embroidered her life, Catherine's lovemaking was of unvarnished simplicity. Once I became aroused, her desire folded up inside her to find its slow satisfaction. She was pleased to lie back and be plundered. I relished her coy, barely detectable responses, pushing myself to the verge of orgasm and hanging there thrust upon thrust until the almost disconcerting imperviousness of Catherine's tranquility was staved open by her belly-deep moans. I felt more certain than I had at any point since my first nights with Camille that I was in love. Yet now that I was older, love felt less pathological, idealized and desperate. I would never tire of Catherine's bottomless intelligence, her endless fund of experiences in places where the world was shuddering. "I'm not even thirty," she said, late that night, "and if I wrote my memoirs they'd be ten thousand pages long."

From the beginning I saw that, even though I had thought of my listless introversion of the year before as a depression, I was outspoken, a little loud, an upbeat personality. Projected against Catherine's battle with welling darkness, I came across as a lively fellow. She remade me as an enthusiastic personality whose zeal dispersed her inertia.

After our first few weekends together – Catherine worked on her thesis in Oxford during the week – a nugget of hard knowledge dropped into my brain. I understood, though I barely acknowledged the insight, that Catherine would never satisfy my sexual needs. As sexually liberated as she had become in her passage across the old East, as much as I loved her roundedness and the delight with which she responded to my rampaging over her body, her passivity did not give me quite enough to wrestle with. Her depressiveness fed her need for her lover's body to ignite hers. If I wanted a woman who delighted in riding on top of me, who took my erection in her mouth and sucked me dry between deliciously menacing teeth, that woman was not Catherine. In fact, it was Leonie. I suppressed this thought. Catherine meant soothing happiness. Leonie meant anxiety and turmoil.

We worried out Hackney's charms: the winding back alleys of blocks of post-war flats, the shining six-storey-high globes of the gas canisters along Regent's Canal that inflated and shrank within their vast steel cages like immense spaceships filling their lungs and exhaling, the facelessness of buildings that were abandoned, or buildings that looked abandoned, but sheltered whole families or small clattering factories, the unfamiliar African or South Asian squashes or tubers in the corner groceries, the cockney specialties, such as salted eels and jellied eels, announced by shops that were stocked with catches pulled out of the canal by the Hackney Hookers. We sat in parks, where young West Indian men from the tower blocks played games of soccer, and read for hours, trading the Eastern European novels we scavenged in second-hand bookstores: Mikhail Bulgakov, Ismail Kadare, Ivan Klíma, Christa Wolf, Ivo Andrić, Andrey Platonov. Catherine, I saw, was my Berlin, the alpha and omega of my quest for the old East. One afternoon, lowering her book, she said, "Thank you for introducing me to Hackney, Kevin. It's brought back something I lost when I left Leipzig. My parents hated me living in Leipzig, and they hated Andreas. For the first time ever, they cut me off. But I survived! That's why it was important for me to go back there last summer, after my parents tried to break up my relationship by sending me to Oxford. My parents control everything except who I sleep with. That's the one area of my life where I make the decisions."

"Why do they want to keep you in limbo?"

"Not in limbo, in childhood." She blushed. "Kevin, if you ever meet them, please don't tell them I told you this, but do you know what they get me for Christmas? Colouring books and little dolls! Presents for a six-year-old girl! When I go to Belgrade, they say,

'How's school, Catherine?' As though I were a child. Their solution to me living in Leipzig was to send me to school –"

"You didn't apply to Oxford?"

She shook her head. "My parents know my supervisor. He told them he was willing to take me on, even though he doesn't think K.R. is a very original poet. He's interested in K.R.'s circle, in his friend Sergei, but for him, it's all in how you count the syllables –"

"The great syllable-counter!" I said. "You've got the same supervisor as Alex!"

"Who's Alex?"

"Alex is the reason I got rusticated."

I had never expressed it like this before – as I had imagined it the night I held a microphone in my fist. As the mist deepened between the tower blocks and two boys slewed through the soccer game on low-slung bicycles, one of them deflecting a shot with his handlebars, Catherine heard the story of Kevin, Leon, and Alex, the graduate staircase at Hamdaw College and the fishbowl quad that crowned it, the arguments between the London Jew and the son of a Russian defector that were so furious they contained a kind of love, while the Canadian served as witness, on the margin and wanting, as Canadians often did, both to claim privileged knowledge and keep his distance. The Canadian assumed the emotions of this engagement as his own, which meant that when the Londoner had a pint too many, as Londoners were wont to do, his friend, still colonial in his reflexive response to an Englishman, not only failed to argue against a foolish prank that the Englishman proposed, which exposed the jealousies underlying the friendship between the Londoner and the Russian, but collaborated in misdirecting the Russian émigré's protegé, a beautiful English public school boy, with the consequence that the boy was run over by a truck. To make matters worse, when the public school boy awoke from his concussion in the middle of Parks Road, rather than taking him to the hospital, the Londoner, the Canadian, and the Russian had taken him to a pub, where he drank a pint and then dropped dead before their eyes. "It traumatized us all. But if I'm going to feel guilty, in addition to being traumatized," I concluded, "I don't know if I should feel more guilty because we caused the accident, or because we took Colin to a pub instead of a hospital, or because we never told Alex, and he still doesn't know why Colin was in the wrong part of Oxford that night. And Colin is dead, while Alex is still suffering."

"Making that speech at the party was your way of acknowledging that." Catherine looked at the grass. "I'm glad you did that, Kevin, even if it got you rusticated. It was your way of showing remorse." She took my hand. That night she murmured, "I think someone should tell Alex what happened."

THIRTY

"IN LENINGRAD I HAD a Soviet boyfriend, and a Lada and a Soviet driver's licence. My boyfriend lived on Vasilevsky Island, across the Neva River from my parents' residence. If I spent the night anywhere other than the residence there would be a diplomatic incident. They raised the bridges across the Neva at two a.m. to let the big ships through. I'd leave my boyfriend's apartment with minutes to spare. I'd get to the first bridge and they would already be raising it, I would race the workers to the next bridge to get across before it was raised —"

As we walked south through Hackney, I thought about Catherine halfway across a bridge between her Soviet lover and her State Department family. I took her arm as we hurried under the railway embankment. To our astonishment, we emerged into a glistening channel of light. The boarded-up shops had been opened. Floodlights and lanterns had been strung along Broadway Market, from Regent's Canal to London Fields. Young women who wore mauve batik blouses and young men with dyed orange hair paraded beneath the lights. It was an East London Art Happening. Husain had opened the off-licence late to catch the business; only the Hookers' pub sulked in darkness. Inside the abandoned shop across the street from my front door the walls were blurred by smoke from burning incense and hung with portraits of topless young men. In the shop next door, young white women with dreadlocks hosted a collection of South Asian-inspired art.

A face in the crowd: a young woman hanging on the arm of a tall, tousle-haired man. "Oi, Kevin." It was Farida. We stopped on the sidewalk. Catherine looked puzzled. As I spoke, I saw Farida's boyfriend write me off as a tiresome Yank. Cross-couple complicity urged Farida and me to spill our news fast. "Pia's getting married ...!"

"And how are you?" I asked.

"I'm done. I'm Dr. Farida. But I'm unemployed. I've moved in with my mate." She tugged her boyfriend's arm. "Have you finished yet?"

"Six chapters written," I said, before the current of the crowd pulled us in opposite directions.

"Kevin," Catherine said, "what kind of accent was that?" I told her. "All these Commonwealth countries!" she said. "I never believed the Commonwealth was real until you told me how you followed your friend because you were Canadian. Shouldn't you just get over having been colonies?" She leaned into me. "I love this light! I am desirous, Kevin."

We left the street and hurried to my apartment. I squeezed Catherine's flesh morsel by morsel. She writhed, her breath sliced into hurried bursts. "Kevin ... Now ..."

As I hitched up my hips, the telephone rang.

Leonie. At this time of night, it could be no one else. Catherine reached up and grabbed my wrist. I pulled away and jumped off the bed. What would I say to her? My distended sexual organ swung limp. The receiver felt cold in my hand.

"There's nobody to fucking talk to," a rough-edged male voice said. "I can't buy somebody to talk to. I can buy food, I can buy women. That's the Russian idea of capitalism; you get a monopoly, you kill the fucking competition, then you bilk the punters ..."

Untangling the telephone cord with my left hand, I made my way back through the curtain. Catherine sat naked on the bed, her pout dispelled by curiosity. Stretching the cord to its limit, I climbed back onto the mattress and kneeled in front of her. "How did you learn how to be a banker, Alex?"

Catherine raised her eyebrows like Leonid Brezhnev. With a teasing smile, she tweaked my dangling penis. As Alex's voice filled my ear, she began to caress me. My breath shortened as the condom filled out beneath the tug of Catherine's hand. She hoisted herself forward, reached around my waist and pulled me towards her.

"Hey, Kevin. You still there, man?"

Catherine yanked herself into a canted-up posture, reached out with both hands and guided me into her at a tilt we'd never attained before. I groaned.

"You all right, man? Fuck, you sound like you've had more to drink than me!"

A wild, unfamiliar light expanded Catherine's grey eyes. I gasped at her tiny, deliberate contractions. The telephone cord biting into my shoulder, I said, "Do you like it there?"

"Everything's *stuff*. Before Russians were about soul and humanity. Now everything's porn and junk. I spend the whole fucking day watching numbers on screens. My clients are these Mafia guys with women hanging over them and fucking body-guards who stand next to them at dinner. The crazy poets and painters my uncle introduced me to ... they're all drunk or dying of cancer. My uncle's dead. He died three months after I got here."

"I'm really sorry, Alex." I meant it. I wished I could stop people in his life from dying. I wished I could give him back the art he craved. "Your other ... uncle ... he's still ... alive?"

"He's in fucking Minsk. Fucking Belarus, man! It's like being dead. Hey – it sounds like you're hyperventilating. Are you smoking up?"

"I'm okay." I reached down to explore Catherine's breasts; she reached up and clasped my hand. "Did you and Leon get your books into the bin? Hey, once you get out of that crazy world you're in –"

"Don't you get it, man? The world I'm in *is* the fucking world!"

"I want you in my crazy world," Catherine whispered, undulating with a slowness that reeled my heart up through my veins.

"Alex," I gasped, "do you have the key?"

"How the fuck am I supposed to remember? I think Leon took it."

The coiled phone cord ate into my shoulder. The cord stretched to its limit, the phone flew out of my hand, ripped away over my shoulder and hit the floor. I cried out; Catherine moaned. I was too depleted to move. When I got up to replace the phone in the receiver, my legs wobbled, and the line was dead.

"Oh, Moscow!" Catherine said. "I'm so nostalgic. You know I have to go back there? My dad wants me to look at K.R.'s papers."

"Do you have money to go to Moscow?"

"My parents will pay. I explain everything to my mom and she takes it to my dad and he makes the decision. I know it's not a very mature way to live when you're turning twenty-nine –"

"What's going to happen when he retires?"

"The State Department will never let my dad retire!" Her pride and innocence startled me. "Some things last forever, Kevin. My parents will always be representing America in the East."

"Don't you deserve your own forever?"

She looked me in the eyes. "You don't have any right to ask me this, Kevin. Don't you have a girlfriend?"

"I haven't seen her in months." As soon as I spoke the words, I regretted my defensiveness, realizing I had missed my cue. What I should have said was: I have a girlfriend and it's you.

As I came in the door on Monday evening, my foot slipped on an envelope addressed in a florid British hand to *Mr. Kevin Carmichael, Esq.* Inside I found a thick white card, bordered in black: *A gathering to celebrate the life of Isaac Zamenhof (1911-1997).* Rain or shine, the celebrants would meet next Saturday at Karl Marx's tomb in Highgate Cemetery. I felt overwhelmed by sadness, yet touched, surprised, flattered, and relieved that Leon had tracked me down. That evening I phoned Catherine, who said she would be honoured to accompany me to the memorial.

I was sitting on the couch, thinking about Leon's father's life, when the phone rang. Touched that Catherine had called back, I said, "Yes, my dear ..."

"How do you know it is me?"

My chest tightened. "I've been waiting for you to call."

"You are not a man. A man would betray me with other women."

"Maybe I've been doing that, too."

"I do not believe you. You are bourgeois. Come to Bonn this weekend and I will make you less bourgeois."

"This weekend I have to go to a memorial service." A long silence. "Maybe the next weekend?"

"Yes, the next weekend you will come."

THIRTY-ONE

CATHERINE AND I GOT on the Tube, transferred to the Northern
Line at Tottenham Court Road, and proved ourselves inept Londoners by riding the wrong train through the fork at Camden
Town. We were already late. Catherine loved the idea of waking
early on weekends, yet she experienced waking less as a return
to consciousness than as a nerve-wracking journey back from a
sad, rainy place where consciousness was unbearable. Rarely
able to summon the energy to sit up before ten a.m., she was
soothed when I went upstairs to the off-licence and bought bread,
eggs, tomatoes, orange juice, and the weekend papers from
Husain. I greeted her with a full breakfast. Today, I had tried to
speed her along. We needed to leave early, and I needed to prepare her for the news that next weekend I was going to Bonn.
We dressed in our best black clothes: she in a jacket and slacks,
pillaged from her sub-fusc. I, with my formal clothes still in
Leon's bin, in a dark suit rented from a Bengali shop. Taking
the wrong fork at Camden Town put us farther behind schedule.
We rode south again, got off and waited for a High Barnet train.
The hike from Archway Station to the Highgate Cemetery was

longer than we had anticipated. We had not visited hilly North London before. After Oxford's manicured gardens, the cemetery's tattered vegetation felt un-English. Shrubs grew untrained, the paths were shadowed by the leafy branches of tall trees. Isolated headstones stood ringed with weeds. We passed family tombs, each with an inverted V over the door. Up ahead, the sombre visage of Karl Marx reigned over a dark-clad gathering.

"It's so good to see him again!" Catherine said. "I feel like I'm in the Soviet Union."

We were greeted by an attractive young woman in a black vest. Uncertain of the etiquette for introducing a friend's ex-girlfriend, I said, "Catherine, this is Emily."

"It's brilliant that you're here. I suppose you weren't expecting to see me? Leon and I had that rough patch. Quite a *long* rough patch. But we're fine now. In fact, I'm the one who tracked down your address in darkest Hackney. I told Leon he had to invite his Oxford mates. He's not very good at that sort of thing ... Do take a program."

We ambled towards the Marx statue.

"Good old Marx!" a tall elderly man said. "He was right about most things." He brushed back disorderly white hair that had fallen inside his glasses. "You see that man over there?" He pointed to an elderly gent who was receiving a program from Emily. "That's Michael Foot."

"The Labour Party leader?"

"Ex-leader, yes. Isaac would have done a more convincing job if he had been willing to compromise ... Isaac and I fought the fascists in Spain! I lost sight of him during the retreat from Málaga. Stukas were buzzing overhead, strafing us. I was sure I'd lost him. We met in Valencia, later, and had a grand old reunion."

"Sir, did you know Kasja Rothman?"

"Not the way Isaac did. He knew her particularly well!"

"And Norman Bethune?"

"Are you Canadian? Is that where your accent's from? Canadians don't realize what a dreadful fellow Bethune was. I've never met a man whose concern for others owed so much to his own ego."

Michael Foot arrived, distracting the old gent. The greyness that hung over the shrubbery was inert, with a throat-coating London blend of mist and pollution. I spotted Leon standing alongside a woman in her fifties whose jaw resembled his. I clapped him on the shoulder and introduced him to Catherine. His eyes beseeched me to clarify which of my girlfriends I'd brought with me.

"Catherine grew up in Moscow, Leningrad, and Belgrade," I supplied.

Catherine's diplomatic instincts came alive. "It's wonderful to see a Marx statue."

"Me da' wouldn't have wanted his service anywhere else."

"You must be tired," I said.

"I'm knackered. It was particularly difficult at the end. Still, I'm very glad I moved in with him. I'd never had so much time to talk to him."

"More time than we older ones got," the woman at his side said.

"Have you heard? I've got a post. At Queen Mary College, down on the Mile End Road, where my uncle was the last Communist councillor."

"We'll be neighbours! I live near there."

"Emily and I are staying in her flat in Notting Hill Gate. Fortunately, the Central Line goes straight across."

He would be living in West London and working in East

London, and I would be doing the reverse. Was it necessary for him to underline that our paths need never cross?

"I'm sorry to ask you this now," I said, though I wasn't. "The night that you and Alex put his books in the storage bin, who took the key?"

"Alex did, of course. I cleared my stuff out yonks ago."

Friends of his father surrounded him. Catherine slid her arm through mine. "It's weird how close you are to those two guys."

"We're mates, as the English say."

"I thought I was your mate. Don't you mate with me?" We walked away, then stopped and turned around. Marx's head floated on a foam of white hair that rode on a sea of black jackets. Catherine's mood grew sombre. "They're all so old. It'll never be like that again."

The day's grey became tinged with darkness. Catherine huddled against me. I suggested we go to a movie. An Eastern European film festival was running in Hammersmith. After making labyrinthine connections on the underground, we arrived in time to see *Colonel Redl* by the Hungarian director István Szabó. Redl, a peasant boy of mixed ethnic background, falls in love with the image of the Austro-Hungarian Emperor Franz Joseph. He writes a poem about his ruler that earns him a scholarship to a military academy. There, he and an aristocratic boy, Kristóf Kubinyi, commit a minor infraction and are beaten together, an experience that bonds them for life. Redl is an incorruptible servant of the Empire; Kubinyi is dissolute and has many mistresses. The only woman with whom Redl is eager to have sex is Kubinyi's sister. Kubinyi, suspecting what has happened, asks Redl a question in slang that the subtitles translated as, "Did you fuck my sister?" As the Austro-Hungarian Empire enters terminal decadence, Redl's code of honour and closeted homosexuality are turned against him, and he is forced to commit suicide. Redl's suicide is both that of the Empire and its ideals of cross-cultural co-operation, and, equally forcefully, his own death, private and unrepeatable.

Afterwards, we wandered the streets in darkness. Catherine, whom I'd never heard utter an obscenity, murmured with a chuckle, "Did you fuck my sister?"

We took the Tube to Notting Hill Gate, where we found a café with antique furniture and pop music playing. As Catherine sipped her vegetarian soup and nibbled at her bean sprout sandwich, I heard a Canadian accent. Alanis Morisette's "You Oughta Know" thudded over the sound system. To my surprise, Catherine knew the words. We murmured them in unison, smiling at each other, until Morisette reached the notorious line where the narrator asks her ex whether he thinks about her when he fucks his new girlfriend. "Don't say that!" Catherine said.

I drew a breath. "Next weekend I'm going to see Leonie. She wants to get rid of me, but we can't let it go without talking in person."

Catherine laid down her spoon. "It goes against everything I believe in, but I don't like this. It makes me nervous."

"It's the only way to reach closure. Then I'll be here for you." I cringed at my own words.

We discussed the trip in calm voices. "Are you looking forward to having sex with her again?" Catherine asked.

I flushed. "I'm looking for closure —"

"Don't lie to me, Kevin. We both know how attractive the Germans can be."

We went back to Hackney. That night, for the first time, Catherine rolled me over onto my back in bed and took my penis in her mouth. She lapped and sucked for a moment, then relapsed onto her side. We lay in the darkness, our breathing too loud. "I'm sorry, Kevin, I can't. Just take me."

On Friday afternoon, I left work with a day backpack and rode the Tube to Heathrow. My Lufthansa flight excavated me from London's depths, bearing me up into Germany's airy expanse. The sun was setting as I arrived at Köln-Bonn. Leonie was loose-limbed and welcoming. As we waltzed through the airport, I realized that at last she had me on her own terms. We sat, side by side in the tram, listening to the clanking of carriages on rails, taking in the shadows of the church spires, the viscous brown of the Rhine, the solidity of the Jugenstil low-rise apartment blocks. She took my hand and placed it between her legs.

In her apartment, she opened a bottle of Italian white wine. "Now we are going to act the way we should act in Poland. It was very stupid of us not to have a nice little one-night stand there. Then the nature of our relationship would be clear."

We finished our wine in bed. She took me in her mouth, making me writhe, then rode on top of me until our flesh was a melted blur and our moans bellowed from a single body. What was going on here was not the resolution of an emotional relationship. I was betraying my girlfriend with a woman with whom I had a strong physical connection. Catherine's needy devotion washed through me. I did not let it interfere with my next erection, my next body-length licking of Leonie's flesh, but I could not ignore it. When Leonie and I said goodbye on Sunday afternoon at the stop for the airport bus, she seemed delighted with her lustful weekend. I pulled her against me hard as I kissed her goodbye. Her wide mouth teased my tongue. I could deny neither the force of the connection I felt to her nor the reality that she would cut me off if I asked to see her on a regular basis. I sat down in the airport bus, the excitement in my flesh evaporating like a trickle of water beneath the hot sun of a Central European summer.

When I entered my basement, I leaned over the phone and dialled Catherine's number. "I'm back," I said.

"Is it over?"

"Yes."

That weekend she came to see me again. Our relationship had become a less romantic, more tenaciously durable beast, capable of containing certain infidelities without cracking. It felt as resilient and twisted as the long marriage into which it might develop.

Spending money I did not have after buying a plane ticket, I invited Catherine to dinner in Islington. Slicing into a cube of tofu, she told me that she had written the first three chapters of her thesis from a different angle, then torn them up. This was the third time she had done this. There had been the historical approach, the biographical approach, and the version that launched straight into textual analysis. "You tore up the manuscript. But you kept the files, right?"

"I deleted them."

"You deleted nine chapters? That's a doctorate!"

"They weren't perfect. I owe it to my parents to write a thesis that is perfect."

Against my will, I remembered Leonie, not her body, but her organized desk, and a paper she had shown me, written in an academic German too dense for me to unravel, that was going to be published in a journal of linguistic theory.

We walked home past silent terraced houses. I did not feel guilty for having visited Leonie — my romantic apprenticeship in the Plateau Mont-Royal had inured me to sexual guilt — but I recognized that I was in the wrong, that Catherine was staying with me because she did not like it when things ended and that at some point I would pay for my self-indulgence. As we entered Hackney, Catherine said, "It's good to be back." She took my hand. We spent the weekend together as we had spent many other weekends in Hackney. Autumn came, then winter. In Oxford, Michaelmas term was more than half over. The year of my rustication had ended, yet my rustication continued. I had neither the money nor the completed thesis to underwrite a return to Oxford. In December, Catherine left for Belgrade to spend three weeks with her parents. "I love Belgrade in the snow!" she said. "Even though it means I don't get tennis lessons from Janko." This was my punishment. Even though she knew that I needed a trip to former Yugoslavia to finish my thesis, she was not inviting me to Belgrade.

Broadway Market was silent over Christmas. Even the eels in Regent's Canal observed a respectful pause, ceasing to plop in the water. When Catherine returned from Belgrade, she said that her father had insisted that she go to Moscow once the weather warmed up. For Christmas, along with dolls and colouring books, she had received an elite library card, awarded to only the most senior Russian researchers, which granted her access to the Moscow archives where K.R.'s private diaries were stored.

"Did you ask for that?"

She shook her head. Her father had pulled strings in Moscow. Her parents expected her to be a superlative researcher, even as they urged her to remain a little girl. I longed to break her out of this lethargic entrapment, to transmit to her my capacity for enthusiasm in a way that would dispel her Great Russian pessimism, her late Habsburg enervation. I longed to pry Catherine away from her parents. "Did you talk to them about putting you on a regular budget and letting you manage your own life?"

THIRTY-TWO

EIGHT WEEKS ON, SIX weeks off. In Oxford, Hilary Term had ended. In Moscow, Catherine's parents had arranged for her to stay with a middle-aged woman named Tatiana Alexandrovna who had an extra bedroom in her flat. Now retired, she had worked as the lead domestic servant during both of the family's postings to Moscow. After Catherine left, I resumed my habit of stopping off at the British Library on my way home. I made hesitant progress on my thesis. I looked forward to the mail that lay in the corridor. Not all of the letters were from Catherine.

Dear Kevin,

Your rustication expired in Michaelmas Term. Auberon tells me that he has not heard from you. I wish to stress the importance of completing your doctorate. Do let me know when you are planning to return to Oxford, whether to rejoin the MCR community, or simply to drop off work with Auberon.

We look forward to hearing from you,

Zed
Mr. Cedric Robinson
Tutor for Graduates
Hamdaw College Oxford

I put in my hours at the Health Authority. I tried to write Chapter Seven. At last I was rewarded with a letter from Moscow:

Dear Kevin,

You have been in my thoughts since I arrived here, hovering like a spirit. You inhabit my consciousness in a way that is eerie. I miss you in many ways, including a very basic, physical way, of course. It's your spiritual presence that clings to me, encouraging me when everyone else is dismissive. I sense your approval at my being here. When I'm here, behind the wall of the old East, like that Thomas Mann character you told me about (though maybe it isn't such a wall any more, alas), I feel as though you're peering over my shoulder. There are parts of your personality that confuse me: how you can be unsure of yourself in many ways and self-confident and inspiring in others, how you seem to be destined to succeed in a way that will always be tinged with failure. But I am very grateful for your understanding. I'm an automaton here, squinting at strangers' (dead strangers') handwriting six hours a day (I'll tell you about my research in another letter). On the bus I relax and experience my only real moments of feeling: a weird stew of tuggings and pictures and internal monologue, sometimes very painful, but pleasant in that it tells me I'm alive and this moment is my life and I can hold off depression as long as I feel something. The core around which those feelings cluster is you.

The days have gained immeasurably in noise, smells, and grit. With Tatiana Alexandrovna, I have a normal, almost Soviet life: washing hanging on the balcony, no hot water, a gas stove. We both come home with big shopping bags (the eternal search for toilet paper!) And I'm glad to have someone to eat with and talk to. She has the problems of a Soviet woman: an ex-husband who's dying of cancer, a father with Alzheimer's who goes wandering through Moscow for hours, a son who was crippled in Afghanistan and now lives in Germany with his wife and whom she misses terribly. I can't compare my troubles to hers, but she and I keep each other afloat. She's very happy I moved in. In the evening, I write in my diary for company. The reason I'm writing to you now is that this evening on the way home I got off the bus two stops early so that I could walk a little more and I went down a side street and suddenly, right in front of me, was a street where nothing had changed. A row of apartment blocks with old signs that no one had bothered to take down. Nothing new or ugly, you would never know that world had ended. If you had been with me, we could have walked straight back into my childhood. I could have taken you with me into the Soviet world.

The country has changed so much. It's true that now that summer is coming, the long hours of daylight give an impression of more joviality and less crime. (I don't care what anyone says, there was no crime in the Soviet Union.)

I'm horrified by the extent of change: kids with earphones and roller blades who wouldn't know what a "Pioneer" was if you asked them, young people who speak sloppy Russian, not even declining the nouns properly (how hard I worked to learn those declensions!). The old Soviet graciousness and slowness and ceremony is gone. I haven't called your friend Alex, but I did go to a birthday party the other day. It was a wonderful, old Soviet extravaganza: food, lots of drink, many friends and relatives, a slideshow of the birthday boy's life, intense conversation. Suddenly at 11 p.m., they all packed up and left! They were tired from work. That never used to happen. Just making enough money to survive exhausts people. They used to be free from those pressures. They used to focus on living and feeling and being close to friends and lovers. Still, I'm sometimes surprised by the old things that survive, like construction workers wearing hats made out of folded newspapers. But the whole way of interacting has changed. On the street I smiled at two young women who were walking past because they were smiling so happily (not something one would have seen in public before), and they stopped me and asked if I was a friend of Jesus Christ and wanted to come to a prayer meeting. Help! Really, I spend most of my time here working, but I live for the moments when I see things that I could show you to usher us back into the world where I grew up. Tonight on the way home I saw a store that advertised "Pizza and Building Materials" and I wanted so badly to show it to you and laugh with you that I knew I missed you a lot.

XXX Love,

C.

Some days the mail brought surprises.

Dear Sir,

You are receiving this letter because your surname suggests that you are of British Origin. We'd like to introduce you to Sid, your British National Party candidate. Sid's a local man. He cares about local problems. We're certain you'll be pleased by Sid's solutions to the troubles that afflict our community:

- A ban on asylum seekers and immediate deportation of those who are already here, living on your tax money.
- The repatriation of Negroes, Pakistanis, and other Alien Races to their homelands.
- The sacking of "trendy" or "right-on" teachers in our schools.
- A ban on the employment of homosexuals and other diseased individuals in jobs that involve contact with the public.

You can meet Sid on Sunday at the pub, where he'll be hosted by the Hackney Hookers …

Some of the letters had Canadian stamps.

Hey Kev!
You must be having a riot over there. Your old man wants to know when you're coming home. I don't think he gets how much fun you're having. Research was always heavy sledding for him. But me, I've been as happy as a hog on ice tracking down old Bethune. McGill and Concordia

332 | STEPHEN HENIGHAN

won't give me cards so I use public libraries and second-
hand bookstores. That's where the pages I've photocopied
come from. You can tell me if I've screwed up, but it looks
like Bethune came back to Montreal around the beginning
of June 1937. So contact, if you get my drift, could have
occurred any time after that, depending on which ladies
the good doctor was seeing. That, and when he left for
China. That'll be the kicker, if I can pin that one down.
I'll keep you posted. Take care of yourself, and enjoy
that thesis.

Fred

For two days after receiving Fred's letter, I skipped going to
the British Library. I snapped back into my routines only after
I received another letter from Catherine.

Dear Kevin,
I was very happy to receive your letter. So much love and
emotion! I could hear your laughter as I read it. It reminded
me of how your good nature scours away my gloom and
allows me to feel, in all that strange amalgam of sensations
that makes up feeling.
    I'm in a muddle, especially about my research, but one
thing is certain — I'm enjoying your tea. I even let Tatiana
Alexandrovna taste it. Of course, it wasn't strong enough
for her, but it helps me to keep afloat, hovering above
the pit (not the ghastly pit of despair of my hospitalized
depressions, but still a pit) that widens and widens at my
back when I see how everything here is changing and how

impossible it will be to change it back to the way it was before. There are more hamburger stands all the time, and also more crime and more people being exploited. I have to keep walking forward so that the pit doesn't swallow me — but forward towards what?

Tatiana Alexandrovna tells me I need to get married. She's such a Soviet woman! They all think marriage is the highest achievement, even though I've hardly ever met a Soviet woman who's had a good marriage. They get married at twenty and by the time they're twenty-five their husbands are drunken womanizers and they're left alone with one or two children. And still they think you're a failure if you've turned thirty (or even twenty!) without marrying. Oh well, it's refreshing that she doesn't treat me the way my parents do. They want me to be a little girl, she wants me to be a married (divorced? abandoned?) woman.

Please tell Alex I will get in touch with him soon. I'm working very hard and I like my routines and I find myself getting "cross" — that's a British word I may adopt, it conveys so precisely how I felt the other day — when people barge in and disturb me. A young Russian businessman who had been in Belgrade appeared at my door, sent by my mother! He's the new kind of Russian: clean-cut, a suit that actually looks Western and doesn't sag, obviously goes to the gym three times a week, speaks English really fast. When I finally got him into Russian he slurred the inflections in a poor attempt to hide the fact that he wasn't sure of some of the declensions. He doesn't drink, but he can't quote Pushkin or Tolstoy either. A real MBA guy, interested in business stuff. We had nothing in common and I got him out of the flat as fast as I could – but even that took an hour. Tatiana Alexandrovna was intimidated by him; her generation of Soviets doesn't know how to deal with his generation of Russians. This specimen visited me because, at a reception in Belgrade, my mother said, "When you're in Moscow you must look up my daughter, she's interested in business, too." How could she? My mother knows I hate business! Oh my parents, they always tell people what they want to hear; the truth is a detail.

Truth, it turns out, is exactly what I have to wrestle with to understand poor K.R. My thesis must be perfect! But that just got so much harder, as I will explain to you. The archive is an amazing place. I think I'm the only person under sixty who has access to the manuscript room. When I was lining up to go in the first day, an elderly scholar peered at me and said, "A very young doctor!" And what did the very young doctor find when she began to work? K.R.'s diaries, above all; also lots of letters to and from his friends, particularly his closest literary collaborator, the nobleman Sergei. It's obvious no one has looked at this stuff because – well, because K.R.'s reputation would be different if they had! I was happily making my way through his diaries, feeling reverent and light-headed at actually holding in my hands the notebooks in which K.R. wrote. I was thinking about his discretion and how he combined being a person from an eminent family with being an artist (a problem that has obvious resonance for me, I know, and I've always accepted that's the reason I'm working on him) when I came across an account of his visit to the steam baths. Yes, it's as bad as it sounds. And it's not as though he left very much for the young doctor – who still aspires to become a doctor – to interpret. No Victorian discretion or elusive metaphors here. He writes, "I went to the steam baths. I invited young Vlad, the attendant, into my stall to sin with me. Afterwards I felt filled with remorse." What a poor, tormented soul he was! His whole life was driven by this passion for men and being a very serious Christian, married with eight children, he felt it was terribly wrong. And Sergei? You guessed it. Sergei (I'm now calling him Sir Gay) was K.R.'s long-time companion. Needless to say, I can't even whisper this stuff to Tatiana Alexandrovna! But the quandary I'm in is: how do I write my perfect thesis now? I wanted to venerate the memory of an old Russian aristocrat by going to traditional old Oxford and writing a thesis based on traditional literary appreciation. I wanted to create an object of beauty, an elegant essay and not something horrible and jargon-filled, just for academics; a work that would keep an older world alive. But there is the question of truth. Unlike my parents – and even imagining ways in which I diverge from them fills me with remorse, like poor old K.R. – I can't tell people what they want to hear. At least not in my thesis I can't. In daily life, I know, I may be more like my parents than I realize. My job is to find truth: a contribution to knowledge. This means understanding K.R., which means submerging myself in Queer Theory and all the modern stuff I'd hoped to avoid. Is there a way I can sympathize with him and understand him without theorizing his condition? Because I'm useless for theory, Kevin, as you know. I'm a good Russian – an old Russian, a Soviet – all feelings and soul, with an intelligence that's intuitive, not theoretical. I know myself that well, just as I know that I enjoy my solitude here, enjoy taking a break from being in "a relationship," even though that doesn't mean I don't still miss you!

> Yours, in a muddle — and with love —
> C.

A few days later, I received another letter from Canada.

> *My dear Kevin,*
>
> *I hope this finds you well. I need to tell you a few things and I think it's better to write them down than to try to squeeze them into a phone call.*
>
> *I suppose I'd better start with what's been on my mind. Last week I had lunch with Joan, and, of course, we talked about you. Joan was on a CBC panel recently. Also on the panel was a very suave young man, Ron something-or-other, who is one of the Prime Minister's advisors. After the taping Ron told Joan that he had studied at Oxford and he knew someone who had worked for her, and, of course, it was you. The troubling part was that Ron seemed worried about you. He said you had been expelled from Hamdaw College! He said it was some sort of ancient punishment that lasts a year, but that the current graduate student president, who's a friend of his, said you hadn't returned.*
>
> *Why didn't you tell me, Kevin? I wouldn't have thought any less of you. I can imagine how your outspokenness would rub those reserved English people the wrong way. I know you wouldn't ask me for help because you think I see you as the repetition of your father, with all his blarney masking his inability to put two pages together.*

*But one achievement of yours that I was always proud
of was your ability to write those long reports for Joan.
When you started to do that, I knew you'd inherited my
ability to stick with a project and see it through. I have
faith in you, Kevin. I know you can finish.*

*Please let's talk about this the next time we phone. I'd
like to hear more about how you're surviving in London.
Are you still with that new girl you told me about? I can't
remember whether she was Russian or American — for
so long those seemed like two sides of the same coin. You
need to set aside time to write! From what Joan tells
me, saving money and living in London are mutually
exclusive. So I'm taking a chance on offending you and
attaching a bank draft for $2500. I know that isn't as
much in pounds. Really, you could have asked me. I'm
far from rich, but I'm not as impecunious as your father,
or as deranged as old Bethune. Just promise me you'll
use the money to buy yourself time to write. Someday you
may want to marry one of your girlfriends, and it will
all work out much more smoothly if you've finished your
doctorate. You can take it from me that a marriage with
an irregular income is a marriage in trouble. Though
even with a regular income, like Marie and Dave have,
trouble can surface. Your sister just seems impatient with
life at the moment. Paul and I are doing fine, though he's
still fighting his ex over the house.*

I send you all my love and good wishes. Let's talk.

*Much love,
Mum*

338 | STEPHEN HENIGHAN

I held the bank draft in my hands, realizing that though I might not have been born to opulence like K.R., or diplomatic privilege like Catherine, I had more support than I realized.

It seemed as though Catherine had been away forever and hadn't written for ages. My life was made up of hospital requisitions. At last, a very fat letter arrived.

Dear Kevin,

Today I was walking through Moscow, lost in my own thoughts, when I opened my eyes and wished I hadn't. The inequalities are so glaring now. The Russians have always suffered, but there used to be a spirit of sharing the hard times. In the Soviet Union there was nothing like the Mafia restaurants I see now, full of frightening-looking rich men and their entourages of bruisers and painted ladies (I think that's the best word — here they really are painted!), everybody smoking and scaring the waiters. Some people had privileges in the Soviet Union, like the right to travel, or a dacha, but since money wasn't important, the differences were muted.

I'm doing battle with an almost overpowering feeling of dissatisfaction. Visions of my healthy life in Leipzig are attacking like enemy planes. Instead of coaxing myself back into the "shape" I want (not just physical, but also mental) I feel numb and defeated. The dissatisfaction doesn't extend in any way to you and me, though I think it's healthy that I've had this time apart from you to see our relationship in perspective. Now that I'm no longer blinded by lustful feelings for you — funny how lust fades after a few weeks, even as one grows subliminally more desirous and nostalgic for the idea of being in a couple — I can see the

two of us more clearly: what I like and what I don't like.
My parents want me to go straight to Belgrade after
Moscow, but I told them there are things I need to do in
England. As you can imagine, one of those things involves
being naked with you!

I was still in a crabby mood when I met your friend Alex.
I phoned him one evening and introduced myself as your
girlfriend. (I realize how rarely I've applied this noun to
myself. Of all the men who have passed through my life,
how many would have said, "Catherine is my girlfriend"?)
Excuse this digression, but naturally meeting Alex as
your emissary – when have I been the emissary of anyone
other than my parents? – has made me reflect on our
relationship as a public event that alters our positions
in the world, my position, especially. I was thinking
about this as I set off to meet him. It made me feel bogged
down, resentful of my onerous role, as though I'd lost my
freedom and needed to take decisive action to reclaim it. I'd
spoken to Alex in Russian on the phone, but when we met
he started talking to me in English. I didn't like him at all.
He's so huge that he's terrifying. He's coarse and crude, not
just because he swears a lot, which I don't like, but because
his English is rough. I know my English can be strange, but
it was as though we were incompatible polar opposites. I
got my English from novels; Alex's comes from the street.
When I asked about the key to the storage bin, he brushed
me aside and said your friend Leon had it. After we ordered
our second drinks – his second vodka, my second tea –
he started speaking Russian and – presto! – we spoke the
same language. His Russian is beautiful: grammatically
perfect, and laced with literary allusions; you can tell he's

spent a lot of time reading poetry. He doesn't think much of K.R., but he's the first person I've met other than my supervisor who has read him. He seems big and tough in Russian, too, but he softens when he talks about literature. I saw a tremendous sensitivity in him, even a wounded quality. I told him he was like the Russians I used to know when I was growing up: a real Soviet. He didn't like the Soviet reference, but he understood what I meant. He told me that he had moved back to Moscow in the hope of living around people like that. He was frustrated in Toronto and Oxford and Harvard because he found it impossible to write in Russian while living in English. Yet when he moved back he felt that Russians didn't live inside their poetry the way they used to. Of course, I knew exactly what he meant!

I'm very happy that Alex is your friend, Kevin, but I'm also puzzled because the part of him that most resembles you, or resembles the parts of you that I love and appreciate, is the part that is invisible in English. The Alex I could imagine you relating to is the Alex I discovered in Russian. Maybe, having grown up in English (or English and French — this gets more and more complicated), you have some sort of radar that I'm denied, which allows you to perceive the sensitive Alex behind the coarse Alex. Anyway, I'm glad we were able to speak in Russian because otherwise I would have wondered why you had sent me to meet him. It's obvious he likes you a lot. He was also very pleased when I told him that I had met Leon. Those dark, intelligent eyes just lighted up. Overall, though, he seemed sad and depressed (digging deeper the pit of depressing thoughts that has opened up during my stay here). The old Russian bohemianism he came here looking for has

disappeared. Some of his colleagues sound like the MBA guy
my mother sent me. (Oh, my mother!) Alex is thinking
of leaving Russia, but he doesn't know where to go. He
says that sometimes he just wants to be really rich and do
nothing. He can't imagine a place for literature and feeling
in the world we live in now. "I think I'm dispirited." As he
said this, I saw his spirit, so sensitive and cultivated, fly up
in front of my eyes and disappear into the air. I felt sorry
for him in the way I feel sorry for K.R. for feeling remorse
for being himself, and even for myself, the aspiring young
doctor who wants to write a perfect thesis and can never
find the right angle. I felt our conversation had ended and
nothing remained but to drag myself home and fall into
a pit of depression. That was when he told me he knew a
couple who still lived like bohemians. Did I want to go out
with them? Right now? I asked. Sure, he said. Of course he
had a portable telephone. I was skeptical and tried to tease
him. "And they won't go home at eleven o'clock?" "Does that
happen to you, too? No, Yury and Mitzi are like my uncle
was. They're like people from before."

You can imagine how eager I was to meet these people
from before! Before I knew it, a chauffeur-driven black
Range Rover had pulled up outside the café. As Alex gave
instructions to the driver, I glimpsed a shadow of the
dangerous Mafia guy in him. I was frightened and told
myself I shouldn't have got into the car. It's all right, I
thought, he's Kevin's friend. Then I felt tired and just
wanted to go home and sleep. I realized this was my
depression trying to trick me out of having experiences
that would drive it away. Once Alex got on the phone to
his friends, I felt better. We drove to an old building in

a district that's still cheap. The elevator didn't work, of course, so we walked up seven flights of stairs to a chaotic loft decorated with paintings and shelves of Russian classics in Soviet editions. Oh, how at home I felt! Yury was a painter with a beard, Mitzi taught German and did pottery. She was Jewish, with very dark hair and eyes. She showed me earthenware vases she had made with delicate little Hebrew inscriptions on the sides. They had wine from the Caucasus. Everybody started to drink except for me, the teetotaller, who's always the diplomatic witness to debauchery (sometimes the participant, too, but without being drunk). Yury seemed to paint full time, and Mitzi obviously didn't teach many hours of German. I made the mistake of asking them how they could survive under capitalism. I felt boring for having asked such a mundane question, so I started telling them about what I'd discovered about K.R. As soon as I opened my mouth, I felt mortified, as though I'd spilled the family secrets. But they were intrigued, and much more open-minded about homosexuality than most Russians. They asked me how I had got permission to read in the archives and I had to squirm to avoid telling them who my father was. Alex was good enough not to give me away. (Or maybe he doesn't know? If you didn't tell him who my parents are, then I'm so impressed. You make me feel like a normal person, Kevin.)

K.R. led us to the subject of decadent nobility. Mitzi said that the difference between the Czarist court and the Politburo was that the court was beset with lots of different vices — gambling, religious fanaticism, homosexuality, womanizing, incestuous intermarriage, and thin blood — while the Politburo had a single vice: alcoholism. Yury objected that alcoholism was an authentically Russian trait. Alcohol nourished the Russian soul! The only good thing about the Politburo was that they were alcoholics! Gorbachev wasn't a normal person because he didn't drink. If he had drunk, he would have been more trustworthy. They were starting to sound like normal Russians, excusing Yeltsin for his failings because he was a true Russian soul, when Mitzi said she felt nostalgia for the nobility. Before I knew what was happening, we were planning to go to one of the nineteenth-century estates that were absorbed into the city as parkland. For a lot of the nineteenth century there were no public theatres in Russia and the nobility went to estates on the edge of the city, like this one, to see plays or go to the opera.

It was two in the morning and there I was with three crazy Russians (once you hear Alex speak Russian, you forget that he's Canadian). Tatiana Alexandrovna had probably already phoned my parents to tell them I was dead. I knew I should go home, but I told myself that if this was the Moscow life I was missing, I couldn't very well refuse it when it came along and swept me away. Alex phoned his chauffeur, who, amazingly, was still awake and even sober when he arrived, and we drove miles out into the suburbs. The mansion in the middle of the park had belonged to a member of the Court. I imagined K.R. and Sir Gay strolling beneath the trees. A third — or was it a fourth? — bottle of wine from the Caucasus was opened. We walked through the shadows and the darkness, laughing and quoting poetry. I would have been worried about our safety except that Alex brought his chauffeur, who I realized (with a chill) was also his bodyguard and a rather dangerous person. He stayed a few steps behind us and was vigilant and ignored our conversation, which probably sounded silly, however much the Russians appreciate drunkenness.

We came out of the trees and there was a small lake. The moon ebbed over the surface of the water. It looked fantasy-like and timeless. I felt I was in the park with K.R., with Pushkin, with the spirit of Russian literature, of which Alex and I were two of the last emissaries. I felt uplifted to be an emissary for literature just as I felt a certain novelty at being your emissary. Anything but an emissary for my parents! (Though I'm proud of being that, too. There is honor in serving America. Oh, it's all so complicated.)

Next to the bushes on the far shore I saw the shadows of swans docked for the night like schooners with their beaks folded into their breasts. I said something half-baked about swans and transcendent beauty, and Mitzi shouted, "We must become the beauty!" Before I knew what was happening, she and Yury were taking their clothes off. I hadn't skinny-dipped in years – in fact, I'd only done it once before – but the idea was irresistible. The water would be cold, but so what? Didn't I always say I preferred a quick plunge into cold water? I may be introverted, but I've never been one for dawdling when others are spontaneous, in new relationships, in new experiences of any sort. For a second the sight of Yury and Mitzi running past me naked paralyzed me. They were both enviably slender. Alex and I avoided looking at each other. Then I thought, isn't this the bohemian life? Their shouts flew over the water and through the trees and resounded off the balconies of the

mansion with a faint echo. They might have attracted
who-knows-what sort of gang, but our security guard –
ex-KGB, obviously – was standing watch beneath the trees.
I took my clothes off and jumped into the water. Oh, it was
cold! I shrieked as loudly as Mitzi. Alex, very deferential
and gentlemanly, avoided looking at me as I ran towards the
water. He moved along the shoreline to where a bush grew
close to the lake, stepped behind a bush, undressed with
movements that made him look gangly and uncoordinated
in a way I hadn't noticed before. He jumped into the water.
A curve of white caught the moonlight. Let's say that Alex
wasn't as skinny as Yury and Mitzi; I can report evidence of
a belly. (I saw something else, too, but I'm not telling about
that!) We splashed and howled in the water. Alex was more
restrained (less comfortable?) than the rest of us. To help
him relax, I quoted some Pushkin: "She dreamt of portents.
She walked across the snowy plain ..." (That's the best I
can do for an English version. You can't translate Pushkin
without abusing him.) Alex picked up where I'd left off,
"... There came a furious, boiling, heaving main." It was
like magic. The verses sent me sailing into winter. I saw
how the park and the mansion would look during a Russian
winter. The poetry created the reality.

When we got out of the water, we were all more
subdued. They were sober and I was at peace with myself.
We were closer than we had been before. It's fun to be wild
together, but wildness implies a distance. Silence can bring
you together, which is something Russians understand
and Westerners usually don't. I jumped up and down on
the shore to dry myself. Mitzi took my hand. "Softly, my
little one. Take your time. Take a walk." We walked naked

through the park hand-in-hand with the men following us, and the security guard following them. Mitzi had a curlicue tattoo on her thigh. It struck me as weird and unRussian. (Also unnatural. I could never get a tattoo. The point of being naked is to be yourself, like an animal.) The moon felt cold then, as my body dried, it seemed to be sending us a discreet warmth. We stopped in a clearing and dressed, the women facing the men. I'm normally so shy. I know you won't believe that, but it's true. I couldn't believe we were doing this. Alex looked at my breasts with appreciation. That's what I felt, not lechery, but a male animal appreciating the qualities of the female. I respected him more because he didn't look away when I noticed he was looking; in that way, too, he's deeply Russian and — sorry to say it, Kevin — not at all Canadian.

Once we got back in the car, it was clear the evening was over. The guard turned into a chauffeur again. We were silent as he drove us back to our apartments. Contrary to my fears, Tatiana Alexandrovna didn't blink an eyelid when I came in at four a.m. Why should she? I was living a normal Soviet life.

The main consequence of this incident (aside from missing a day in the archives) is that skinny-dipping has abolished the remoteness from lust that I had achieved during the last few weeks. I am desirous, Kevin! I am in urgent need of a roll in the hay. I'm starting to think I've got enough material on poor old K.R. and had better come back soon.

XXXX, Love,

C.

THIRTY-THREE

S LYOGKHIM PAROM.

I came home to find a card lying in the hall with these words written in firm letters on the back. Beneath, a familiar hand had scribbled: *That means "with light steam." It's an encouraging comment you make to someone on his way out of the shower — or the steambaths (poor K.R.!) I hope to say "s lyogkhim parom" to you very soon! Much love, C.* I turned the postcard over and saw a picture of onion domes.

The next day, after work, I stayed on the Central Line one stop past Bethnal Green, getting off at Mile End. I crossed Regent's Canal, walked to the bright new Arts building of Queen Mary College, opened the front door and entered the lobby. "Where do you think you're going?" a uniformed guard asked.

"Dr. Zamenhof?" I said. "In the History Department?"

The guard lifted the receiver of his phone and dialled an extension. "Sir? There's an American bloke dressed like a ragamuffin here to see you."

I was given permission to go upstairs. I found Leon in a large, bright office with a seminar table in the middle and a window that looked out over the canal. He wore a white shirt open at the neck and a tailored black jacket. "Become a regular East London lad, have we?" he said, studying me.

"The rest of my clothes are in your bin —"

A look of resignation gripped him. "I imagine we'll be seeing our Alex soon. He's fed up with Moscow. Says he's going to California. He'll need to liberate his Russian library."

"We have to tell him, Leon." This was what I had come here to say. "We sent him off the rails by killing that boy. We've made him into a fucking stockbroker."

"Don't be so utterly tiresome. You're obsessed with something that happened yonks ago."

"You've shrugged it all off, haven't you?"

"We all have our crosses to bear." He slid a stacked pile of pages towards me: proofs for the book he had written based on his D.Phil. thesis. The words on the first page were: *To the memory of my father, Isaac Zamenhof.*

"Why didn't it affect you, Leon?" I sat down beside him at the table. "You know we should have taken that boy to the hospital, not to a fucking pub. What happened to Jewish guilt?"

"It's not that I don't realize we did something we shouldn't have done," he said in a slow voice. "Maybe two things we shouldn't have done: making the phone call and taking him for a pint. Nor that I fail to see that the result of our actions was a fatal accident — though the connection's rather tenuous. But I cannot, for the life of me, see how it would help Alex to tell him this now. I'm sure he's forgotten the whole thing."

"On the contrary, this *whole thing* caused him to lose faith in poetry."

The afternoon sunlight glimmered on the canal. Leon didn't

reply. When I couldn't stand the silence any longer, I said, "Are you still back together with Emily?"

"We're married! Sorry not to have invited you to the wedding. It was strictly a registry-office affair ... Our last defiance of Emily's family! From now on we're beholden to them. They're buying us a house so that the offspring can be raised in circumstances appropriate to their maternal lineage."

"You're buying a house? Around here?"

"No. In fact, the house they've found is in Muswell Hill." He shrugged his shoulders. "It'll be a quiet spot to raise the little nippers."

Alex had a chauffeur and Leon was buying a house in North London's upper bourgeois hilltops. I looked down at my scored slacks. "You must enjoy working on the street where your uncle was elected as a Communist."

The words sounded more bitter than I'd intended. Leon said, "Look, when we met at Hamdaw it was less than three years since the Berlin Wall had fallen!" He flashed a smile, lifting his head in one of those Jagger-like poses that had earned him damp-eyed stares from the women of the graduate staircase. "You *think* you're adrift because of your vexed guilt. But you'd be adrift in any event simply because the bipolar world we grew up with has shattered. You know what I say? I say don't worry, new divisions will come along and you're not going to like them one little bit. The West will be gripped by some new oppressive ideology that's even more repellent than anti-Communism."

He handed me a business card with the blue crown of the Queen Mary and Westfield crest in the corner. "Here's my email. Send me a message and I'll write to you if Alex turns up in London."

I slid the card into my wallet and left. Walking up Regent's

Canal, I thought of Leon going home to Emily in their Hill —
Notting Hill, soon to be Muswell Hill — as I returned to my
basement. The next day, after work, I went to an internet café
near Oxford Circus, sat down among Russian and Turkish restaurant workers and Italian and Spanish students of English as a
Second Language, found that my Hotmail account had been
closed due to inactivity, opened a new account and sent Leon a
message. I waited two days, went back to the café and found his
reply:

> Right, Kevin. We're in touch. I'll let you know if I hear from Alex.
> Leon.

I tried to write my thesis. I was stuck on page two of my penul-
timate chapter, unable to analyze a country I had not visited. At
last, the phone rang and I heard Catherine's voice.

She came to see me that weekend, her face undeniably hers
though not precisely as I remembered it. We made love as soon
as she came in the door, and again when we woke up in the
middle of the night. In the morning I went upstairs to Husain's
off-licence and bought the weekend papers, bread, orange juice
and eggs. We spent the morning discussing stories in the papers.
I had expected her to talk about Moscow, but her mind was
already concentrating on her visit to Belgrade. Former Yugoslavia
had seized the headlines again since war had broken out in Kosovo.

"Kosovo feels far away in Belgrade." We were sitting on my all-
weather carpet. "I've never met a Serb who's been there. The wars
in Croatia and Bosnia were more intimate. It was horrible. People
had family in those places ... Belgrade is more provincial than
Moscow, but it's my home, too. It was wonderful growing up
there, even though when I was a teenager I had a weekly appoint-

ment with the CIA guy at the embassy. I had to tell him everyone I'd met that week, including boys I hadn't told my parents about. I hated it! I used to cry and cry, but in the end I always gave him the names, then he would come back and tell me which of my friends were security risks I wasn't allowed to see again. But I don't blame my parents. When I'm with them, fun things are always happening. Last time, we flew to a place called Tivat for the investiture of the new President of Montenegro. As we approached Belgrade on the way back, fog closed in and we were denied permission to land. We had to fly to Budapest. We didn't have our passports, but the Hungarians let us into the country, and we pigged out on Mexican food at a restaurant. My parents really miss Mexican food! The next day, when the fog didn't clear, the embassy in Budapest drove us to the border. We had to wait until Janko, my dad's driver, drove through the fog to the Yugoslav side of the border, then brought our passports across so we could re-enter the country. I felt so good driving back to Belgrade with my parents and Janko! Those are the times when I feel I have a home."

She got to her feet and rummaged in her pack. "Kevin, I have something for you." Out came a manila envelope with a hard, cardboard back. "If you'll accept it," she said in a murmur, startling me with a girlish blush.

Inside the envelope I found a single sheet: the eagle-festooned letterhead stationery of the United States Mission to Yugoslavia. An old typewriter had pecked out the words:

I would like to invite Mr. Kevin Carmichael to visit me in Belgrade.

Below was a scrawl which Catherine said was her mother's forgery of her father's signature. Yugoslavia, ostracized from the

West by Slobodan Milosević's murderous rampages into Croatia, Bosnia, and now Kosovo, was an invitation-only visa country. I couldn't get in unless someone important invited me. And now someone had. Catherine had given me the ticket that I'd never bought in Gloucester Green, not to Berlin, but to Yugoslavia, where my thesis, my own personal trilogy, might find its conclusion.

I quit my job. I took my passport and the letter of invitation to the Yugoslav consulate on the third floor of a building near Earl's Court. The consulate was guarded by a tall, surly man who wore a pistol in a holster. Security cameras targeted the battered hardwood floor, chain-smoking visa officers disappeared behind frosted-glass panels and reappeared hours later. I filled in the visa application form: *Country of Birth, Country of Nationality, Ethnic Nationality*. I hesitated at the last question. Irish, French, a dash of Iroquois, rumours of a great-grandmother who had been German or Polish or maybe Ashkenazi, I was too mongrelized to have anything so uncompromising as an ethnicity. In Montreal, I had been an *Anglais*, pigeonholed by my mother tongue; in England, I was a Yank, condemned by the Brits' tin ear for foreign accents. I reasserted the primacy of the nation-state by writing: *Canadian*.

THIRTY-FOUR

THREE WEEKS AFTER CATHERINE handed me the letter, we flew to Belgrade via Rome. We landed and waited for our luggage to be X-rayed. Having cleared customs and immigration, we walked into the lobby and were met by Catherine's mother. "Oh, my mother!" she had said as we boarded the plane in Rome. All the way across the Adriatic, as our fellow passengers smoked in defiance of Alitalia's regulations, she spoke of her mother's illnesses, daily handfuls of pills, lapses into drinking, sudden flight to Washington for an operation, then, after she was told to take it easy, her return to Belgrade and equally sudden departure on a seven-city speaking tour of Kosovo — were there seven cities in Kosovo? — to encourage ethnic Albanian women who lived in the middle of a spreading war to educate their daughters to be independent.

I spotted her before Catherine did, a short-legged woman with high cheekbones and a deep-hued complexion in which Native American ancestry was more evident than it was in her daughter. Her face was rumpled with exhaustion, yet her shortness, thrown into relief by the tall Serbs striding past her, did not diminish her indomitable authority.

The ambassador's wife hugged her daughter. "How's school going, Catherine?"

I received the courtesy of a brief greeting before we walked out into the cool, sunny autumn air. "Edith's driving," the ambassador's wife said.

"Not Janko?"

"He has work to do for Dad."

"Edith," Catherine murmured, "has been my dad's secretary since I was born. She's from Arkansas. I don't think she's noticed that we're not in Arkansas anymore."

We walked to a nondescript sedan. An obese blond woman with big hair permed into large curls, gold glasses, a gold chain around her neck and a gold watch on her wrist, sat at the wheel. "Howdy, Baby! How's school?"

"It's not school. I'm a thirty-year-old doctoral candidate."

"Gettin' all grown up, huh?"

Catherine and I sat in the back seat as the car dived into the green gullies that spilled creepers over decaying socialist apartment blocks reminiscent of those I'd seen in Hungary and Poland. *Beograd* — "white city" — was white only in its obsession with ethnic purity. It was a gloomy, atmospheric place of steep inclines, abundant foliage, and smog-eroded stone facings. The ambassador's wife mentioned that Senator Bob Dole had been staying with them until this morning; I would stay in Senator Dole's room.

Catherine squeezed my arm to signal to me not to react to this plan to prevent us from sleeping together. I responded by joining the conversation, "Richard Holbrooke was here earlier this year, wasn't he?" The British newspapers had discussed the visit of President Clinton's Special Envoy to the Balkans with their customary irony. *The most dangerous ballistic missile in the Balkans is in Belgrade tonight*, one journalist had written. *His name is Richard Holbrooke*.

When her mother failed to respond, Catherine said, "That was tense. Dad and Holbrooke don't agree. It was difficult, wasn't it, Mom?"

"Special Envoy Holbrooke negotiated a peace agreement in Kosovo," the ambassador's wife said.

"But Dad doesn't think it's going to work, does he?"

"How's school going, Catherine?" Edith said.

We went uphill into the white villas of the Dedinje district. Catherine pointed out where Milosević had moved across the street. Having exhausted his statutory two terms as President of Serbia, the dictator had named himself President of Yugoslavia, retaining power by changing official residences. The buildings in Dedinje belonged to embassies or very rich Serbs. The tall white mansions had curious upside-down-horseshoe-shaped windows on their upper floors. They were surrounded by high fences and fronted by booths armoured with reflector glass. Rusted little Yugo hatchbacks painted the blue-and-white of the police were stationed at every corner.

When we arrived, Catherine led me up four flights of stairs to her room, an unfinished, student-like flat under the eaves. "You can move in here in a day or two. For now, put your luggage in Senator Dole's room. Oh God, my mother! She encourages me to have sex so that she won't feel guilty I've been deprived by the weird life she's given me, but when something gets serious she tries to separate us. It's all so Quaker."

I kissed her, then stepped back to survey her built-in bookshelves lined with books in the Cyrillic alphabet. Catherine, too, had a Russian library. Interspersed with the books were photographs of

Catherine playing in the snow in Moscow as a child, photographs taken in adolescence in Belgrade and at her boarding school in Austria. There was a photo of her parents as fit, dark-haired people in their twenties.

"When the fighting in Kosovo got bad early this year, the residence was evacuated. America owns an enormous warehouse in Amsterdam. They sent huge trucks here through Croatia. Every item was removed from the house, its location noted, then all of our possessions, and all of the furniture and china and silverware belonging to the government, were driven to Amsterdam. When Holbrooke's cease-fire came into effect, the trucks came back from Amsterdam and everything was put back in place. This room has been dismantled and sent to Holland since the last time I was here, but you'd never know it. They've even put my books in the right order."

I said nothing. This Catherine, the daughter of ambassadorial miracles, unsettled me as the Russian Catherine intrigued and attracted me. She touched my arm. "I want to play tennis. I can't believe Janko didn't come to pick me up!"

We walked downstairs. Catherine's father emerged from his office in the company of his right-hand man, a pudgy, boyish, forty-year-old named Jack. As they passed, a uniformed US marine leapt to attention and bellowed, "*Suuh!*" Jack, like Catherine's parents, rode between the floors of the ambassadorial residence in the gleaming elevator that ran through the middle of the villa; Catherine made a point of using the stairs.

We converged in a large kitchen with Jack's wife and four-year-old daughter. Serbian women dressed in aprons offered us spicy, meat-filled rolls called *bureks* on plates emblazoned with the US eagle. Edith grabbed two *bureks* and sat down by herself at the end of the table. Everyone observed a respectful silence as

the ambassador and his assistant divulged scraps of their conversation. The big-bellied bulkiness that made Catherine's father
avoid the stairs was tempered by a bearded, bespectacled face
that would have appeared too professorial for the State Department had his glasses not been black-framed and utilitarian, and
had he not been bald on top, with tufts of hair stranded above
his ears and tendrils scurrying down the back of his neck. Even
in a white dress shirt and a red tie, he looked like a hillbilly who
would be happiest swilling moonshine on a stoop in the Ozarks.
His southern accent was intact, laced with rural raunchiness.
"That's just batshit," he said, in response to Jack's recitation of
the explanation they had received from Milosević about how half
a dozen Kosovo Albanian bodies had ended up beneath the sand
of a riverbank.

"Dad," Catherine said, stepping forward, "this is Kevin."

Granting me a nod and a wave that did not coalesce into a handshake, the ambassador talked about his most recent meeting with
Milosević. A former international banker who had worked in
New York, Milosević acknowledged the ambassador's fluency in
Serbian, yet insisted that negotiations take place in English. Jack
took up this thread, explaining, as though I were unaware of it,
the disintegration of the language formerly known as Serbo-
Croatian into distinct tongues written in different alphabets. "The
kids here learn both alphabets, but Milosević pushes for everything to be in Cyrillic. He's isolating young people from the rest
of Europe."

Hungarian-language schools in the Vojvodina region, Jack said,
had to negotiate their survival on a school-by-school basis, offering the government proof of loyalty in order to continue teaching
in Hungarian. Catherine's expression begged forgiveness. "Dad,
have you noticed Kevin's visiting us?"

"Sure." His eyes scanned past me. "You gonna last longer than her other boyfriends?"

"I think I've already outlasted most of them."

Jack, who was roughly three years my senior, smiled with avuncular condescension. "You're from Montreal? I guess you don't know much about Yugoslavia in a place like that."

This would have been the end of our meeting – Catherine was edging us towards the door – if Edith, who had added two more *bureks* to her plate, had not said, "They don't know squat about Yugoslavia, but that doesn't mean they ain't got Communists. What was the name of that Communist outfit your dad was with, Kevin?"

"My father?" I was too astonished to continue. Catherine and her mother had gone still.

"Him and that journalist friend of his who read Chairman Mao's little red book."

Nick, I thought, as Catherine took another step towards the door. The ambassador, though feigning absorption in a conversation with Jack, was observing us with discreet attention. I remembered my father and Nick arguing about Mao and Marx in the kitchen, bottles of Molson Canadian in hand. I had no memory of Nick's Maoist campaign for city council, though I supposed my father had pasted up posters for this quixotic enterprise, which had earned Nick a few dozen votes. In later years, Nick changed his drinking habits, heading to fancy bistros where he schmoozed with a millionaire press baron; a famous novelist, and even a future prime minister, who secured him the Progressive Conservative nomination for a suburban riding that he was supposed to win but lost by five thousand votes. The conservative Nick was no longer my father's friend. By the time Nick died of cancer in his fifties, everyone had long ago forgotten his youthful flirtation with Maoism – except, it seemed, the CIA.

My head reeled that Canadian lives of such harmless bohemianism merited the attention of the US State Department. "Frankly, Edith," I said, "I don't think it's any of your business what other people read."

Catherine's grimace threatened to collapse into catatonic retreat. Her mother's impassive mien warmed into a smile as I went on, "My father has read thousands of books. What makes you think that a thin collection of slogans would influence him more than all those serious works?"

The ambassador shook hands with Jack and wheeled his belly and beard out of the kitchen. Edith returned to her *bureks*. Catherine went out the door and up the stairs. I followed, catching up to her on a landing where an eight-foot-tall abstract painting of Chagall-esque colours was leaned against the wall. We breathed in silence, unable to look at each other. "That painting," she said with a coy smile, "is by one of my Russian boyfriends."

"I don't give a fuck about your boyfriends. What was going on down there?"

Catherine looked ready to wilt. I reminded myself that this wasn't Leonie, with whom I could have set-to arguments. Catherine's response to anger was total withdrawal. "Edith runs security checks on all of my boyfriends."

"Edith? Come on. She's just the big-mouthed messenger. Who's the CIA guy? It's Jack, right? He knew I was from Montreal."

Catherine closed her eyes. "Kevin! You know I'm not allowed to talk about this."

Until she uttered these words it hadn't sunk in that even her personal life was property of the US security state. "Eighty votes in 1971 for a Montreal Maoist who became a conservative and was once a friend of my father's makes me a mortal threat to the mighty US of A?"

"You can't say those things, Kevin. We're here to serve America." The wide line of her mouth wavered. "I just want peace. I want ease and succour."

"I'll give you succour."

She smiled. "You can do that tonight. What I want now is tennis! Janko owes me a lesson." She called one of the Serbian ladies, who came to the bottom of the stairs. In a mixture of Serbian and English, Catherine asked that Janko meet her at the tennis courts. She led me to a large, third-floor study and told me to wait. Ten minutes later she returned in white shorts and a T-shirt, brandishing a tennis racket and carrying a canister of balls. When I got to my feet, she laid a hand on my arm. "No, stay here. I am not an athletic person. If you see me playing tennis," she said, her voice dropping, "you'll never want to see me naked again."

"I doubt that."

"You are forbidden to watch me play tennis. Wait for me here."

I went to my room, retrieved my copy of Ivo Andrić's *Bosnian Chronicle*, then returned to the study. I examined the floor-to-ceiling bookshelves. Here was another Russian library, but also an American library, crammed with books on the history and politics of the United States. There was a gleaming samovar, a framed photograph of Catherine's mother in animated discussion with Hillary Clinton, and, mounted and framed, the citation that her father had received from President Bush for his handling of the break-up of the Soviet Union.

I had been reading for half an hour when the ambassador's wife came in. "Where's Catherine?"

"Getting a tennis lesson." Seeing a frown rumple her inscrutable face, I said, "Apparently, I'm forbidden to watch."

My attempt to lure the ambassador's wife into a shared appreciation of Catherine's foibles failed. She regarded me with a shrewd look which, though defined by a sour pursing of her mouth, was not devoid of sympathy. She opened a door at the back of the study, entered a small office, then closed the door behind her.

Catherine returned almost two hours later, sweaty and red-faced, but relaxed and upbeat. She went upstairs to take a shower. When she returned, it was time for supper. The ambassador and his wife were dining out. The Serbian ladies served us in the kitchen, taking pains to provide Catherine with a vegetarian meal. In the Serbian dining repertoire, where most main courses included pork and any item that was not actually meat was either slathered in meat sauce or submerged in a greasy stew, this required ingenuity. As she ate her potatoes and salad, I asked her why Janko hadn't returned to the residence with her. "Did he not even work up a sweat?"

"The garage is next to the tennis courts," she said. "He showers in his flat upstairs. He has a little CD player; it's very cozy. He has a flat in town, too, where he lives with his wife and kids."

After dinner, Catherine instructed the serving ladies not to lay out breakfast for us. Her Serbian was less confident than her flawless Russian, yet it was clear that the message had been received. We walked through Dedinje, observing the five-storey villas in the dusk. "We can do our own shopping and cook on the hot plate in my room. I am an independent adult!" She reached out and took my hand. "I'm sorry they ran a security check on your dad, Kevin."

"I'll get used to it." As we returned to the residence, my

strongest feeling was one of relief at having reclaimed her gracious warmth. I kissed her. We necked on the street corner until we realized that two policemen in a Yugo were laughing at us.

Before joining Catherine, I went back to the room that had been occupied by Richard Holbrooke, Senator Dole, and now me. I brushed my teeth, then stepped onto the balcony. Framed by the crooked limbs of the beech trees, a pair of tennis courts stretched below. Abutting the farther court, at the edge of a path that led back into a garden bordered by thick hedges, stood a stone garage whose second storey rose to a peaked roof.

I went up to Catherine's room and was met with a soft embrace. "I'm happy to be back in Belgrade. I had my first sexual experiences here as a teenager." She kissed me. "I think it's time for another sexual experience."

As we began to make love, she was already aroused. Her deep-sea English depression had been evaporated by the steam of the shower that I smelled on her skin. A future in which Catherine's depressions would dissolve remained within reach. The thought filled me with joy. The dim morning light, obscured by the eaves, found us dozing in a naked embrace. The door opened with a creak. I heard a throaty gasp. "Catherine!"

The ambassador's wife stood in the doorway.

"Mom!" Drawing the covers up to her shoulders, Catherine said, "It's not exactly a secret that Kevin and I have been sleeping together for two years."

"Catherine! Think of the staff."

Bare-chested, I sat up. "It didn't do my staff any harm."

Catherine giggled like a schoolgirl. The ambassador's wife stared at me for a long time. For all her practised inscrutability, I detected a judgement going through the process of revision. I realized that she did, in fact, have an assessment of me. A man your thirty-year-old daughter has been dating for two years is a man who may become part of your family. Even time-defying diplomats, eternally rejuvenated by new three-year postings, must recognize this. I watched Catherine's mother's noncommittal mouth and dark Cherokee eyes. I imagined that my response to Edith had impressed her, and that my coarse pun had erased that good impression. A Canadian, in any event, was an awkward proposition: too fifth-business, too much an attic-dweller, stranded north of recognizable landmarks. The ambassadorial couple, who had sabotaged Catherine's relationship with Andreas the East German, would expect their daughter to marry an American, preferably a diplomat, or, as second best, some anodyne Washington think-tank type. But they knew, also, that diplomacy depended on compromise. Beneath her disapproval, I sensed a contradictory yearning for communion in this short, imposing woman. I realized that, even more than the ambassador, she was the orbit around which this villa spun. "I'm sorry," I said. "I shouldn't have said that."

"And I shouldn't be shocked, I guess. But if you don't mind, we'll leave your stuff in Senator Dole's room."

THIRTY-FIVE

BELGRADE BEGAN AT THE bottom of the hill. The villas petered
out into a busy intersection. Before we could get there, we had to
negotiate breakfast. When we reached the second-floor kitchen,
we saw that though Catherine's instructions had been understood, they had not been obeyed. Breakfast had been laid out for
us with shiny cutlery and ambassadorial china. Smiling ladies in
aprons beckoned. I poured bran flakes into a white bowl where
a gold-embossed US eagle hovered at the milk-line and fifty gold
stars circled the rim. We ate in silence, then escaped.

At the splayed intersection below the entrance to Dedinje,
stalls sold bus tickets, cigarettes, and pornographic magazines.
Asking for tickets, Catherine leaned over the front of a stall
and came face-to-face with a livid spread of six forked female
crotches stacked on top of each other like trophies. She backed
off. We walked over the bridge that crossed the highway. Packed
buses spewed black fumes as they struggled up the long hills. We
passed the file of grimy embassies, including the US Embassy,
where Catherine's father went to work every day. Then came
the government office buildings, their windows clogged with

wooden shutters. On the nearby apartment blocks, the shutters were rotting and the grey-pebble walls were smeared with soot. Everything looked closed; government employees hadn't been paid in over a year. Downtown, a sparse selection of international chains kept their doors open alongside local shops that sold dowdier, more affordable merchandise. The opposition press was alive. Catherine translated a Cyrillic newspaper headline for me. An interview with the British Defence Secretary, headed with: *Milosević is Not for Democracy. Your Future is Dark.* I picked up an opposition paper on a newsstand. When I opened it, every second page was printed in the Latin alphabet. It couldn't be every page, an eager young man who rushed up to practise English explained, because that would attract accusations of disloyalty. Alternating pages in Cyrillic and Latin allowed the editors to argue that they wished to be Serbs yet speak to the world. Everywhere we went, people thanked us in broken English, *Gastarbeiter* German, or archaic French for coming to visit their forgotten country. We saw no other obvious foreigners, no one who was not dressed in the formal, spruced-up lumpiness of Serbian fashion. The pang of isolation was as palpable as the black smoke that belched from the buses and congealed into a substance that was nearly as solid.

The rush hour began at noon. The streets clogged bumper-to-bumper with Yugos that boxed in the hissing buses and made the sashed traffic policemen standing at the intersections blow their whistles. Catherine said that civil servants came into the office in the morning in order to retain their jobs. Yet, in the absence of a salary, they felt no compunction to put in a full day's work. At noon everyone drove home for lunch and stayed there.

In the British Library I'd read about Belgrade's Museum of the Revolution, the last surviving Communist museum in Eastern

Europe. We found the building a short walk down the street from the Parliament. But we had arrived too late. The twin brass plaques, inscribed with the museum's name in the Latin and Cyrillic alphabets respectively, had dulled to near illegibility. A freshly painted sign next to the open door announced in English and Serbian: INSTITUTE OF GENOCIDE STUDIES. A hopeful flutter in my chest – were the Serbs confronting their responsibility for the massacres in Bosnia? – fell to earth with a thump. A display window showed off the Institute's publications. The books, printed in English, included: *The Suffering of the Serbs in Sarajevo*, *Our Kosovo Origins*, and *Serbs: The True Story of Europe's Greatest and Most Persecuted Race*.

On the way home we entered a grocery where the smell of raw soap, the sight of toilet rolls packaged in crinkly pink paper and dubious-looking canned vegetables reminded me of the surviving Communist-era stores I'd visited in Hungary and Poland. We pushed a tiny grocery cart that was identical to those I'd seen on my earlier trip east; the carts looked comically small in the hands of towering Serbian shoppers. The women's hair was dyed with henna and shocked into fraying perms, the men had the largest, blackest moustaches I'd seen. There was little evidence of gleaming Western brands horning in to compete with the frumpy socialist provisions. In retreating into hyper-nationalism, Milosević had locked in a pre-1989 landscape. This, I imagined, was what Marshall Tito's Yugoslavia had been like: the same drab goods as elsewhere in the Eastern Bloc, but larger quantities of them, enhanced by the freedom of movement that allowed one or two members of each family to work in Germany or Austria and bring Western goods home. Catherine loaded bread, orange juice, and cheese into our little cart. The bill came to thirty dinars: eight dollars. On a Serbian salary this would be expensive.

We took the long way back to the embassy. Catherine led me into a district of square houses set behind wrought-iron gates, with red shutters and grated windows. The houses were built into a steep hillside. The lower floors were basements at the front, but opened onto ground level at the back. Catherine's family had lived here during their first two postings to Yugoslavia. "Back when Belgrade was livelier and the clubs downtown weren't run by the Mafia. I used to sneak in the gate with some boy doing military service I'd picked up. I'd tell him to go down the hill, then I'd go inside and say goodnight to my parents. Once they had gone to bed on the top floor, I would open the French window of my room at the back —" She smiled, meeting my eyes. "I liked to feel connected to where I was. Men gave me a way of achieving that."

We reached the gate of the ambassadorial residence, waved to the guards in the security booth, then went up the drive, past trimmed bushes and bright green lawns as close-cut as a marine's scalp. As we entered the wide front hall, the ambassador's wife was closing a door. "Catherine!" she whispered. "The opposition leaders are here. Could you talk to them? Dad can't stay. He's getting ready for dinner with the Norwegian ambassador." She sighed. "They keep going back to what their parties did to each other fifty years ago. Dad sits there and says, 'I understand that —'"

"'— but people in Washington don't understand it. What can we do that will get people in Washington on our side?'" Catherine gave me a bright-eyed look. "That's what my dad says to people he's negotiating with. And it usually works."

While Catherine admired her father, she worried about her mother. It was the ambassador's wife who, at the age of seventeen, had met a soft-spoken Southern boy who had completed a two-year hitch in the Marines, where he had been assigned to guard duty at the US Embassy in Tokyo. He watched the diplomats going in and out of the embassy doors. He sure thought those folks had swell lives, but he figured he would never get to be one of them. The woman who became the ambassador's wife convinced her new boyfriend that they could get into Berkeley and pursue their dreams. She, the scholarship winner, submerged her ambitions, as her husband did a master's degree and she became a Foreign Service wife. A tangle of sympathy, uncertainty, exasperation, fear, guilt, and compliance surfaced in Catherine's eyes as her mother sent her in to entertain the leaders of the Serbian opposition.

I followed her into a lavish ground-floor room furnished with high-backed armchairs and dark-red sofas inlaid with discreet arabesques of gold thread. A grandfather clock in the corner accentuated the setting's Habsburg air.

"This is our daughter, Catherine, who's a doctoral candidate in Russian literature at Oxford," the ambassador's wife announced to the three leaders. "And this is our friend, Dr. Carmichael, who is a consultant to the British National Health Service. He can answer your questions about maintaining a public health system in a free-market economy."

I caught Catherine's pitying look, but the thrill of meeting people whose names and faces I'd seen in the pages of *The Independent*, *The Observer*, and *The Sunday Times* overrode my trepidation. I shook hands with the leaders of rump Yugoslavia's opposition parties. Mr. Djindjić, the Democrat, was dressed in the uniform of a Western politician: navy blue suit, white shirt, red tie. His thick, blow-dried, light-grey hair extended over his forehead like a starched, tainted sheet. Only his hard, combative face disrupted his smooth veneer. Mr. Drašković, the Royalist novelist, was a tall man in a brown polo neck sweater and a darker brown jacket of a heavy, rough weave. His narrow features, which had appeared in the newspapers after he had gone on a hunger strike in Milosević's jails, were muffled by sideburns that descended to a long, sharp beard. His hair, parted in the centre, fell to his shoulders. Mrs. Pesić, the Social Democrat, had rumpled, short, blond hair. She wore a pale dress, a dark cardigan, and serious-looking glasses. I was aware that she had been imprisoned by Tito rather than Milosević.

"Do you favour a single-payer model where income tax supports the health system," she asked me, "or is it more efficient to demand that citizens pay a deductible for each visit?"

All three opposition leaders spoke English. Drašković's was the roughest, but even he was able to debate policy in gruff barks. "I think the deductible has a pernicious effect," I said, accepting the role in which I had been cast, "because it deters the poor from seeking medical assistance. A universal health system produces a healthier population, fewer sick days and greater productivity." Sentences I had written for Joan came flowing back. Catherine watched me with a puzzled, not entirely comfortable, smile.

"Dr. Carmichael is from Canada," the ambassador's wife said.

"Of course!" Mr. Drašković said. "Because in America you do not know about public health! You know only about public guns!"

"Every Serb has family in Canada," Mrs. Pesić said in a diplomatic tone.

"In Niagara Falls!" Mr. Djindjić offered a campaign grin.

"American senator take me to Niagara Falls," Mr. Drašković said.

The other two leaders turned to him with keen attention. I could see them struggling to continue in English as they asked Drašković which senator had given him this boondoggle. The three leaders compared the hotels where they had been lodged in

Washington, D.C. and New York. This allusion to their political activity gave me the opening to ask how they saw the Serbia – the Yugoslavia? – that would emerge after Milosević. Did they envisage a return to a federation?

The opposition leaders' wary looks told me they had different positions on this issue. Mr. Drašković laughed. "I want Serbia with hotel like I stay in Vashington."

They were off, extolling breakfast buffets, airport transit lounges, restaurants where they had been wined and dined by congressmen. They raved about prime rib, Florida orange juice, cherry cheesecake, and airport limousines. The space these images of the West occupied in their imaginations unnerved me.

"It's very good to see the three of you together," the ambassador's wife said. "We look forward to working with you to find a way to prevent what is happening in Kosovo from escalating."

We accompanied the leaders out of the reception room and onto the front steps of the residence. The ambassador's limousine pulled up to take them home. The driver who hopped out to open the door was a tall young man with brilliant black hair and rugged cheekbones. When the limousine pulled away, I asked Catherine, "Was that Janko?"

Her mother fixed her with a stare. "Yes," Catherine said.

"Why didn't you say hi to him?"

"Not in front of the opposition leaders."

As we returned to the entrance hall, I thanked the ambassador's wife for letting me attend. "It was an honour to meet Vuk Drašković."

"I think a bomb went off in Vuk's brain," she replied. "As for Djindjić, he runs his party like a Mafia boss. Vesna Pesić is the only democrat of the bunch."

She disappeared in the direction of the elevator. I shared with

Catherine my disappointment at the subject of the opposition leaders' conversation. "Vuk's a writer," she said. "He's very knowledgeable about Serbian literature. Probably the others are, too. I don't know why they're so obsessed with *stuff*. Milošević is the same. In the middle of negotiations he'll start talking to my dad about comic strips or Walt Disney movies."

In the morning, we hid away in the garret and feasted on grilled-cheese sandwiches cooked on Catherine's hotplate, washed down with sugary orange juice.

"At last," she said, "I'm here as an independent adult."

"Would you like to be independent and go travelling with me?"

"Kevin! I came here to spend time with my parents." We were sitting cross-legged on the floor. "You can go on your own if you want. I won't be offended." Seeing my dismay, she said, "I'm worried about my mother. She doesn't look well. And I want to play tennis!"

We finished our brunch. Catherine went downstairs to confer with a serving lady. She came back smiling. "Janko can give me a lesson in half an hour."

She crossed the room, pulled her tennis whites out of a drawer and began to change. I went to her side and touched her naked waist. "I want to watch your lesson."

"I told you, Kevin," she said, pulling her jersey over head, "I look funny when I play tennis!"

"You think I've never seen you look funny before?"

"Wait for me in the study. We can go out this afternoon."

After she left, I went down to Senator Dole's room. I edged close to the balcony and heard the hollow whock of tennis balls. I decided not to trespass on Catherine's trust by leaning out and looking. As soon as I reached the study, I regretted my compliance, reminiscent of my passivity with Camille, with Leonie. When would I stand my ground in a relationship?

"Another lesson?" The ambassador's wife came in.

"I thought we were going travelling, but tennis seems to take precedence."

Her expression was impervious to my acquired British irony. "Catherine said you have an academic interest in Yugoslavia. You need to see the country."

"Catherine's worried about your health. And she wants to play tennis."

"There's been way too much tennis around here."

She made a gruff gesture, then caught my eyes as though expecting me to reply. When I said nothing, she continued, "Most of the people who spend their lives worrying about my health will die long before I do." She lifted her chin in what I felt was a declaration that she had not given up on me, that we might yet become collaborators. "Would you like to use my computer to read your email?"

She opened the door at the back of the study and led me into a windowless office where the walls were hung with framed photographs of her and the ambassador meeting important figures in US, Russian, or Yugoslav politics. My Hotmail revealed a message from Leon, written three days earlier.

Oi mate. Alex rang last night. He seems awfully set on this business of moving to America. He's chundered with Moscow. I'm not certain how he plans to clear out the bin, if it comes to that, but I told him I'd lend him a hand. Give me a ring when you're back in London. I trust the land of the ethnic cleansers is greeting you as one of its own. Leon.

I wrote to him about the Institute of Genocide Studies. In a way that I hoped sounded firm, I added that Alex's return would give us all a chance to have a good natter. Hearing footsteps on the stairs, I left the office. Before I could meet Catherine on the landing, a squat figure had intercepted her. Mother and daughter stared at each other, locked together as though their profiles, separated by a jigsaw, had found a posture in which to return to a primordial meshing. Feeling I was intruding on an intimate scene, I retreated to the lounge. When Catherine came in, five minutes later, her body exhaled the steam of her shower. Her hands hung at her sides like those of a contrite schoolgirl. "My mom and I are going out for lunch. The Holiday Inn is still open. It has a spa. We're going for a massage and a pedicure." A sheepish smile. "My dad's coming home from the embassy. You'll have lunch with him."

It took me a moment to grasp that the Ambassador's wife had made a decision about my visit. I had joined Catherine among the ranks of those whose lives were manipulated by ambassadorial planning. My Canuck hackles rose at the notion of my existence being legislated by the US State Department, yet I could not stem a pulse of gratitude. Like the opposition leaders, I was moving through a world constructed by Americans.

Twenty minutes later, the ambassador's rollicking Southern accent filled the front hall. A woman in an apron came in. "*Molim,*" she said, and beckoned me to follow her downstairs, past the abstract painting on the landing. We went down a passage where she opened a door and ushered me into a high-ceilinged dining hall lined with glistening oak panels. A portrait of President Clinton hung at the end of the room. The dining table, of a thickly varnished, red-hued wood, seated twenty. Two places had been set. The serving lady indicated that I should sit to the ambassador's right.

The marine bellowed, "*Suuh!*" as the ambassador left his third-floor office. I heard the elevator sigh down one floor. The ambassador came in wearing a grey suit and a red tie, his scant hair mussed over his ears. He trundled his belly in front of him like a wheelbarrow. I waited for him to seat himself before I sat down. He acknowledged the courtesy with a nod. Pouring us each a glass of ice water from a jug on the table, he said, "My wife says you're doing a case study of this country, so I guess you know this is where the nineteenth century ended and the First World War began. And goddamn if the Cold War didn't unravel here, too."

Seated to his right, facing the room's only window, veined with discreet bars, I received the muted midday glow as an emanation that seeped around the ambassador's mountainous bulk. "In Canada, the First World War is a defining national moment —"

"Just the same as in America."

"You weren't in it for that long."

"April 1917 to November 1918, long enough to —"

"We were in it from the beginning."

"Your people spent four years sloppin' around in the mud going nowhere. We came in and won that war."

"It's still a defining moment. Canada lost as many men in the First World War as the United States did in Vietnam."

My final word — that word that never failed to make Americans pause — brought this border skirmish to a close. A man in a black jacket carried in a silver tureen and dished us each a generous serving of an extremely rich Serbian soup that tasted like hot, liquefied pork grease. We slurped in silence.

The soup was followed by an unSerbian lettuce-and-tomato

salad, then by a main course of large pork chops, baked potatoes, and carrots. Wiping his beard with his napkin before beginning to slice his pork, the ambassador said, "You haven't finished your dissertation."

"I've got a hundred and eighty pages that my supervisor has approved. If I can travel here and take some notes, I'll be able to finish writing up the last two chapters."

"I don't understand why it takes people so long to finish doctoral dissertations. Some of those reports you wrote for your old boss were almost as long as a thesis, but they only took you a few weeks."

At least he wasn't pretending that he hadn't read the security report on me. I realized that in the ambassador's eyes I had certain assets. I was a think-tank guy of the sort who was likely their second-place choice for Catherine's future. Was this why the ambassador and I were having lunch?

"Catherine has always been a stellar student. I'm not saying that because she's my daughter. I recognize that my son doesn't have those gifts. He's happy as a police officer back in the States and that's fine. But Catherine ...! She's got to finish. I only ever wrote a master's thesis —" He turned in my direction, the sun glossing his sideburns. "Can you explain to me why she's not getting it done? You know her pretty well now."

He looked at me through his glasses, as though wanting to make sure that I appreciated the concession he had made. "Catherine could be finished by now," I murmured, "but you have to be a little pedantic to write a dissertation. You have to think you're right and everyone else is wrong. Catherine's too flexible. She writes chapters, then tears them up. It's as if she doesn't know how to take a firm stand."

I saw I'd entered a patriarchal marketplace where daughters

were bartered off to men who offered the right wares. In the absence of her parents' approval, Catherine was going nowhere. I believed the words I'd just spoken, yet I refrained from telling the ambassador that Catherine was afraid of finishing because it would mean ceasing to follow her parents around the old East.

"She's got to take a position and argue for it, even if she thinks it's batshit."

"I encourage her to keep what she writes, but each time she gets disenchanted, she deletes everything."

As the waiter entered with coffee and cherry cheesecake on a silver platter, the ambassador slumped back in a posture that indicated that this part of our conversation was over.

"How many more postings do you have before retirement?" I asked.

He gave me a startled look. "Last time I was back in Washington, I had a meeting with Secretary Albright. She remembered me well, I'm pleased to say. She told me I was being considered for another posting at ambassadorial level. If that comes through, I'll hit retirement age in the second year of my next posting. They'll let me finish the posting, of course, but," he said, allowing himself a sly Southern smile, "I'm kind of hopin' they'll let me do one more after that."

"Have you thought about where you'd like to retire to?"

"Maybe D.C.," he said, reaching for his coffee. "Our son's there and I could get some consulting work. I just don't know if I want to be in the middle of all that if I'm not going to be an ambassador anymore. So maybe California, where my wife's from. Or maybe Florida, where my wife's dad retired to. Or it could be Maine, we went up there one summer." He laid his hands flat on the banquet table. "How the hell am I supposed to know? Other folks always told me where to live."

He's just like her, I thought. *Or she's like him.* That was why Catherine wasn't going to finish her dissertation. She was like her father.

THIRTY-SIX

THE NEXT DAY, CATHERINE and I left on a train for Vojvodina, a semi-autonomous region of rump Yugoslavia with a large Hungarian population. As I looked at her beside me, and at the young women reading Harlequin romances in Magyar who sat across from us in the second-class carriage, I savoured the ambiguous fruits of an emotional victory. I had played on Catherine's Achilles heel, her subservience to her parents, to get my way as I had never got it with Camille or Leonie. The benefits of my alliance with her mother had been evident from the moment the two women had returned, steamed and pruned, from the Holiday Inn. Catherine had taken my hand and told me we could go travelling. She chose our initial destination, and her mother facilitated our departure, deputing Edith to drive us to the station, but they were my plans that were being fulfilled.

We stepped off the train and tramped around a deserted resort town on a lake. When we entered hotel lobbies, receptionists addressed us in Hungarian; since the beginning of the war, no other foreigners had set foot here. Once they heard Catherine's Russian-inflected Serbian, or, worse, our murmurings in English, room prices tripled or quadrupled, even though the hotels were empty. Giving up on the lakefront, we hiked to the edge of town, where my backpacker travel guide said that there was a Sport Hotel — one of the economy hotels that the old Eastern Europe had built for young people. The two-storey, whitewashed building stood in a field on the edge of town. Overflowing dumpsters, surrounded by splashes of garbage, crowded around the entrance. The windowsills of the upper-floor rooms were lined with empty brandy bottles. Men in T-shirts and dark jackets lounged in the doorway. As we approached, women opened the windows and confronted us with challenging stares. One woman leaned out of a ground-floor window, picked up a bottle and threw it at me. It glanced off my leg and fell in the grass.

"It's a refugee camp," Catherine said.

I kicked the bottle of Slivovica. A pall descended over us. I was travelling with Catherine at my side, yet at our glimpse of the Sport Hotel, her spirit decamped. She was there and not there; her body, too, slipped out of reach. We found a *Sobe* sign, indicating rooms for rent. Once we had paid our eighty dinars — about twenty dollars — for the night and sunk into a big double bed in the back room of a farmhouse, it felt as though her body lay beyond the crest of a wave.

In the morning I admired her as she stood in the pale blue jeans she wore for travelling and a purple sweater with a sagging polo neck. I hugged her and kissed her on the lips. She held herself against me in stillness. "Let's find breakfast."

This was impossible. The concept didn't exist. Yugoslav travellers set themselves up for the day by smoking an unfiltered cigarette. "The reason I was looking forward to coming here," Catherine said, "is that when I was sixteen, my best friend was an ethnic Hungarian girl." They had travelled to this town to stay with the girl's aunt. "I had this ridiculous idea that I'd run into her and we would be friends again." One night, the girls had planned to go to a ball across the border in Hungary. They spent Saturday afternoon trying on dresses and make-up and giggling about what Hungarian boys would be like. They were practising dancing in high-heeled shoes when a limousine stopped outside the door. Catherine's mother appeared, flanked by security guards in blue suits. She ordered her daughter to collect her belongings and return to Belgrade. In two minutes she was out the door; she never saw her friend again.

"Her aunt lived in one of those villas we walked past yesterday. It looked deserted. I'm sorry I wasn't able to explain, Kevin. When I saw it was empty, I felt empty, too. I guess they moved to Hungary. The old way *was* better, in spite of what it did to our friendship. People didn't get driven out of their homes because of their culture."

"But why did your mother —?"

"The CIA guy at the embassy got a report that some of my friend's relatives in Hungary were members of the Communist Party. So I wasn't allowed to see her. I cried for days —"

We travelled to Novi Sad, a 1960s socialist vision of the future. We rode a bus down a broad boulevard of symmetrical apartment blocks. Catherine thrilled to the socialist vestiges: advertisements constructed of plastic letters ratcheted to steel frames on the tops of buildings; working men's cafés where one grabbed a tray and, for pennies, received a bowl of greasy, filling soup; gargantuan statues to "heroes of the working people of Vojvodina."

The tram took us as far as the river. Most of the old city lay on the opposite bank of the Danube. We struggled across the long, dramatic Liberty Bridge in buffeting wind. Huge gusts swept down the river, sang through the steel cables overhead and flung us against the girders. Catherine squinted out over the wide river at the red-roofed old town. "The wind makes me feel alive!" Her fingers gripping the girders, she said, "Are you asking yourself how you ended up here?"

"I'm thinking that my relationship with you became possible when I met Leon and Alex. You're the female principle."

"I'm sorry I haven't been very female for you recently."

We struggled across the Liberty Bridge. In the old town we found a *Sobe* in a garret with sagging twin beds and a small window that looked out over an ancient square where Serbian soldiers in blue ceremonial uniforms performed goose-stepping parade-ground manoeuvres. We stayed in Novi Sad for two nights. The longer I travelled, the less certain I became of what I was looking for. The stodgy meals of pale bean broths that turned an orange hue and chunks of lamb submerged in soups paunched my bony frame; Catherine's robust body thinned. Every soup she ordered was larded with fat; pizzas announced as vegetarian arrived dotted with pepperoni and bacon. Our health faltered; we got colds. In the smoky passages of trains, we fought for the right to open a window and received lectures from Yugoslav passengers that cold air destroys the lungs and causes pneumonia while cigarette smoke makes lungs strong and healthy. In the countryside that passed beyond the windows, we saw makeshift white shrines to the war dead and blocks commemorating martyrs from three years before mingled with monuments from the thirteenth century. There were farms, but no livestock. Hungry people had eaten all the animals.

On our next train, Catherine opened a Serbo-Croatian grammar her parents had bought in the 1970s. A woman reached forward and touched her knee. *"Ma chère mademoiselle,"* she said in a French unused since the Second World War, *"la langue que vous étudiez n'existe plus."*

The Serbo-Croatian language no longer existed, and neither did the country it embodied. We were not in Yugoslavia, but in Serbia, ruled by Slobodan Milosević and watched over by Catherine's parents. At the next stop, a man got in and unfolded a tabloid newspaper. A full-page interview sprawled around the photograph of a familiar face. "Don't look now," I said, "but he's reading an interview with your mother."

Mistaking the language we were speaking for German, the man remonstrated, *"Diese Frau mag nicht was in Kosovo geschieht. Kosovo ist unsere Heimat!"*

Catherine and I glanced at each other, knowing well that Catherine's mother did not like what was happening in Kosovo, and unsurprised that this man regarded the region, which it was unlikely he had ever visited, as his ancestral home.

"Diese Frau," Catherine replied, *"ist meine Mutter."*

As the man sputtered that Kosovo was his true home and no one would beat him, and Catherine asked in German if he had ever been to Kosovo and he admitted that he had not, I thought that the country I needed to see was not Serbia, but the former Yugoslavia.

We hopped off at the next station and read the schedule posted on the wall. A train from Belgrade to Zagreb would pass through in half an hour. We were going to Croatia.

The train was only five cars. Service on this route had just resumed after having been suspended during the Croatian and Bosnian wars. The land was flat, the dark soil supporting tall stalks of corn and unharvested sunflowers rotted black. Our progress was grindingly slow. We shared our compartment with an elderly couple. The man was in his seventies. He sat upright and alert, his eyes magnified by large glasses. His arms bulged with what looked like tumours. The woman was small and clad in black, her grey-streaked hair scraped back off her forehead. When Catherine tried out her Serbian, the woman told her, with a bitter light in her eye, "We are refugees."

They were Serbs from the Krajna whose home had been destroyed by the final Croatian offensive of the war. The resettlement in Serbia they had been promised had left them living under a tarpaulin in the foundations of an unfinished building project. The man had a brother in Zagreb whom they hoped would take them in. The woman showed us her only identification, a typed letter on United Nations High Commission for Refugees letter-head stationery that stated her name. The man wielded a sheaf of documents, including a newly minted Croatian passport. Since the rubble of their home, which had been levelled by Croat mortars, was within the now-enlarged borders of Croatia, he had not been allowed to trade in his expired Yugoslav passport for the Serbian passport he desired. "I must carry the passport of *those people!*"

The train stopped at the border. The man who came in to examine our passports was tall and young with punkish side-burns extending from beneath his uniform cap. He grunted; everyone reached for their documents.

"Hey, cool — Canada!" he said, in shockingly perfect English as I extended my passport. "Where you from, man? Toronto?"

"Montreal."

"No way! I'm from Kitchener. Born and raised. When the war started, I knew where my duty lay. I came over here and served my country. My parents always told me this day would come. Once we got our own country, I figured I'd stay here and defend the border." He handed me back my passport. "You'll love Zagreb, man." He flipped through Catherine's passport, thickened by extra pages and scores of visas. "Hey, guys, have a great time."

He turned to the old man, regarded his passport and grunted challenging questions. He was rougher with the old woman, tossing her UNHCR letter back into her lap. He ordered the refugees to follow him off the train. Out the window, we watched them cross the tracks to an office.

"There's a Canadian who doesn't have an identity crisis," Catherine said.

Tight-lipped, I replied, "That's not my understanding of multiculturalism."

"It makes me despair when I remember what this country was like." Her soft voice respected the stillness that had settled over the train. "It's like Russia. Before, there were babushkas in the Moscow subway who helped people board the trains. 'Not too fast, comrade, you may slip.' 'Lend a hand to the comrade mother with her baby.' 'Another train will be here soon, comrade.' Those ladies were everything I loved about the Soviet Union. And this time, when I went back —" her voice caught "— they were gone! I couldn't believe how much I missed them." As I hugged her, she said, "It's the same here. It's never going to be like that again."

She looked at me with a panicked expression. I tightened my hug until she gasped for breath.

The elderly couple returned to the compartment. The old man was calm, but the woman was furious. She made so many bitter comments that the man told her to be quiet. He slipped a Croatian kuna note, adorned with a portrait of a priest, out of his wallet. "This priest was a fascist," he said, as Catherine translated in a hushed voice, "like Tudjman!"

"You must never say this in Croatia," the woman said.

Outside the train, towns were clustered in the folds of fin-backed hills, each handful of houses dominated by the spire of a Catholic church. New churches were being built above the pink, two-storey houses that were under construction. We had seen similar refugee-housing projects in Serbia, but here the houses were large and plentiful – and many of them were finished, with glass panes in the windows and washing on the line. For the first time, we glimpsed livestock: cows, chickens, geese, a few grubby sheep. When the train arrived in Zagreb, we stood up and shook hands with the refugee couple. "*Do vitenje,*" I said, uncertain whether I was speaking Serbian or Croatian.

Catherine and I stepped out into the cool air. The dark green mountains set the Habsburg squares into harmonious niches. I was back in the post-Mitteleuropa world of Budapest and Prague. Western brand names were everywhere. No longer unique in our foreignness, we heard the voices of German tourists and Australian backpackers.

"I was here before," Catherine said. "The soil is the same, but it's a different country."

"Wasn't it always different? Look at the architecture. By coming here from Belgrade, you go from the Ottoman Empire to the Austro-Hungarian Empire. Yugoslavia was built across a fault-line."

"I used to feel as at home here as in Belgrade. Now I feel like a Serb!"

We found a rundown, overpriced hotel and lost sight of each other in a sagging, king-sized bed. Late at night, rain began to fall. I woke to the sound of grapeshot drumming against glass. Had war resumed? I lay still, listening to the fusillade. In the morning I realized that I had heard the sound of chestnuts, blown off high branches, falling onto cars parked in the street. From the window of our room, I saw sidewalks plastered with leaves. A thick, grey fog blotted out the mountains.

When Catherine rolled over, I glimpsed the grey tint around her gills. "Oh my God," she groaned. "I just want to lie here. If I close my eyes, it'll all go back to how it was before."

"Let's go down to the coast," I said. "Think of the sunshine!"

It took an hour to get her out of bed. In Croatia, breakfast was not a problem. There were Slavic cafés that sold *bureks*, Viennese cafés that sold *Apfelstrudel*, and French cafés that sold croissants. We opted for the *bureks* and ate them while walking through murky streets where huge banners on public buildings blazed a slogan that Catherine translated as *God heed Croatia!* Posters of Pope John Paul II were everywhere, reminding me of the summer I had met Leonie in Poland. That summer I had ascended into a realm of air and light and freedom; now I stood high in the mountains, wrapped in cool, dingy fog. My airy perch had darkened. In a reversal of my earlier venture eastward, I must descend towards the sun.

"I hate this country!" Catherine said, as soon as the lettering on the bus terminal came into sight. "Do you see what they call a bus station? A *kolodvor*!! A 'wheel-yard!' It sounds ridiculous. There's a perfectly good Slavic word for bus station, *stanica*, but they can't use it because it might sound Serbian. They invent some ridiculous word to pretend they speak a different language!"

We entered the gleaming, ultra-modern terminal. When Catherine asked at the information counter about buses to the coastal city of Split, her Russianized Serbian was rebuffed by English, "You should take the 11:30. That one is an express."

The bus to the coast passed through towns of houses with steeply pitched red roofs where bullet holes spattered the stucco façades. We entered the town where our travelling companions of the day before had lived until three years earlier. The streets bustled with new investment, the Croatian shield stood on every street corner and newly built Catholic church spires reached for the sky; the idea that thousands of Serbs and their ancestors had inhabited this town for most of recorded history did not seem credible. Every Christian Orthodox church and monument had been razed; the Cyrillic alphabet had been banished. The radio broadcast the same news over and over. Even without knowing the language, I was able to discern the theme: "The President of the Croatian Republic, Dr. Franjo Tudjman, today –" The news itemized Tudjman's activities as he cut ribbons and opened conferences in provincial towns.

In the late afternoon, we glimpsed Split through a niche in the mountains: the busy port, the market streets turbulent with humanity, the ranks of ugly high-rises behind. We were dropped on the waterfront where buses and boats came and went. In the market, every kind of fruit, grain, meat, egg, bread, and garment was being vociferously sold and bought in a loud tumult of bartering. After austere Belgrade, the abundance of merchandise assaulted the senses more violently than the sunlight. "How do they do it? There aren't any beggars."

"No beggars," Catherine said. "That's a sure sign of fascism."

I felt her personality warping. In England she had considered irony cruel and ungenerous. I knew that she blamed her bitterness on me. We walked to the Roman emperor Diocletian's palace. The locals inhabited the building as part of their daily lives, leaning against a pillar to sell shirts, stacking boxes on the checkerboard marble floor. We sat down on an ancient stone. "I didn't sign up for all this travelling," Catherine said.

Was she talking about our trip, or her life with her parents? The ambassador's wife had obliged Catherine to go travelling with me in full awareness that I, not she, would shoulder Catherine's resentments; she had infiltrated a time-bomb into our relationship in the knowledge that when it exploded Catherine would scurry home.

"You invited me here."

"I invited you to Belgrade to meet my parents." She gave me a disconsolate look. "Where do we go now?"

"Hvar." My travel guide described it as a beautiful offshore island. An island would isolate us from the ravages of Balkan history. On an island, I could have her to myself; on an island, too, anything that went wrong would be my fault.

We rode a ferry for two hours through searing sunshine that reverberated off the blue Adriatic. We sat in seats that looked back at the dwindling shoreline. I held her hand. At the port in Hvar we were met by a woman who led us to a clean room with a balcony overlooking the harbour, the islets in the bay, the boats and the brown, packed-together buildings of the old city. The architecture of the square behind us advertised its Venetian origins. We had left the East. When the door closed behind the landlady, I knew everything was going to be all right. The old town was exquisite, there was hiking nearby. The sole drawback was that the daily ferry back to Split left at seven a.m., an hour at which Catherine found it nearly impossible to get out of bed.

We sat on the balcony and watched the sunset glide across the water. Catherine held my hand, then jumped up and took a photograph of me. I imagine that photo as illustrating a state of contentment I never experienced with her again. That night, at the restaurant, the vegetarian pizza lived up to its billing; the salad that accompanied it was fresh and green. The lamps whose light polished the cobblestones siphoned the greyness out of Catherine's jaw. As we climbed the outdoor stone staircase to our room, I pulled her against me and kissed her. "I do like you a lot, Kevin," she said. "I'm tired now, but tomorrow I'll feel desirous again."

I kissed her, then stared at the brown stonework of the ceiling until I fell asleep.

A light in my mind. A light where there shouldn't be light. The bathroom light. It was on. I struggled to open my eyes, then tried to close them again.

"Are you all right?"

Catherine had dropped her cosmetics bag. She was picking up tubes, o.b.'s, gels. "I have to get the ferry."

"What are you talking about?" My body groaned for sleep. The bedside clock said it was four a.m.

"My mother's dead. I saw it in a nightmare."

"You know she's not really dead," I said. "You can phone –"

"The only phones are in the post office. It doesn't open until eight o'clock. What if I phone and my mother's dead? The ferry will be gone and I'll have to wait twenty-four hours to get out of here ... I have to go, Kevin!"

I hauled myself out of bed and stood next to her. "Catherine, it was a nightmare."

"I've dreamed things before that have come true. You don't know how many illnesses she has." She bunched her hands into fists and closed her eyes. "I saw it so clearly. I know she's dead!"

I laid my hands on her shoulders. She resisted by wilting inward. "We parted on bad terms. She does so much for me. I should show more appreciation."

"How much more appreciation can you show? You subordinate your whole life –"

"*Don't criticize my mother!*"

She shook herself free of my hands. "She's not dead," I murmured, longing to go back to sleep.

"You can't know that. Oh my God, what if she died and I wasn't there — What kind of daughter am I? Kevin, I have to get that ferry!"

I threw myself down on the bed, too tired to move. Catherine had killed her mother in her mind to get revenge on her for having colluded with me, and on me for having colluded with her mother. Any man who became her life partner would have to betray Catherine by collaborating with her parents.

I didn't consider letting her go. I knew I would go with her. That was my weakness. If I had stayed in bed, she might have come back to me on the afternoon ferry, but I was too needy. *Perdre le nord*, the Québécois said of people who became disoriented. Without Catherine, I would lose not my north, but my east.

We griped as we packed. I had paid the landlady for two nights. At six-fifteen we woke her up and asked her to return the fee for the second night. Speaking to us in derisive German, she refused. We walked down to the port, bought tickets, and got on the ferry. I felt desolate as I watched the exquisite Venetian harbour slide away in the morning gloom. The sun came up, turning the Adriatic a bright blue that hurt my eyes. Catherine and I travelled in silence, neither of us sleeping.

On the waterfront in Split, telephones were mounted in the wall close to where rattletrap buses left for the run along the coast. Catherine bought a phone card from a kiosk and dialled the number of the ambassadorial residence in Belgrade. A serving lady put her through to her mother. Their conversation was brief. "She's fine, of course. She's busy. She didn't have time to talk."

We stood in silence. Buses revved their throaty engines, steve-dores unloaded cargoes of fish, tourists photographed men selling hats on the steps of Diocletian's palace.

"I want to go home."

"We'll go home," I replied, feeling a gruff authority return to my voice, "but we're not going back the way we came. We're going to take one more trip together. We're going to Bosnia."

THIRTY-SEVEN

THE BUS DRIVER, NEVER resting more than one hand on the steering wheel, talked on his portable telephone, lighted cigarettes, scratched his head, swung wide on curves as we gasped at the rocky bays. Glacier-hacked mountain ranges kicked rough accordions of rock skyward. Below, on the right, the Adriatic spread bright blue then bright green. Here the hill-tumbled towns of red-tile-roofed houses were free of bullet holes. *Sobe / Zimmer / Rooms / Camere* signs were everywhere. I watched a tall young man in swimming trunks haul himself up onto a pier, pull off his snorkelling gear, and hose himself down. The vignette glowed in my mind until, at the town of Ploče, the bright world vanished.

We drove into a swamp lined with petroleum tanks and poor, shabby apartment blocks. I had lured Catherine on this trip by pointing out that returning across Bosnia was a more direct route to Belgrade than doubling back via Zagreb. But only in theory. I didn't know whether we could cross Bosnia. But I knew that Bosnia, with its cultural multiplicity and its war, was the East I needed to understand.

Only six passengers remained on the bus as it wound through

the swamp that met the Neretva River where black sewage gushed into the water. A line of stopped trucks marked the Bosnian border. The driver parked, got up, and walked back through the bus, collecting passports. Only Catherine and I did not have Bosnian passports. The driver disappeared. When he returned our passports, no stamp had been added. We had not officially left Croatia or entered Bosnia. We were crossing into a zone that was in revolt against the Dayton Peace Agreements. Calling itself the Croatian Republic of Herceg-Bosna, this illegal Croat mini-state had seceded from Bosnia. Not being a recognized country, it could not stamp passports. The Bosnian government did not stamp passports in Mostar, where effective Bosnian control began, because this would legitimize the existence of Herceg-Bosna.

Within five minutes of crossing the border, I saw that in Herceg-Bosna I had descended to a nadir that marked some sort of end to the journey that had begun the day I had watched a quarter of a million people march past my balcony. As the bus drove through low-lying, residually marshy land where hills began to hump up on either side, Croatian flags were wrapped around the hydro lines that hung over the road. Billboards displayed enormous photographs of the leering warlords who ruled Herceg-Bosna.

On the outskirts of Čapljina, surrounded by barren fields, a police cruiser was parked in the middle of the road, its double blue lights flashing. A hundred metres farther on stood another pulsing police car. Between the two cruisers, uniformed police were frisking men who were spread-eagled against halted vehicles. The bus driver hit the brakes, did a U-turn and followed back alleys towards the town centre. The driver yelled requests for directions out the window and nearly ran oncoming cars off the bumpy dirt streets. The fire-scorched, formerly white stucco houses of ethnically cleansed Bosnian Muslims had crumbled; the few houses that remained intact were splashed with the letters H.K.

"*Hvratska kuča*," Catherine murmured. "Croatian house." The mortars had spared the homes of Catholics. A huge, propped-up white cross stood on the hill above the town. The bus crossed the green river into the battered downtown. Bullets had punched through the latticework of the angled wooden blinds that projected out from the apartments' windows. Small buildings lay crumpled in pools of rubble. It was mid-afternoon, but nothing was open. Amid the dirt and dust that filtered into the bus and settled beneath our clothes, an extravagant new town hall rose from dinginess like a hallucination. Stridently Croatian in its pseudo-Habsburg architecture, gaudy in its fresh coat of electric blue paint, the building presided over a domain of colourless dust, ruins, potholes, and a few men digging.

Between Čapljina and Mostar the land lay flat along the banks of the broadening Neretva River; the hills pushed higher. Every roof had disappeared from what had been solid two-storey, red-tile-roofed farmhouses scattered over the green fields. Windows gaped; the bullet-pocked walls accentuated the houses' abandonment. A burnt-out car sat in the middle of a field. Croatian flags flapped on the wires. The warlords' faces smiled at us from billboard after billboard.

"You're Catholic. Didn't you tell me you had something to feel guilty about?"

"I don't want to think about that now." I resented her associating me with this nightmare, resented her lashing back at my having taken advantage of her moment of remorse to bully her into making this journey. *We Are All Bosnians Now.*

As we approached Mostar, military jeeps with "MP" in white

letters on the hood or "SFOR" – the UN Stabilization Force – on the side zoomed past. The plain outside the city was spotted with petroleum storage tanks. Mostar was in ruins. Buildings had been pounded by artillery until their features had melted like those of a plastic mask subjected to a blowtorch. Among the dun-coloured walls that enclosed yards of rubble, it was impossible to guess to which century or style the buildings had belonged.

The driver braked to cross the temporary metal bridge that had replaced the curved bridge, built by Turks in the sixteenth century, that the Croats had destroyed.

Debates in the Hamdaw College MCR filtered back to me. Mostar! I thought. I'm in Mostar!

The transition from the Croatian to the Bosnian side of the river was unforgiving. The driver eased across, the metal plates creaking under the wheels, and parked on the Muslim side. The teenagers who hung out at the new bus station – the only restored building in sight – as though it were a suburban mall, looked thinner and browner than those on the opposite side of the river. Yet this couldn't be true, the tragedy of this hellish landscape was that there were no racial differences among the people who had tried to blast each other out of history. Muslims, Serbs, and Croats emerged from the same Balkan melting pot. As we got off the bus, I saw half a dozen women, huddled together on a bench, wearing hijabs of vestal whiteness.

I went back to my seat and pulled my camera out of my pack. I hadn't taken any photographs on this trip. The landmark of Mostar demanded documentation.

"I can't believe the bridge is gone," Catherine said, her running shoes chiming on the slanted steel sheets. "I came here as a teenager with Yugoslav friends. It was so beautiful!"

We ambled towards the centre of the bridge. The enormous

green mountains, whiffs of cloud teasing their summits, plunged into the fast-flowing Neretva. I took my camera out of my pocket and lined up a shot of the peaks.

"My friend!" A dark, wiry man in a tracksuit bounded out of the bus station, waving his arms. "*Sobe!* You need *sobe*, my friend."

He stepped in front of me, waving his hand before my lens.

"*Vorsichtig*," Catherine murmured to me, warning me to be careful. "*Er kann gefährlich sein.*"

He turned on her. "I no *gefährlich!*" He pushed up against me. "Give me your camera, my friend." His moustache was ragged, his tracksuit grimy. He smelled of dirt and tobacco. "My children need food. War is *gefährlich*. My house *ist kaput*."

"Forget the photo, Kevin."

Catherine was right, yet I wanted a panoramic view of the mountains to certify my arrival in Mostar, the inverted Mecca of my pilgrimage. I ducked past the man's gesticulating arms, got to the edge of the bridge, and raised my camera. The man pushed in front of me. I heard the green water pouring through the canyon, glimpsed the rubble heaped on either side of the river and tried to dance away from the madman. Catherine approached the Croat end of the bridge, where the man and I were hopping around like deranged brothers, jumping as high as we could, I to get my photo, he to block it.

The madman hit her. Spinning in a full-force leap with his arms extended like the whirling dervish of Bosnian lore, he clobbered Catherine in the back of the head with his closed fist.

Catherine toppled straight forward without putting out her hands. Her forehead hit the metal surface with a clang that drove a stab of fear into my ribcage.

"*Gefährlich!*" the madman said, as though he had illustrated a point.

He staggered backwards. Catherine moaned. The bus driver came out of the station, shouting at the top of his lungs. The madman yelled back. I was in Bosnia and didn't understand what anyone was saying. I rushed to Catherine's side and dropped to my knees.

"You are a stupid, stupid man." Over my shoulder, the driver swore at the madman. The sound of the water pouring through the gorge below seemed to grow louder. The teenagers smoking under the overhang of the bus station jeered. The madman fled. Between us, the bus driver and I hoisted Catherine into a sitting position. "My head hurts." Her next words were in Serbian. The driver and I got her into the bus station and sat her on the women's bench. One of the young women got up, bought a Coke, and persuaded the man at the soft drink stand to chip ice off the inside of his freezer and put it in a plastic bag. The woman returned, smiling from beneath her white hijab, and offered Catherine Coke and an ice pack. Ever the diplomat, Catherine drank the Coke, which I knew she hated, and pressed the ice to her forehead.

"*Hvala*," I said, thanking the woman. "*Hvala*."

I bent over Catherine. I wanted to put my arm around her, but refrained out of respect for this bench of shrouded women.

Tears stood in her eyes. She sipped the Coke. The big, tough-looking driver was speaking to her in a consoling voice that I felt unable to match. When she lifted the ice pack from her forehead, I saw a raw blue bruise. The man at the soft drink stall brought her a fresh ice pack, the driver uttered a command, and we all boarded the bus. When I reached out to take Catherine's hand, she kept her small fist clenched. "You have no discipline. I could have dealt with a situation like that when I was six." She leaned forward, wincing in pain. "We're going to arrive in Sarajevo after dark. I just want a doctor to tell me I'm going to be all right."

I slid my arm around her shoulders in the juddering bus. As I longed to give her a full hug, she crumpled into tears. "I feel so sorry for that man —"

"The bastard hit you."

"The driver said he was a schoolteacher. A shell killed his wife and four children."

My children need food. Having starving children was the delirious fantasy of those whose children had been blown to pieces.

Beyond Mostar the destruction grew worse. Every brown wall had been pounded into obliteration. The land turned greener and brighter. Ragged boys gambolled at the roadside, trying to cadge lifts. Billboards boosted "the Coalition" — the Bosnians' multiethnic response to Catholic and Orthodox warlords. The valley narrowed. Beyond a miraculously intact dam, the road ran along the edge of the river, wound against the cliff-face, and darted through tunnels. SFOR military trucks, transports, and jeeps passed going in the opposite direction. A long bridge across the river had been dynamited; a metal cage had been laid over the remnants to keep the route open. SFOR soldiers deployed behind warrens of sandbags stood guarding the replacement bridge. The bus slowed to a crawl. I looked out the window into the eyes of a thin, fair peacekeeper, standing at attention with a Ukrainian flag on the shoulder of his uniform. He looked as though he should be in high school.

The bus drove into a long tunnel. When we came out the other side, we were in an idyllic mountain world where it was hard to believe that war existed. "It's like Switzerland." Catherine squeezed my fingers. The afternoon light gleamed on huge hills of dense forest, prosperous mountain towns untouched by destruction. The river was wide and deep, sliding into vast, still lakes. For the first time, we saw the spindly spires of mosques. "Before the war," Catherine said, "you saw lots of those in Mostar." The area was like an Islamic wonderland. Yet, here, few of the women wore hijabs.

Over the next hour, the dark forests shredded into desultory outcroppings of industrial ugliness that carried us to the outskirts of Sarajevo. We saw the thicket of high rises in the distance, then the long tram line that led into town along the edge of the highway. We arrived at six-thirty. The small bus station was deserted. No one rushed up to offer *sobe*. We walked to the Holiday Inn and were given confused instructions on how to find the accommodation office of the BosniaTours agency. The siege of the city had ended two years earlier, yet the buildings that were receding into darkness looked battered. As we walked away from the Holiday Inn, fifty or more people were bedding down in blankets or sleeping bags to spend the night on the grass behind the hotel.

In the narrow streets of the older neighbourhoods, almost everything was closed. "This city used to be bustling," Catherine said. "It was lively, it was fun." Sensing the weakness in her voice, I reached out to put my arm around her shoulders. Her body remained stiff. "You're the one who wanted to go to Bosnia. And because I had just done something stupid, I felt I wasn't in a position to say no to you." She glanced up at me. "We're completely different, you know. You want problems because you think you'll learn from them. I've got enough problems. I just want peace. The side of me that you find attractive is the part I'm trying to get rid of."

Past experience having taught me that once a woman developed an analysis of how I was not like her, any argument was counter-productive. I said nothing. We walked to the Bosnia-Tours office and found it closed. As I laid my hand on the door the high, broken ululation of the call to prayer shattered the dusk. The moan intensified the streets' emptiness. On a street called Marshall Tito — a name long since removed from streets in Serbia and Croatia — we found buildings with the lights on.

Catherine stumbled against me. "Oh my God."

"What's the matter?"

"Kevin, this is really embarrassing." Closing her eyes and leaning into my chest, she whispered, "I've just wet my pants."

"What?"

"It's that hit on the head. My brain's misfiring." She hugged me. "I don't want to die, Kevin! I need to go home!"

Terror ripped through me. Before my eyes Colin crumpled onto the table at The Eagle and Child. No. Not another hemorrhage. Not Catherine. This couldn't happen again. I must not be responsible for another death.

Before I could speak, Catherine had stepped into an open doorway. In the light, I saw the stain on her pale blue jeans. A man and a woman were tending a store where brandy bottles stood on shelves behind the counter. The prices were in Deutschmark. Catherine approached the woman, who wore a casual headscarf, and asked her directions.

"I'm going to the embassy," she said when she came back.

"Catherine, we can get a hotel — Did you ask about a doctor?"

"I want to go home."

The US Embassy was home? Yes, it was; it always had been. Following her through streets that grew darker as they wound into a residential district, I tried to press practical points. "Won't the embassy be closed?"

"I can talk to the marine."

"What marine?"

"There's always a marine on duty. He'll find me a doctor."

After five minutes, as we returned to the area around the Holiday Inn, the trees fell away and the building stood before us, enormous in its classical white lines, glaring lights, and sprawling grounds enclosed by high, wrought-iron bars. It looked like a caged city block from Washington, D.C., captured and airlifted to the Balkans.

Catherine approached the security booth, spoke to the guards in Serbian and got them to wave us in. We stepped inside the gate. As Catherine had promised, a US marine arrived, a walkie-talkie bobbing from a cord at his belt. "How can I help you, miss?"

She told him whose daughter she was. The marine snapped into action. When Catherine explained what had happened to her, he subjected her forehead to the most perfunctory scrutiny before whipping the walkie-talkie to his mouth. "*Suuh!* Daughter of Head of Station Belgrade is here. Reports an attack on the bridge at Mostar. Injuries sustained. She needs a doctor, *suuh.*" He motioned to Catherine to follow him. "Come right on in, miss."

As I followed her, the marine stepped between us. His face was broad and bland and pale. "Who are you?"

"I'm her boyfriend."

"You're not married? You 'Murrican, suuh? Are you a citizen of the United States?"

Catherine disappeared into the bright glow of the security lights. They set the vast lawn agleam with a sheen that made the grass look like astroturf. "No, I'm Canadian."

"This is 'Murrican territory. If you're not married, you're not a legal couple." His walkie-talkie crackled. "*Suuh!* Unattached foreign national, suuh ... *Yes, suuh!*" He nodded to me. "You stay here."

"Catherine!" I shouted. "This is ridiculous."

The guards escorted me out the gate. The marine accompanied Catherine towards the embassy building. When I looked back, her silhouette had melted to a dark blob at the core of a vast field of light.

THIRTY-EIGHT

I STUMBLED ALONG UNEVEN sidewalks in the dark. In this residential neighbourhood, many of the trees and mansions had survived the siege. I got lost and wandered around in circles. Deprived of Catherine's soothing voice, I was agitated and confused. I found my way back to Marshall Tito. On a side street, a nineteenth-century house had been converted into a hotel. A single room, negotiated in the German I had learned sitting next to Catherine, cost thirty Deutschmarks. My room was made of bare pine boards so bright and unfinished that I got a splinter in my finger. I made a mental note of this detail and of the details of the people I saw at the doner kebab stand where I bought my supper. I thought of how I would relate each of these encounters to Catherine, repairing the rent in our shared memories. "God forgive me," the protagonist of *Sword of Honour* said at the end of the last volume of the trilogy. As Waugh's character did his Yugoslav penance, so I would do mine. If I hadn't felt guilty about her concussion, I would have fought harder not to be separated from her at the embassy. Remorse would earn me my reunion with Catherine. All night I kept waking and listening for her breath.

In the morning light, Sarajevo was strange and enticing. In the old city, the cobblestones that had been blasted during the siege were being laid again. The streets were full of café tables, rendered incongruous by the mountains and minarets that rose behind them. The cafés were full, as though no one had to go to work. I wandered into the market, where hut-like stalls displayed a wondrous variety of clothes and handicrafts for sale at high Deutschmark prices. Nearly everyone was a foreigner, even some of the market vendors were anomalously blond representatives of Norwegian or Irish NGOs. Uniformed soldiers from Spain, Germany, and the US surveyed the wares. Finnish policemen and Italian *carabinieri* bargained in gruff voices, serving as the first line of consumers. At the café tables, bureaucrats spoke in Euro-English.

"He will not agree to organize the workshops in this manner."

"We are obliged to raise the productivity quotient of this program."

How Catherine would have mocked them! Passing stooped young Muslim men filing into a mosque, where green-bordered funeral announcements in Latin script were preceded by flourishes of Arabic, I walked until I found a small shopping mall with a restaurant in the basement. Having left my hotel with the vague idea of exploring Sarajevo before getting a bus to Belgrade to meet up with Catherine, I had ignored breakfast. I entered the restaurant just before noon. The menu was printed in the Bosnian variant of the ex-language of Serbo-Croatian. Seeing me hesitate, the well-dressed waiter shouted in the direction of the kitchen. A young woman in blue jeans emerged. "Need some help, do we?" she said in English with a London lilt. Her dark brown eyes regarded me from beneath a stylish page-boy haircut. "Are you just travelling around, then?"

I told her I'd been travelling with my girlfriend, who'd had an accident and had gone ahead to Belgrade for medical treatment. She smiled, then ordered me a vast lunch that started with a thick soup and an enormous salad. She asked whether I minded if she sat down.

Emina's family had been scattered by the war. At seventeen, she had been accepted as a refugee – "asylum-seeker," she said, using the derogatory British phrase – and had completed university in London while trying to locate the surviving members of her family. "Two years ago when I came back, this city looked horrible. This year, it looks better. Sarajevo is the one place in Bosnia where the three cultures are still living together, so foreign governments can justify sending aid here. Now, if you didn't lose immediate family members, you can get on with your life. It's hard for people like my mother; her parents and her brother were killed. We are looking after my uncle's wife and little girl. They sleep in my room and I sleep on the couch. Now I am an asylum-seeker in my own home!"

Her father owned the restaurant. He lost money on a day-by-day basis, but made big profits on banquets hosted by international organizations.

My soup and salad were succeeded by a breaded veal cutlet with cucumber. After the cutlet came a Bosnian *lonica*, a peppery stew served in a clay pot with a tight-fitting lid.

"How are you getting back to Belgrade?" Emina asked.

"On the bus."

She shook her head. "Nothing here is that simple. The bus to Belgrade leaves from a Serb suburb." She paused. "My father's Serb friends moved there. He talks to them on the phone, but he doesn't go to visit them because someone might damage his car. I wanted to go because CDs are cheaper, but it's hard to find a taxi driver who will take you, and if they hear my accent, I could have problems."

"I can't get a bus to Belgrade unless I can pass for a Serb?"

"You have to take the overnight bus to Zagreb," Emina said, as the waiter placed a strong coffee in front of her. "I'll take you to the station. I'm seeing my boyfriend this evening, but I'm free until then."

I ate baklava and a flan slathered in cream. I would have to take the route that I had denied to Catherine, double back to Zagreb and catch a bus to Belgrade from there. "Did your boyfriend stay here during the siege?"

"Yes, his father is a Serb who fought in the Bosnian Army. A lot of Muslims were suspicious of him, but he was able to do it. There are some Serbs in the Bosnian Army, but no Croats."

I tried to remember everything she said so that I could share it with Catherine. I wished she were here to speak to Emina in her own language. When the waiter brought my bill, the un-expectedly reasonable price made clear that I had received a reduced rate.

Emina, in high spirits, walked me around Sarajevo. Her young woman's pleasure in entertaining a man alleviated my anxieties, assuring me that when I saw Catherine in Belgrade, everything would be all right. Turning a corner, Emina pointed to a hilltop at the end of the street, "Until three years ago, the Serb artillery was right *there*." A little farther down the street, "My grandmother was blown up on this corner. The rest of us were in different countries, so none of us found out until months later." Later she touched my arm and pointed to a building where framed photo-graphs of Zagreb and Dubrovnik hung in the glass window. "This is the Croatian Cultural Centre. You see! You couldn't have a Muslim Cultural Centre in Zagreb or Belgrade. Someone would throw a bomb at it."

I had come to Bosnia in search of the dark core of my world. The bridge in Mostar had given me this, in more violent shades than I had wished. Emina revealed the tenuous persistence of the layered world of before. After two hours, she walked me to the little bus station and ordered me a one-way ticket to Zagreb. I paid and received a tiny cardboard ticket and a grooved metal slug that opened the turnstile to the platform. Emina looked at her watch. "I've got just time for a spot of coffee before I go to the mosque."

We went to a dingy café with a television in the corner. There were no women or foreigners. All the men were smoking. Fending off stares, Emina ordered two espressos. "I couldn't come into a place like this by myself, and my boyfriend refuses to bring me. After living in London, though, I have this odd idea that women should be able to sit wherever they please." We shared London experiences until Emina slid a headscarf out of her pocket. "Evening prayer. I have to go."

"I thought you were seeing your boyfriend?"

"First mosque, then boyfriend."

"You can be a Muslim and have a boyfriend?"

"Why on earth not? I don't throw every detail in my parents' faces the way English girls do. There are questions they know better than to ask and I would never answer."

As we entered the street, the eerie ululation of the call to prayer reverberated through the cobblestones. Emina extended her hand. "Have a good trip. I hope you get back together with your girlfriend."

She hadn't believed my story for a second. Night came on.

The bus to Zagreb was a double-decker German luxury liner. The driver's assistant told me in German to keep my feet off the seat because the bus was imported. All night we were kept awake by Steven Seagal movies. In each movie, Seagal blew away dozens of bad guys, his gun blasting at high volume as we drove through cities like Bihać, where the most furious battles in recent European history had been fought. In the morning, I stumbled out and bought a ticket on the eleven a.m. bus to Belgrade. The trip took all day. As the Serbs wouldn't allow a Croat bus to besmirch their homeland, we had to cross the border on foot with our luggage, show our passports, explain our business, then climb into a beat-up Serbian bus. Most of the passengers were Croat women rippling wads of one-hundred-Deutschmark notes. They were going shopping in Belgrade, the last redoubt of rock-bottom East Bloc prices. The woman sitting next to me, though, was a Serb who had gone to Zagreb to find a job. After telling me this in German, she opened a tabloid newspaper. At the top of the front page, Catherine's face stared at me.

I grabbed the paper. "What does it say?"

My neighbour explained that this was the American ambassador's daughter, who had been attacked by a Muslim terrorist. "The Muslims are not Europeans. We will throw them out!"

I felt sick at seeing Catherine's face hung out for public viewing. She looked pale and startled. The fact of her following in her mother's footsteps as Balkan tabloid fodder made her feel unreachable. Watching the Croatian shoppers regard the rough-and-tumble Belgrade skyline as it approached in the evening light, I shared their nervousness. For the first time, I had doubts about what would happen when I saw Catherine.

In the bus station, I found a huge taxi driver with a drooping moustache. *"Dedinje,"* I said. *"Das Haus von dem amerikanischen Botschafter."* The second time I said it, he understood. He suggested a price that was probably far too high, then reduced it when I offered to pay in Deutschmark. We crossed the bridge over the highway, turned the corner and went up the hill into the white villas. The driver braked as we passed Milosević's villa with the Yugo police cars parked in front. When we reached the ambassadorial residence, the driver stopped and gave me a quizzical look. I paid him, hoisted my compact backpack and walked towards the security booth. I gave the guards a nonchalant wave. They waved back, as though I had just stepped out for a stroll. I walked up the drive, past the lawns gleaming beneath floodlights, opened the front door and walked into the entrance hall. Yugoslav women in aprons appeared. *"Molim,"* I said. *"Gdje* Catherine?"

One woman held up her hand while the other hurried towards the elevator. I listened to the ticking of the grandfather clock and the shifting of the marine's boots two floors above me. A few minutes later the elevator whined again, the door opened, and Edith came out. "I was just tryin' to figure out what to do with your stuff."

I had forgotten about Edith, her big hair and big belly, clattering wrist bangles and glinting gold watch. "You can leave my stuff where it is. I'm going upstairs to see Catherine."

I started past her. She grabbed my wrist with a meaty palm of perspiring Southern warmth. "Catherine's in the military hospital in Germany. She came back from Sarajevo in the limousine last night. The doctor suspected a concussion, so we got her onto a flight this morning. That was a real big hassle you got her into! The ambassador figured you'd do a better job of lookin' after his little girl." She shook her tumbling hairdo. "When's your flight back to England?"

"Three days from now," I murmured. "Catherine isn't alone in Germany, is she? Her mother went with her?"

"The ambassador's wife has a real busy schedule. She can't change it just like that."

"You sent her to a hospital in Germany by herself? Don't you care about her?"

"The way I see it, we all care for her a heap better than you done."

"I want to talk to the ambassador's wife."

"I'll make a note of your request."

A woman in an apron hurried out of the kitchen, picked up my pack and headed up the stairs. A second woman beckoned to me. As I was hungry, I followed her into the kitchen. The Serbian food was good, though not as savoury as Bosnian fare. I sat alone in the high-ceilinged white kitchen, feeling severed from love and friendship. When I had finished, I walked upstairs and found my way to the room that had been occupied by former Senator Bob Dole, and Special Envoy Richard Holbrooke, the most dangerous ballistic missile in the Balkans. I looked in the bag of my belongings that had been brought down from Catherine's garret and found a fresh T-shirt.

A woman in an apron came to my door, "*Molim.*" I followed her to the third-floor study. The ambassador's wife and I exchanged wary glances. Sitting down in the middle of the couch, she waved me to an armchair. She wore baggy dress pants that accentuated the shortness of her legs. Her dark eyes observed me across the ruffled collar of her blouse. Perched on the lip of a cushion that was too large for her, she looked like a tiny Turkish pasha overseeing the Ottoman occupation. I bent towards her like a supplicant. We spoke in a desultory way about Bosnia. "They haven't developed any infrastructure or manufacturing," she said. "The whole economy is service industries for soldiers and NGOs. When the foreigners go home, they won't have any customers."

Sensing that she was skirting a conversation, in time-honoured diplomatic fashion, I said, "Do you want to hear what happened to Catherine? My version?" She indicated neither yes nor no. I went ahead. She listened without comment. "I shouldn't have tried to take the picture," I concluded. "It was the only photograph I took on the trip."

"I guess you have a souvenir."

Her drooping cheeks were innocent of ironic intent. "When is Catherine coming back?"

"It's a light concussion, you'll be happy to hear, so they'll probably send her home in a few days. A person who's suffered a concussion needs rest. She'll stay here until she's better. At least I hope she can stay here. I hope we can all stay. The fighting in Kosovo has started again —"

She slipped into the kind of conversation with which she was comfortable. I interrupted her, "Is there a phone number where I can reach her?"

"When she comes home, you can call her here."

"You mean there isn't a phone number at the hospital, or you're not willing to give it to me?"

The ambassador's wife paused. I marvelled that this no-nonsense little woman, with her Cherokee cheekbones and just-folks directness, had become the unofficial empress of the Balkans. In her hesitation I detected a resurgence of our complicity, until she said, "Hospital phone numbers are for family members. You are not family." Then, offering me the concession that would forge a diplomatic compromise, she said, "Would you like to check your email?"

I stood up, feeling as though I had left my innards on the seat of the chair. Was it possible, in late 1998, for a mother to break up her daughter's relationship when both the daughter and her lover were over thirty? *A still stream.* I heard Alex say. *You know that from now on Onegin's life won't be worth shit.*

The ambassador's wife left me at her computer. I scrolled through two weeks of spam and found a message from my mother announcing that my sister had split up with her husband. The event left me cold; my own relationship mattered so much more than a suburban marriage gone stale.

As I was about to turn off the computer, a new message appeared from Dr. Leon Zamenhof. Next to the sender's name was a red exclamation point.

Oi, mate. I just tried ringing your flat and answer came there none, so I suppose you're still in Slobo's State of Ethnic Purity. I've got a rather odd development to report. I'm here working late at the uni and the co-op rang with their knickers in a twist because a moving agency turned up at my old digs, carted off the storage bin and announced they were sending it to, of all places, the DHL office in Amsterdam. Alex's name was on the invoice.

He certainly wields considerable clout these days! I rang the co-op, but it's too late. The bin, which is the property of the collectivity, is off to Holland, on its way to California, I reckon. All this happened at four o'clock this afternoon. If you want to reclaim your belongings, you had better get to Amsterdam by

tomorrow. Otherwise, mate, I'm afraid you've seen the last
of them.

I wrote him a terse note of thanks. I thought about how the villa's furniture, down to the swivel-chair I was sitting in, had been driven to Amsterdam the last time war had broken out in Kosovo. Before turning off the computer, I looked up the address of the Amsterdam DHL office. *Hornweg 64.* It was west of downtown and appeared to be difficult to reach by public transportation. I went in search of the ambassador's wife and found Edith. "Could you drive me to the airport in the morning?" I asked. "I'm going to change my ticket."

"Sure," Edith said, with a big-mouthed smile. "It'd be a pleasure."

THIRTY-NINE

THE MORNING LIGHT SLANTED through the glass walls of the quiet Belgrade terminal. Many airlines had cancelled their services to Yugoslavia, making this feel like the airport of a much smaller city. The Alitalia counter was deserted but for a gruff middle-aged Serbian woman. I explained to her in halting German that I no longer wanted to go to London, but to Amsterdam. She scowled at me, lifted the receiver of the phone and spoke in Serbian. *"Zweihundertachtzig Deutschmark,"* she said.

I had little money, but fewer choices. Not to catch up with Alex was unthinkable.

I peeled off three one-hundred Deutschmark notes. I had one more left, along with about two hundred US dollars. I didn't want to think about how I would get back to London. On the flight from Rome to Amsterdam, I fell asleep. I was still groggy when we landed. The sunlit corridors of Schiphol Airport dazzled me. After the Balkans, everything felt bright and crowded. I smelled the crisscrossing odours of waffles and sausages, took in familiar logos and others I had never seen before. I felt as out of place as a man in a sheepskin coat. I missed Catherine and the self-assured reserve with which she encountered the world's strangeness. People brushed past me; announcements blared in English and Dutch. I put one foot in front of the other and shuffled forward through the crowds. I felt disoriented by the ease and efficiency, the absence of political slogans, walls pocked with bullet holes, warring alphabets, or religious excess.

I picked up my backpack at the luggage carousel. It was two-thirty in the afternoon. I walked to the taxi queue and got into a cab, tense with anxiety that I was making a fool of myself. Even if Alex was at the DHL office, how would I get my stuff back to London? The taxi skirted the city centre, stitching from one point on its western fringes to another. From the highway, I glimpsed drab apartment blocks, sprawling parks, a station along a light rail line where hundreds of bicycles were locked at racks, a sign to a golf course. The DHL office was located at the base of a rectangular peninsula bordered by canals to the east and west and a river to the north. I felt as though I were entering a trap.

The taxi pulled into a yard in front of a series of closed loading bays. DHL trucks, yellow with red logos, were lined up on the edge of the yard. The offices were in a nondescript two-storey building. I paid the driver with my last hundred-Deutschmark note and received a wad of Dutch change. I stuffed the money into my wallet next to my remaining US dollars. It was a cool, windy day. The taxi disappeared and I walked to the office.

Behind the reception desk, two tall, bored men in DHL shirts looked up.

"I am looking for a friend," I said. "His name is Alexander Spokoynov —"

The unshaven man on the right glanced at his partner. They exchanged a few words in Dutch. "The Russians?" he said. "They are in the back room. They have been there since almost two hours."

The clean-shaven man swung up a hinged segment of the desk and waved me through. We walked down a corridor and into the cavernous warehouse. An Afro-Caribbean man in a helmet drove a forklift across the warehouse floor, lifted a pallet piled high with boxes and transported his cargo towards the loading bays. The stale dryness of the air heightened my sense of unreality.

At the back of the warehouse, two crewcut men dressed in dark tracksuits lounged in front of a door. The Dutchman looked at me. "Tell them they do not have the right to shut the door. We give them this room to make one package. They must not shut the door. It is forbidden. Tell them this in Russian!"

I felt gutted by ignorance. How much more solid my friendship with Alex, my love for Catherine, would be if I knew Russian! I tried to dredge up Russian words. "*Brat* Alex," I said. "*Tovarisch* Alex. *Spasiba.*"

I insinuated myself between the two men. They clamped my arms with practised expertise, holding me fast.

Before I had time to react, the DHL man said, "This is forbidden! I will call the police!"

They must have understood the word "police," because my burning arms, aching where they had the night Stan and the security guards had marched me out of Hamdaw, were freed. "Cool," one of the Russians said. He offered a mockery of a smile. "*Nyet* police. Cool, man."

The DHL man shrugged his shoulders and backed off. The second Russian gave me a curtailed wave, inviting me to follow him through the door.

There are doors you step through and can never step back out of. Even today I struggle to understand what I felt when that young thug let me into the windowless staging room where

Alex sat on his knees, surrounded by his Russian library. A third, slightly older man in a tracksuit was with him. Grey hardback books lay in rows on the concrete floor. I glimpsed the gold Cyrillic lettering that had glowed behind the glass wall of Alex's room beneath Oxford's cloudy skies. This Alex's face was bloated by comparison with the Alex I had seen the night I had earned my rustication. The thickness of his neck had blurred the lean set of his jaw. His hair, longer than that of his crewcut comrades, curled over his ears. His mouth was pinched in a disconsolate expression, and his cheeks were mottled. In his hands he held a bore. His left hand capped the top of the bore, while his right hand gripped the S-shaped handle and rotated the awl-like point at the bottom. Beneath the bore was an open book.

I was so startled to see him that I failed to grasp what he was doing. My escort closed the door against the DHL man's protestations.

I looked again. Alex was hollowing out a book.

He ignored me, shouting at the guys in tracksuits in the voice of a boss. The young guy who had accompanied me into the room left. Alex and I were alone with the man who was closer to Alex's age. At last Alex looked at me. "What the *fuck* are you doing here?"

"I came to get my stuff."

He waved at the end of the room. My clothes and paperbacks were scattered on the floor. My High Table suit lay apart from the rest, flat on its back like a deflated corpse. "Take it and get the fuck out of here." He remained on his knees, rotating the bore. "We've fucked up. We thought we could do this fast. It's taking way too long and those fuckers are getting suspicious."

He lifted the bore and blew on the cavity he had excavated. Fragments of print-smeared paper flew up into the air like dark confetti. He turned to a suitcase at his side, opened the lid and lifted one of a heap of transparent baggies filled with white powder. He pushed the baggy into the hole in the book and closed the cover. He set the book on a pile on his left and reached for a fresh book from a pile on his right.

"Who's that?" I said. "Chekhov? Tolstoy? Maybe it's the book you read to me that night — the one that quotes Pushkin's line about the rest of your life being a still stream?"

"I have to fucking finish this job or we're all going to fucking rot in jail." His right hand swirled. The dry, paper-smell in the air reminded me of the Duke Humfrey's Library in Oxford. He looked at me from under his brows. "If you don't want this guy to throw you out, help me."

"Alex, you lived for literature —"

"It's all fucking finished. Everything you and me and every literate person back to the Greeks lived for. I saw the future in Moscow. Brutality and coke and fucking unbelievable amounts of money and bodyguards with AK47s and women you pay for and computer screens you stare at until you can't think or imagine. That's what's coming. Either you get a ton of money or you get crushed. I know where I want to be!" He gasped, blew a fresh litter of paper into the air, stuffed a baggy into the cavity and closed the cover. "Goncharov may have been a fucking civil servant, but he wrote a book long enough to put a baggy in!" He spoke in Russian. The other man stepped forward. "Help me, Kevin. Or else get the fuck out of here."

I glanced at my scattered belongings. I hadn't come here for this miserable hoard. I breathed in the stale air, saturated with paper-shavings. Specks of Dostoevsky, Bulgakov, Gorky, Bitov, Tolstoy, and Pushkin stuck to my throat causing an arid thirst. The moment I touched the books, I would be criminally responsible.

The man's hands tightened on my right arm. I was sick of people throwing me out. If I let this thug eject me, I would never see Alex again. I stepped forward, shook my arms free and set my backpack on the floor. I picked up three books from the pile on Alex's left and put them into the box. Then I returned for three more and bricked them in as tightly as those below. I laid the loaded books in neat rows in the DHL box. The other man hefted the boxes onto a stack he was building on a wooden pallet that had openings on the side to accommodate the tines of the forklift. We worked in silence until Alex said, "What do you care about these books, man? You can't read Russian."

He lifted the head of the bore and blew away more tainted confetti. "Catherine says I'd understand your personality if only I spoke Russian."

"Catherine! You never know what that woman's thinking."

The edge in his voice reminded me of *Colonel Redl*. I tried to meet his eyes. "Did you fuck my girlfriend?"

"I'm sorry, brother, just once –"

"The night you went skinny-dipping?"

"No. No way, man."

"Catherine said that when she took her clothes off, you looked at her like a man who appreciated a woman."

"She told you that? Holy fuck, hold onto that woman, man." The swivelling movement of his hands on the bore paused. "Fuck, we've got fifteen baggies left!" His right hand spun around, shredding spools of paper. He packed cocaine into *Dead Souls* and *Crime and Punishment* and *The Golovlyov Family*. I put the bulging volume in the last box. "I phoned her after. I sent my car over for her. I'm sorry, man."

"It was her choice. Our relationship hasn't been one hundred per cent faithful on either side."

"That sounds more fucking realistic than most relationships." He leaned forward to blow away shards of paper. "It just happened once. I didn't call her again and she didn't call me. It sounds kind of perverted, but I think we both missed you. "

This was, possibly, the second time that Alex and I had slept with the same woman. An intimacy that was also resentment roiled inside me. I wanted to be close to him to erase his closeness with Catherine. The dual image of Catherine riding a US government limousine back to Belgrade from Sarajevo and riding Alex's chauffeur-driven Range Rover to his Moscow apartment wrenched my mind. For a strange moment, I wanted the packing of defaced books to go on forever. I was as unsettled as Alex was relieved when we finished and stood up.

He whined out an order in his high-pitched Russian. The other man hurried forward and they lifted the last box onto the pallet. My High Table suit, paperbacks, jeans and T-shirts remained abandoned on the far side of the room. "Take your fucking stuff. We're shipping these boxes and we're getting the fuck out of here."

He laid his hand on the door handle. As he opened the door and we slipped out into the vast main space of the warehouse, a desultory shout echoed from the front of the building, the sound muffled by rows of ceiling-high racks stacked with boxes and huge containers. I gripped the sleeve of Alex's black leather jacket. "Alex, the night Colin died, what was the poem you recited?"

"It was *Onegin* — you know that."

The part at the end when Onegin realizes that Tatiana will never be his. What a strange requiem for a dead young man!

The mystery of it pulled me towards him. "Alex, Leon and I —"

A shout in Russian. The man who had been in the back room with us bolted past, running towards the front of the building. Alex and I dodged sideways, until we were able to peer around the end of a row of stacked boxes.

At the front of the warehouse, where light from the reception desk poured in, Alex's three accomplices were in a dancing stand-off with four police officers.

A reverse avalanche of heat poured up my legs. My face and body began to sweat. My legs were trembling. *"Leon and I killed Colin,"* I whispered. As the words came out, I understood why I had persisted in taking that worthless photograph on the bridge, why I could find redemption only in killing the union that might save me.

A shaft of cool logic penetrated my scrambled perceptions. If I left my backpack behind, I would be the first member of this gang to be identified. I turned around, lunged back into the room and swung the pack onto my shoulders. When I stepped back outside, Alex had cut to the left, edging towards a wash of light along the warehouse's side wall: an open loading bay. My heart was not so much thumping as squirming. Alex started to run. I ran after him.

"Did you hear me?" I gasped. "Leon and me ... And Colin ... He'd been to Moscow."

My breath was gone. My need to reach Alex flung me forward. My pack wasn't large or heavy, but it was an extra weight. I ran in spite of it. Alex cut around boxes that the forklift driver had piled on the lip of the loading bay. He jumped. I heard a grunt.

I stumbled, felt sweat all over my body and drove myself forward until I came out onto the dimpled metal of the loading bay. Alex had fallen beneath the wheel of a truck. A parked truck.

He lay still, then pulled himself out from beneath the vehicle and began to run. The lip of the loading bay clanged beneath my feet. I heard a whine and a shout. I turned around. The fork-lift was driving towards me. When I turned to look out again, Alex had vanished. I realized I was at the front of the building. Hornweg, and a wide highway behind it, were across the park-ing lot. Cloud had closed in without dimming the sun. Conscious of the pack jolting on my shoulders, I crouched down and, pivot-ing on my palm, slid over the edge of the loading bay, hung there by my arms for a second then dropped onto the tarmac of the parking lot. I ran out to Hornweg. Traffic hurtled past. I looked back and saw the forklift driver staring at me from under his yellow helmet. I bolted forward. A horn honked. I rushed onward with my head down until I fell on my hands on the grassy median. I gasped for breath, hauled myself upright, waited for a gap in the traffic and ran across the highway. On the other side there was a double row of trees. I staggered in exhaustion against a slender trunk and looked back at the loading bay. The driver was gone. My breath was drawn short by the off-kilter moaning of Dutch police sirens. I had to get away from this peninsula before the police cordoned it off. I had to find Alex. We hadn't finished our conversation.

Behind the trees was a path where bicycles sped past. A pedes-trian lane ran alongside the cycle lane. Sweating, I headed south. I tried to move as fast as I could without attracting attention. Not even in Holland did people wear backpacks to go jogging. Beyond the path lay a bay of murky water, obscured by huge warehouses. Barges steamed through the bay; enormous, corru-gated metal containers were piled on the docks. The sirens' howling subsided. By now the police would have arrested Alex's accomplices. If they caught Alex, I was finished. This morning

I had woken up in a room that had been occupied by a former United States Senator; now I was a fugitive. If I was caught, my rustication would be cited as the first stage in a downward spiral. The best I could hope for was weeks of detention, questioning, legal problems, a prison sentence for aiding and abetting. My breath contracted in my throat. Catherine in hospital, I thought, and me in jail.

As the muffled sun began to fade into the late-afternoon clouds, a damp cold came up through the earth. Having flown in from the fringes of the Adriatic, I had forgotten that it was late November. Through the trees, I saw a police car go past. A routine patrol, or were they looking for us? I continued down the path. I had never felt more isolated or alone. The path curved past warehouses. The angle from which I was looking at the docks told me that I had left the squared-off peninsula and was walking along the water's edge in the direction of downtown. I was still a long way from tourist Amsterdam, snared in a net of highways and industry, where a man with a backpack would attract attention. I heard dipping and moaning sirens; two police cars raced along the highway. As soon as they arrested Alex and got my name, I would be the object of a manhunt that I had little chance of eluding.

The trees grew sparser. I was visible to anyone who drove past. The water was closer on my left. The day turned greyer. The path became a sidewalk that ran along the edge of a busy road. There were docks and warehouses on my left. As the first smudge of dusk smeared the clouds, I was amazed to spot an Ibis Hotel, its cheerful red logo the emblem of lower-middle-class European travel. This was a place where a backpack would blend in. I brushed down my clothes and ran my hands through my hair. I walked into the lobby, where an Asian receptionist in a blazer was giving directions to a blond man in English that was native to neither of them. No one paid me any attention. I stood still, enjoying the luxury of breathing normally. I took off my pack and sat down in an armchair to consider my next move. Then I realized it was obvious.

I loitered by the door. When a taxi pulled in to drop off a man in a business suit, I stepped out and hailed the driver. What could be more mundane than a man with luggage stepping out of a hotel to get into a taxi? Knowing nothing of Amsterdam, I asked the driver to take me to the train station. I assumed it would be downtown. As the taxi swung onto the highway, I felt an eerie elation, as though I were being lofted into space. I was free, I was safe. Relief lowered my defences; exhaustion engulfed me. I was woken by a voice hammering into my brain, "You do not sleep in my taxi!"

"Sorry, I was up late last night."

"You come here for the smoke or the girls?"

"The girls," I said.

He laughed. The taxi slowed as we entered narrow streets where water glinted in the darkness and trams clanked along tracks. I glimpsed quaint old walk-ups stumbling against each other along the banks of the canals. I wondered where Alex was. Even if he had got away, he had lost everything. He had studied at Oxford and Harvard and become an investment banker. Now he was a criminal. Yet his greatest loss, his most unforgivable crime, was his destruction of his literary culture.

The taxi got stuck in traffic. Telling the driver I would walk to the station, I paid him with the Dutch guilders I had received as change from my first taxi ride. I walked through the centre of Amsterdam, feeling exhilarated and free. There were tourists everywhere; nobody looked twice at my pack. The glare of neon heightened my post-Yugoslav culture shock. I wished I could share my re-acclimatization with Catherine. I burned to confess to Alex. I dipped down closer to the water on an inlet and found myself staring at a transparent cube with a woman inside. She made eyes at me and ran her fingers over her lips. The thought of Catherine locked in a military hospital with tubes in her arms filled me with tenderness. Starving, I walked into a pub with a TV over the counter. I sat at the bar and ordered Indonesian noodles and spicy beef with a tangy soup. I watched the Dutch TV news and was unable to discern any reference to a drug bust. The food soothed me, then my panic returned. I had to find Alex, yet I also wanted to be free of this mess, confident I could board a plane without being arrested.

Two Brits in black leather jackets sat down next to me and ordered Pilseners. Spotting the backpack at the foot of my stool, one of them said, "What's the matter, mate? Couldn't find a hostel?"

They boasted that their hostel had a lounge reserved for pot smoking. Irritated, I paid, left, and walked into Amsterdam's uptown core. Hostels appeared; the fourth one where I asked had a vacancy. The price was more than that of a Yugoslav *sobe*, but I had enough guilder to cover it. When the middle-aged man at the reception desk asked for my passport, I began to sweat. He returned my document after making a copy of the photo page. If the police were looking for me, they would eventually find out where I had spent the night. I walked down the hall to a whitewashed room that contained four steel-framed bunkbeds fitted with taut white sheets. A voluminous blue duvet covered each bed. I clipped my backpack to the frame of my bed, walked down the hall to the men's toilet facilities and took a shower. The shower was grimy, but the warm water bore me to the edge of sleep as it sluiced away my sweat. As drowsiness overcame me, I felt helpless and panicked. My empty, spartan room was a prison cell. I put on my swimming trunks and a T-shirt. It wasn't yet nine o'clock, but, as my bout of nerves subsided, my energy drained away and I fell asleep. I woke at two a.m. when two stoned Irish girls stumbled into the room, turned on the light and flopped against each other as they got ready for bed. It was four a.m. before anyone else arrived. I lay awake and tried to figure out where Alex had run to. He couldn't cross the English Channel or get on a plane. The only direction in which the borders were open was east.

At seven a.m., with the bunks sagging with comatose young people, I got up, slipped down the hall to the washroom, and shaved. I would be less likely to be taken for a fugitive if I didn't look like one. I dressed and carried my pack to the front of the hostel. Breakfast, a generous ration of sliced meat and cheese, dark bread, and coffee, was laid out in a side room. I forced myself to sit down and eat. I had a few guilder left and two hundred US dollars. My Barclay card might work in the banking machines, but, like the photocopy of my passport, it would betray my whereabouts.

Outside, the clubs on the square were silent. Stolid clerks and secretaries cycled to work through a whitish morning mist. When I walked to a corner store to spend my remaining guilder on a phone card, the dark-skinned man behind the counter addressed me in English without bothering to find out whether I was Dutch. Not only had I flown from Europe's south to its north, but from its past to its future; from history as tyranny, minute gradations of ethnicity that demanded division, destruction and slaughter, to a drugged, porn-gorged, global-English-speaking haze of self-gratifying individualism.

I tried to put myself in an academic frame of mind. I was about to phone Oxford. One always phoned an Oxford don on the hour because it was the only time when you could be certain you weren't interrupting a tutorial. At nine o'clock sharp I slipped my card into a pay phone on a quiet street corner and dialled the Hamdaw College Lodge. "Could you put me through to Mr. Robinson?" I asked the porter. After a series of clicks, Zed's voice answered, clipped and forbidding.

"Are you coming back to submit?" he said, when I had identified myself.

"At the beginning of next term. But that's not what I'm ringing about." A police siren howled. I lowered the receiver to waist level, my palm sweating against the hard rubber. My legs were shaking too hard for me to move. The police car shot past. My chest shuddering, I lifted the receiver. "Zed? Sorry about that. A police car went by."

"I heard. What an odd siren. Have you returned to Canada?"

"I know you keep tabs on Hamdaw graduates," I said. "I'm looking for an address —"

"If I can help you, I shall."

He was as good as his word. Two minutes later I hung up and walked to the station to look for a long-distance bus. No one asked for identification when I bought my ticket. Yet I was no longer in Eastern Europe, where US dollars were king. My offer to pay in dollars resulted in my being directed to an exchange booth. For an extortionate commission, I divided my dollars into guilder for the ticket and Deutschmark for farther east. The bus came in, I sat down next to a window at the back.

We left the city. Nobody tried to stop me.

428 | STEPHEN HENIGHAN

The clouds grew thicker and blacker as the bus drove east. Dark rain fell. We skirted cities and crossed borders. No one asked for a passport.

As signs in German appeared, I thought of Catherine. Would my route pass close to the US military hospital? I wondered whether she and I would ever again make love in a basement in Hackney. How badly I needed her! I longed to tell her everything that had happened since she had vanished into the glow of the US Embassy in Sarajevo.

Late in the day, when the grey of the clouds was merging into the grey of dusk, the bus entered Berlin, where, without my having set foot here, my wanderings had begun. A shiver ran through me as I remembered sitting on Camille's couch, watching men hammer at the Wall. *The fall of the Berlin Wall is crucial, absolutely crucial, to us.* Leon was right, as always. The breaching of the Wall had released a quarter of a million protesters onto Rue St-Denis and dispatched me on a journey that was ending here, where the Wall had been gone for one year short of a decade. Along its former course stood huge, raw, shiny building projects. Concrete buttresses thrust up above the roads, fangs of wood protruded from tarpaulin flaps, trucks groaned up to the foundations of new buildings, and everywhere there were teams of construction workers – hard-bitten, un-German-looking men with olive skin and dark moustaches. It was late in the day, rain was falling, yet the activity was relentless. The seam of unfinished buildings gouged a bright path through the grey city.

The bus dropped us in the former East. As I stepped down onto a sidewalk, which I would have been forbidden from treading for most of the first three decades of my life, I thought of Catherine retreating with Andreas behind the wall of the old East. The ambassador had received his first posting at ambassadorial level at the East Berlin Embassy that the United States had maintained for a year after the Wall fell. Thoughts of Catherine led me to Alex — was this unavoidable now? Catherine wasn't the only woman we both knew. Alex's history with Hamdaw women was more complicated than it appeared. This was the intuition that had brought me to Berlin.

I walked through streets where the apartment blocks' grey, flaking stucco looked as delicate as the fabric of abandoned wasps' nests. The street lighting was sparse. Tinny little Trabants, so fragile that I could have put my hiking boot through their doors, mingled with Škodas and Ladas. I turned a corner. A shiny, sandblasted new café projected its glare into the night, scattering tables over the sidewalk. The rain had dwindled to a drizzle that cooled my cheeks and moistened my eyebrows. A pair of determined café-goers huddled over sputtering candles beneath an awning, warming their hands on mugs. I asked the couple directions. When I failed to understand their replies, there was no recourse to English. On this side of Berlin, the second language of anyone over fifteen was Russian. I walked on. The statue of the founder of the East German Communist Party loomed over an avenue. A cul-de-sac ended in a grey stone building that was long enough to look low even though it was three storeys high. The building's lobby was drab. A shiny new panel containing a buzzer system had been installed in the wall. I buzzed the number Zed had given me and waited.

A German voice answered. "*Ich bin Kevin Carmichael von Hamdaw College,*" I said. "*Ich möchte —*"

The connection was cut. I felt an ebb of relief and realized I was dreading this meeting. The door opened. A woman carrying a cloth grocery bag entered the lobby from the street. She directed a question at me. Unimpressed by my attempt at a reply, she said, "*Sie sind keine Deutscher!*" You're no German.

I wasn't any German! She closed the door behind her, ensuring that I would not be able to enter the building.

The door opened. A head poked into the lobby. "It *is* you. Why did you speak to me in German? You didn't speak German when we were at Hamdaw."

Her jaw had thickened, lending her a stern handsomeness. Her flesh looked less milky than I remembered, though she wore her blond hair in the same short style as she had six years earlier. Her long legs no longer jostled with adolescent coltishness, but held her high and commanding. "Come in," she said, as I failed to speak. "We can talk in my flat."

Which meant we had something to talk about. I followed her down a narrow corridor of bare stone. She explained that before — in this city everyone understood what *before* and *after* meant — this building had been the residence for the workers of the adjacent factory.

She opened the door. Her flat had a squared-off, doll's-house quality, with meagre little counters and low doorways that Christa had to stoop to pass through. The same pressboard cupboards I had seen in Poland lined the walls.

I realized no one else was here. It felt like a stab in the stomach.

"You are late. Alex left this morning." A wave of red spilled through her cheeks as she uttered his name.

I thrust my hand against the wall. "But he was here?"

"He was here last night." Her blush deepened.

"I have to talk to him. Where did he go?"

Christa's face hardened. Her eyes flinched with distrust.

"Did he tell you where he was going?" I watched her fixed expression drain her face of colour. "Of course he's going east.

That's the only direction he can run in. The problem is that he's going to have to show his passport to cross the Polish border."

"He had another passport." Her words emerged in an involuntary exhalation. "Come into the kitchen. I'll get you something to drink."

The kitchen had a utilitarian iron basin of a sink painted an off-white shade, a gas stove and a small fridge. We sat at a table that had been pushed against a wall of bare stone. Christa opened the fridge and produced a box of orange juice. Having expected a beer, I smiled. I remembered her beseeching Alex to play Twister.

"This other passport," I said as I sat down, "was it in a different name?"

"Yes. He showed it to me. He shouldn't have done that, but he was very alone."

"I was with him in Amsterdam —"

"Yes," she said with the calm that was the prerogative of her large body. "He told me."

I detected a knowingness in her manner; it grated on me. "People often tell each other everything when they're in bed together."

I regretted my words as soon as I uttered them. She was a nice woman, she had let me into her flat after not having seen me for six years, and she was sharing confidences with me. In spite of my harshness, she didn't blush or get angry. "Are you surprised? Three times at Hamdaw he came around the balcony to my room at night. He was having problems with Susan. The first time, I was terrified. I had never done that before. But I knew he was the one I wanted even though I would never be his girlfriend. I made a decision to accept love when it was available." She laid her hands flat on the table.

"I understand." But I didn't. Neither Christa's behaviour nor

432 | STEPHEN HENIGHAN

Alex's made sense. *Sometimes it's not about infidelity destroying a relationship, but about compulsive flirting wearing it down.* Not even Susan had suspected that Alex was unfaithful to her. Or perhaps she had known, in the unacknowledged way one senses a long-time lover's betrayals without being told about them. I had known that Catherine had slept with Alex, though I hadn't admitted to myself that I knew. Sitting across from Christa, the reality of those bodies forking together – his enormous and incipiently paunchy, Catherine's appetizingly round – clubbed me with a palpable immediacy. *I think we both missed you.* How often a third person's presence was implicit when two lovers made love! The person one of them was fleeing from, or vicariously longing for, brought the bodies together. If I had been the phantom facilitator of Alex's coupling with Catherine, who had Alex been seeking by sleeping with Christa?

"Did he talk to you about what I told him in Amsterdam? About me and Leon –?"

"He didn't mention Leon. Where is Leon now?"

He had kept the deepest secret to himself. Or he hadn't understood what I had tried to tell him. The tension in our conversation waned as we spoke about Hamdaw acquaintances. Once Christa had satisfied her curiosity, she said, "Alex found a newspaper article about Amsterdam. You can take it with you."

She stood up in that way which encouraged me to leave. As she handed me a folded section of *The International Herald-Tribune*, I said, "Do you know where he's planning to go?"

"He didn't tell me, except that he would be entering Poland. After he showed me his other passport, I asked him not to tell me anything more." Half a head taller than me, she regarded me with a stern expression. If the police came, she would have to tell them that she had seen me as well as Alex. I thought of Alex tiptoeing around the upper balcony of the fishbowl quad as Decibel Doug had tiptoed to Cindy's room.

"I need to talk to him!"

I slid the *Herald-Tribune* into my pack. Christa gave me directions to Unter den Linden and the Brandenburg Gate. I thanked her and accepted her loose-armed, hard-elbowed hug. As our bodies separated, the buzzer rang.

Christa froze. She gave the buzzer a cursory jab. Heavy feet advanced up the stairs.

Alex stopped as he reached the top of the stairs. In spite of a squint, he looked better than he had in the back room of the warehouse. The cool, damp Berlin night air had frizzed his hair and brought out the colour in his cheeks. His limbs looked gangly, his step rejuvenated in spite of his paunch. He gave me a punch in the shoulder that was hard enough to be either affectionate or angry, then closed the door behind him.

The three of us stood in the entrance to Christa's squashed little flat, cramped as the interior of a Trabant, squeezed as the borders of the old East Germany had been. We were too embarrassed to speak. I was abashed by the confession that awaited me. Alex looked mortified. If I had located him, so could the police. In succumbing to the temptation of a second night with Christa, he had made the kind of sentimental lapse that gets clever fugitives arrested. Christa, whose pale face was turning red again, had lied to me by saying that Alex had left. She had put him in jeopardy by letting me in. Realizing she had made a mistake, she had hoped to get me out the door before Alex returned; the contradiction between the need for secrecy and the desire to confess had tripped her up. She turned redder and redder. I saw her delving for words, perhaps wishing that there was a language that she and Alex could speak to each other that

I would not understand. As she remained silent, I explained to Alex how I had found him. "It was a guess. A guess only someone who knows you well could have made. Aren't you taking a chance by walking the streets?"

"I was stuck in here all day while Christa was at work. I needed some fresh air." He shrugged his shoulders. "There's nobody out there. East Berlin is empty."

"And tomorrow morning you'll leave for Poland. You'll stay with Jerzy in Warsaw, then go on to Belarus." Alex's route took shape in my mind as I spoke. It hadn't occurred to me before, yet it was obvious. It was two hours from here to the Polish border. Once he reached Warsaw, it was only two hours to the border of Belarus. In Minsk, sheltered by his uncle, he could live below the radar of the Moscow Mafia, to whom he owed millions for the cocaine impounded by the Dutch police. No one would think to look for him there. In that country, which had been severed from Europe, he could not be extradited to Holland or the United States. A country that had not changed, that remained much as it had been before, would shield him from threats from East *and* West. *Fucking Belarus, man! It's like being dead*.

"Nobody knows where I'm going." Now that I had mentioned Jerzy's name in front of her, Christa would be more of a security risk if the police came. That was my foolish lapse. The sooner I got out of here, the safer Alex would be.

"I'm leaving," I said, "but there's one thing I have to tell you. Leon and I killed Colin. I can't not tell you that. Our friendship forces me to tell you that, even though telling you may destroy it... I started to tell you when we were leaving the warehouse ..."

"Do you think I heard anything you said then?"

Having started, I had to go on. "Leon and I were jealous of him.

We phoned Lady Margaret Hall and left a message for Colin to come to Hamdaw for Bessborough's party rather than meeting you. We'd had a few drinks ... And then we encouraged him go to the pub instead of the hospital ..."

Alex stared at his feet. Christa's body looked stiff. We were all still standing in the doorway. I couldn't pronounce the next words I had to say. I struggled with a dry throat against silence and dishonesty. In love, I had deceived and been deceived without bringing a moral judgement to bear on my acts or those of others. The historical context for moral judgement was dissolving, yet now I needed it back.

My voice snagged in my throat. "It's not just Colin's death. That was an accident ..." At last I found a way of expressing what I needed to say, "Our responsibility goes beyond Colin's death. That phone call was the catalyst for everything that's happened since. You wouldn't have left Oxford if Colin hadn't died, Alex. You would have finished your D. Phil. You wouldn't have gone to Moscow —"

"I wouldn't have become a fucking trafficker. That's what you mean." He continued to gaze at the floor.

"The death of a young man ..." I struggled for air. "It was like your brother's death all over again."

"*Shut the fuck up about my brother!*" He straightened up with the clank of a buckle on his leather jacket. "You don't know what the fuck you're talking about."

I saw that he hadn't realized I knew, and that Christa hadn't known either. She huddled back into the kitchen doorway, too low for her lanky frame. She braced her hands against the sides of the doorway and bowed her head.

"You don't understand anything. Who the fuck do you think you are? Fucking Raskolnikov? All of this was going to happen anyway."

I was silent. Christa said, "At Hamdaw you were always the two Canadians."

"That didn't mean a thing. We never knew the same stuff or had the same culture." He caught Christa's eye. "It's like we're from different countries. Anyway, there are no more countries." He waved in my direction. "Look at these fucking Germans trying to reunite a country! It's all bullshit."

I felt ill. By tainting Alex's relations with Christa, I had put his escape at risk. I realized how badly I yearned for him to get away. I didn't care what he had done, I didn't want him in jail.

"If I wanted to make sure I'm gonna escape, I'd kill *you*! You could walk out of here and go straight to a fucking police station —"

"I'd never do that."

"I can't know that." His rage surged up again. "You think I haven't ordered people killed before?" Christa shrank back into the kitchen, her head withdrawing between her shoulders. "In Moscow, some people had to be eliminated. I didn't do it. I didn't see it happen. But I chose to move to Moscow. Don't come to me saying that all your sensibilities have been wrecked because some fucking phone call destroyed my life. I'm not your victim. You can't imagine what I live with."

"Now I understand why you destroyed your Russian library."

"Oh, we're back to literature as a moral force. Well maybe it *is* a moral force. Maybe it's because I've read Dostoevsky that I'm going to let you walk out of here and assume that, because you've read Dostoevsky, too, you won't betray me."

"I confessed because I've read Dostoevsky. I won't betray you because I've read Tolstoy."

"Fucking intellectual." He gave me a punch in the shoulder that knocked me against the wall. I laughed. He hit me again, in exactly the same place. This time it wasn't a joke. The blow stung. I stepped back. He moved forward a pace, raised his hand, then dropped it and turned away.

"Get the fuck out of here."

Christa had retreated into the kitchen. Her sobs scraped against the bare walls. My confession, though it had done more harm than good, had at least increased the likelihood that Alex would cross the border tomorrow morning. Having pried him loose from a woman's embrace, I had dispatched him to the care of men: Jerzy in Warsaw, his uncle in Minsk. I would never see him again.

He opened the door. I walked past him without touching him or looking back. My shoulder registering the painful echo of his punches. What he and Christa would say to each other after the door closed was unimaginable.

As soon as I heard the door shut behind me, I regretted not having told him that Colin had made it to Moscow before his death. Not once but twice. Though the revelation would have stung him if I had let it slip when we were in Oxford, I had the feeling that now he might find it soothing.

It was too late. I couldn't go back. We would have no more conversations.

A damp chill bored into my bones. I had nowhere to hide. I thought of Catherine lying in a sterile military hospital. I thought of her returning to Belgrade and recovering by playing tennis. I quickened my pace.

At the end of Unter den Linden stood the Brandenburg Gate. The photographs I'd seen since childhood had been taken from the West, with the Berlin Wall behind it. Now I was approaching it from the East, and the Wall was gone. I walked under the gate and turned right into what – almost since I was born – had

438 | STEPHEN HENIGHAN

been no-man's-land, a vast space around the Reichstag. *He's the sort of tosser who tells you the Jews burned down the Reichstag.* My first conversation with Leon. I knew I would never tell him about my last conversation with Alex.

The new civil service district along the Spree River was going up in a glare of twenty-four-hour construction. Saws and drills and the whine of metal on concrete, transparent tarpaulin draped over scaffolding and lighted up from within, trucks pulling in and pulling out again. The Reichstag was awash in light and dwarfed by buildings not yet unveiled. As I crossed no-man's-land, where fleeing wall-jumpers had been shot down in the glare of searchlights, the halogen lamps' glare reverberated with the sad howl of Turkish music. The East I heard was not the East I knew. In the light by which men from this other East were building the future, I sat down, opened my pack and pulled out the newspaper.

The *Herald-Tribune* was crammed with news of Kosovo. Holbrooke's ceasefire agreement was in shreds, the North Atlantic Council had issued activation orders for limited air strikes against Serbia. I was worrying about Catherine's return to Belgrade when I saw —

Russian Literature Drug Traffickers Arrested

Police in Amsterdam have arrested three men at the city's DHL office in a bizarre attempted drug smuggling incident. Ivan Ryzhov, 23, Dmitry Izmailov, 24, and Alexei Kharitonov, 34, all of Moscow, were taken into custody when they were surprised filling hollowed-out volumes of classical Russian literature with bags of cocaine with an estimated street value of $7 million. DHL officials became suspicious when the men took more than two hours to prepare the shipment, which was to be sent to a Russian Orthodox church in San Francisco.

The group's ringleader, and owner of the Russian library, identified by police as a former student of Russian literature at Oxford and Harvard universities, escaped. His whereabouts are unknown.

At large is Alexander Spokoyʏᴏᴠ, 29.

According to witnesses, a fifth man, who entered the DHL office while the traffickers were preparing the package, was an accomplice. Reported to be in his thirties, he did not speak Russian and spoke English with a heavy accent. Only the back of his head is visible in CCTV images. His name, nationality, and current whereabouts are unknown.

FORTY

"THERE'S NO FRIGGIN' WAY they could've screwed!"

Fred stood up from the chesterfield and crossed the living room. "You've been a real inspiration to me, Kevin." He looked at me through his horn-rimmed glasses. "Bethune came back to Montreal after his adventures in Europe. Kinda like somebody else I know! June 6, 1937. In nothin' flat he heads off on a speaking tour to raise money for families of men who fought in Spain. By January 1938, he's in China with Mao Zedong's Communists. Your mum wasn't born until 1940. There's no way Bethune and your grandma could've screwed. Their only chance was in 1937, and that's too early. Maybe something happened then, but it didn't get your grandma pregnant."

"That's the end of that," I said, looking out the window at the balconies of the adjoining apartments. "So much for my hereditary connection to socialism."

I had returned to Montreal at Christmas. That night in Berlin, I walked until I found a banking machine; the *Herald-Tribune* had given me the courage to withdraw money. In a punky district of former West Berlin, I found a hostel. In the morning, the bruise on my shoulder making it almost impossible for me to move my arm, I went to a barber shop and tattoo parlour, where I had my hair cut as short as that of the dyed-blond punks. The back of my head no longer looked as it did on DHL's CCTV. I rode a bus to Tegel Airport and made the rounds of airline counters until I found an affordable ticket to London. I returned to Hackney broke. The temp work I got was less steady than my old job at the Paddington Health Authority. I was barely able to cover my rent. My life was reduced to waiting. I waited for Catherine to return to England; I waited for the police to question me; I waited for DHL to return my clothes and books; I waited for inspiration to write the last two chapters of my thesis. I waited and waited, and I was still a man in his late thirties who worked for scraps in offices where most of his fellow temps were fifteen years younger than he. I was no longer saving money, I no longer knew whether I had a girlfriend, I no longer communicated with Leon or Zed or Auberon.

Catherine and I, though we had each other's email addresses, had never got into the habit of using them. Like my bonds with Leon and Alex, my love for Catherine was rooted in literary conversation and handwritten letters. I phoned the ambassadorial residence in Belgrade. "*Dobro jutro,*" one of the serving ladies answered. She told me that Catherine was in Germany. Could I speak to the ambassador's wife? She was out. And Edith? Edith was in a meeting. So it was each time I phoned. *Molim,* I pleaded. *Molim molim molim.* One day in December, a serving lady replied that Catherine was in her room. I asked to speak to her and waited, as I had been waiting for weeks. The gloom of my basement closed in on me as I thought of Catherine descending from her garret. I drew a sharp breath as the receiver was lifted. "Sorry," the Serbian lady's voice said. "Catherine in Germany." She hung up.

One night a week later, as I was figuring out whether I would have enough money in my account to cover the next month's rent, the phone rang. "Where are you?" I asked.

"I'm here, supporting my parents in a difficult time." We talked about the war in Kosovo. As a result of his disagreements with Richard Holbrooke, the ambassador had been sidelined. Christopher Hill, US ambassador to Macedonia, had been put in charge of negotiating with Milosević. Hill was tall, young, athletic, with a full head of hair and a patrician New England accent; Catherine's father was old, bald, so fat that he looked shorter than his height, and spoke in a modified hillbilly drawl. If this crisis broke the wrong way for him, she whispered, he might be forced into early retirement.

"Will NATO bomb Serbia?"

"If they do, it will be as though one part of me is bombing another." A few minutes later, she said, "So this is what I am thinking about, Kevin. I'm not thinking about us very much. I used to think about you all the time and now I don't. It's not because of Mostar, it's just that I'm here and this is the centre of the world right now and my parents really need my support."

"I'll wait for you."

"If they bomb, we'll be evacuated to Washington. Don't stay in London on my account if it's easier for you to write your thesis in Canada."

That was the end of my English life. I came back to find the walk-up in St. Louis-du-Mile-End full of boxes. My mother and Paul were moving into a new condo in the Plateau Mont-Royal. Marie had moved to Calgary, apparently with another woman, a topic that my mother refused to discuss. Unable to afford the now-condo-ized Plateau, I rented an apartment in St. Henri, not far from my father and Fred in Verdun. I ensconced myself in the city's depths. I taught English as a second language to Québécois secretaries and salesmen for sixteen hours a week, divided between two different night schools. I covered my rent and groceries and not much else. After London, Montreal felt circumscribed. I lived vicariously, by reading international newspapers in the Concordia University library. I read every article I was able to find on the war in Yugoslavia. One day, I read a short piece in *The Independent* about a human rights activist who had been jailed in Zimbabwe. A shock went through me when I saw that it was Farida. The article mentioned an Amnesty International letter-writing campaign to secure Farida's freedom. I scribbled down the details, promising myself that I would write a letter. Though my fellow Hamdaw colonial was often in my thoughts, my letter remained unwritten. Three weeks later, *The Observer* reported that Farida had been released into exile in South Africa.

Less than two weeks after I moved to St. Henri, NATO found the pretext it needed. In a village called Račak, the Serbian Army had massacred forty-three Kosovo Albanian farmers. The ambassador made a statement deploring this atrocity. The North Atlantic Council mobilized. The next evening, on my way to a class, I went to an internet café and sent Catherine my new address and phone number. I told her that I missed her. In the morning I read that though many Serbs had closed ranks behind Milosević, fitful anti-government demonstrations had broken out in Belgrade. I realized that the ambassador, with his daughter at his side, was campaigning to win back his privileges.

At the beginning of March, the phone rang. An immense

silence, then a woman in tears. "Janko's gone! Milosević's people said they'd kill him for collaborating ... My dad had him ... him and his wife ... and children ... evacuated. They're being given green cards and new identities. I'm not allowed to know their new names!" Her voice crumpled. I was startled by the volume and bitterness of her weeping. Would she ever cry for me as she was crying for this other lover?

Her lover. I had said it, if only to myself. Janko, whose flat over the garage Catherine had described in such detail, was gone. The ambassador had rid himself of this irritation. *There's been way too much tennis around here.* He was fighting back, concentrating all of his bearded good ol' boy gruffness and passive-aggressive hocus-pocus on undermining Christopher Hill, Slobodan Milosević, and other threats to his career. Janko had been the foe most quickly dispatched.

"I'm sorry." This was the first time I had heard Catherine cry.

"Thank you, Kevin. Thank you for listening." She caught her breath. "You're a real friend."

That pushed me over the edge. "I'm not your fucking friend! I'm your boyfriend, and it made me feel like shit that you were sleeping with Janko. I love you."

She didn't reply for a long time. "None of my boyfriends ever sounded so committed – or so foul-mouthed! Thank you, Kevin. There's no one else I could have called."

"Our relationship –"

"Oh, what is to be done?"

"I remember the last time you asked me that question."

"I was still seeing Andreas then. It makes me blush to think about it."

Had she blushed in Janko's apartment because she was see-ing me? "A married man who works as a chauffeur is not your

future, Catherine. Your dad knows that." I trembled at my diplomatic obsequiousness.

"The world is ending here, Kevin. The Amsterdam warehouse
is getting trucks ready –"

A warehouse in Amsterdam. I had so much to tell her. She
began to talk about the peace negotiations in France. The American R with which she pronounced "Rambouillet" drove home the
gulf between us, a gulf I was more aware of in language-conscious
Montreal. Her voice perked up. "My dad's preparing a plan for
the evacuation of American government employees and their
dependents. I asked him if the plan applied to me. He said, 'No,
you're an independent adult.' It was the nicest thing he's ever
said to me! That's how I want to be; in the same country as my
parents, but recognized as an independent person."

I never again heard her voice from the East. Two weeks
later, Christopher Hill forged a peace agreement at Rambouillet.
At the last minute, Russia and Yugoslavia refused to sign. Serbian militias blasted Kosovar villagers. The television returned
again and again to images of the Račak Massacre. Five days later,
Richard Holbrooke, the most dangerous ballistic missile in the
Balkans, returned to Belgrade, and to my old room. He and
the ambassador went to see Milosević. Disdaining the ambassador's fluent Serbian, Milosević told them in English that he
would never retreat on the issue of Kosovo as part of Serb-ruled
Yugoslavia. The United States of America, Milosević said, was
the accomplice of Islamic terrorists. Holbrooke was furious. He
left the country. A few hours later, the bombing began. NATO
bombed Belgrade and Kosovo; they bombed the Chinese Embassy,
and the factory that made Yugo cars. At the end of the first week,
they bombed the Liberty Bridge in Novi Sad. As I stared at its
truncated destruction on my 16-inch television screen, I heard

the sound of the wind in the girders as Catherine and I were bounced against the railing by gusts howling down the Danube. *The wind makes me feel alive ... my relationship with you became possible when I met Leon and Alex. You're the female principle ... I'm sorry I haven't been very female for you recently.* A bar of uncertainty inside me twisted and snapped. I went to the internet café and wrote Catherine a long email, pleading with her to tell me that she was all right.

A few nights later the phone rang. It was my mother. Though I had returned to Montreal to be with my family, I'd had limited contact with them. My return made them uncomfortable. As my father, fearing that he had transmitted the unfinished thesis gene to me, had fobbed me off on Fred, so my mother had been cautious about communicating with me. She and Paul had built their new life on the assumption of their children's absence. The only member of my family who had become ubiquitous was my ex-brother-in-law, Dave, now Montreal's most prominent Angryphone. It was hard to open the pages of the *Gazette* – and harder still to read *La Presse* or *Le Devoir* – without seeing Dave's face contorted into an expression of fury as he evoked former Yugoslavia, threatening to partition the Island of Montreal to preserve English-only zones where the blue fleur-de-lys flag, like the French language, would be banned.

"I'm calling," my mother said, "because there's something we have to discuss."

I had been avoiding the Plateau, where every street corner was piled high with memories. The next afternoon I wandered through my old haunts, observing their transition from *bohémien* to *bourgeois*. My mother and Paul's new condo was on the ground floor of a Montreal walk-up triplex that had been extended back over what had once been a *ruelle* – a narrow alley between two streets. My mother came to the door. I kissed her on the cheek and went to sit in the sunroom in the addition. Dirty March snow lay outside the French windows.

My mother sat down opposite me. "I'm afraid I have bad news. Joan is ill —"

"How ill?" A jab in my heart.

"Very ill." My mother tried to meet my eyes, then failed and looked at the floor. "She has a few weeks at most."

"Why didn't you tell me?"

"I only found out myself last week. Joan's sister Harriet phoned. Harriet says Joan didn't tell anyone because she's been depressed about the political situation —"

"The last time I talked to her, we disagreed." I stopped. Joan had been my mentor, my mother in the public sphere. "Is it cancer?"

My mother nodded. "They did a double mastectomy, but it metastasized. Harriet wanted to move her to a hospice, but poor Joan got pneumonia." She stared at the snow bank then looked me in the eyes. "We should go and see her."

She didn't want to go alone. This was something we could do together to break down the distance between us. She had phoned the Montreal General to confirm their visiting hours.

That evening, I taught an after-work English class. As I walked to the Métro, I thought that my rustication was not over, would not be over until I finished my thesis. I went to an internet café. Catherine's name gleamed in my inbox.

Bombs depress me. In Washington. Phone below. S lyogkhim parom. C.

With light steam. An encouraging comment you make to someone on his way out of the shower. Hope carried me home. I phoned Washington, D.C. "Catherine can't come to the phone," the ambassador's wife said, her American accent blaring in my re-Canadianized ears.

"She's depressed again, like she was when I met her. Being with me made her better."

"We all appreciate your concern, Kevin. It's real good of you to call. Call again next month. She'll be ready to talk to you then."

I hung up and threw myself on the couch in despair. The telephone rang. "Kevin," Fred said. "Turn on CBC radio right now."

I flipped the switch on my ghetto blaster and listened to a measured British documentary that made the case that the Americans, working with the Kosovo Liberation Army, had faked the Račak Massacre to justify bombing Belgrade. The documentary's sources included retired major generals both British and Canadian, liberal and conservative newspapers, BBC reporters and a European Union investigation that had discredited the Americans' claims. When the program ended, I sat in the dark and wondered whether the ambassador had collaborated with this charade from the start, or whether his initial opposition to it had been the source of his arguments with Holbrooke. He had gone along with this lie, I suspected, to save his career. What had Catherine known and not told me? I pondered the silences between us. Years later I was assured that, in spite of its impeccable provenance, the British documentary was Russian propaganda. I no longer knew what to believe. The world of immutable facts and firm belief through which I had moved in the years after the end of the Cold War was eroding; we had entered a time in which any truth could become indistinguishable from a lie.

In the morning, I came up out of the Guy-Concordia Métro in front of the statue of Norman Bethune and caught a 165 bus up the diagonal slope of Côte-des-Neiges to meet my mother at the Montreal General. We entered the ward where Joan was being treated and walked past open doorways. Hospital beds had branched into vast, armoured, wire-sprouting contraptions, watched over by peeping computer screens. In some beds, white-haired, grey-faced figures sat up, talking to visitors. Trolleys and waste bins were parked along the walls of the broad corridors; yet rather than the bustle of activity I had expected, I found an air of abandonment. We got lost and couldn't find anyone of whom to ask directions. Each room harboured its private huddle of tragedy, on which it felt wrong to intrude.

When we got to Joan's room, she lay inert and deflated beneath the sheets. Anyone would look small and crumpled, I thought, surrounded by so much wire and metal.

Then I realized she was dead.

"Three minutes ago," the nurse said. "We are waiting for her sister before we send her body to the morgue."

"I don't believe you," my mother said. She was crying.

"I show you the body," the nurse said in a voice tinged with defiance. She stood up from the computer where she was filling in a form on the screen. I glimpsed a blank for *Time of Death*. A bold-faced green line crossed the muted computer screen above Joan's bed.

My mother couldn't look at the bed. "If only I'd come earlier, she'd know ..."

"She is dead," the nurse said. "If you come, if you do not come, she does not know."

She pulled back the sheet. I was relieved to see the body in the bed was not Joan. This shrivelled, sag-fleshed husk bore no resemblance to the elegant woman with the pronounced dark eyebrows and wavy grey mane who had graced panels on so many public affairs programs. Once I overcame my shock that the body was naked, I took in the tiny, pouched stomach, the red circles on either side of the sternum, the bared teeth and shaven skull from which a prickle of white thatch protruded.

"That's not her," I said.

"Dead people look different," the nurse said. "In my country, we see many dead people."

I couldn't rip my gaze away from the body. "What is your country?" I asked.

"My country is Serbia."

My mother gave me an accusatory look. I reached out to hug her; she veered away, sobbing and shaking her head. Joan's sister Harriet came around the corner. A composed woman, who worked as an actuary, she was taller and fairer than Joan, the grey in her hair blended with residual licks of light brown. Finding my mother in tears, she yielded the role of the bereaved for that of the comforter. They were both more at ease this way. Harriet was spared the indignity of losing her composure and my mother was able to redeem herself for her neglect.

After Harriet had signed papers and the husk that the hospital referred to as Joan had been taken to the morgue, we went downtown in Harriet's Mazda and had tea on a side street below Ste-Catherine. I thought about Joan for days: her solitary, self-sacrificing life, which had substituted nation for family, her early academic success, her campaigns, the withering of her following, her marginalization. When we were campaigning against Free Trade, our discussions had lasted for whole afternoons. Much of my understanding of the planet I inhabited came from Joan. Since leaving Montreal, I had begun to disagree with her, yet had never felt comfortable distancing myself from her sufficiently to stake out a distinctive terrain.

Two days after the funeral, Harriet phoned. "Kevin, there's a clause in Joan's will that says that if you accept, you inherit the Independent Canada Institute. As you know, she always wanted you to take over."

"What would I be inheriting?"

"There's a lease on the office at McGill with two years to run, one full-time employee, two graduate student assistants, and a list of volunteers. There's a contract to do a survey for a union, a little grant money ... Joan's financing was trickling away. If you have a particular direction in which you'd like to take the Institute, a way of reinventing and re-financing it, even if it's not the direction Joan would have taken, this might be a challenge you'd like to take on."

Stretching the phone cord, I walked to the window. On the street below, the snow banks had shrunk to gritty white patches. Spring was coming. NATO was still bombing Belgrade. Soon, the ambassador's wife said, I would be able to talk to Catherine. A particular direction. Like the ambassador, this was what I lacked.

"The person I was ten years ago," I said, "would have taken it on ..."

"Make your decision and send it to me in writing." She gave me an address. "One more thing," Harriet said. "There's a girl from the CBC who wants to do an interview about Joan's life. I don't feel up to it. You worked with her —"

"No problem," I said, glad of the opportunity to compensate for having disappointed Joan's expectations.

I was finishing my letter when the phone rang. "This is Melissa Bradshaw from CBC radio," a self-assured voice said. With a jauntiness that shook me out of my despondency, we discussed times and places for the interview. "I'm in Verdun," she said, when I told her where I lived. "If I leave work early tomorrow, I could come by your place around four."

In the morning, I mailed the letter in which I renounced my inheritance. I could have accepted Joan's bequest, led ICI in a more moderate yet still progressive direction, finished my thesis, picked up part-time teaching at McGill or Concordia, and slipped into a comfortable, limited niche in Montreal society. But I did not want to be tied to Montreal. I wanted to be free to follow Catherine.

When the CBC reporter rang the buzzer and came upstairs to my apartment, I was glad that I had put on one of the dress shirts I had bought to teach in. Under her spring jacket, the journalist wore a blue blazer and a white blouse. She was dressed in a blue skirt, black pumps, and black stockings, not a hair out of place. "Melissa," she said, extending a hand. "Pleased to meet you." She set down a black bag containing recording equipment and gave me a smile whose crookedness felt daring by contrast with the manicured symmetry of her clothes and hair. Her voice trailed off. "Do I know you from somewhere?"

"La Cabane," I said, pinpointing the location. "Seven years ago, with Jake Mendelsson."

"Oh my God!" She blushed. "You know about my secret life! I expect you to tell me a few secrets during this interview, or we'll never be even."

A microphone appeared, cradled at a diagonal in a stand. She set the stand on my wobbly dining room table, then scampered to the wall to plug it in. "You know about the older man I dated at nineteen. Not even my best friends know that. You owe me big-time!"

Seeing that it was up to me to either dampen this ebullience or stoke it up, I said, "Would you like a glass of wine?"

"I'm not at the office ... why not?"

I produced a bottle of cheap French red wine from the *dépan-neur*. We sat down on opposite sides of the wobbly table. "Tell me a secret," she said.

"When you're overseas," I said, "and you meet someone from a different city in your country, you're obliged to share a nationality."

She looked me in the eyes, her levity yielding to a more serious expression. "When you're in Montreal," she said, moving her hand across the table as though advancing a chess piece, "you can have a completely different idea of nationality from the people next door."

We drank most of the first glass in silence. By the second glass, I was trying to tell her everything that had happened to me since we had met at La Cabane. She asked me when I had last seen Catherine. Befuddled, I ticked off the months on my fingers. Six, seven, could it be eight months ago?

"Sorry to break the news, but she's not your girlfriend anymore."

"She was evacuated. She suffers from depression. Once she's out of hospital —"

"It's important to know when a relationship's over. I broke up with my boyfriend three weeks ago because I knew it was finished. *Finito. Kaput. Fini, tabarnac. J'ai cassé avec lui!*"

I laid my hand on hers. When we did the interview, three hours later, we were naked and had made love twice. Melissa held the microphone in front of my face with her right hand, while her left hand stroked my chest, extracting confidences from me about my work with Joan in an era that had vanished.

Melissa was an intelligent, passionate young woman with a lovely body. Though this was only a one-night stand, I was a lucky dog. Yet, as we had been grappling towards my bed, I had suffered a moment of panic. Melissa had stripped off her bra. The sight of unfamiliar breasts — large, with disproportionately small nipples — raised the words she had spoken to me earlier in front of my eyes like a warning sign. It told me that the moment I caressed her naked breasts, a stage of my life would end. Going to bed with Melissa was the end of Catherine and Leonie and Kumiko and Pia, the end of Alex and Leon; a return to Canada, the conclusion of my wanderings and my efforts to snatch back before from after. It might even be the end of after. It was a force I could not resist. I fell on my knees on the uneven parquet floor, fitted my palms against either side of Melissa's soft belly and ran my tongue up her body until I felt her breasts nestle against my ears.

THE END OF AFTER

"IN A GLOBALIZED WORLD," Simon said, "you have to move fast. If that's true of history, it's even truer of industry and education, the two pillars of British society that I'm here to talk about tonight."

He sipped his glass of water and shook his clipped grey curls. When I had written to tell Tina that twelve years after entering the D.Phil., I had submitted my thesis, she had responded by informing me that the day after my viva, Simon would be the keynote speaker at a Hamdaw fund-raising reception. I must come! Would Leon come, too? When I emailed him, taking the opportunity to congratulate him on his promotion to Senior Lecturer, he replied:

The only thing that would lure me back to Hamdaw at this stage
would be if Alex reappeared from whatever hole he's bolted down.

I had not told Leon that a year after my return to Montreal I had written to Christa. She had received an unsigned postcard from Minsk, her last word from Alex.

"In Britain we have a history of fine educational institutions that despise the people who make our country work. During my own days here, I stood precisely where I'm standing tonight and proposed measures of which I'm now properly ashamed. As we get older, we develop more perspective, and perspective, I must say, is something we shall need if we are to adapt British education and industry to our new century."

The formally dressed alumni seated on folding metal chairs ranged in age from twenty-five to eighty-five. At the back of the room, I spotted Zed. He had written to me, on learning that I had submitted, to wish me luck on my viva. Fortunately, this had been a low-key affair. My external examiner, from the London School of Economics, had been scornful yet forgiving. I was now Dr. Carmichael. Auberon, ever the diplomat, his thinning hair and expensive suit identifying him as an emerging Big Beast of the SCR, took me out for a drink at the King's Arms. What benefit, he asked, would I gain from completing a doctorate at forty-four?

I told him that three years earlier I had been hired as a full-time Cégep history teacher. As I explained the role of the Cégep – after high school, before university – he nodded his head, appearing to feel that I had found my level. I had remained in St. Henri, buying into one of the first abandoned factories in the area to be gutted, sandblasted, and renovated for condos. Gentrification had continued, doubling my condo's value. My job was undemanding, the salary decent. My MA put me in an upper tier of the salary scale; a completed D.Phil. would lift me to near the top of the scale. Having little else to distract me, I began to write. Yet, rather than the final chapters of my doctoral thesis, what emerged was: *Compatriots from different cities, when they meet overseas, are obliged to share a nationality. I was from Montreal and Alex was from Toronto ...* It took me two years to write the story of my wanderings. Only when I finished did I return to my thesis. I blazed through my last two chapters in three months.

"We all lost our heads for a bit after the Cold War. It was a time of barmy schemes and unrealistic idealism. Well, that's over," Simon said, giving the audience a stern look. "We are no longer so idealistic as to imagine that our way of life does not have enemies.

"Privatization will make education more responsive to the needs of the public. Soon students will pay high tuition fees. If Hamdaw College wishes to support all the students we would like to see study here, we will need to build up a truly impressive endowment."

As Simon made his fund-raising pitch, I grew mutinous. When his talk ended, there was applause. Everyone stood up, Tina rushed over and kissed me on both cheeks. "Kevin! I can't believe you're a Cégep teacher! You're not married? You don't have children?"

I shook hands with Simon. "Do you remember my last speech in this room?" he asked.

"I liked that one better." Before he could react, I said, "I'm going to say hello to Zed."

"Frightful racket in here." A heap of de-elasticized sock had collapsed over Zed's right shoe. "What say we take a walk?"

We stepped into the damp Thames Valley night. The studious, stony silence of Oxford engulfed us. "I never thought I'd set foot in the Ho Chi Minh Quad again."

"They don't call it that anymore." Zed chortled. "Name fell out of use three or four years ago. It survived for thirty-five years, then vanished overnight. Students today don't challenge the Fellows as your lot did. Now it's, 'Yes, sir, yes, sir, three bags full, sir.'"

We walked into the front quad. The statue of the founder in her stone gown slipped behind us. "Do you still eat at High Table?"

"I enjoy dining, but some nights Dennock and I are alone like an old married couple. High Table is dying. The new generation of Fellows want to get home to their families. Don't want to be in College until eleven o'clock every night."

We walked in silence past the empty quads of All Souls College. "I don't suppose," he said, as we came out onto the High Street and turned towards Carfax Tower, "that you've heard from your Russian friend since he filled his books with drugs? I gather the police never found him."

"No," I said. "All of that was my fault. Mine and Leon's, though Leon never accepted it."

"Zamenhof has done frightfully well. He's a major historian of the Left."

"Because he never allowed himself to feel guilty." As we stood beneath Carfax Tower, with black taxis idling in the glare of the streetlights, I told Zed about the prank that had caused Colin Blake's death. "That's why I burst into Bessborough's party and made that speech. That's why Alex went off the rails —"

He touched my arm, directing me away from the stench of exhaust. We walked through deserted back streets where our voices resounded on the cobblestones. "If there's one thing I've learned as a historian, it's that small decisions do change large destinies. There's no use in pretending they don't. Zamenhof is wrong to say it all would have happened in any event. But some other dreadful event might have occurred. His brother was murdered, that was bound to come out in one form or another. Even destroying his books might be a symptom, if his brother wrote poetry. At this stage I would say you've done your penance and should get on with your life." We swung around a corner. "It's private life that saves you from despair. Did you marry that girl from Moscow?"

Only after three months of calls to the house in Alexandria, Virginia – this was what my phone bills said – was I able to speak to Catherine. We began to talk every day or two, until we both depended on these phone calls. One night we tried to have phone sex and broke into shared laughter. "Come and see me," I said.

She asked her parents to approve her plan. A ticket to Montreal was purchased, then cancelled as the ambassador, disgraced and facing forced retirement, snared an invitation to an important dinner. To make the best impression, he must arrive as a family man. It fell to Catherine to certify the family's Eastern European vocation, "Our daughter, Catherine, who is a doctoral candidate in Russian literature at Oxford University."

Catherine sparkled at the dinner. She asked her parents to repurchase the ticket to Montreal as a reward. Twice more the ticket was bought and cancelled. The ambassador received an invitation to meet with Secretary of State Madeleine Albright. Two weeks later, he was named ambassador to Bulgaria. Catherine's ticket to Montreal was cashed in to pay for a ticket to Sofia. Or so she told me, as she took a break from packing. She was so excited about going to Sofia that I saw it was pointless to remind her of her promise to come to Montreal. In that sense, I let her go. I let her go because I did not want to dent her happiness at returning to the East. In this way, she, and the East, would always be with me. I adopted Catherine's conviction that some things lasted forever.

A year before my return to Oxford, Mr. Djindić, the Democrat, now Prime Minister of Serbia, was assassinated. Catherine filled my mind for days, causing me to lose interest in my work and the people around me. But it took an event in which her family was directly involved to drive me to write to her again.

For six months I dated – her word – an alienated Torontonian who was living in Montreal. During the holidays, she whisked me off to the city to which she longed to return. In her sister's Etobicoke living room, I read an article in the *Toronto Star* about the overthrow of the elected government of Eduard Shevardnadze in the Republic of Georgia. The sight of the ambassador's name airlifted me out of my surroundings. The *Star* reported that the Rose Revolution that had overthrown Shevardnadze had been orchestrated by the US Embassy in Tbilisi. The crowd that burst into Parliament and forced Shevardnadze's resignation had chanted slogans not in the Georgian language, but in Serbian, the language of the demonstrators' strategists, who had been flown in from Belgrade by the man who, as Head of Station there, had plotted the downfall of Slobodan Milosević.

My relationship with Catherine, I saw, had been granted air and space to breathe because, during the era that Simon had just proclaimed ended – the long decade between 11/9 in Berlin and 9/11 in New York – our desires for the contours of the pre-1989 world had run parallel. Yet I had been in love with a woman whose father, in his unassuming, good ol' boy way, incarnated the United States' foreign interventions and covert operations that Joan and I had spent years denouncing.

Had I punished myself for Colin's death by falling in love with my enemy?

I was ready to make peace with having lost her.

I wrote Catherine a letter that expressed an absence of bitterness that I knew would appeal to her Quaker soul. I addressed it care of the ambassador, Embassy of the United States of America, Tbilisi, Republic of Georgia. I mailed the envelope to an address

I found online for the United States Department of State. Early the next year, when my thesis was almost ready for submission, an envelope with US postage appeared in my mailbox. Inside I found a photograph. I longed for a recent photo of Catherine. What I received was a picture of snowy mountains. *I'm working here, two hours outside Tbilisi, in one of the most beautiful, primitive places on earth. I have my own job. I'm exactly where I want to be: supporting my parents in the country where they are working, yet recognized as an independent person. This is how you must always think of me. You must know that I could never blame you for what happened in Mostar, and you shouldn't blame yourself for Oxford. None of it is your fault. You won't hear from me again.*

"No," I said to Zed, as we walked up St. Giles. "We didn't marry."

"Then you should marry somebody else. Speaking of private life, I ought to be getting home."

He shook my hand and walked to a mini-bus stop. Secure in the knowledge that no past time was worthy of my remorse, I headed back to the inn in Jericho where I was staying. Tomorrow I would return to Montreal.

AUTHOR'S NOTE

THIS STORY, LIKE THE fictitious characters it portrays, adheres in its chronology to the historical record of the 1990s. I've taken small liberties with other chronologies, for example, by advancing by a few weeks the release date of Bruce Cockburn's song "Mighty Trucks of Midnight." Very small changes have been made to the locations of some streets and buildings in East London.

I thank Jennifer McCartney for sending me a copy of Paul Prescott's book *We Saw Spain Die: Foreign Correspondents in the Spanish Civil War*. I'm grateful to John Jantunen and Alex Good for their comments on earlier drafts of this novel, and to Sarah Jensen for her rigorous copy edit. My greatest debt is to Marc Côté for an incisive structural edit that brought the book together.

We acknowledge the sacred land on which Cormorant Books operates. It has been a site of human activity for 15,000 years. This land is the territory of the Huron-Wendat and Petun First Nations, the Seneca, and most recently, the Mississaugas of the Credit River. The territory was the subject of the Dish With One Spoon Wampum Belt Covenant, an agreement between the Iroquois Confederacy and Confederacy of the Anishinaabe and allied nations to peaceably share and steward the resources around the Great Lakes. Today, the meeting place of Toronto is still home to many Indigenous people from across Turtle Island. We are grateful to have the opportunity to work in the community, on this territory.

We are also mindful of broken covenants and the need to strive to make right with all our relations.